The Truth About Dating

a novel

By Julie Christensen

ISBN-13: 978-1461094586
ISBN:-10: 1461094585

Cover art and design by Jennifer Maginn

For my parents, who always encouraged my dreams.

In memory of Rosemary.

Acknowledgements

Thanks to Stacey Wodehouse, amazing friend and the inspiration for Izzy. To Cindy Foster, writer and editor extraordinaire. To Diane, Stephen, and Amy for just being you. To Jennifer Maginn, who designed the awesome cover for this book. To my earliest readers, Denis Fitzpatrick, Kim Schairer, John Ellison, and Betsy Runnion. Thanks to Amy, and to Brenda Hoover for proofreading the new edition of this book. To everyone who wrote reviews when my novel made it to the quarterfinals of the Amazon contest. And to Jerry, for your beautiful style of critique and that last, zinging line.

The book, **Finding A Husband After 35**, by Rachel Greenwald, is published by Ballantine Books and is available at major booksellers.

Table of Contents

Chapter 1
Dating Advice for Single Women

When I was six-years old I wanted to be a ballerina. At the age of eight I switched to marine biologist. By high school I was going to be an artist, living in a Manhattan loft, showing my work in Paris and Tokyo. My family and I would live half the year in the city and the other half in the mountains. (I'd already decided in the fifth grade that I'd marry at age 27 or 28 and have 3-5 children and a dog.)

So I never dreamed that at age 38, I'd be working as an audiologist in Omaha, Nebraska, still single, without children, or a boyfriend, or even a dog. Instead of painting my next masterpiece or walking my children through Central Park, I was sitting in a darkened sound booth, playing tones into the ears of my last patient of the day, a 77-year-old woman who was congratulating herself every time she heard a beep. BEEP. "Yes, there it is," she muttered. "And again. Ha! Yes, my hearing has always been excellent."

Unfortunately, her hearing wasn't excellent anymore, which she must have known because as I was going over her test results, she interrupted to tell me that she wore hearing aids.

"Where are they?" I asked.

"In my purse."

"Why aren't you wearing them?"

"Because they don't work. I paid $6000 for these aids and they have never been any good."

"Why didn't you return them at the end of your trial period?"

"I wanted to, but that man said I would start to get used to them." She'd gotten them from a hearing aid dispenser in town, the kind of place that targets the elderly with full-page ads in the paper.

"The sound of a flushing toilet makes me nearly go through the roof," she announced. "My family is sick at how expensive they were. My daughter said, 'And you still can't hear us.'"

"You have to go back for more adjustments," I said. "Sometimes it takes months to adapt to hearing aids. But it can be done, as long as you're persistent."

"Dear, what was your name again?"

"Quinn Malone," I said.

She gripped my arm as she stood. "Don't get old, Quinn," she said after she'd finally managed to stand up.

I hear that line all the time. "I'll try not to," I said.

"When you're old, people try to take advantage of you. But I'll go back to that man and get these things fixed. Are you married?" she asked.

"No."

"Miss Malone, you're never going to meet a man in this profession. Too many old people. Take my advice. Go back to school and learn shorthand. That will get you a man. Wear a short skirt and cross your legs as you take dictation. You'll be married off in no time."

I had on a calf length skirt that must have targeted me as an old maid. "Okay. Well, thanks for the advice and please call me if you have any other troubles with the hearing aids."

"I will," she said. She let go of my arm as she headed out the door. She was laughing to herself and muttering, "That's good advice. Stenography."

They say your life can change in the blink of an eye, but for the past eight years I'd been in Omaha, Nebraska living the same life, day in and day out. I had a good job, at a national center for audiology. And in spite of what that 77-year-old said, I saw more than just old people. In fact, my clinic specialized in pediatrics. But I hadn't had a boyfriend since I'd moved here. I hadn't even had a date. Can you read between the lines, Reader? I hadn't been laid in eight years.

I can't say I'd even tried that hard. I hadn't done the bar

scene since my twenties. I didn't do anything social except hang out with my girlfriends, usually in our homes. And now it was 4:45 on a Friday afternoon and my only plan for the weekend was watching a Buffy the Vampire Slayer marathon from Netflix. The 77-year-old was right. I was not going to meet a man anytime soon. The news media was full of stories about how hard it is to get pregnant after the age of 30, forget 35. And now I was 38. My biological clock was ticking away, causing a low level of desperation that made me feel depressed and hopeless. It's hard to initiate major life changes in a state of panic.

So I started small. On the way home from work, I made a list in my head of life changes I could make to meet men.

> 1. Move to a city with more like-minded men. Portland, Seattle, and Albuquerque would be full of men who liked hiking and camping.
> 2. Get more involved in the independent music and film scene in Omaha. But I wasn't sure how to meet those people. The first question most people ask you is what high school you went to. I went to high school in NY and Omaha can feel like a club for insiders only.
> 3. Join the community theatre. Omaha has the biggest one in the country, I'm told.

I tapped the steering wheel. My ideas were lousy. I wasn't going to move and I wasn't going to make inroads with the cool people in Omaha. Instead of going straight home, I decided to go to the art store. If nothing else, at least I could start a new painting this weekend. (Yes, I did attempt to live my dream. I studied painting at Pratt Institute in Brooklyn. Ten years after graduation, I went back for a master's in audiology because I couldn't make my living off being an artist.) I still painted, but I didn't even attempt to sell my work anymore.

I don't know why I can't meet men. I'm not bad looking. I'm funny and fit. And I have a retirement fund and no credit card debt. In my twenties I dated. I even had a serious relationship with someone but, well, it didn't work out and I don't like to talk about it. Maybe Omaha is to blame, but it seems that the

older I become, the fewer men I meet. It doesn't help that I'm
a little introverted and around men I can be nervous and tense.

My cell phone rang as I pulled into the store parking lot. It
was my best friend, Izzy Jaramillo. She's a speech pathologist
and lives eight blocks from me. "I drove by the paint store on
the way home from work and decided to re-paint my kitchen,"
she said. "Want to come over and help? I've got wine and I
can order pizza."

"Sure," I said, relieved to have something to do tonight.

"I'm still at the store. I'm trying to decide between a Granny
Smith green and a tomato red. Can you meet me at my house
in an hour or two?"

I hung up with her and headed into the art store. I only
needed canvas and some stretchers, but I found myself
wandering through the aisles, looking at frivolous
merchandise, like decorative envelopes. I was playing around
with some glitter ink pens when the bell on the front door
dinged and a tall, dark-haired guy strolled in from the street.
He was outright handsome. He had on jeans, a t-shirt, and
some moccasin-like shoes. We had a moment of eye contact.
He looked at me like, "Wow, who are you?" and headed my
way. His glance made my cheeks flush red. I looked down at
my pens, wishing I was looking at something more
intellectual, like, say, linseed oil. When he was a foot away, he
crouched down to examine a pile of drawing pads that sat on a
lower shelf.

Recognizing the golden opportunity at my feet, I tried to
remember if I'd shaved my legs recently. I should be better
about shaving when I wear skirts to work. I don't always
bother if there's just a light stubble. One of my ex-boyfriends
used to call it my Don Johnson look. I could hear the hot guy
on the floor next to me flipping through the stack. He'd be
finished in another minute. My brain scrolled through a list of
one-liners. I thought of and dismissed, "Hot enough for you?"
and "I like your shoes," finally seizing on dropping my keys,
so that he could hand them back to me. I got a firm grip on my
keys, took a deep breath, and...suddenly I felt something wet
and cold on my calf muscle. A tongue. The man was on the
floor, licking my leg. I dropped my keys and screamed. The
man on the floor beside me leapt backward. Too late, I saw

that the storeowner's miniature collie was also on the floor behind me. The owner and other customers stared at me in alarm. "Sorry," I stammered. "The dog licked me." How could I explain that I thought the man had licked me? I turned to go. The man on the floor handed me my keys.

"Not a dog person?" he asked as he stroked the collie.

I love dogs. I thought you were licking my leg. I left the store without answering him.

So Omaha cannot take all the blame for my single status.

As soon as I got home from the art store, I looked up the community theatre's phone number and called. They connected me with their volunteer coordinator, a woman named Nancy. I explained about volunteering.

"Sure," she said. "We'd love to have you. We do ask that you commit to an entire production, which is about two-months of your time. Our next run begins in a week, so you could come down this weekend. Training will take about six hours. Then you'd work about three hours, four nights a week, Thursday through Sundays, Sunday being the matinee."

I thanked her and hung up without committing. I did want to meet people. But did I have to sacrifice all my free time to do it?

When *Sex and the City* was on television, my married friends used to moan about how much they missed dating, how boring their lives were, how much work their husbands were, and how they wished they could be single, like me. The naïve little darlings! Real life dating is not like what you see on television, unless you watch Liz Lemon, on 30 Rock. In real life, if you're in your 30s or 40s, it's a full-time job to even meet men, much less date them.

But I wasn't going to let some 77-year-old lady read me like a book and badger me into becoming a stenographer. I was going to take action. Tonight I'd hang out with Izzy, but starting tomorrow, I was going to find a way to meet a man, get married, and have children. This book that you're reading or listening to chronicles my two-year journey into dating. In this book, you will read the truth of dating, not Hollywood's glam version of singlehood. It's not all doom and gloom, but if you pass this book on to your married friends to read, I guarantee that they'll never romanticize your single life again. They might even start to sympathize with your plight.

So I sat at my kitchen table, racking my brains for other ways to meet men. What about blind dates? Blind dates reek with the scent of desperation covered up by a thin layer of adventurousness. You have to be brave to go on a blind date, but your courage is probably motivated by a baser emotion. Mine was fear. I was scared I'd run out of time to have children.

I knew I needed to be proactive about my dating life, or lack thereof. Back then, I thought I had control over my singledom. That, with a little effort, I could meet the man of my dreams, or at least, a nice guy I could marry.

Chapter 2
Blind Dates

Why do blind dates get such a bad rap? I've always wished that more people would set me up on them. When I decided to be proactive about dating, I petitioned everyone I knew to set me up with someone, starting with Izzy while we painted her kitchen Gazpacho Red. No one had any prospects. Well, that's not quite true. I take a painting class from an artist in town, named Jack. His friend, Eli, paints there too, along with another regular, Kate. Jack and Eli are of that class of men who stayed in shape after they got married. Jack is about 50. Eli is ten years younger. They are intelligent, nice men who love their wives and children. And yet, they have terrible judgment about men.

Case in point: When I asked them about a setup, Jack and Eli suggested a friend of theirs: An unemployed, 50-year-old artist with a drinking/rage problem. (Off-road rage, as I like to call it.) His M.O. is to appear, rant all over you, and leave. That was the best offer I got. Kate, also married with children, understood why their friend wasn't a viable option, but didn't know any single men.

Left to my own resources, I'll never find a man. I'm too comfortable in my quiet little world. My magazine stand at home is overflowing with New Yorkers I haven't read yet. I paint. I'm learning to knit. And attractive men make me befuddled. When I see a man that I feel drawn to, it's like, well, it's like my soul leaves my body and the soul of my 13-year-old self jumps in to take the helm. If a guy tries to engage me, even just smile at me, I'm terrified, I'm speechless, I'm sweating. I feel like I'm wearing braces again. I want to keel over and puke. (You remember the licking dog story from Chapter One. Did I need someone to set me up, or what?)

Finally, a co-worker, Lona, recommended someone she knew from her second job. Lona is 22 years old and she has two jobs because, somehow, between the ages of 18 and 21, she managed to work up a $35,000 credit card debt. Now she's enrolled in a program where they educated her about budgets and cut up her credit cards. She has to pay for everything with cash or check. She's on the ten year plan to be paid off, but is trying to speed things up with the second job.

Lona and I had just finished doing a hearing test on an 18-month old with pink eye. We were de-germing at the sink when she asked me. "Are you still looking for blind dates?"

"Sure. What have you got?"

"My co-worker, Ted. He's just the nicest guy."

"Why don't you want to date him?" I asked.

"Well, he's 40."

I understood.

"I thought I could give him your number, and have him call?"

"Yeah. I'd love it," I said. I shut off the water. My next patient, a 6-year-old, was waiting. "Thanks for thinking of me," I said.

Ted called and we made plans to meet for dinner. I was so hopeful that I wore a skirt and shaved. He wanted to pick me up, and since Lona knew him, I agreed and gave him directions to my apartment.

I live in a four-unit building. I love my apartment. It's a two bedroom, with a large living room and five closets. The place is owned by a woman in her seventies, Agnes, who's a real powerhouse. Her building is immaculate. She's the kind of landlady who calls you because she notices that your garage door opener is sticking and might need to be replaced.

I'm the only renter under the age of 60. My downstairs neighbor on the west side is a 72-year-old woman with teddy bear vases in her window. Hanging from her door is a quilted kitten holding a heart that says, "Welcome." Both my downstairs east and upstairs west neighbors are 68-year-old, retired men, Buzz and Walter. They never talk. I rarely talk to any of them, except a friendly hello.

The only real negative is that the kitchen is small and the walls are thin. I hear Walter's radio like he's playing it in my closet. Walter is a frail man who gets up at 5 a.m. every morning, walks downstairs and unlocks the street door. At 9:00 at night, he goes back downstairs and locks it. I'd made the mistake, shortly after moving in, of greeting him in the hallway with, "Hi, how are you?"

"Not well," he replied. "I have terminal bone cancer. It's extremely painful." Walter wore giant glasses that magnified milky eyes. They blinked as he waited for my response.

"I, er, am sorry," I said.

"I can't eat because I've lost my appetite." He had a pasty complexion and he smelled of mothballs.

"Is there anything I can do?" I asked.

"There's nothing anyone can do. It's terminal." He blinked at me for a few seconds longer.

"If there's anything you need…"

He opened his door and went inside. I wondered who was taking care of him. According to Agnes, he had no family in town. As far as I could tell, no one ever came to visit. He left every Thursday morning at 7:30 for something, but other than that, he always appeared to be home. Of course, since I worked during the day, he had 9 hours that I couldn't account for. Maybe friends did come over.

On the night of my blind date with Ted, when I was finished getting ready, I sat in the living room with a book. I was too nervous to actually read, though. Butterflies were jumping around in my stomach. At 7 o'clock on the dot, I heard the street door open and footsteps tramp upstairs. They paused in front of Walter's apartment, and then moved on to mine. Instead of ringing the bell, he knocked. Taking a deep breath, I put on a smile and opened the door. He looked nice. He was slight and fair-skinned. He was wearing beige polyester pants and a silk shirt with zigzags of color. His shoes were loafers with tassels.

Okay, Reader, I think I know what you are thinking. That I'm superficial. But I'm not really motivated by looks. At least, not that much. I know that people become beautiful when you love their personality. Men I've thought were unattractive became beautiful to me once they started making me laugh. The problem with Ted was that he was 40-years old but dressed like my grandpa. Maybe that's what people mean by chemistry.

We did the meet-n-greet. He complimented my apartment, and we were off to the restaurant. As we sat down to dinner, I tried to be open to the possibility that chemistry could develop.

T: "So, Lona said you paint?"
Me: "Yes. How about you? Are you into any arts?
T: "I write."
Me: "I didn't know that. What do you write?"
T: "I've written several episodes of Star Trek."
Me: "You're kidding. You're a professional writer! Wow."
T: "I sent the episodes in, but they didn't use them."
Me: "Oh, gotcha."
T: "I'm a big Star Trek fan."
Me (jokingly): "Do you dress up in those outfits and go to conventions?"
T (serious): "Sometimes."
Silence.
T: "Do you like Star Trek?"
Me (honestly): "I've never seen a single episode."

Our date continued, but this narrative will not. I'm not going to torture you with the rest of our chemistry-free encounter. You'd probably either 1) lose all hope about your own single status and the power of blind dates, or 2) become so bored that you'd fall asleep. Either way, you'd stop reading, and then you'd never find out about what happened to me later.

When it rains, it pours. The next morning, one of my patients and his wife told me that they wanted to set me up. They had come in for a hearing aid adjustment.

"Now, my doctor is telling me this hearing loss is no big

deal," Archie said as they walked in the room. His wife, Edna, was right behind him.

"Huh?" I asked.

"He says I have presbycusis, and that it's normal for my age, so he doesn't know why I need hearing aids." Archie was in his early seventies. He had a shock of white hair that usually stood on end. He leaned across the table at me. "So, what do you say?"

"Well, presbycusis is just a fancy word for older-age-hearing-loss."

He started laughing at that.

"I had to get reading glasses last year," I said. "It normal for my age, but that doesn't mean I don't wear the glasses."

"I can hear," he said.

"I can see," I said, "just not close-up." Then I added, "You can hear but you can't understand."

He slapped the table with his palm. "Exactly."

"That's because your hearing loss is in the high frequencies, where consonants are. So you hear speech, but it sounds mushy."

"I'll tell you something," Archie said. "These suckers were hard to get used to." He was talking about his hearing aids. "But once you've worn them for a while, you wonder how you got by without them."

"He never takes them out," Edna said.

"Except to go to bed, and to bathe." He smiled. "You've done a hell of a job for me."

"Did you tell your doctor?"

He slapped the table again. "You betcha!"

"By the way," Edna said. "You're single, aren't you?"

"Yes," I said, perking up.

She bowed her head a little, to add suspense to what she was about to say. "We know the perfect man for you," she said.

"He's the son of our very good friends," Archie said.

"He's very successful."

I wanted to ask them a couple of questions, like "Is he liberal? Is he religious?" But I don't like my patients to know my politics or religious beliefs, so I settled for, "Neat."

"Can we give him your work number?"

I didn't think that would be a conflict of interest, since I'd never seen him as a patient. "Sure. What's his name?"

"Chris. Chris Tompkins."

"Terrific. Thanks! I really appreciate you thinking of me."

Chris called a week later.

"Hi Quinn. This is Chris."

I was just at my desk for a few minutes between patients. I'd answered the phone while checking my email and listening to a hearing aid I'd just gotten back from repair.

"Hi," I said, not knowing who he was but thinking he was a patient.

"What's up?" he asked.

"I'm sorry," I confessed. "Who are you?"

"Maybe I should call back when you're off planet moon."

This confused me even more because the moon isn't a planet. I continued to pause and then he said, "This is Chris Tompkins. My parent's friends set us up. Is this all coming back to you now?"

"Most people I've never met before give me more than a first name to go on."

"Never mind. Listen, my parents and their friends said you were something special, and I'm going to trust that and tell you right now that I'd just as soon forego a bunch of empty phone conversations and meet for dinner. What do you say? V. Mertz?"

It was one of the more expensive restaurants in town. *Why not?* I figured. I mean, I really wanted to meet someone. "Sure," I said.

"Terrific. How is Friday? Say, seven?"

"That works." I'd have to miss TLC's Friday night line-up, but I could live with that.

"Great. My Saab is in the shop. Will you mind driving?"

This took me aback, since I would have preferred separate cars. But I'm a modern woman and he came with references. "Sure. Where do you live?"

Chris's apartment was in Dundee, an old, well-kept Omaha neighborhood. A lot of the apartment buildings in that area are charming. They have open courtyards and gargoyles. Some of

them remind me of monasteries. His was a sixties-style
building, square and cement. I could hear the TV blaring when
I knocked at his door, 2B. A man in an undershirt answered the
door. He was nice-looking with short, light brown hair and
greenish eyes. He had a slight potbelly bulging over his jeans.
He was holding a beer can. Budweiser. "Quinn, right?"
 "Yes. Chris?"
 "So, is Quinn short for something?"
 "Yes. Quinnley."
 "Your parents wanted a boy?"
 "It's a girl's name or a boy's name, like Chris."
 "Well, la di da."
 I probably should have turned around and left. But I really
wanted to make this date work, so I just gave him a level stare.
He broke off eye contact and cleared his throat. "Uh, I'm just
getting ready. Let me put a shirt on," he said. I stepped inside
and peeked at my watch. I wasn't early. In fact, I was five
minutes late. His small living room was packed with two
recliners and a sofa. A big screen television took up half the
room. Newspapers were strewn across the floor. There was an
empty plate on the floor and a KFC container stuffed with oil-
stained napkins next to it. The television was blaring a football
game. It always annoys me to have a television running while
I'm visiting someone. In my mind, the television should be
turned off as soon as company walks in the door. It's like
taking off your baseball cap in class. It's just good manners.
 "If I'm catching you at a bad time," I called into the
bedroom, "we can always reschedule."
 "Not at all. I'm starved."
 "It's just that I don't want you to miss your game." My
passive-aggressiveness was failing, as usual. I don't know why
I bother; it never works for me.
 "Nah, my team's not playing."
 "Ok, then," I said quietly, to myself.

 The wait staff at the restaurant was excellent. The food was
good, too. Even our conversation was okay. Chris turned out to
have traveled a lot, and we spent most of the evening
comparing notes on different European towns and cities.

"I loved Rome!" Chris said. "It was my favorite city in Italy."

"Mine too," I said. "But I was only there for four days. I was so homesick for NY when I was in Venice. Rome felt closer to home."

"Are you a city girl, then?"

I shrugged. "I miss public transportation. And the variety of people. But I think I'm happiest when I'm standing in a forest of ponderosa pine. I love the smells of the outdoors."

"Me, I'm a city guy. I like my indoor plumbing, my television, and my espresso."

I laughed. "Sure. Say, what did you think of the toilets in Europe?"

"The one thing they don't do better than us. They suck."

"Try being a girl," I said. "In France, half the toilets made you squat and pee into a little hole. The first time I went to the bathroom, I thought I'd walked into a shower stall."

"Yeah," he said. "That would be hard for a girl. How did you do that?"

"Not easily." I said. "I once peed on my shoe, in the south of France. In Cannes, I think. Or Nice."

"Did you see the Picasso museum there?"

"Wasn't that the one with the giant Roman head on its side?"

"Yes. That's the one." The waiter brought us our check. I reached under the table to grab my purse.

"Uh-oh." Chris said.

"What's wrong?"

"I forgot my wallet."

"Oh, that's okay," I told him. "My treat." I scanned the bill as I slid my credit card into the holder. The total was high. His entrée was almost twice the price of mine and he'd had two beers to my one. I don't know why this annoyed me, but it did.

I drove him home. Getting out of the car, he paused. "I had a really nice time," he said.

"Me too." I lied. Although, he hadn't been all bad. The conversation was interesting.

"Do you want to come in?"

To your rat's nest? "It's late."

"Okay. Well, I'll call you."

Why do men always finish with that line? Don't they know

that line is the mother of all bad lines from men? "I'll call you," is man-speak for "I don't have the courage to tell you to your face that I'm uninterested. So I'm going to tell you something to get me out of here, and when I get home, I'll never think of you again."

But I underestimated Chris. He *did* call. And invited me out for dinner the following week. "*With* my wallet," he'd added. I didn't want to go. But on the other hand, it seemed unfair to refuse. He obviously wanted to prove to me that he could pay for a meal. And, wasn't the conversation pretty good? The day before our date, he called to cancel. A good friend of his had just showed up from out of town.

"Oh," I said. I thought his voice sounded funny.

"Actually, that's not completely true." Ah. Here we go. "The truth is that I met someone else the same time I met you," Chris said. "And we hit it off better than you and I did."

Translation: we had sex, I thought.

"So, I think it's better if you and I just remain friends."

"Sure," I told him, trying unsuccessfully to remove the emotion from my voice.

"Okay, I'll call you then."

We hung up. I said to the wall, "I'll never hear from him again." Then I burst into tears.

Post-Blow Off Analysis (Aided by best-friend, Izzy, who has a boyfriend, but still understands):

"You are crying because you've been rejected, not because *he* has rejected you," she said.

"Well, maybe."

"Definitely. It hurts to be cast off, no matter whether you *liked* the guy or not."

"But Chris was a loser, and yet, he thought he could do better than me. He spent an evening talking to me and decided that he didn't like me."

"He's a dumb ass," Izzy said.

The good news is, within a day I was completely over the hurt. Usually, I take months, and with one guy, years, to get over romantic rejection. This guy took 24-hours. It was freeing, really, to recover so quickly.

So, see, Reader? Blind dates aren't all bad. No, I didn't get a man, but I learned a lot about myself. I did some good work on my psyche. I got the chance to do what men do, pick a person up, take him to a restaurant, pay for the meal, and drive him home. I even got the offer of sex thrown into the deal. Ahhh. It's refreshing to go on blind dates. It keeps you on your toes and teaches you that you aren't as special as you thought you were.

Chapter 3
The Problem with Novels

Irresponsible writers are perhaps the main reason why educated women are still single in their thirties. These writers create men who are so incredible, so brilliant, sexy, perceptive, and good in bed, that woman actually start to think they should hold out for men like this.

I'll name a couple of the ones I'm holding out for: Diana Galbodon's Jamie (great big, muscled Scottish clansman who can fight off five men alone and bring a woman to orgasm with ease), Barbara Kingsolver's Loyd (intelligent, great arm muscles, tall with black hair to his shoulders, gentle, good with dogs), Janet Evanovich's Joe Morelli (let me just pour a glass of water down my shirt as I talk about him–Trenton cop, gorgeous, dates a very spunky woman and takes a lot of crap from her, owns a cute little home that he inherited from his aunt, has some issues that he carries around with real stamina), and finally, Elizabeth George's Lynley (Scotland Yard Inspector, Earl, golden hair, dressed to kill, drives a silver Bentley, extremely sensitive, tortured in love, kind, generous, able to function in a hostile environment without taking things personally).

Every single one of the men above (with the possible exception of Lynley) is a hard-body. All are champions in the female orgasm. These men are much more dangerous than someone like Jane Austen's Mr. Darcy. Austen gave Darcy flaws; he was arrogant and obnoxious. Contemporary authors pretend to give flaws. For instance, Evanovich will comment on how Morelli's eyes have a look about them now that makes a woman think twice before approaching him. (Cop eyes that have seen a lot.) George reports that Lynley can no longer run a seven-minute mile and he needs reading glasses. Lynley also has massive amounts of guilt that make him feel the need to continue his very disheartening job as an inspector at Scotland Yard. But women don't care about flaws like that; they are part of the appeal.

If the authors of these characters were men, at least we'd have a hope in Hell. At least I'd know there's a man out there who aspires to something like his character. But these are women creating their ultimate fantasies.

The perfect man isn't out there, obviously. But the right man might be, and he probably isn't a good swordfighter or a Bentley owner. And…does any guy know how to give multiple orgasms, or are those a work of fiction, too?

Chapter 4
You Won't Meet a Man
Planting Rhubarb

I first heard about speed dating from Eli, in painting class. Since he's married, it's no surprise that he'd recommend a night of torture for single people and think it sounded like fun.

Painting class happens every Thursday night. Our conversations in a nutshell:

Jack—I just downloaded a huge collection of obscure Johnny Cash songs.

Me—You know, they are prosecuting people for that.

Jack—There are 3 million people on that site every time I log on. How are they going to get us all?

Eli—You can find out who's being prosecuted. Just log onto the federal government's web page. Actually, you can buy most songs now for just a dollar on several sites. I'm waiting for them to do that same thing with DVD, at some point. My wife just got the first five seasons of Buffy on DVD. Those television series get pricey.

Kate—Who's Buffy?

Me—The Vampire Slayer.

Kate—The what? (Did I mention before that Kate, a brilliant redhead, knows absolutely nothing about pop culture, even though she's in her late 30s? You'd think SHE'D be the single one, but no, married with two kids.)

Eli—I think you should try this speed dating. They get equal numbers of men and women. Then you sit down across from one, talk for four minutes, and move to the next one. You meet a room full of people, all in one night.

Me—I'd rather be slayed.

Izzy had heard of speed dating. "I know one or two people who've done it," she said. "But what about Internet dating? It seems less gimmicky."

"Are you nuts? That's dangerous. Any psycho could be doing the Internet."

"A lot of people do the Internet, Quinn. I know a handful of people in serious relationships that began online."

I told relayed some horrifying news stories I'd heard on television but she wasn't swayed.

"Everything's a risk. But maybe Speed Dating is better for you," she said.

"Neither way is an option." I told her.

Izzy smiled. "You'll meet someone. You have to. You're amazing. You'll find a guy who's amazing too."

"You think?"

"Sure. Maybe a deliveryman. Or, does the meter reader have to come inside to take his reading? Maybe you'll have a gas leak, and the gasman will recognize you as his other half."

"Just because you're in some sort of happy relationship. When you were single…"

"I had a blast," she finished.

Izzy was lying through her teeth.

"You have no idea what's it's like for me," I said. "I'm four years older than you."

"Enough with the eggs. You've got plenty left. You have plenty of time."

"You just don't understand," I said.

"Oh, I think I do. Sal is nowhere near ready for marriage. Just because I have a boyfriend, doesn't mean I'm on the verge of starting a family. Oh, did I tell you? Melissa, at work, is getting married next month. That's the third wedding in six weeks. She told us at lunch yesterday. She said, 'I know this seems sudden, but when you know, you just know.' God. She looked so happy. And everyone was so happy for her. I wanted to tell her, 'You think you're going to live happily ever after, but it's all a lie.' She is so naïve."

Izzy was married at 21, divorced at 28. It was a devastating, heartbreaking divorce from which I don't think she's even remotely recovered. She met her boyfriend, Sal, when she was 31, and although she wants to get married, she also believes that all marriages are doomed to failure. She's full of contradictions like that. She's joyful, but very sad. She's kind, but very angry. She reminds me of a rock with veins of silver and other minerals through them. She has these very different streaks that, viewed all at once, are strikingly beautiful. Some of the veins are small, hard cores of cynicism. Others are overwhelming streaks of generosity. Even though I'm older sometimes she feels like my elder. One time, a medium looking at past lives told her that she was on her very last life before Nirvana. She has moments of wisdom that make me believe the medium was correct. If you don't believe in reincarnation, then you could make the argument that she is tougher than me because her life has been less sheltered. She hasn't always had it very easy. The hard knocks have left their traces, but they only make her compassion for others even more startling. She would give me anything, including her last dollar.

But she is the last person I'd want at my wedding. "I'd like to tell that girl," Izzy was saying, "'You think he loves you? You think he'll always be around to fix your car and shovel your sidewalk? Good luck with that. You stupid, naïve little girl. There's no such thing as happily ever after!'"

"Are you going to the wedding?" I just ignore Izzy's anti-marriage rants. Debate is useless.

"I'm going to bring Sal. Maybe it will force the issue."

"Force him to decide to commit to a lie?"

Izzy shrugged. She has no shame about the conflict between her desire to be married and her belief that all marriages are empty promises. Hope springs eternal, I guess.

"You should leave Sal home and see if there are any eligible men at the wedding."

"Hmmm. That's an idea."

Izzy is 5'10" with blue eyes and blond hair. Spanish surname, handed down from a great-grandfather, but she's a total Scandinavian babe. Men love her. It makes me sick. She's a real charmer, too. In terms of male interaction, she's much more advanced than I am. I'd rate her skills at an 8, on a scale of 1-10. I'm a 3. Maybe a 2. Okay, fine, I'm a 1.

My other best friend, Ann, lives downtown. She rents a loft in an up-and-coming area where developers have been restoring warehouses. Nearby is an entirely restored warehouse area that draws tourists and high rents, called the Old Market. The Old Market has unique, local shops, very few chain stores, and lots of Goth teenagers wandering around, wishing they were in SoHo or Seattle. Ann's neighborhood mostly just has drunks and homeless shelters.

Ann's an early riser, like me, and we sometimes meet at 6:30 a.m. for a leisurely coffee before work.

"Speed dating sounds like a nightmare," she said. "What are we, cattle?"

"Yes! Exactly," I sipped my coffee contentedly. "I'm not that desperate."

"And yet…"

"What yet? There's no yet. There's just nothing good about it."

Ann nodded. She has long black hair, like me. People always mistake us for twins, even though our bone structure is different. She is petite. Her wrists are the width of quarters and she's a head shorter. But people see the dark hair and the fair skin and stop looking. Ann is a college-educated retail worker who doesn't know what she wants to be when she grows up. Her jobs change with the seasons. Right now, she's a sales clerk at Williams Sonoma. "And yet, maybe this would be a way to broaden your social circle," she said.

"Do you want to do it with me?" Ann hasn't had a date in years. She claims she isn't even looking.

"Sure," she said.

"Really?"

"Yeah. Just as soon as I'm finished shoving needles in my eyes."

My office mate, Lucy, is, as Bridget Jones would say, a smug-married person. She's thirty-three and has been married for four years to her grade school sweetheart. Status on single male friends they know: all losers.

"What kept you so long?" Lucy asked. It was 12:30 and I was only just back from clinic.

"Faker." I sat down at my computer to check my email. Every once in a while, a child or adult tries to fake a hearing loss. They really tick me off because it takes time to break a faker, and in the meantime, other patients with real hearing loss are kept waiting. Or an audiologist misses half her lunch.

"Was it that 13-year-old girl?" Middle school girls are notorious for faking hearing loss.

"No. She had a moderate, unilateral loss. This was the 24-year-old guy. Workman's comp." Lucy and I have most of our conversations with our backs to each other. It's the nature of office life with computers.

"Have you heard of speed dating?" Lucy makes rapid subject changes without warning.

"It's not for me." I was eating a cheese sandwich and deleting spam. What was up with speed dating? I felt like:

Knock, knock.
Who's there?
The Universe.
The Universe who?
The Universe thinks you need to speed date.

"It was on the news last night. It sounds like fun. You meet up at a bar with equal amounts of men and women. Each woman is seated with a man across from her. A bell rings…"

"I know." I turned around in my chair. "I'm not interested."

"It sounds like fun to me!"

"That's because you're married and don't have to actually do it."

"I miss dating."

"That's because you never dated."

"I wish I had," she said.

She was wearing a white sweater with little teddy bears on the front. She had matching teddy bear earrings and teddy bear socks. The dating world would eat her alive. "I'd trade places with you in a heartbeat," I told her. "Would you with me?"

"Husbands are a lot of extra work!"

Everyone says this to me. I can't tell if they are trying to make me feel better, or if they truly mean it. "Extra work? Are you kidding?" I asked. "Right now, I cook every meal. I clean the house. I do all the shopping. I take the car in to the mechanics. I pay all the bills. I go next door for store-bought lemon cake and instant coffee when my dying neighbor invites me over for a visit. I'm tired of doing everything myself!"

"Your neighbor is dying?"

"Yes." I opened my knapsack and took out an apple. "He has started inviting me over for cake and he is not a conversationalist. We have many, long, drawn out silences. When he does speak, it's to correct my grammar and complain about how my generation is destroying the English language." I took a bite. Crunch, crunch.

"Ernie would never have gone over there. I would have done it. And while I was gone, he would have either been watching television or making a mess in the kitchen I'd just cleaned." She picked up a chart. "Believe me. I worked a lot less when I was single."

"You were never single," I snapped and turned back to my computer. I was unreasonably angry with her for having had the same man since she was 12.

"You could have fun," Lucy continued. "Act all serious, but then ask silly questions like, 'What's your favorite flavor of ice cream,' and write down what they say, as if the flavor hinges on a call back from you."

"Or your favorite season of Survivor," I said, against my better judgment.

"Just do it for laughs. It's an experience to tell your grandchildren about." She paused. "But you won't get grandchildren if you don't date…"

I gave speed dating more thought as I worked through my afternoon clinic. I had a new patient at four o'clock. Lonesh. Both parents came, which doesn't usually happen. I mispronounced his name when I called him from the waiting room.

He rolled his eyes at his parents, turned to me and said, "Low NESH."

"Sorry, Lonesh." I said, with the correct emphasis.

"It's okay," he replied. "Everyone always gets it wrong. Let's get started, shall we?" Reader, did I mention he was six?

Back in the audiology sound booth, I got the history from his parents. They had no hearing concerns, but Lonesh had failed two school hearing screens. As I set Lonesh up for testing, I asked him questions in a soft voice. "So Lonesh, how old are you?"

"Six."

"Ahh. And what's your teacher's name?"

"Mrs. Mrs. I forget."

I smiled because I've yet to meet a six-year-old who can remember his or her teacher's name. But he understood everything I said, so I was pretty sure he was feigning a hearing loss. *Two in one day!* I thought. Three minutes into testing, I thought differently. Lonesh's hearing thresholds were normal in the low frequencies. As I moved up to the higher pitches, his hearing became progressively worse. That's not a hearing loss that a six-year-old would ever fake. I started to register the parents sitting behind me. I needed to take a read of them because I was going to be giving them some hard news in a few minutes.

They were well-dressed, professional-looking people. Their glasses alone looked to cost about $400 each. Both were texting on Blackberries while I tested Lonesh. In spite of their son's unusual name, theirs were plain-Jane. Joan and Ron. Lonesh had a moderate sensorineural hearing loss in the high frequencies. I took him out of the sound booth and showed him to some books that he could look at, just outside the booth. Then I turned to the parents. They were probably about my age. Both were good-looking, with more style than you usually see in Omaha.

"Well, the hearing test I did agrees with the others. Lonesh has a hearing loss in the higher frequencies. That means that even though he can hear you when you talk, he is probably missing the higher pitched sounds, like t, sh, s, f, th, and c. He might hear some of these, but they will be very soft, like a whisper." I paused to breathe. I've been giving parents bad news on hearing tests for years, but it still makes me nervous. They seemed to be taking it all in, so I kept going. "It's a sensorineural loss, which means that it is unlikely to improve." They continued to look at me. Neither one had any visible reaction. Up until this point, they were just hearing a lot of gobble-gook that's easy to dismiss. My next few sentences would change that. "Has anyone talked to you about how we would treat that?" He had three previous hearing tests, after all.

"No." They both shrugged.

Damn. "We would treat that with hearing aids. Hearing aids will help make those high-pitched sounds louder. It won't restore his hearing to normal, like glasses can make vision normal, but it will make a lot more of those sounds audible to him." The parents were unreadable. "Do you have any questions?"

"So," the mom began, "he'll just wear one?"

"No, he'll do better with two. He has two ears, and the loss is about the same in both. With two, he'll do better in background noise and he may be able to localize sound."

"And he'll just wear them at school?"

"He'll wear them full-time. Just like glasses."

"And how long will he have to wear them for?"

Forever. "He'll wear them his whole life, probably, just like glasses."

"Does insurance pay for them?"

I shook my head. "Almost never. But you could call your company to check."

"And how much do they cost?"

"Per aid, there is a range that goes from $1400 to almost $3000." The mom visibly balked at this. Who could blame her? "But we can start by putting Lonesh in a loaner aid. We have a loaner hearing aid program here that we use to fit kids right away, while their parents come to grips with everything and figure out finances. And there are some good funding sources, if you qualify, that will help you pay for the hearing aids."

"We won't qualify," Mom said. "But that doesn't mean we have $6000 lying around."

I nodded. "He probably won't need the most expensive ones and you'll have some time to prepare. He can wear the loaner for a few months while you work out how you'll pay."

The father was silent throughout the entire interchange. I looked at both of them when I talked, but he never made eye contact with me. We chatted some more and then I took them over to the Ear Nose and Throat doctor, or ENT, for short. By now it was five o'clock. There's never enough time scheduled for these newly identified hearing losses. While they waited for the doctor, I passed behind them and overheard the mother say to the father, "If his teacher doesn't have a problem, then I don't know why…" They were still coming to grips. That's why it was good to have ENT directly after me. Doctors have much more authority with the general public and their opinions carry more weight. She would recommend hearing aids and this would make them trust me more.

So, parents learn that their child has a permanent disability. And in the same conversation they realize that they are going to have to pay out at least $2000, if not more. And hearing aids are not even going to "fix" the problem. Their kid will hear better, but he won't hear everything.

I hung around in the back hall of ENT while the doctor talked to the parents. When she finished, I went in to take ear impressions. "I'm going to squirt this goopy stuff in your ears," I told Lonesh. "You won't be able to hear anything once it goes in. In about five minutes it will get hard, and I'll take it out. Then I'll send it off to a factory that makes the ear molds that go in your ear." I had already shown him the different colors the ear molds could come in. Of course, his mother wanted something discreet–skin colored. Lonesh wanted a yellow and red swirl. Whenever possible, I let the kid choose the ear mold colors. It's the kid that has to wear the aids all day long. He or she might as well feel cool.

As soon as the ear impression material was in his ears, Lonesh said, challengingly, "I can still hear you." His mom asked him a question, moving her mouth with no sound. She asked something to do with pants—I got that much.

"You asked me what pants I have on!" Lonesh said. "See? I told you I could hear you!"

"He can hear us," his mom told me. It's funny how people are. She'd already forgotten that she'd turned her voice off when she had talked to him. She wanted to show me that he could hear, but he'd been lip-reading. Denial is not always rooted in rationality.

"He's a good lip reader." I said to Lonesh, "What's your brother's name?"

"Rantall!" he said.

I put my hand in front of my mouth to block his view. "Do you have a dog?"

"What?"

I turned to his parents. "He's a smart little boy. He's using lip reading to fill in the blanks. When a child is bright, like Lonesh, he will perform well in spite of his hearing loss. What you'll find though, once he gets hearing aids, is that he is less exhausted by the end of the day. He's exerting a lot of energy to communicate, and if he has a boring teacher, or if the subject matter doesn't interest him, he'll be less likely to exert the energy it takes to listen." This seemed to resonate in the mom. Maybe they'd gotten that complaint before.

Sometimes I give too much information. I couldn't tell with these parents when to stop talking because the mom was engaged and the dad was disengaged. When in doubt, I always ramble. "You'll probably notice," I continued, "that his comprehension breaks down in difficult situations, like when there are a lot of people talking at once, or a lot of background noise, or when there's distance between him and the person he's talking to."

"Should we stop at the grocery store on the way home?" the mom asked the father.

"Is there one near here?" he asked.

"There's that Bakers, just before Ames." I took this to mean that they had taken in all the information they could handle and I shut up. When the ear impressions were out of Lonesh's ear and in the box, they packed up and headed home. I left just a few minutes after them. The offices were empty and security was closing down the building.

I couldn't wait to get home. It was Friday. I had a pork chop marinating in soy sauce, olive oil, and vodka. I was halfway through a lightweight, cotton sweater I was knitting for myself. That would be my evening. Dinner and knitting to the lineup of Friday night sitcoms. I tried to imagine how it would be to go home to someone. Schlepping up the stairs and opening the door to the smell of dinner cooking.

"You're late, Hon. Long day?"

I could see myself dropping my bags on the floor as I sat down at the kitchen table. Maybe he would put a glass of wine in front of me as I said, "Long day! New ID at 4:30. I'm exhausted."

As I pulled into my garage for real, I felt a pang of self-pity about my empty apartment upstairs. I sat in my car for a minute after my garage door had already closed. Okay, time to get going. The interior light that came on when I opened my car door seemed desolate.

Walter was in the basement, folding his laundry. He did his wash every Friday morning at five, like clockwork. The other tenants had dryers, but Walter hung his clothes on two lines he'd strung across the basement. Every Friday morning, on my way to work, I'd walk through walls of threadbare sheets, fraying shirts, and faded boxer shorts.

Tonight, he was folding his last sheet as I entered from my garage.

"Hi," I said. "How are you?"

"I'm not well. I have terminal bone cancer," he said.

"I know. I'm sorry."

"It's very painful."

"Is there anything I can do?" I asked.

He blinked. "There's nothing anyone can do. It's terminal."

I nodded. "Okay. Well, I'm going to go upstairs." I turned to leave.

"I've been meaning to mention the basement waste container," Walter said.

"Huh?"

"Right there," he indicated a plastic garbage barrel, filled three-quarters of the way with dryer lint. "I'm very weak. I can't drag that out to the curb any longer, and it's almost full."

I didn't know why Walter, who didn't have a dryer, took it upon himself to take out the lint, but I didn't ask. "I'll do it."

"I have almost no strength left in my hands."

"Okay." I slung my bag over my shoulder and headed upstairs. I didn't want to grow old alone. At the top of the basement steps, I unlocked my mailbox and took out an assortment of bills and junk mail. There was one envelope from my college roommate. No letter, just eight haphazardly snapped pictures of her two kids. The pictures were full of bright smiles. There were shots of them in a pumpkin patch, others of them playing on their front lawn, and a few of them in their pajamas, ready for bed. Both kids had my friend's eyes. The photos reminded me of a former co-worker, an audiologist where I did my fellowship training. She was happily married, with three kids. When I thought of their house, and their kids, the inside of my chest hurt from jealousy. "I want what you have," I had told her one day, during a lull in the usually busy clinic. She was standing in the doorway of her sound booth. In that clinic, your office was your sound booth. No windows, but a lot of peace and quiet.

"What have you done to meet people?" she'd asked. "Have you joined any clubs?"

"I'm not really a club person," I'd told her.

She'd nodded. "When I first moved here, I had no friends for the first six months. I couldn't meet anyone my age, male or female. I don't know...I'm kind of shy. Not really outgoing by nature."

I had nodded. I'd understood completely.

"My apartment, at the time, offered garden plots, and in good weather, I spent every evening in mine. I'm a real green thumb.

Anyway, I don't know why, but one night, out of nowhere, I was knee deep in soil and I realized, 'I'm never going to meet anyone, staying home on a Friday night to weed my rhubarb.' I joined the ski club the next week, and that's where I met my husband."

At the time, my response had been, "I don't like to ski."

Now, five years later, I opened the door to my apartment in Omaha, Nebraska. Complete silence. It was time to give speed dating a try.

Chapter 5
Speed Dating

The 4-Minute Date people had rented out an entire bar. I had dressed up in my best color, black. I was wearing a bold red lipstick. I sat in the parking lot and gave myself a pep talk. "You want to meet people." I looked at myself in my rearview mirror. "You can do this."

On the way inside, I passed a yellow Trans-Am with the license plate "I4HUSKR." You have to live in Nebraska, or be a football fan to understand or at least be aware of the rabid intensity of Husker football fans. On game day, the whole state wears red. My stepmother bought an Omaha t-shirt when she and my father came here to visit. Back in Florida, a man passed her in the grocery store and told her "Go Big Red!" She had no idea what he was talking about.

Inside the bar, there was a registration table where the organizers were signing people in.

"Don't tell the other participants where you work or live," a 20-something woman with frizzy blond hair and a wedding ring said as she took my money. "Don't tell them your last name." She handed me a sheet of red paper. "This is your score sheet. Each participant has a number. Write down his number when he sits. At the end of four minutes, you give them a fumble or a touchdown. When you turn in your score sheet, we tally the votes. Any couple that touchdowns each other gets their picture and email sent to each other. You take it from there."

I was number seven. Lucky seven! I took this as a good sign, got a pint of Guinness, and found my table. The tables were small and round. Each one had two chairs and a numbered placard. Speed dating came for all age groups. This organization had evenings for mid 20s to 30s, mid 30s to 40s, and mid 40s to 50s. Thirty to forty would have been ideal, but they didn't offer this option. After careful consideration, I had opted for the mid 30s to 40s. Thirty seemed too young, but the upper range of 40 seemed too old.

To calm my nerves, I set about meeting the women on either side of me. Number six was a schoolteacher. Number eight was an internal medicine resident. The resident was 39. She had a nerdy, bookish look that I found charming. She seemed like the kind of person who would always keep an interesting conversation going. The schoolteacher was 34. She had that midwestern perm that makes 25-year-old women look like soccer moms. I thought that men would choose her more than the resident, because she looked more predictable. I wondered where I fell in. Both women seemed more nervous than me, but I doubted they were. I can fake confidence well, and I was pretty sure that I was more terrified than anyone around me. I specifically didn't look around at the men because I didn't want to form any preconceived notions. The question I'd finally decided to ask was, "What's your dream life?" I figured it would give me insight into their long-term goals.

They started late, which didn't help my nerves. The first man sat down and the games began. He was number seven also. The male number seven.

Me—Hi. Uh. I have a question prepared. Do you have a question you want to ask me?

#7—Uh, no.

Me—Okay. Well, here is mine. What's your dream life?

#7—Uh, gosh, that's a hard one. I don't know. To live in Western Nebraska.

Me—Oh, do you like it out there?

#7—I grew up in Western Nebraska, near mmmmrh (unintelligible).

Me—Where?

#7—Western Nebraska.

Me—Yes, but where?

#7—mmmmrh.

Me—I can't understand you, where?

#7—(laughing) You're not from Nebraska, are you?

Me—No.

#7—Let's see (sizing me up). You're from Iowa? (Creative thinker, Iowa is just over the river from Omaha.)

Me—No.

#7—Then where?

Me—New York.

#7—New York?

Me—Yes.

#7—New York?

Me—Yes.

#7—New York???!!

Me—Yes.

#7—THE New York?

Me—Yes.

#7—Ugh.

#8—Hi, I'll need you to write your number on my list. I'm legally blind.

Me—Okay. My name's Quinn, nice to meet you.

#8—I can tell your age by your voice.

Me—How old am I?

#8—I knew you'd ask me that. Let's see. 32.

Me—I'm 38.

#8—Yes, I could tell. I also don't judge people by their appearances, because I'm blind. I just see their insides. My blindness is not hereditary so I won't pass it on to my children. But I wouldn't mind passing on the human knowledge I've learned from being blind. It's very interesting to see how people treat you when you're blind. I only use my cane at night, and people are much nicer when I have the cane. Otherwise they say things like, 'What are you, blind?' and I tell them, 'Yes, as a matter of fact.'

Me—Why don't you use your cane during the day?

#8—I don't like the way people treat me.

I could hear my neighbor on the left, the teacher, questioning the men just before they got to me. She had the kind of voice that carried. She did the same routine with each one.

"Are you religious?"

"Well, yes."
"Christian?"
"Uh, yes. Protestant."
"Practicing?"
"Y-yes."
"Weekly attendance at services?"
(Meekly) "Sometimes."

By the time they reached me, some of them had broken into a sweat. I thought they'd enjoy my easy question, but it seemed to cause them as much anxiety as the schoolteacher's drilling.

Me—What's your dream life?
#1—I don't know.
Me—What would you do, if you won, say, 30 million dollars?
#1—I don't know. Make sure my kids are taken care of. I can't really think of anything else. Buy a home. Uh, oh, and help people.
Me—Do you have a question for me?
#1—What do you do?
Me—I can't tell you that. I signed a statement saying I wouldn't reveal where I worked. So did you.
#1—What? When?
Me—When you walked in here.
#1—(annoyed) Everyone else has been telling me where they work.
Me—Well, they've been breaking the rules.
#1—I work at Colson's.
Me—You shouldn't tell people that. Any one of the women here could be a stalker.
#1—I'm not worried, (placing his hand on his breast, over his jacket) I've got a gun.
Me—(thinking— "Where's that damn bell?")

#2—Where you from?
Me—NY.
#2—I been there once. What a rat race. Those people there, they're like little ants crawling around an anthill. They look like a swarming mess, but somehow they all know where to go.

#3—How old are you?
Me—I'm 38.

#3—I'm 60. Got three grandchildren.

Me—Did you know this was supposed to be for mid 30s to mid 40s?

#3—Yeah. Last week I did the twenties one. Didn't meet anyone.

#4—Hi, where do you work?

Me—You can't ask people that. You signed a statement saying you wouldn't. It's against the rules.

#4—Well, everyone's been asking me how old I am. That's breaking the rules.

Me—Is it? I don't remember that in the statement.

#4—It's in there.

Me—Well, here's my question. What is your dream life?

#4—Wow. That's tough. I don't know. I guess it's to have more corvettes. I own three.

Me—Is that your corvette in the parking lot? The red one with the 'I4HUSKR' license plate?

#4—Yup, that's me. One of my other ones says BOY TYME. I wanted IM4NURU, but of course, that was taken.

Me—What's NU?

#4—What's NU? (incredulous)

Me—Yes.

#4—You're not from around here, are you?

Me—Nope.

#4—You from Iowa?

Me—No.

#4—(shock). Then where? Kansas?

Me—New York.

#4—You live in NY?

Me—No, I live in Omaha.

#4—Then you're FROM Omaha.

#5—I've got three kids.

Me—Oh really? What are their ages?

#5—22, 25, and 27.

Me—(thinking—is your oldest one single?)

Me—What is your dr—

#6—"No!"

Me—(confused) What is your drea—
#6—"Yes!!"
Me—(laughing.)
#6—Wait, I have one more.
Me—Okay. What is your—
#6—I don't know!
Me—What is your dream life?
#6—Hmmm. I like that. Let's see, I'd travel, try to spend some time helping other people out. Buy a house somewhere quiet. What's your dream life?
Me—I'd buy a house in the mountains, have a big family, make time to paint.
#6—You're an artist?
Me—Yes.
#6—What medium?
Me—Oils
#6—Cool. What mountains?
Me—Well, I like New Mexico.
#6—Oh, New Mexico is great! (smiling sheepishly) You're really pretty.

Touchdown!

"So, the whole thing cost me $28, not including the beer, and I met one guy. Luckily, he gave me a touchdown, too, or the whole thing would have been a bust."

"You've exchanged emails?" Izzy had stopped by my office to pick me up. We were going out to dinner, but my ENT clinic was running late, so I had to hang around till they were sure that the last patient wouldn't need a hearing test. Since it was after five, most of the department had already left. Izzy was kicked back in Lucy's chair, her long legs practically touching the opposite wall of our tiny office.

"Yes, and it turns out that he writes poetry!"

She grimaced. "Stay away from writers. They'll mess you up." Her ex was a writer.

"No, it's perfect, because he's creative, but not in the same area as me, so we won't need to compete. I'll have my painting and he'll have his poetry. Quinn and Bob, the painter and the poet."

Izzy looked unconvinced, but she moved on. "Does he have a real job, at least?"

"He's a factory worker."

Izzy let a pause pass before she said, "And he knows you have a master's degree?"

"Well, no. Not yet. It's not like I'm going tell him that in my first email!"

She was silent.

"And we already have our first date planned. And it's a great one. And he's the one who thought of it." I paused but when she didn't speak, I continued. "We're going to a poetry slam! And he's going to perform!"

She was silent.

"And that means that he's got guts. Courage is more important than similar educational backgrounds. And for all I know, he has a master's degree too, in some obscure, unmarketable subject like ancient farming methods in eastern Nebraska."

"You are right, courage is admirable," Izzy conceded. "And he must have guts to perform in front of you on your first date." That's Izzy, brushing all concerns under the rug and bucking up to support my denial.

"Second date, really," I said.

The slam was at a tiny yoga studio/tea bar that hosted the event monthly. If you've never been to a slam, it works like this: Poets who want to perform sign their name to a list. The MC picks a few people in the audience to be judges. Each poet gets up and performs a piece. The judges vote, ice skater-style, holding up score cards (1-10). The audience is encouraged to cheer or hiss, depending on their opinion of the scores. There are usually at least three rounds. Slammers don't just get up and read their poems. They perform the poem. They are part actor, part rapper, part performance artist.

Bob and I met a little early, at a nearby diner. He was wearing jeans and a t-shirt. His shoes were heavy work boots. Did I mention he had long brown hair? He was nice looking except that his face had a lot of scars from acne or chicken pox. I ordered a glass of wine, he got coffee. "I don't drink." He told me when the waiter walked away.

"Will my wine bother you?"

"No. Not at all. I've been clean and sober now for three years."

To me, "clean" implied hard-core drugs, not just alcohol. While I was processing this, he said, "Heroin, cocaine, no crack, though."

"Oh, good."

"Yeah. My son's going through a similar issue, but he hasn't made the commitment to sobriety yet."

"Your son drinks?" When he'd first said "son," my visual image was a six-year-old boy. Now I was picturing a first grader with a beer.

"Drinks, among other things."

"How old is he?"

"22."

"How old are you?"

"Forty-seven. How old are you?"

"Thirty-eight."

"Ah." We both stared at each other for another look.

Bob asked, "Do you have kids?"

"No, but I'd like them."

"My child rearing days are over."

Obviously.

"Do you want a lot?" he asked.

As if we could find some kind of compromise. Well, if it's just one... "Yes," I told him. "A whole passel."

He looked disgruntled. Kind of how I felt.

"So did you score any other touchdowns?" I asked.

"Yeah. One other. She's 45," he said, accusingly. Then he relented. "How about yourself?"

"No. I fumbled everyone else."

"I'm the only one you picked?"

"Did you look at the other men? Half of them could have been my father, the rest looked like criminals. The women seemed better."

"Yeah, you ladies did get the short end of the stick that night."

Still, we went to the slam. And I had to give him credit for dating women his own age. The slam was a small group of about 15 people. We grabbed some folding chairs in the middle row, center, and settled in. The first person to get up and read was a woman in her early 40s. Her hair was in a tight perm. That soccer mom look I mentioned earlier. In her hand she held a sheet of paper. She looked wholesome, like she would serve us apple pie after she read her poem. The room was silent, waiting for her to begin.

"You say you love the smell of my apartment.
Gingerbread, you say.
You could eat me up.
And you eat me.
You lick and suck and taste.
You hump and whine and groan.
But now you don't like gingerbread anymore.
My gingerbread man ran away.
But when I find you, I'm going to bite off your head."

My face had turned bright red in the middle of her piece. I couldn't look at her, I was so embarrassed by the poem.

"What is this, a therapy session?" Bob asked in a low voice.

I had to agree. So did the judges. 4, 7, 3. A couple of people in the audience booed at the judges. They were the compassionate people in the crowd, chiding the judges for being unnecessarily harsh.

The next poet was a man who looked about 30. He had thick, dark brown, shoulder length hair. He climbed onstage with no script in his hand. His voice was animated:

"Early on Sunday morning, NPR breaks into the regularly scheduled program, Europe Today, to announce that Saddam Hussein may have been captured, alive! They are broadcasting LIVE. When Weekend Edition starts, LeAnn Hanson is still the anchor, but it appears that the previously scheduled program has been scrapped so that we can hear, every minute, on the minute, that Saddam was found in a "snake pit." That he didn't put up a fight. That he seemed defeated. That he had $700,000 in cash. That he told the soldiers he wanted to negotiate. That he was found in a snake pit. That he didn't put up a fight, that he seemed defeated, that he had 700,000 American dollars…"

The poet started talking faster and faster, like a malfunctioning robot, his arms sticking out and shaking.

"SaddamhasbeencapturedbyAmericantroopshewas-
foundinasnakepithedinnaputupafightheseemed-
defeatedhewantedtonegotiatehehadsevenhundred-

Americandollarssaddamhasbeencapturedby-
Americantroopshewasfoundinasnakepithe-
dinnaputupafightheseemeddefeatedhewanted-
tonegotiatehehadsevenhundredAmericandollars-
hewasfoundinasnakepit—"

Then he exploded. His just seemed to burst open and fall. His body slammed into the floor so hard that the platform shook. "He's gonna have bruises," I whispered to Bob. Lying on his back, the poet continued:

"What? No Puzzle Master? I was waiting for the answer to lasts week's puzzle."

He rolled over and sat up. He voice was so subdued I had to strain to hear him.

"I'm sitting in my kitchen, drinking coffee, listening to NPR's coverage about Saddam, but I'm also sitting on my sofa, remote in hand, watching the twin towers implode on every channel. Sixty-four stations. I'm watching the plane crash and then the towers implode. On. Every. God. Damned. Channel. MTV. The Food Network. Comedy Central. And it feels like, for the rest of my life, no matter where I am or what I'm doing, I will always be, sitting on my sofa, watching the twin towers implode. I can't bear another media blitz. I can't hear five different analysts speculate on why Saddam surrendered, or what impact his capture will have on the war."

He got back on his feet.

"My therapist would say I'm suffering from post-traumatic stress disorder. At work, on that day, we saw it all unfold, live, on a small black and white. After a few weeks, everyone around me had moved on. I felt like my arms had been amputated.

Is it because I used to live in New York? Because I took the subway to the World Trade Center stop every day? Rode the long escalator ride to the surface and passed all the people coming in, as I made my way out, to a diner a few streets away, where I worked as a waiter? Brought coffee and the lunch specials to people who are now ashes on the streets of New York?"

He was miming the escalator ride and the walk.

"But then our regularly scheduled programming came back and I could sink into oblivion, with the Simpsons. All was right with the world. After awhile, I thought I could feel my arms again. The following spring, I saw a car hit a dog. He was obviously a stray. A mutt. He was already dead when I got to him."

The poet was back on the floor, stroking an imaginary dog.

"God. He looked so unloved. His whole side had been ripped open. I let my vision blur so that I didn't have to focus on the blood. His head was still warm. Another driver stopped. 'Is that your dog?' she asked.
'No,' I told her. 'He's a stray.'
'Did you hit him?'
'No. That motherfucker drove off.'
'Do you want me to call someone for you?'
'For me? Why?'
'Because you seem upset about the dog.'
That's when I realized I was crying. Gushing. My face was soaking wet and snot was pouring out of my nose."

He screamed his next line.

"I'm not crying about the fucking dog!"

The audience seemed to do a group freeze, like we were all afraid to breathe. He was standing and yelling now.

"I'm crying because the fucking twin towers are gone and everyone who was inside them is dead. Every fucking one is dead!"

He watched us, for a minute. We stared back at him, immobile. Then, his voice returned to normal.

"I frightened that lady. She jumped backwards and ran from me. So maybe I do have post-traumatic stress disorder. But did I get it from the event? Or from CNN?"

As he stepped off the stage, I felt certain that this man was destined to be my husband. My insides were crumbling around me, the way they do at the start of a major crush. The kind of crush that makes you inarticulate and awkward every time the object of your affection approaches you to chat. He sat a few seats away from me. The judges held up their scorecards: 9, 10, 10.

Bob was next. He carried the poem up with him, to read.

"The winter comes. Brown leaves curl.
The sky gets steely gray. I wonder where you are."

His left foot was tapping nervously while he talked. He didn't look at anyone in the audience, but at his piece of paper.

"You left in the rain and it's in the snow that you stay away.
The snow piles high. But I stoke my own coals."

A couple of people in the audience laughed at that line, but Bob didn't seem to hear them.

"I stay warm.
Death is all around me, but I know that spring will come.
Spring is under death.
Spring with green buds that poke through the cold soil.
My ship will come back, when the ice in the harbor has melted or broken."

Scattered applause. 7, 6, 4. He sat back down. My future husband, a few seats away, leaned toward Bob and said, "Excellent, man. You're getting better and better." Bob had been coming to this slam for several months.

"Thanks, man," Bob replied. He looked defeated, though.

"Good job," I told him. "That one judge is a meany."

Bob walked away with third place, but I would call it an award by default. There were only four competitors. The first prize went easily to my future spouse. His award was a wooden monkey, painted gold.

He held it up like it was the World Cup. "I want to thank all of you for this honor," he said. He was making the most of the campy award. "I especially have to thank my wife, Maria, who I know is thrilled to have this monkey for our very own." He nodded toward a young, woman with funky glasses in a long skirt. Married. At 30. Married too young, before he'd had a chance to meet his soul mate: me. Bob and I got up to leave. The poet and his wife stayed on, chatting with everyone.

"Ahhh. Too young for me anyway!" I muttered.

"What?" Bob asked.

"Nothing."

"Would you like to see more of my poetry?" he asked. "I could email you some."

"Sure," I said.

I went on the 4-minute date and all I got was some lousy poetry.

"Be glad that she will be the one who's woken at 2 a.m. because his creative drive is gone and he needs to replay the first three years of his childhood to process through the loss."

"Not all writers are crazy," I argued. "You had to see him. He was amazingly talented. And hot. And political."

"You dodged a bullet, my friend," Izzy said.

I didn't believe her for a second.

"So you'll just have to try again," Lucy said at work on Monday. "Do the 4-minute date thing until you meet a good guy."

"More than half of them were pushing fifty," I told Lucy. "The other ones looked utterly beaten by life. They looked like they had almost gone under, and the 4-minute date was something they were doing as a last shot before giving up on life completely."

"Well, you met one nice man." Lucy said.

"Yeah. A recovering drug addict."

"Well, if he's recovering…" She stopped and admitted defeat. Then she zinged me with the kind of useless advice that is typical from someone who doesn't date. "You have to kiss a lot of toads before you meet your prince."

"Says the woman who married her grade school sweetheart," I replied.

Chapter 6
Top Ten List of
Useless Advice for Single Women

10. You should enjoy being single while you can. I wish I still was. I miss dating new men.

9. If you smiled more, you'd get a man.

8. You need to wear more make-up.

7. You're lucky to be single. Having a husband is like having another child.

6. Get a dog and walk him in the park.

5. Join a church singles group.

4. Do what you enjoy and you'll meet the man for you.

3. You have to kiss a lot of frogs before you find your Prince Charming.

2. Stop being so picky–you can't have it all, you know.

1. As soon as you stop looking you'll meet a man.

For any smug-marrieds who are still reading this novel? None of these things work! None. So from now on, when single people complain to you, try telling them, "You are right. My heart goes out to you. It's a jungle out there. I wish I had some useful advice, but all I can say with confidence is, 'Hang in there! You may or may not overcome!'"

Chapter 7
Petitioning the Universe to
Avoid the Bar Scene

I was sitting at home on Friday night, knitting in front of the television, when the phone rang. I looked at my watch. Ten o'clock. Everyone I know knows not to call me past nine. I'm usually in bed by nine.

"Hello." I could hear loud music in the background. Wrong number.

"Quinn?" Man's voice.

"Yes?"

"Hey. What's up?"

"Who is this?"

"It's Chris."

"Who?"

"Chris. Remember? We went out on a date?"

Ugh. Chris. Reader, I'm not very good with names, but how could I forget blind date number two, where I got stuck with the bill and then dumped? "Oh. Hi," I said.

"So," Chris asked, "What's happening?"

Top Three Cardinal Rules for Men:

Never say, "I'll call you," if you're not going to call.
Don't check out other women when you're with a woman.
Never, ever call a girl from a bar, drunk. Especially one you've dumped.

"Chris, what do you want?"

"Whatcha doin' tonight? You want to come party with us? The whole gang's here."

What gang? Not my gang. "Chris, you woke me up. I'm going back to bed. Good-bye." I hung up. So, guy who dumped me calls me on a Friday night and I tell him he woke me up. Spinster. Or, drunken guy calls me from a bar and I hang up on him. A much better take. Spinster, or SPIN-ster? Eh?

If anything, the 4-minute dates seemed to have reduced my quality of life, rather than improved it. Bob was emailing me his latest poems, all of which, apparently, focused on a woman he'd loved. Who'd left him. In winter. They were long, rambling, and trite. I was running out of positive feedback that wasn't an outright lie.

I decided I needed some kind of reward for my efforts, so I signed up for a Continuing Education class. If I won the lottery, I would major in Continuing Education, going the whole range from *Perform Simple Repairs on Your Car* to *Raise Your Own Bees*. For now, however, I thought I'd just stick with one class. I could have taken the advice of many, many people, and signed up for a Continuing Education class that would be filled with men. There were options, namely, *Beer Brewing*, *Whiskey Tasting*, and *Carpentry*.

But I already knew, from previous experience, that these classes would be 80% women. I knew, without going to any of the sessions, that those women would come in full makeup, low cut blouses, and cleavage. That they would do whatever it took to sit next to the two to five men who attended. I knew that at least two of the men in attendance would be unavailable. Two would have serious social boundary problems. And at least one would think he knew more than the teacher and insist on making corrections, adding information, or telling anecdotes about his own beer/whiskey/carpentry experience. If there was an interesting man in class, I'd never get near him. He'd spend the hour surrounded by a circle of aggressive women who would as soon slice off my right hand as let me share a band saw with any of the good men in the room.

So I signed up for a class called "*Affirmations: How to Attract Prosperity*." We met at one of the high schools, in what looked to be a ninth grade biology classroom. This group was, predictably, all women. I was the youngest by ten years, not including the teacher.

She looked to be about 26. She wore a cashmere, turtleneck sweater, a wool skirt, and boots with 4-inch heels. She closely resembled Malibu Barbie. I guessed this was the New Age look in Omaha. She sat on top of the teacher's desk and said, "Good evening. My name is Brandy. Congratulations for making a decision to give yourself a happier, healthier life." She handed out paper and pencils. I'd come with my own notebook, specially bought for the evening. "Write this down," she told us, from the desktop. "I know what I want. I ask for what I want. I receive what I ask for."

The class scribbled. "To get what you want, you have to release what you don't want, to create a vacuum." Brandy's feet must have been killing her in those heels. "I want you all to write down three things you want to release," she said. "I'm going to give you ten minutes."

For the first seven minutes, I couldn't come up with a single thing. I thought about my job, where I lived, my art degree. I thought about the paintings I worked on at night and over the weekend, and how I'd gotten a degree in audiology so that I could live comfortably, while still making art. Finally, I wrote.

Inability to talk about/sell my art
Lack of limberness
Max

I should explain that Max is an ex-boyfriend, my first real love, and even though we broke up years ago, and I haven't heard from him since the breakup, I unconsciously compare all other men I meet to him. That is, I compare other men to his good qualities. His bad ones I basically ignore.

About the limberness. I've been doing yoga for several years now, and I still can't touch my toes. I've never been able to touch my toes. Even in the first grade.

When we were all looking up at Brandy, she hopped off the desk and gave us more instructions. "Now, let's fill the vacuum with something positive. Look at your list. Make another column next to it, and write down the exact opposite of each thing on your list."

Inability to talk about my art —- Excitement describing my art to others

Inflexibility —- Ability to touch my toes
Max —- Freedom from missing Max

The list got me thinking. Was this really all I wanted to change about myself? No, but some of these goals seemed obtainable. What would stop me from attaining these goals and then making more lists? As if she was reading my mind, the teacher then said, "There is nothing you can't get, as soon as you know what you want to ask for." She began to pace around the room. "Your car's breaking down, but you can't afford a new car. Well, do you want a new car? No, you just want a car that runs perfectly. So, find a good mechanic." The class digested this. "Does anyone here believe that men always leave?"

Out of 15 people in the class, seven women raised their hands. Brandy spoke carefully and compassionately. "If you believe that men always leave, you will either attract men who leave, or you will drive away men who stay because you must be right." She was silent for a moment. The class was silent. When she spoke again, she spoke very softly, and slowly. "You…are…that…powerful." She cocked her head. "If you weren't afraid, what would you accomplish?"

We were all wrapped around her New-Age finger now. I was scribbling furiously. From now on, in every tough situation, I was going to ask myself "If I had no fear, how would I act?"

"This applies to absolutely every part of your life. You can make a list of affirmations that will get you anything you want. A new job, a new home, a man." At the last word, there was a collective inhalation in the room. The excitement was palpable. Brandy could feel it. "That's right," she said, "if you make a list of what you want in a man you will get it. A word of warning when you petition the Universe: Be clear and detailed. Ask for absolutely everything you want. Ask for him to be single, or you'll get everything you want, but he'll be married with three kids."

We got ready to make our lists. The list was supposedly for anything we wanted in life, but I would have bet that 98% were making a list of their ultimate man.

"One last thing," Brandy said. "Ask for everything you want. Then ask for more."

What I Want In a Mate:
Male

32-44
Fluent in English and Spanish
About six feet tall
Lanky, but muscular
Challenges me
Very intelligent
Witty
Innate kindness
Innate sense of justice
Confident
Good taste
Non judgmental
Easy going
I can relate to him the way I relate to Izzy
Goal-oriented
Functions efficiently under pressure
Extrovert
Good father
Is waiting to have kids with the woman he marries
Good problem solver
Respectful
Good manners
Is free of nicotine
Is free of illegal drugs
Is good with money but understands that money and happiness are different

Brandy said that the Universe doesn't understand negatives, so you have to couch all requests in positive terms. Otherwise, when you ask for a man who "is not married," you'll get a man who "is ~~not~~ married."

I took my list home and used my notebook to make daily affirmations about this man. According to Brandy, I was supposed to write out this list, every day, until I got what I wanted.

I called all my friends for suggestions on my list. Izzy added, "Gentle," "positive manner," and "articulate." Ann added, "I love him." My mother added "Not cheap" (which I changed to "generous"), "Respects my beliefs," and "I respect his beliefs." I modified "good father" to "being a good husband and father is more important to him than societal judgments or financial considerations." This is because part of my marriage plan is that my husband and I will each work half time and stay home with our kids the other half time.

When I read my list to Lucy, she said, "You're asking for an awful lot. This guy, if you actually got him, wouldn't you be a little intimidated by him?"

"No."

Lucy shrugged. "Well, good luck. If you ask me, you are setting yourself up for disappointment."

I just reminded myself of what Brandy said. "You are one million times more powerful than you've ever let on. Ask for everything you want, then ask for more."

Chapter 8
Internet Dating - The Profile

The daily affirmations gave me hope. But I didn't meet any men.

Izzy made a good point. "You can't just write a list and expect everything to come to you. You're going to have to make some effort to get out there and meet the Universe halfway."

"I did the 4-minute dates!"

"And now you get to give up? Do you really want to sit home every night watching Dawson's Creek reruns?"

"Don't mock a show that you've never even watched!"

"Okay. I'm sorry. But seriously, Quinn. What kind of effort are you going to put forth?" She was over at my apartment. We were supposed to be watching a movie, but instead we were discussing the state of my love life.

"I thought that maybe a neighbor would move out and the man from my list would move in next door."

"I've been checking out men from Omaha on Match.com and there are some real cuties."

I was interested in why Izzy was looking at men on an Internet dating page. Did Sal know? "No," I said. "I'll never do Internet dating."

"Just log on and take a look." She stood up. "Let's look now."

I stayed seated. "My computer is too slow."

"We're just sitting around anyway. We'll talk while it loads."

I pushed up and got my laptop from my bedroom and we set up shop in the dining "nook." Walter was coughing, next door. I didn't even notice anymore, but it was irritating to Izzy. "What is wrong with him?"

"The walls are thin."

"He needs to cut dairy out of his diet."

I logged on to Match.com and we started scrolling through profiles. Everyone had a username, tagline, and a written section. About 70% had pictures. Izzy was correct; there were some men who seemed kind of funny and cute.

"Let's write a profile for you," Izzy suggested. "You don't have to post it. But I think it would be good for you to sort out what exactly you're looking for, and how you want to represent yourself." When she put it in those terms, it seemed like a reasonable suggestion. We spent the next two hours writing mini-novels for the two main sections: "About Me," and "About You."

If you are uninitiated, here's how Match.com works: you set up a page that describes you, including pictures, if you wish. Most Internet services work the same way: you write a paragraph about your personality and another about your ideal match's personality. You can check off hair and eye color, profession, education, salary, etc. Once your profile is posted, people can search for you by city, age, religion, eye color, hair color, body type, whatever. You give Match.com an email address, and if a person wants to write to you, they email Match.com, who forwards the mail to your address. By going through Match.com, the writer never sees your actual email address. You can scroll through profiles and receive messages from others for free. You only pay if you want to initiate contact or respond to an email.

The hardest part of the profile was thinking up a good username and tagline. One guy that I saw used the tagline "I run with scissors." I wanted something funny like that. In the end, we settled for Quinn Painting as the username, with "Introverted but funny artist," as my tagline.

Here's my profile, in full.

ABOUT ME:

Hi. I'm a painter, as you might have gathered from my tagline. I mainly do portraits and landscapes, in oils. I studied painting in NYC in my late teens and early 20s. Later on in my 20s I got a Master's degree in a healthcare field because I wanted to be a little more financially stable, and I also wanted to be able to paint for me, not to pay the rent. As an adult, I have moved around a lot and lived in Europe as well as all over the US. My favorite place to live in is New Mexico, because I love the beauty of the desert and the laid back, open-minded culture that prevails there. I'd like to eventually return to the southwest. I'm an early riser. I love to cook, especially dinner parties for friends. In my free time, I enjoy movies (especially art films), poetry slams, hiking, eating out, yoga, theatre, reading (literature, mysteries). Things I'd like to start doing: Tai Chi, glass blowing–I'm sure there's more but I can't think of it off the bat. My friends would describe me as hardworking, but with my priorities mainly intact (I'm a little too driven, but I'm working on this!). It's hard to write about myself. Here's a quote from one of my girlfriends. (She's pretty honest, a little biased but different enough from me in personality that I think she paints a well-rounded picture). "Quinn has it so together. She had an art show of 20 paintings while in grad school–how does anyone do that? She does a lot of things that most people would be afraid to do, like move to new cities, take new jobs. She takes care of herself; she's healthy and smart about money. She knows herself, what she wants to work on and where she wants to go. She's gorgeous. And she cracks me up."

ABOUT YOU:
I love men who are compassionate, funny, and happy with themselves. Athletic, thriving in a job that helps others, not addicted. Are you a good conversationalist? Do you live an alternative lifestyle (no I don't mean a hippie commune! More like, you're willing to drop down to half time at work in order to write your second novel or raise your children). Do you like to camp? Hike? Travel? Read away your entire Saturday? Do you have a strong network of friends who think you're awesome? Can you go off on your own, or out with your friends, without me having to always come along and are you unthreatened by my strong ties to friends and my need for having time to myself? Do you like good food? Are you smart about money but understand that money doesn't make you happy? Are you liberal, politically? If any of this rings a bell, let's talk. If you're not any of this but you think I should still know you, write me anyway.

Some of you may have noticed that I was heavily influenced by Alanis Morrissette's lyrics for the song "21 Things I Want In a

Lover," off her album, Under Rug Swept. Alanis is one of the few songwriters who sings about the process of being in relationships. Her lyrics focus on self-analysis and growth. She has lines like, "it's a cycle really, you think I'm withdrawing and guilt tripping you. I think you're insensitive and I don't feel heard." Alanis crams as many words as possible into each verse. It's why some people love her and why others can't stand her.

"This profile is pretty cool," I said to Izzy.

"Yes. It's you, in a nutshell."

We sat at the table, looking at the computer screen. "You know," I said, "I don't see why I shouldn't just post it."

"You might as well. It's too bad you don't have a picture."

"I do have a picture, from my sister's wedding." She'd just mailed it to me a few weeks earlier. Little sister's wedding, I might add. In the picture, my hair is professionally done. I have on make-up. False advertising, maybe, but still. It was me, looking good. Once I'd fished the picture file out of my sister's email, it uploaded in seconds. We double-checked the profile.

"Looks good," Izzy said.

I clicked Make my profile visible. A note popped up to say they would review my text and picture and post it within 48 hours. "Well. That's that," I said.

"This is going to be fun!" Izzy said.

I continued to petition the Universe every morning with my coffee. When Lucy asked me how my "manhunt" was going, I ignored her sarcasm. "Beautifully. I'm taking risks, and risks are always rewarded."

"Yeah, it's pretty risky to write an impossible list of traits on a piece of paper every day."

I hadn't told Lucy, or anyone, about the match profile yet. I wanted to see how it worked out first. Ok. I was embarrassed.

"Damn, I can't believe it!" Lucy was talking to her computer. "This house," she said, turning to me, "is on the market again."

Her computer screen was up and open to a realtor's website. A cute little bungalow was for sale.

"We made an offer on that house, three years ago, and we lost it because some guy paid in cash."

"You're kidding. How much cash?"

"Well, we bid $68,000 but the house ended up selling for $67,000, in cash."

"I hadn't realized real estate was so cheap in Omaha."

"It depends on the neighborhood. This was a borderline area. Prices are still high in the more desirable locations. And now the buyer is re-selling it for ninety-four thousand!"

I almost fell out of my chair. "Seriously? That's a $27,000 profit! In three years!"

"This is why the market is so messed up!" Lucy said. "Greed! And I'll bet he didn't even make any improvements. It was in great shape, three years ago."

"What's that web page you have up?"

"The real estate site. I'll send you the link."

"And you can search for houses?"

"Sure. By price, neighborhood, bedrooms, fireplaces, garages, hardwood floors. You name it and you can search for it."

Hmmm. Sounded familiar.

Match's 48-hour waiting period took away instant gratification. Ideally, five minutes after I hit visible, my soul mate would be the first person to contact me. Instead, I forgot about the posting until almost a week later. I was at my desk, writing a report, when I thought, Hey, what about that match.com thing? I had set up a Hotmail email account to receive the Match emails. I logged in over lunch. Seventy-four messages were waiting. I stared at the inbox for a few seconds, then finally clicked on one.

Username: RUtheOne?
Tagline: A Great Guy
Wowza! You are the best looking woman on this site. You simply must email me. You're fantastic and I think you'll say the same about me, once you've seen my profile or met me in person. The camera is not kind to me, so don't pay much attention to my picture. If we meet, I will treat you so fine. Everyone I've ever dated says that I am a great listener and very sensitive. Email me! Please!

I logged off and called Izzy. Izzy's work as a speech pathologist requires that she travel between group homes and other places, so she was always reachable by cell phone.

"This is Izzy Jaramillo," she sang, unsuspectingly.

"I have more than 70 Match.com messages in my inbox." I told her. "You started this mess, now you can clean it up. My email password is viggomortensen123. I'll talk to you when you've got the list narrowed down to ten." I hung up and walked away from my desk in case she called me back.

Chapter 9
Match.com - The Quest Begins

If I was going to rewrite this chapter, I'd call it, "The Uphill Climb, That Takes You to the Top of an Anthill, Begins. But I don't want to bias you too soon, so forget you just read that sentence.

Working together, Izzy and I had the emails separated into three groups by the end of the week. Definitely Nots (40); Sounds Good But May Have Issues (22); and Yes, Maybes (12). The tricky thing about Match is that many men wrote almost nothing in their emails to me. Others wrote novels. Izzy and I debated whether to include the short writers in our good list.

Izzy–"If they can't be bothered to work a little, I say, move on."

Me–"I'm trying to imagine what I would write to a guy, and I think I'd want to say, 'Hey, it's in my profile, go read it and tell me what you think.'"

In the end, though, Izzy won with the argument of, "If he can't put the effort into writing a nice paragraph in his initial email, he's probably not communicative." The other hard thing about Match was finding great emails from funny guys, then pulling up their profile and discovering that they were:

twenty years older than me
smokers
divorced with children
politically conservative

only dating women their age or younger (usually, their dating range was 18 years to their age, or 18 years to two years over their age)

"What about the children thing," Izzy argued. "So what?"

"I could consider it," I agreed. "It's just that I envisioned this guy and me doing all of that for the first time, together." So we kept men with children in the Sounds Good But May Have Issues box. Older men were Definitely Nots, as were men with messed up dating ranges.

"Why not conservatives?" Izzy asked. "You're closing yourself off to so many men that way, and a lot of those guys are really nice."

"But I'm a liberal."

"Who cares?" she said. "It's just politics."

"You'd date a conservative?"

"Of course. I've dated many."

"Politics for me is like religion for others. Some people only date other Catholics or Jews. I only date liberals. It's the gay rights thing," I said. "And the death penalty. I feel very strongly about those issues. And stem cell research. And universal health care."

"So you can't date someone who doesn't agree with you? How would a difference of opinion in those areas change your lives in any way?"

"I want to raise my kids with my basic principles."

"Your kids will decide anyway, when they grow up."

"That's true of religion, too. You still raise them in yours, though."

Izzy shook her head. "Okay, conservatives to be judged on a case-by-case basis."

I shrugged. "Okay. Add smokers to that list, too."

From the Yes category, I couldn't fathom emailing all twelve, so I began with three.

Username: Pickme!Pickme!
Tagline: We're running with the shadows of the night!

Username: YesYesandYes
Tagline: Love me? Love my dog!

Username: MedicalMania
Tagline: Doctor in search of love

We started with Pickme!Pickme! His profile went like this:

About Me: Well, my second grade teacher wrote on my report card that I was funny like Danny Kaye. Yes, you know, Danny Kaye, the comedian from the forties? Never mind. That same teacher told me I was droll. Mrs. Jacobs. She was great. She turned me on to Roald Dahl. My all time favorite book is James and the Giant Peach. You should be open to naming our first son James.

I feel compelled to warn you about a few traits. First, I dance like Tony Randall on crack. Second, I like to talk to people, but I can seem quiet until I get to know you.

I'm in the Air Force, so I do relocate sometimes and am away for periods on assignment.

About You: Jeez, I have no idea. You aren't some sixty year old, disgruntled postal worker with a tagline that says "Fresh and fast." If we email for a while, and then you decide to move on to greener pastures, that's fine, but do me a favor and say so, okay? It's no big deal, but I'd like you to tell me you won't be engaging in any more conversation.

"Does he seem bitter?" I asked.
"He's just been burned by people he's talked to on the Internet," Izzy said.
I was looking at his picture. "He's not bad-looking, but gosh, he looks so square. Straight-laced."
"You like funny. And he is funny."
"I do."
So I wrote. Izzy revised.

Dear Pick me! Pick me!,
Hi. Thanks for your email. ~~I notice that you list yourself as conservative. I'm liberal. I'm writing anyway, because I know some people who call themselves conservative just because their parents did, without actually holding the same belief system. I'll give you an idea of my belief system. I am in favor of stem cell research, I'm pro-~~

choice, and I want to preserve the arctic wildlife refuge. I think that *war with the Middle East will only cause more terrorism. I'm in* *favor of gay marriage. So, still interested?*

By the way, *your profile was really funny. I read it to my girlfriend (the one who contributed a comment to my profile) and we laughed our asses off. How long have you been in Omaha? Would you say that the military life suits you? Are you flexible in your belief system?*
Quinn

Within two hours, Pick me! Pick me! (a.k.a. Lance) had replied to my email by saying that he was flexible in his belief system. He said we could talk about specifics in person. He was from North Carolina and was a computer engineer for the US government.

"Maybe I'll see how this goes, before I bother emailing the other two guys."

"Great idea. Put all your eggs in one basket," Izzy said.

"Writing to him was exhausting. I need a break."

"Come on," Izzy said, sitting down in my kitchen/Internet café nook. "I'll help. We have a template now. We can knock these other two off in less than 15 minutes."

We compromised on one email. YesYesandYes lived three hours away in Missouri, but he was from New Mexico and he was liberal. Also, he looked athletic and kind of sexy. He wasn't as funny as Lance, but he wasn't a dud, either.

For a few weeks, Lance and I sent a flurry of emails back and forth. He was hysterical in every one. Sometimes he was so funny that I laughed aloud. My laugh sounded strange, echoing through my empty apartment. I wondered if Walter could hear me. We finally agreed to meet for dinner. I was kind of excited about meeting him. I mean, who doesn't love to laugh? I figured I'd be laughing all night. Our plans were for six, and I arrived right at six on the dot, even though I parked a few blocks away to prevent him from seeing my license plate number (in case he turned out to be a stalker). As I approached the restaurant, I saw him standing by the door. He looked just like his picture. He watched me without expression as I approached. Up close, he still didn't seem to recognize me, so I said,

"Lance?"

He nodded. "Restaurant is full. It's a 20-minute wait."

I took another look at his grim countenance and suggested we wait in the bar. An hour and a half later I was hunched over a toilet in a bathroom stall, calling Izzy on my cell phone. But I'll get back to that in a minute.

At the bar and I ordered a Corona. Lance ordered a coke. "Do you not drink?" I asked, thinking *another addict*?

"I drink," he replied.

I waited a bit for him to elaborate. He didn't. "So," I said, "have you ever been here before?"

"Sure. All the time. I love this place."

"What's good here?"

"Anything's good."

"What's your favorite?"

"I like everything on the menu."

Silence, then I asked, "How was your day?"

"The usual."

"What's a usual day?"

"Get up, go to work, come home."

I carried the dialogue down little dead ends like this for twenty minutes before deciding that the Funny Man was going to have to work a little harder. I vowed not to say another word, to force him to carry his side of the conversation. There was a clock with a minute hand on the wall right behind his head. We sat in dead silence for a full three minutes and eight seconds before he asked me how long I'd lived in Omaha. Those three minutes took three hours off my life.

I'd like to say that the evening improved, but it didn't. The conversation was stilted. I don't think he smiled once. I felt like a lush, drinking my beer while he drank soda. "You aren't much like your emails," I told him, toward the end. "I don't think you've made one joke tonight, but your emails are hysterical."

"It's easier to be funny when I can revise before sending."

The ending of a bad date is always the worst part. How to separate without hurting someone's feelings or letting guilt make you plan another date. Thus, the phone call to Izzy, from the bathroom. Of course, she wasn't home. So I called Ann. She wasn't home either. I left Izzy a message. "It's horrible. It's torture. I'm dying here. He's nothing like his emails. I wish I could sneak out right now, through a window in the bathroom and run home to the book I'm reading and a cup of cocoa." What I didn't know was that, while I was in the stall, talking with an answering machine, Lance was paying for our dinner.

A Note About Paying For Meals On Dates: This practice is old, and I think it came about back when women didn't have jobs, or didn't make much money. It was a good practice, back then. Now, it's antiquated. I can pay for a meal just as easily as a man can. So I don't approve of the practice. Fair is fair. That said, I find it very charming and gentlemanly for a man to pay for the meal, once. On our first date. However, if I don't want to date the man, if I, for instance, never want to see him again, and would rather be home cleaning my bathroom than eating with him, then I don't want him paying for me.

When I finally forced myself to exit the bathroom, Lance was at the cashier by the door with his wallet open. For a split second, I thought he was sneaking out and I felt relief. "How much was the meal?" I asked him when he returned. I was reaching into my purse.
"That's not important."
"Yes, it is. Lance, I want to contribute to this meal."
"It's not necessary."
"Thank you," I said, realizing I'd forgotten to be gracious. "You're a real gentleman, but please, may we go Dutch?" He refused, so I gave him my lecture about women paying their share.
"Not in my world," he said.
"Fair is fair. Why shouldn't women help pay?"
"Not in my world."
Fine, what are you going to do? You try to help out these men who are getting the short end of the stick, but he wasn't ready for it. So he paid. And because he paid, when he then suggested we go out again, I said "yes," even though I was screaming "no" on the inside.

Chapter 10
You've Got Mail

Dear Quinn Painter,
First, let me say that your picture is lovely. Second, I must
add that I know how to treat a lady. I hold open doors. I
bring roses on the first date. In bed, I am what many women
have called, an artist. You paint your canvas, I will paint
you, if you know what I mean.

Dear Quinn (as I am assuming that is your name), I am a
horse when it smells good.

Dear Quinn Painter,
You have the best profile online. I am finally getting over a
painful break up from a long-term relationship but now I
honestly feel better than ever. I am looking for someone
who is foremost, honest. And who is looking for their
soulmate. Yes, at the age of 54, I still believe I can find her.
Could you be her? If any of me sounds right for you, then
maybe, just maybe you are the girl I've been searching for
my whole life. Why don't you email me and we'll find out.

Hi, please email me. I'm pretty sure that you and I will be a
great match. You are really beautiful. I don't have a picture
up, and I haven't put much time into completing my profile,

but don't let that stop you from emailing me. Take a chance! If you do, we could meet for lunch. I would even buy you lunch, but it would have to be in 45 minutes because I can't take more time than that off from work.

My darling, we haven't met yet, but you will know you are THE ONE if you enjoy walking barefoot in the rain, drinking wine as the sun sets in front of you, holding hands in public, staring dreamily into the eyes of your ONE TRUE LOVE. When you find me, you will hold me close and not let me go. I will only do everything in my power to make you the happiest woman alive.

Quinn Painter,

After finally ending a long-term relationship last month, I feel that I am truly ready to settle down with The One. I'm sick of the bar scene. I like women who are good listeners and who can comfortably wear jeans but also be at ease in a ball gown. I have a very important job that prevents me from being able to post a picture, but I'm quite good-looking and I'm sure you will not be disappointed.

Chapter 11
Looking for a Man is like House-Hunting

"**I**'m not sure I like Internet dating," I told Izzy.

"Why not? You've gone from no prospects to nearly 100 potential dates."

"It seems like a lot of work for very little payback."

"Well, keep your options open. Still put yourself out there in other ways. Why don't you join a gym?"

"Uh, maybe. But I have a better idea. I'm going to buy a house."

"A house?"

"Yeah. A house."

After my conversation with Lucy about Omaha house values, I'd read *Real Estate for Dummies* from cover to cover and gotten a realtor. Her name was Flora. She was in her early sixties, but stylish and energetic. I wanted old Omaha. I wanted neighborhoods with old homes with wrap-around front porches and walk up attics. Also, old homes were the only affordable houses in Omaha. I'd been approved for a $100,000 loan, but, based on estimated mortgage payments from my broker, I couldn't spend more than $85,000. Yes, Folks, Omaha has housing that cheap and even cheaper in some old neighborhoods. Flora knew old homes. She lived in a 1907 Greek revival house. Not a neighborhood I could afford, but it bordered places that I could buy into.

I found the house of my dreams on our first outing. It was the last of five homes we'd viewed. The first four looked good on paper, but when you stepped inside, you were hit with wall-to-wall wood paneling, or the smell of cat urine. Or just an overwhelming feeling of despair, possibly from bad paint jobs by renters, or the other two-bit ways that people destroy the beauty of an old home, in order to redecorate with a part of themselves into their living space. I was appreciating my apartment, until we walked inside the two-story, brick Tudor from 1924. There were matching stained glass windows on either side of the front door. The entranceway had a cast iron mail slot and tiled floor. We stepped into the living room and marveled at wall-to-wall hardwood floors, a brick fireplace, French doors that led to a sunroom on the left, and pocket doors between the living room and dining room. I was speechless. The kitchen was enormous. In addition to the sun, living, and dining rooms, there were two bedrooms on the first floor, in the back. Both bedrooms had crystal doorknobs and large closets. The upstairs had been converted into a rental unit with its own entrance. It was a charming one bedroom, with two built-in bookcases, a small kitchen and bathroom. The house was $85,000.

"Rental income, too," Flora said. "Or, it looks like it would be easy to convert back to an upstairs."

The attached garage opened into a giant basement. Central air had already been added. "This place just gets better and better," I said. "Do you think the fireplace works? I want to make an offer."

"You've only seen five houses. Do you want to look around more?"

"Why? How could I do better than this? That rental unit could help pay my mortgage." Already, I was envisioning myself as a laid back, reliable landlady. I was going to emulate my current landlady. The tenant would love me. I might actually make a profit off the house, if my mortgage payment, minus the rental, was less than my apartment rent. Maybe I could use the money for weekly massages. No, I'd save it for repairs. If my renters were good, I'd even drop their rent to keep them. I could imagine the conversation. *"You guys have been such good tenants."* It was a young married couple. Both in graduate school, working on their dissertations. *"I'm going to lower your rent by $100 a month."*

"You have no idea how awesome that is going to be for us," the *wife says.*

"Well, thanks for being good tenants," I'd say. And then I'd leave before they could thank me anymore.
"Quinn, did you hear me?"
"Huh?"
"Let's go back to my office to start the paperwork."

On the drive, she swung through Dundee, an old, hip neighborhood where progressive, wealthy, young white people lived. "If I were you," she said, "I'd put that home on the back burner and start hunting in this area." She pulled up in front of a giant brick house with a black wrought iron fence and a For Sale sign. "You belong somewhere like this," she said. "You could have a painting studio upstairs, you could garden, and walk to galleries and coffee houses."

"Well, if I had $250,000 to spend, I'd agree with you. But I don't." I was feeling kind of angry. My house was a steal, even if the neighborhood was sketchy.

With a sigh, Flora gave up and started driving to her office again.

I offered $81,000. The whole process took more than an hour. Flora faxed the contract to the other realtor and drove me home. "So, we'll know in 24-hours?" I asked, as I got out of her car.

"More or less," she said. "But I'll talk to the realtor tomorrow and tell him what a sweet, young thing you are, and how you are trying to purchase this house all on your own."

When I got home, I make a quick assessment of my furniture. I didn't have that much, but I'd definitely need help moving. I thought I could load everything I owned into a medium-sized truck.

I called my landlady. She answered on the first ring. "Hi, Agnes, it's Quinn. I wanted to let you know that I've been house hunting, and I found a house and made an offer on it. I don't know if they'll accept, but I thought I should warn you that I might be leaving."

She didn't miss a beat. "Quinn," she said, "I have always said that paying rent is like throwing your money down the drain. Now give me the address so I can see this place for myself and make sure it's okay." It's amazing how many people will stand in and be surrogate family members for you when you live in a city alone.

After I hung up with Agnes, I checked my cell phone voicemail. I'd given Yes, Yes, and Yes, whose real name was Dick, my cell phone number in an email the day before because he was going to Albuquerque and wouldn't have email access. He left this message:

Hi Quinn. This is Dick. I'm standing on top of a peak in the Sandias. The air smells like a crisp, sweet apple. I'm looking around at the colors, there's sage green, orange, brown, light and dark brown, blue sky of course, and a reddish, rust colored plant. It's so beautiful here. I'm going to send you a postcard, so you'll have to give me your address. (Good luck, buddy boy. There's no way some stranger from the Internet is getting my address, not even if he was sending me the mountain itself!)

I'd been putting off calling him, but…well, now was as good a time as any. It was working out to be a big night. First the house, then the first conversation with a potential mate. I was really nervous, terrified, actually, but I pushed it aside. I stood at my front window and dialed.

When he answered, I introduced myself as Quinn from Match dot com.

"Hey, Quinn! We meet at last! At least, our voices meet." He was so friendly that I felt myself start to calm down.

"How's Albuquerque?" I asked.

"It's great. Last night, I saw the Lobos game. Then I went out with a bunch of guys from my fraternity and bought them all drinks."

"Were a lot of guys you went to school with at the game?" I asked, imagining him with a crowd of his old buddies heading over to their old fraternity house.

"Nah. Just me." Suddenly, my picture shifted, to a 32-year-old man, buying drinks for a bunch of 19-year-old boys, dropping pearls of thirty-something wisdom into their drunken ears. I don't know…it made me kind of sad. While I was processing this, he said, "Omaha is only three hours from me. And I've never been there. I'm thinking of driving up for a weekend. What do you say? Would you act as tour guide?"

"Sure," I told him, panicking. "That would be great."

"What is there to see in Omaha?" he asked. "I guess it doesn't matter, since I'm there to see you, anyway. I was never one for small towns."

"Omaha isn't that small," I said.

"It's small for me," he said.

"It's bigger than Albuquerque," I told him.

"Really? Are you sure?"

I was sure.

"How about the weekend after next? I'll drive up on Friday night."

"Okay, then!"

Reader, I did tell Izzy about the house bid first. I am, after all, a modern woman. At least, I try. But we quickly moved on to Dick's impending visit. "I'm worried about this," I told Izzy. "What if he wants to stay at my apartment?"

"Has he asked?"

"No, but he might. I mean, hotels are expensive."

"You can offer to pay half. But he's not going to ask to stay at your apartment. He wouldn't expect to."

"So you think that's okay?"

"Of course it's okay."

My painting class mirrored this theme. "No way he stays with you," said Jack, peering at me over his bi-focals.

Eli agreed. "But I bet he won't ask," he said. "It would be unsafe for him, too. He's the one who's going to be alone in a strange city."

"I think we should take a road trip to Missouri and check this guy out," Jack said, threateningly. "We'll just show up, knock on his door, and invite ourselves in. Let's see how he handles that."

I amused myself with this vision, of Jack and Eli showing up at Dick's door and making themselves at home on his living room couch. It would have been fun to see how much mettle Dick had but, in the end, I found out before any road trips were necessary. Things fell apart over the course of the next two phone conversations. The first took place four days before he was supposed to visit. We had talked for 20 minutes, and were just about ready to hang up when he said, "So, I feel like a heel for asking this, but can you send more pictures?"

"What?"

"I thought," he continued, "now that I'm coming and all, that you could send me more pictures?"

My face flushed, from my forehead to my neck. I flashed back to the moment in second grade when Melissa Johns ratted me out for eating paste.

"What would you want more pictures for? You're meeting me in five days."

"I'd just like to see more of what you look like."

"Why? So that if you don't like the pictures, you don't have to drive three hours?"

Dick paused. "That was incredibly stupid of me. I'm sorry. Look, I'm a guy. We're all jerks. You have to be willing to forgive me for stupid comments."

I was silent.

"Can I get a second chance?"

A stronger woman would have told him not to come. I couldn't do that. I'd had such high hopes for him. He was from New Mexico! "Okay, but just this one time."

Meanwhile, the owners of my dream home had countered with a price of $82,500. I accepted! Pending home inspection and FHA approval, of course. The home inspector couldn't come for ten days. "And nothing happens until the FHA inspector signs off," Flora said. From what I'd heard, FHA tended to focus on cosmetics, like cracks in windows and banisters on the stairways. I needed them for the loan, but the regular home inspection was the one that mattered.

In the meantime, I went shopping for clothes to wear for my weekend with Dick. We talked again on Thursday night.

"So, three hours is a long drive," he said.

"Yes it is."

"So, if things go well between us, any chance I could spend the night at your place?"

I'd actually role-played this exact thing happening with Izzy, so I knew exactly what to say! (Tell me my worrying isn't helpful! Izzy was humoring me, but here I was, using it!) I just slipped the tape in and pressed play. "Listen, this has nothing to do with you and I hope you don't take this personally, but in this day and age, I can't do that. I can help you find a hotel room, and I'll split the cost, but I can't let someone I just met spend the night in my apartment."

Long silence. "Well, I guess I can see your point." In a tone that said he actually didn't.

"Thanks for understanding," I said.

"Sure. I completely get it. I have friends in Lincoln that I could stay with, except that they just had a baby, so…" Silence.

I waited him out. I was a duck. The guilt was rolling off my back like water.

"So," he continued, "I don't think they'd want me as a guest."

"I can recommend some good hotels."

"I guess I could call my friends and ask them anyway…"

Thirty seconds passed. *Quack, quack*, I thought.

"You know," he continued at last, "maybe this weekend isn't such a good idea. Three hours is a long drive." He was trying to force my hand.

"I thought you said earlier that you didn't mind driving."

"I don't. But I think that this is a long trip to make after all the driving I've done this week. I'm not sure what to do. I'm wondering if we can we postpone this trip for another weekend?"

"Omaha will always be a three hour drive." I told him. "You might as well decide now whether you want to make it or not." I tried to sound nonchalant, but I wasn't sure I was pulling it off.

"Yeah. I guess I don't want to make the drive. Is that okay?"

"It's not for me to say. You do what you want." I couldn't end without a parting shot, though. "I just wish you hadn't been so indecisive. I cleared my weekend for you."

"I know. I'm really sorry."

Like I had any kind of weekend plans to clear.

"He didn't want to make a three hour drive unless he was going to get laid," my painting class said. I tended to agree.

I sighed. Looking back on our calls, I realized that our interactions seemed to go downhill after I mentioned that I had made an offer on a house. His voice developed a harder edge, and he'd started talking about how he was looking at homes too. Actually, in retrospect, we probably weren't well matched. He did a lot of bragging about how much money he spent on things. He'd actually told me he was looking at cars that cost $120,000. I could never, in good conscious, live with a man who drove a car that costs more than a house (a house in Omaha). And that, "I'm okay and my expensive stuff proves it" mentality is bad news. So, as everyone kept telling me, I knew I dodged a bullet. But it still sucked. It *hurt*! I was deeply disappointed. And back to square one with no one on my plate but Lance.

Chapter 12
Getting Closed-Out on Match

On my second dinner with Lance, I decided to pin down his politics.

"So, you call yourself conservative."

"Basically."

"Because I'm a liberal."

"That's okay."

"Well, I think so. But I don't usually get along very well with conservatives."

"I'm not that conservative."

"Oh?" *Could this be true?* "Let's compare some notes. What's your opinion on drilling in the Arctic Refuge?"

"We have to. The oil is more important than a couple of animal species."

"What we really need," I said, "is to find alternative energy sources so we aren't so dependent on the Middle East."

"Well, my friend Davie would say that drilling is the only way to free ourselves from Saudi Arabia and nail them for their anti-American terrorists."

"Gay marriage?"

He shuddered. "That's just wrong."

"Why?"

"Because it is."

"So you think that some people shouldn't have the same rights that you have? Doesn't that sound like segregation in the fifties?"

"I just know that gay marriage is wrong."

"Stem cell research?"

"Uh. I'm opposed."

"Why? Stem cell research could potentially cure Childhood Diabetes."

Poor Lance was sweating. "I wish my friend Davie was here. He is great at arguing his points."

"But we're talking about your beliefs, not Davie's. If you can't even argue your reasons, then how do you know what you believe?"

He shrugged. "I just do."

"I really don't know if this is going to work, Lance. Your conservativism is a real issue for me."

"You say it like it's a disease."

"I just mean that I feel strongly about my beliefs and you don't seem to even understand why you have your beliefs."

"I don't think much about politics."

I looked at my hands. "Tell me about your job," I said, because we hadn't even given a waitress our dinner order.

"You aren't stuck with Lance," Izzy said. You've got 72 more men to get through."

And about 30 new ones every week. "They're all weirdoes."

"Not all. What about that doctor guy? What was his name? Medicine Man?"

"MedicalMania. But he is in his forties." I don't know why forty seems so scary to me. Probably because it's not that far away.

"You're 38!" Izzy asked. "And when Mary Russell meets Sherlock Holmes, he's in his 60s."

That's a reference to Laurie King's Mary Russell mystery series. She revives the character of Holmes for her stories. And Izzy is right. When the guy is right, the package matters very little. MedicalMania liked to hike, ate organically, and was smart. He was handsome, and alternative looking. The only negative was a line in his profile that said, 'I am a very young looking 44-year-old.' I don't know why that sentence bothered me. It was like he was trying to sell himself in this superficial kind of way...like a woman saying, "My bust size is..." Izzy thought I was overreacting, but it made me wonder about his self-esteem. Still, I emailed this man. Why not? The other two guys seemed great, but weren't. Why not try someone who seems questionable and hope he's great?

I kept my email simple. Just wrote thanks for the email and asked him what a typical day at work was for him. His response came the next day.

> *Hi, Quinn. Nice to hear from you. A typical day for me would be to rise early, go for a run with my dog, then head in to work. I'm a radiologist, so I don't do rounds. That means no early mornings (yea!). I divide my time three ways: research, clinic, and teaching. I am part of a practice so I get good vacation, about six weeks a year. This enables me to travel around the globe, and also back to my hometown of Santa Fe. I find that, while I enjoy the Midwest, I often need a southwest-fix for the colors, smells, and food. Also, the people. You've spent time in New Mexico, haven't you? That was one of the things that attracted me to you.*
>
> *What's an average day for you? What kind of job do you have? I see that you work in healthcare and with children. What do you do?*
>
> *Jacob*

I love the name Jacob. It's in my top ten list of favorite male names:

1. Jeremiah
2. Max
3. Jacob
4. Josh
5. Benjamin
6. Zach
7. Seth
8. Victor
9. Evan
10. Jack

"Third time's the charm," Izzy said when I forwarded her the draft of my reply to Jacob. "I've got no corrections. You're getting better and better at this."

"Hi, Jacob. Thanks for your message. Yes, I've spent time in NM. I lived in Albuquerque for five years. I love northern New Mexico. It's my favorite place in the world, and where I'd eventually like to end up living.

Thanks for explaining what you do in your job. I'm an audiologist. My patient load is about fifty-fifty adults and children. In a typical day, I might test the hearing of a 4-month old, a 2-year-old, a 10-year-old, and an 87-year-old. I fit hearing aids, and could fit any of the above ages, on an average day. I also do vestibular testing on dizzy patients.

I notice in your profile that you like to hike. I wonder if you could tell me good places to hike here? I used to hike the Sandias all the time, when I lived in NM. This part of the country seems to have nothing. But maybe I just don't know about it? Looking forward to your reply, Quinn."

I waited a day to send it, so as not to seem too eager.

He didn't respond after a day. I was patient. I figured he was just playing it cool. Or he was busy. Or he was not the kind of person who checks his email often. On day seven, I decided to not let my insecurities take over. I wrote him another note.

Hey, Jacob. How's it going? Things are good here. I've had a great week. I went to the Tori Amos concert last night. She inspired me to get up early today to paint for two hours before work. Later tonight, I'm going to a wine tasting party that a friend is having. Then, this weekend, I'm just going to relax–take some long walks, paint some more, read. I'm reading an awesome book–The Hazards of Good Breeding. Do you know it?

I hope this email finds you well and that you're having a good week, too.

Take care, Quinn.

He never responded. And that was that. I couldn't call, or run into him, or ask his friends. I felt so powerless. I mean, I wanted to hear why he wasn't interested. And how could he ignore such sincere and open notes? If he met someone else, why couldn't he write and tell me? It seemed so unfair, to not get any response. But maybe people don't seem real to Internet daters. What else could explain it? If he met someone else, why not drop me a line to say so? If he wasn't interested, well, that'd be harder to say. But what in my letter could have made him lose interest?

I vowed that I'd never do that to someone online. If I'd been interacting with them, and changed my mind, I'd tell them so.

It reminded me of Lance's profile. I had laughed at his comments about telling him if you didn't want to email anymore. My sympathy for Lance was increasing by the minute. And to think that I'd thought he seemed bitter when I first read his profile. How the worm turns!

Chapter 13
How to Dump a Man in Five Easy Steps

"I burn with pain, with the pain of your absence. My tree has no leaves. But my roots sink deeper, searching in vain for a vein of water. Searching as the wind howls through my empty branches."

I was still getting poetry from Bob, the speed dater. I was unsure what to do with him. I would send him brief notes like, "Your poetry is really coming along. I especially like when you don't hit me over the head with your symbolism." But I was running out of things to say.

The women on *Sex and the City* had sex in *every* episode. Me? I get Bob and Bob's poems.

One day, in mid-December, a week before my home inspection, Bob wrote without a poem attached.

"Hey, Quinn, would you like to accompany me to my office Christmas party?"

"Bob, I thought you were seeing the other girl you met at speed dating?"

"Yeah, well, we just broke up."

So why not fall back on good ol' Quinn? Let her suffer through the office Christmas party even though she's not dating material? What a perfect ending to an all-around, lousy night of speed dating! I was annoyed, so I deferred responding until after I saw my next patient.

Debbie was 37, just one year younger than me. I'd followed her for about two years. She had a conductive hearing loss, which meant that her hearing nerve worked fine, but the mechanical part of her middle ear, the ear drum and three bones behind it, were stiff from otosclerosis, and stopped sound from getting to her nerve endings.

Typically, an otologist can correct this loss with surgery, but Debbie had some health problems that make her a poor surgical candidate. I don't know what they all were, but for starters, she was missing an eye and had no teeth. Even so, she was still a pretty girl. Today, when I went to the waiting room to get her, she had a cane. I knew she was a meth addict, but there were probably a lot of other things going on, too.

"What happened?" I asked, once we were inside a room.

She shrugged, giving me a toothless grin. With her eye patch, she looked like a pirate. "Stroke, I guess. I don't really know."

I nodded. Now that she'd said something, I thought I could see the left corner of her mouth turned down. She had reduced mobility in her left hand, too.

"I was in western Nebraska, with JJ." JJ was Debbie's boyfriend. He came with her sometimes and always struck me as a loser. "We had a fight, and he left. So I was stuck out in the middle of nowhere for five days. I couldn't get home because I didn't have any money to call anyone."

I didn't ask her how she'd been eating.

"Finally, I hitchhiked home with this guy. He left me off in Aurora. I got a couple more rides and when I got home, I tracked JJ down and went after him with a hammer." The way she told the story, her voice was sweet and kind of shy, like she was talking about losing an assignment for school. She smelled strongly of Ivory soap. She looked up at me with her big hazel eye. "I roughed him up pretty good, on account of catching him off guard. He was asleep." *Jeez. Remind me not to cross you*, I thought.

I waited to hear about the stroke, but she never came around to it. "Anyhow, now I can't get my left hearing aid in, because my left hand doesn't work that great."

We practiced putting the aid in with the right hand until she was proficient. "These hearing aids just make everything sound so much better," she said. "You are so good to me, Quinn. I don't know how to thank you."

"It's my job, and besides, I enjoy it. I'd like to see you back in a week, to make sure you are doing okay with the hearing aids." I stood up and she followed me, hobbling to the door. "Do you need to call someone for a ride?" I asked.

"No, un-uh. JJ's waiting for me in the car."

When I got back to my desk I opened my email and typed Bob a letter.

> *Bob,*
>
> *Cool! So, I take it you changed you mind about having kids?*
>
> *Quinn*

I never got another poem from Bob again.

In the first 3 months of putting my profile up, I'd gotten 5,756 hits. That's the number of people who opened up your profile. About 150 of those people had emailed me. My first three encounters were busts. "But good experiences," Izzy reminded me. "Let's think about what you've learned. First, that Lance wasn't bitter, but sick of getting blown off."

"Yeah," I said. I was still sore about the whole radiologist-blow-off.

"You've also learned how to correspond with the opposite sex. You've gotten much better at writing them and showing off your personality."

"True."

"So, on to the next group. Why don't we do five more?"

How to pick five out of the growing list I had, with more emails coming in every day. And no one sounded what I'd call stellar. Here's a sampling of what I read on a daily basis:

Well, I'm back in the saddle again after having my heart broken by my girlfriend of ten years.

My ideal match is a young and slender male with minimal body hair, OR tomboy female. He/she loves intellectual pursuits, including chess, gardening, and non-fiction reading.

I'm a teacher and coach for middle-schoolers. I am looking for someone who knows how to be a winner in the game of life. There are too many quitters and people who blame others for their misfortunes.

I was full of self-pity. "There's no one out there for me."
"Nonsense," Izzy said. "I'll pick out the five, you just email them."
"No, never mind. I'll do it." Eventually.
"Just forget about that doctor. Who knows? Maybe he died."

I loved my apartment, but I was starting to appreciate the idea of a house. When I got home, Walter was listening to *As It Happens*, from Canada Public Radio, on NPR. I like that show, but it doesn't mean I always want to hear it. I ate a peanut butter sandwich and climbed into bed by 8:30. The BBC World News was on next door, but when I shut my bedroom door, I couldn't hear much. I tried to read, but by 8:35 I had turned off the lamp. It was kind of early for bed. But I felt exhausted. "Just one of those days," is what I would have said to a dog, if I'd had one.
The phone woke me at 9:35. "Hello?"
"Hey Quinn, it's Chris."
"Who?"
"Chris."
Him again? "Chris, what do you want?"
"I wanted to invite you to a party on Friday night."
"I'm busy Friday. Thanks anyway. Goodnight." Why did he reject me but insist on pestering me? Of course, I couldn't fall back asleep again until 11:30.

In the morning, I went to yoga before work. I was annoyed at Chris but also worried that I'd been rude. But during yoga, all was forgotten.

I do Bikram yoga. The room is hot, which helps loosen my muscles. Bikram yoga is like Xtreme Meditation or something. The positions are hard, but your focus is tranquility. You can't maintain a pose without balance, strength, and flexibility. A lot of the balance is mental. If the person next to you sways or falls, you could fall just from seeing them go down. When I'm in a hard balance pose, I visual that a chair is under me, or that I'm leaning on a mantel. Or that my feet have sprouted 12-inch metal spikes that are sunk into the ground. When I'm exerting all my strength to hold a pose and focusing all my energy in maintaining a sense of calm, I don't have time to think of anything else. In Bikram, you aren't even supposed to scratch an itch. (You think, "Oh, I have an itch. Interesting," and co-exist with it.) The mental focus Bikram requires is like a 90-minute break from all my life's worries.

"You are a fleck of dust," my instructor said, "and a universe." Chris was no more than a buzzing fly that I heard across the room, but didn't really pay attention to.

In my car, after class, Dave Matthews Band was on the radio, playing "Crush." I felt calm and loose. The violin part went perfectly with the way my body felt. If you've never done yoga, just listen to that violin piece to know what coming out of yoga feels like. Complicated in a loose, smooth, transitioning, beautiful way.

As I entered my building from the garage below, I saw Walter, carrying his groceries upstairs. He must have left to shop at 6 a.m. He was inching upstairs, one step at a time, resting his bags with each step.

"Would you like me to give you a hand?" I asked. I scooped up his bags and carried them upstairs.

"Thank you," Walter said. "But the real concern I have is the snow. I need to get out of my driveway."

"Agnes has that man come to plow," I said.

"The plow man leaves a few inches in front of our garages. I used to shovel that myself, but now I don't have the strength. I don't need to go out every day, but I can't be housebound this winter. I have doctor appointments. I need to purchase my medicine and food."

"I'll shovel your drive," I said.

"Why, I couldn't ask."

"You didn't. I'd be happy to. It will be good exercise."

"I'll pay you, then," he said.

"No need," I said. "It will only add a couple of minutes to my morning."

"Fine," he said. Like he was doing me a favor.

I smiled and let myself inside my apartment. I truly didn't care that he didn't say "thank you." You gotta love yoga!

"And then there's Chris," I told Ann. "Now he's called twice and woken me both times. I'm like a grandma, asleep in bed when everyone else is up and out."

"Those were bootie calls," she said. "He hung up with you and went on to the next number." We were having coffee at our usual downtown hangout. I've wondered for a while if the owner didn't have a crush on Ann. He seems friendly, but she's adamant about not dating. I can't tell if she is afraid or honestly not interested. She had on a silk shirt, rain slicker, capris, and Tevas. She does not know the meaning of *dress for success*. "There are two possibilities, either the woman he chose over you didn't put out, or she's out of town."

I could only marvel at her cynicism.

"The only way to get rid of these men is to be blunt, Quinn. Subtlety doesn't work on men."

"I practically hung up on him," I told her.

"You need to be more explicit. You know what, let's practice. I'll be you. You be Chris. Or Lance."

"Let's start with Chris," I said. "He's easier because I really dislike him. Brrring, brrring."

"Hello?" Ann said, with a pretend yawn.

"Hey, is this Quinn? It's Chris."

"Chris, I hear voices in the background. Are you calling from a bar?"

"Yeah. I wanted to invite you out."

"Chris, let's get something clear. Calling drunk from a bar is not the way to win a woman's heart. You've ruined your chances with me, but I'm telling you this for the next woman you meet. Now, go back to your friends and don't call me again." Ann smiled. "See how easy that is? Your turn. I'll be you."

"Hello?"

"Hey, Quinn. It's Chris," Ann said, in a drunken, surfer dude voice.

"Hi Chris. Are you calling from a bar?"

"Uh. Totally dude. There's a great band here. Want to come out and join us?"

"No, Chris. I don't."

"Okay. Sorry man. Jeez."

"Chris, don't call me drunk from a bar again. It's rude. Good- bye."

"Pretty good," Ann critiqued. "You forgot to tell him never to call you period."

"It's just that that seemed so mean. Isn't it implied?"

"Nothing is implied with men. Now, let's get rid of Lance. 'Hi Quinn,'" she said. "Want to grab dinner on Friday?"

"Actually, Lance, I don't know if…yes, I'd like to, as a friend."

"No, no, no. That will never work," Ann interrupted. "You have to be blunt. 'No, Lance. I can't have dinner with you because I'm not interested in dating you. I wish you the best of luck with future dating. Take care and goodbye.'"

"Just cut him off like that? I wanted to stay in touch with him."

"You can't. He won't let you. That When Harry Met Sally theory is true. Men can't be friends with women. If they think they have a shot at dating you, they put out friendship. If there's no chance of dating, the friendship is over."

I didn't believe her. "I don't believe you."

She shrugged. "Okay, learn the hard way."

I was quiet for a few minutes. "I told him I thought he was on a lower moral plain. Who would date someone who thought that?"

"It's either A. He doesn't care because sex will be fun, regardless of how much you despise him, or, B. His other pickings must be pretty slim."

I agreed to go out with Lance the next time he asked. I planned to break up with him; I just needed to do it face to face. I didn't dress up for this date. I wore jeans and a black LL Bean cotton sweater. No eye makeup, just lipstick. I began with a serious talk about his politics.

"I just don't think we'll ever get past it," I said.

"I'm fine with us having different politics," he said.

"But I'm not. Haven't I already made that clear?" I asked. "How would we ever raise children?"

"We would each give them our opinion."

"So, you and I would explain our different opinions on gay

marriage to our four-year-old?"

"We'd wait till he was older."

I decided on a different tack. "What other types of women have you met online?"

"Let's just say that none of them have seemed very, what's the word? Sane."

"Really? Give me some examples." I was curious about my fellow women on Match.

"Well, the first woman seemed nice. She was beautiful. She was a med student, so I figured she was smart. But she went to the bathroom on our third date and tried to kill herself."

"What?"

"Yeah. I guess she had taken a bunch of pills. They called an ambulance and took her away."

"Did you ever see her again?"

"I tried, once. I went to the hospital. But she told me to take a hike."

"Jeez."

"The second woman was okay. Except that she was about 10 years older than she said."

"How old was she claiming to be?"

"Thirty-five. But she was easily 45 and could have been even older. She had those spots on her hands, like my grandmother. And jet-black dyed hair. The next woman got so drunk on our first date that she threw up in my car. The next couple seemed okay, but they didn't want to date me after the first date."

"Why?"

"One said I looked too much like her ex. The other one, well, I might have inadvertently been watching the football game on the television behind her head while we were talking."

We were at a bar/restaurant, during this conversation. There was a television mounted behind my head. "You haven't been doing that with me."

He took a swig of his beer. "I learned my lesson."

"Sooner or later you'll meet someone who's a good match for you."

He shrugged. "What about you? Have you been meeting a lot of men?"

"Some."

"How many emails have you gotten?" he asked.

"About 150. The first 80 or so of those came in the first 5 days. It's slowed down since then."

His eyes widened. "Are you kidding?"

"No. How many have you gotten?"

"Twenty-five or so total in six months." He shook his head. "So how many dates have you had?"

"You were the first date…"

His eyes perked up. "Really?" I could tell he was proud of himself.

"Because your profile was so funny," I said. "Then there have been a few men I've corresponded with, but so far, those have fallen through."

"One hundred and fifty."

"A lot of them are freaks," I told him.

"As freaky as my dates?" he asked.

"No," I conceded. "Not yet, anyway."

Lance looked defeated.

"You are really nice, Lance. But it's not going to work with us."

"Why not? We get along well. And we're both pretty normal."

"Yes, but your political opinions offend me. Also, you seem to loathe your job, but you won't quit because the pay is good. I could never live that way. And I don't want my children to grow up with a father who's already defeated by life."

"So, you didn't say what we role-played, because you didn't want to be mean?" Ann asked.

"I wanted to be honest. But not mean."

"And telling him he was defeated by life was the nice way to break up with him."

"I messed up. Damn. I thought that being honest was the best way out."

"It was. You just didn't have to make a full disclosure."

"See, this proves that I can't talk to men!"

"Well, you got yourself out. You'll do better next time."

"There's not going to be a next time. Internet Date No. 4 is just going to have to be a keeper. I can't deal with anything less."

Chapter 14
Internet Date Number 4

Dear Quinn Painter

Your profile is the most engaging one I've seen since I've started on Match. You are a great writer. I'm a big fan of art, although I don't do any myself. I used to draw in high school. I suppose you've gotten a million emails so far, so I'm not holding out much hope for a response, but let me tell you a little about myself, just in case. I'm 34. I'm a carpenter. I didn't go to college, instead I apprenticed with a master carpenter for four years. Now I have my own business. I make custom furniture. I also volunteer my skills at several homeless shelters in town. On a good day, I will rise early, and go with my dog on a long hike or bike ride. He's a chocolate lab, named Hershey. (Not my name choice— I got him from the pound and he came with the name.) Then I work in my shop for several hours. Go to a job site for more work. Head over to a shelter to repair a broken bunk bed or pinch-hit a plumbing problem. I usually wrap up the day watching television or reading a good book, with Hershey asleep at my feet. Oh, did I mention I love chocolate? (giggle, giggle).

So, any interest? If so, I'd love to hear from you. If not, no problem. Good luck in your quest.

Cheers, Jim

I responded without even showing the email to Izzy. It was the same email I'd sent to the radiologist, more or less. He replied the next day.

> *Quinn,*
>
> *Thanks for your email! Great to hear from you. Say, are you free tonight? I just got a call from one of the shelters–volunteers are replacing their roof, and they are desperate for more manpower–their goal is to get the whole roof finished before dark tonight. I was planning on heading over at 3:30. Want to come? Are you spontaneous?*
>
> *Jim*

We met at the shelter. I took vacation to leave work early and got there shortly after four. We had about an hour of daylight left. For a mid-December day, it wasn't all that cold. Low 50s, although the temperature was already beginning to drop as the sun went down. I was nervous but just ignored it as I parked my car and locked up. He was waiting outside the shelter. He was much better looking than his online photo. He had dark, glossy hair that he swung out of his eyes with a shake as I approached.

"Quinn?" he asked, with a smile. He was in good physical shape and he had a friendly, casual feel to him. I felt good about my appearance. I was in jeans, sneakers, and my second best color, a navy blue sweater. My hair was in a ponytail. Personally, I think I look best in jeans.

All of a sudden, I realized I'd forgotten his name. "Hi...nice to meet you." Shit! I racked my brain but I couldn't come up with it. He was Internet Date #4!!!

"Likewise," he said. "Here's a hammer. Let me take you around back."

About ten people were already there, working. Some were on the ground, organizing the supplies and directing others. About four were on the roof. I thought of my own home, which was three days from inspection, and I couldn't help but smile. I loved that house already. I shook my head and refocused on the house in front of me. I'd never actually replaced a roof, but the foreman showed me how to align the shingles and hammer them in place. My date was working a few feet behind me.

"Who did you come with?" the foreman asked as he passed me by. "Uh, I came with …" I used my thumb to point to the Guy behind me.

"With me," the Guy said. "She came with me."

"Hey, how are you?" the foreman asked.

"Great, Joe. Just great."

I turned to look at the Guy. Could he tell I'd forgotten his name? He smiled at me. "The last time I roofed a house was in the ninth grade," he said, as he hammered.

"Was it your house?" I asked.

"Yes. Our barn, actually. My father is such a perfectionist that he made me go back up and realign half of them. They had a slight curve and it bothered his anal-retentive sensibilities."

"On a barn roof? Who would ever even see it?" I asked.

"He would, while he drove around on his tractor."

"That is a real commitment to order." I said. I didn't want to bash his dad.

"Well, he had a point. I mean, it did look better."

I glanced behind me and saw that his shingles were perfectly aligned. Mine were slightly less so. "Do you think my shingles are okay?" I asked. "They seem a little crooked."

He glanced up at them and frowned slightly. As he opened his mouth to speak, the foreman popped his head up. "They look good. We're not expecting perfection. We just don't want the roof to leak." My date shrugged and went back to work.

We finished the roof just at dusk. I went into the shelter to use the bathroom and wash my hands. There were three little kids running around. The oldest looked to be six or seven. She was yelling at the other two kids to stop following her and go back to their mom. The other two kids were about two and four years of age. All three kids had a look of stickiness about them, like they'd recently eaten dessert.

"Did you know there are kids here?" I asked The Guy as we headed toward our cars.

"Oh, sure. There are lots of kids here. Lots of families. Mostly single moms with kids. They stay in a different area from the men."

I nodded, like I got it, but I was in shock. I had never heard of children in a homeless shelter. Weren't there better options than that, for most kids?

I thought of his name on the drive home. Jim. He sent an email the very next day.

> *Quinn,*
>
> *I don't want you to get a big head, or anything, but I think you are swell. Can we have a formal date, where I wear a tie and buy you dinner?*
>
> *Jim*
>
> *P.S. Your car made a terrible squealing sound as you drove away. It sounds like the fan belt. I can fix that for you.*

The day of our formal date, I breezed into the clinic with a smile for everyone.

"What are you so happy about?" Lucy asked.

"Me? Do I seem happy?"

"You look like Mary Sunshine."

"Oh, I don't know why. Maybe it's because everything is finally going right for me. I have my home inspection tomorrow. I have a date tonight! With a total hotty. That could be the reason. A carpenter hotty."

"Carpenter?" Lucy asked, wrinkling her nose.

"Yes. Like Jesus," I said. That stopped the line of criticism I could see at the tip of her tongue. I turned smugly back to my computer and began a report.

My first patient of the day was a seven-year-old boy. Jonathan was a bright little thing, with curly black hair and big brown eyes. His mom was young and pretty, with some lines around her mouth that suggested too much sun.

"We already have a hearing test," she said. "They told me he needed a hearing aid, and to come to you."

A quick glance at their chart told me they lived about an hour south of Omaha, in a little town called Weeping Water. We started with a repeat hearing test, and my results were identical to the last test.

I stepped out of the sound booth for a minute to grab a hearing aid from our hearing aid lab. When I came back inside, I unhooked Jonathan from the headphones and brought him into the test side of the booth, to sit next to his mother.

"Jonathan does have hearing loss in both ears. In the highest frequencies, sounds have to be at least 70 decibels before Jonathan will hear them. That means that, even when you are sitting next to him, he won't always hear every part of what you say."

"He understands everything we say to him."

"Yes," I nodded. "His hearing is normal in the low frequencies, so he hears a lot. But he's got a severe hearing loss in the high frequencies."

I put the mom in the sound booth, with Jonathan next to her, and played a soft, tone through the speakers. "Can you hear that?" I asked the mom. She nodded.

"Can you?" she asked Jonathan. He shook his head.

I started raising the volume, in ten-decibel increments. Jonathan could hear the sound when it got, roughly, to the level of a vacuum cleaner. His mother looked at him in disbelief. "You couldn't hear that before?"

I brought them into a counseling room to talk some more. "What he's missing are mid and high frequency sounds. Mostly consonants. So if I said, 'Look at the cat,' he might miss the 'c' sound. He'd have to guess, 'Did she said 'hat,' 'bat,' or 'rat.'"

"He can hear the word cat," his mother said. "Jonathan, what's a cat?"

"Like Kitty," Jonathan said. She looked at me triumphantly.

I nodded. "Good job, Jonathan. And you're right," I said to the mom. "He will hear and understand some speakers better than others. And some words. Especially when people are near him and there is no background noise. But he'll still miss a lot of words, and he won't be able to overhear conversations very well. Overhearing is a big part of how children learn language, and also how they learn about different societal rules that are unspoken. Like, if everyone in class has to ask the teacher permission to go the bathroom, and he doesn't hear others ask this question, but just sees them leave, he will just leave too. Then the teacher will say that he isn't following directions, but unless she sat him down and explicitly told him the rule, he wouldn't know about it."

The mom nodded. Her eyes had glazed over, so I decided to move on. "Hearing aids would help improve his ability to hear those sounds." I turned to Jonathan. "How do you feel about that?"

He shrugged. I rephrased my question. "Do you want a hearing aid?"

"No," he glanced sideways at his mother.

"What is bad about them?" I asked.

He shrugged. "They look funny."

I nodded. "I have one in my ear right now," I told him. "Can you tell which ear?"

He looked at me in surprise and peered at my ears. He shook his head.

"No."

I turned so he could get a better look at my right ear. I was wearing a behind-the-ear hearing aid, the only style we fit on young children.

"Ugh. It's so big. Can't he get one of those little ones?"

"Kids grow so fast, that he would outgrow all the other sizes every year, or so. With this style, we just replace the ear mold."

"Will he need it for school?" she asked.

"Yes. In fact, this size will allow the school to hook a transmitter into his hearing aid, so that he'll hear his teacher's voice a little louder than anyone else in the room."

His mother frowned. "When I was a girl, just the retarded kids wore hearing aids like that." Jonathan balked.

I nodded. "Uh huh. Sure. Um, any kid with hearing loss wears this style." I took a deep breath. No point in getting angry at dumb stuff that a parent says in a stressful situation. "We fit hundreds of kids every year," I said. "Some are in the honors society, some are artists, or musicians, or football stars. But they all wear this style of hearing aid."

I sat down on the floor so that I was eye-level with Jonathan. "We could get a color that blends into your hair," I said. I took the aid off my ear and put it on his. "Your hair is a little short, but if you let it grow even another quarter of an inch, I think you could hide your hearing aid very well." I used my fingers to comb his hair over the aid, then handed him a mirror. "Show your mom," I suggested.

Jonathon climbed onto his mother's lap. She inspected the aid on his ear without comment.

"I know a little boy, well, now he's a teenager, but he got his first pair of hearing aids at the same age that you are," I told Jonathan. "He went to school with the hearing aids in his ears, and when he came home, they were gone!"

Jonathan's eyes widened. "Did he lose them?"

"No. He told his classmates that they were miniature radios. During recess, he sold them to his classmate for two dollars."

Jonathan got a laugh out of this. His mother started to cry. She was a silent crier. I looked up to see tears streaming down her cheeks. A second later, Jonathan saw them too. He patted her back. "What's the matter, Mom? Don't cry." I could see that Jonathan understood that his mom was crying about him and his hearing loss. He probably thought he had some control over it, that if he'd worked harder during the hearing test, he wouldn't have a hearing loss. His mom didn't mean any harm, she was just trying to deal with this very sad news as best she could. But she was showing him that something about him was making her cry. And he was too young to realize that it was nothing he could change and that it was nothing that was wrong with him.

Back in my office, I called the manufacturer of the hearing aid we'd ultimately settled on, and ordered a pair for Jonathan. After entering the order in our computer tracking system, I leaned back in my chair. It was 10:12 in the morning, and I was exhausted. Patient care can really wear you out. I took a moment to picture what my house was like, across town, at this exact moment. It would be completely still inside. At this time of day sunlight could be streaming through the rooms, making starbursts on the walls as it went through the crystal doorknobs. The vision of the silent rooms full of sun calmed me. I opened my email. There was a message from Jim, the carpenter.

> *"Hi Quinn. A friend of mine has an art show that opens tonight. Could we add some culture to this dinner by visiting the gallery after we eat? No hard labor, this time."*

Reader, I really liked this guy. He was fun, and the idea of a date with him energized me for the rest of the day.

We were meeting at a restaurant in the Old Market area, my favorite part of town. The Old Market reminds me of a mini-SoHo before Pottery Barn and other national chains took over all the stores. Old Market is still completely local. Or, almost completely. Jim was taking me to the only chain-restaurant in the neighborhood. I don't know why anyone would choose a chain when we had our choice of locally owned French, Mexican, Italian, and Persian eateries. Jim apparently had bad taste in restaurants. But that was no big deal. I figured, once he ate somewhere good, he'd never go back to a chain again.

Jim had worn jeans with a blazer and tie. I had on a long black skirt, with a black velvet jacket. "I look like a hobo," he said.

"No, you've got a jacket on. You look great."

"I should have worn my chinos."

"I'm not concerned, so you shouldn't be either."

"I just wish I'd dressed nicer. I was picturing you in the jeans you wore to Habitat, and I dressed according to that. What was I thinking?"

"You look great. Really. So let's drop it, okay?"

"Fine." He fingered his water glass. "God. I should have worn chinos."

"Tell me about your friend."

"Henry? Oh, he's a really talented artist. He's amazing. Wait till you see his work."

"How did you meet him?"

"Down here. At one of the coffee houses. It turns out that we live in the same building. One of those warehouses by the bridge."

"You live in one of those lofts?"

"Yes."

"That must be so neat." Several of the warehouses had been renovated into loft apartments. They were expensive, but, I figured, a carpenter probably made pretty good money, if he could find his niche.

"A far cry from a farm house. My parents think I'm a lunatic, living in this place. All my mother could comment on was the lack of natural light."

"There's no natural light?"

"'It's like you're in a coffin, Jim.'" He was mimicking his mother, in a high-pitched voice.

"There's no natural light in your loft?" I asked again.

"One room has light. The rooms behind it go deep into the warehouse. There are no windows that far in."

"But isn't it all open, like a loft?"

"It's got high ceilings. Two bedrooms. One bath. My parents are always that way. They just don't get that I'm different from them. It's always 'Ask God what he would do.' As if God would have any idea what it's like to live my life, right now. They hate Hershey. I actually have to kennel him when I go home to visit."

"Well, not everyone's a dog person."

"Next time I go home, he's coming. And he's staying in their house. They are going to have to deal with me *and* my dog. I'm fed up with them. I haven't been home for two Christmases now, and that's why."

"How is it to have a dog in an apartment?" I asked.

"In the past, I've always spent Christmas with friends. Or, ex-friends, now."

"Why ex-friends?"

"I'm seriously considering suing them," he said. "In fact, I probably will hire a lawyer. I made them some cabinets. I offered to make them for free. They just paid for the wood. But they were so picky, with so many changes, that I asked for a little extra money. They balked. The cheapskates."

"How long had you known these people?"

"I'm not going to be taken advantage of. I don't tolerate users."

While Jim talked, he didn't make eye contact with me for more than a second or so at a time. His eyes were wandering all over and his fingers were nervously handling his silverware. I felt that if I could just get his eyes to stay still on my face, we'd be able to have a nice conversation. "I've got a good life, though," he said. "I work. Love my job. I volunteer between 10 and 20 hours a week. That works out to 520-1040 hours a year."

"That's amazing."

"You probably think I'm tooting my own horn."

"Not at all. I'm just having a hard time having a conversation with you. You are jumping so fast, from topic to topic that I feel like we aren't having any sort of dialogue."

His eyes were on my chin. "Well, tell me about yourself."

"Well, I'd like to do that. But I have a few questions about some of what you've been saying first. Like your parents. Where do they live?"

"Just outside of Kearney."

"So you grew up in Nebraska?"

"Yes."

"And do you have brothers or sisters?"

"Eight, all together. All of them just perfect replicas of my parents. They all live close by. I'm the only one who broke out and moved to Omaha. They absolutely hate Omaha. They think they'll be shot the moment they step over city limits. But they have to learn to accept me, just as I am, Omaha and all. I'm a good person. I volunteer more than anyone else I know. I can't tolerate people who won't give back. If you don't volunteer your time to some cause, you aren't a good person. It's that simple. I'm not perfect. My father thinks he's perfect. And sure, his tools are cleaned daily, his barn is swept, my mother's kitchen is shiny and spotless. Cleanliness is important. I'm pretty neat. I don't think I could live with someone who's messy."

He was like a bunny rabbit, darting all over a lawn. It was impossible to relax in a conversation with him. I finally gave up attempting to dialogue, and just let him rant. I couldn't even take comfort in the food. It was precooked, frozen, and re-heated.

The gallery was walking distance from the restaurant. I was realizing that Jim and I hadn't really talked at the shelter. His actions were what I'd liked about him. And his emails.

"Do you go to a lot of art openings?" he asked me.

"A fair amount," I told him.

"Then maybe you've seen my friend. Henry Patrick."

"I'm not good with names. I might recognize him when I see him."

And I did. Henry was a tall, beautiful man. He had blond, wavy hair that stopped just above his shoulders and large, red lips. He was slender. He was gay. He looked straight out of a Carravagio painting. He approached us as soon as we walked in the door.

"Jim! Darling!" He took Jim by the shoulders and kissed both his cheeks.

Jim glowed under Henry's attention. "Henry, I'd like you to meet Quinn."

I got a handshake. "Hello, Quinn. Aren't you a dear, here with our little Jim." He stared at me, long enough that I became uncomfortable. When I broke his gaze, he reached over and squeezed

Jim's left shoulder. "You'll have to promise to be good to Jim," he said to me, his hand still on Jim. He studied me a minute longer, then gave Jim's cheek a pat, and left us.

"Isn't he great?" Jim gushed. We started to walk around the gallery. The place was packed. We stopped for plastic cups of wine. As I drank, I eyed the other gallery goers. There were lots of interesting-looking people milling around. Omaha had a young, hip crowd, but they were a tight group that didn't seem to need fresh blood in their fold. Henry was doing the room. He was flamboyantly gay, an unusual trait in the Midwest, as far as I had seen.

The walls of art were hard to see through the crowds. When we elbowed through, though, I could see that the work was good. Henry did portraits. Loose, gestural paintings that seemed to capture a person's features in ten strokes or less. With Jim at my side, I moved from painting to painting, marveling Harry's skill. "He's talented," I said to Jim.

"He's a genius," Jim said.

Halfway through the gallery, there was painting of Jim. It was one of the larger pieces, about four feet by six feet. Jim was sitting in a chair that was turned backwards, with his arms hanging over the chair back. He was shirtless. The painting emphasized his good looks, actually, it exaggerated them, just a tad. He had a sensuous, but sleepy look, like he'd just woken up after a long night of sex. People were looking at us, recognizing the model. I turned to Jim. "Wow. This is you."

"Yeah," he turned a little red. "I posed for it a while ago."

"It's incredible. How long did you have to pose for?"

"I think it was a total of about 20 hours. We did it in two hour increments, more or less." He looked at his feet. "It's weird to see it up here. It's been hanging in Henry's bedroom for months. Now that it's on display for the world, I guess I wish I'd worn a shirt."

"Well," I said, "shirtless, we get to see how good Henry is at painting flesh tones."

Jim nodded. "Henry is just so incredibly talented. And he's an amazing person. I feel honored that someone like him is friends with someone like me."

That's when it hit me: Jim had a crush on Henry but didn't seem to realize it. Suddenly, I understood the piercing stare Henry had given me. He had been thinking, *Here comes our Jim with another girl. Keep dreaming Jim. Until she grows a penis, she'll never be able to satisfy you.*

"You really like him, don't you?" I asked Jim. His gaze drifted across the room to where Henry stood, surrounded by a group of five other men.

"How can you not? He's got it all."

Chapter 15
My Dumping Skills Improve

"Your home inspection has to be rescheduled." It was Flora.

"What? Why?"

"Apparently the guy fell off a ladder. He's in the hospital with a concussion."

I started to cry. I couldn't help myself. I was so disappointed. Plus, I think I was a little over-wrought. Buying a house is stressful. "Is he okay?" I asked, over-enunciating to hide my tears. I didn't want Flora to know what a baby I was.

"He's fine. But we're looking at another week out."

"Are the sellers upset?"

"They said they're fine with it. The guy is in the hospital. What else can they say?"

I took a deep breath. "Sure. How could they not understand?"

My downstairs neighbor and Walter both played Husker football games so loudly that I felt like I was at the stadium. Even though they frequently blasted the same television shows, they never socialized with each other.

Encounters in the hall with Walter invariably went like this:

Me: "Hi, how are you?"

W: "Not well. I have terminal bone cancer. I'm in a tremendous amount of pain."

Me: "Yes, I know. I'm sorry. Is there anything I can do?"

One day, he said, "Can you make pies?"

"Sure. Can I make you a pie?"

"Do you make it the right way? With a homemade crust?"

"Uh, yeah."

"My mother used to make a pineapple pie. It always cooled you off, on a hot, summer day. The recipe was printed in the newspaper."

"I'd love to make that pie for you, if you still have the recipe," I said.

"As long as you'll do it right. I gave it to someone a while back and she used a store-bought crust for it."

"Well, I'm sure I won't do as well as your mother, but I'll try."

"People today just don't take the time to make a good pie."

"No, they don't."

He came by later, with the recipe. I had to go to the grocery store for most of the ingredients. It was a very processed recipe, calling for things like instant vanilla pudding mix, but it wasn't all that difficult to make. When I stopped over with the pie, he said, "Please, come in and share this with me."

His apartment was the mirror image of mine, but his walls were painted a 30-year-old green. I remembered that my landlady said that he never wanted improvements, because he didn't want his rent to be raised. She had to fight with him to install central air, and according to her, he never used it. It was true that he had a window unit air conditioner in his living room. I stood in the hallway, taking off my shoes, while he bustled into the kitchen to make coffee and cut the pie. On the floor, next to the door, lay a manila envelope. In large letters, someone had penned, "To be opened by whoever finds me dead or severely incapacitated."

"Coffee is ready," Walter called from the kitchen. I walked through the living room, which was done up rather nicely in fifties-style furniture. He had a corner-nook that was obviously just for reading, with a funky black chair and a reading lamp. I sat down with him in the kitchen nook, at a worn, Formica table. His coffee was instant. I don't like pineapple, never have, so I held my breath for each bite, to reduce the taste. "I don't know if I've told you, but I have terminal bone cancer." His milky eyes watched me, unblinking.

"Yes, you have mentioned that," I choked.

"It's very painful and I have very little appetite. I've been losing weight, but I can't seem to make myself cook." He took a bite of the pie. "Was this crust made from Crisco?"

"Butter," I said.

"My mother always used Crisco."

I nodded. What else could I say? "So you're from Omaha?"

"Yes. I had one brother and one sister, now deceased."

"I'm sorry. Do you have friends in town?"

"There are some people from church, who check in from time to time. I don't want to be a burden to anyone," he replied.

"I don't think anyone would think that," I said.

"I have a nephew," he said. "But he's a ner-do-well."

"What a shame." I said.

"He threw his life away."

"Is that your only relative?"

"No, there's a niece, in Milwaukee."

"Does she ever visit?"

"I could hardly ask. She's very busy with her own life."

I glanced out the window. "It's getting cold," I said. "It smells like snow."

"I wanted to discuss the matter of the lint in the basement," Walter said. "I haven't got the strength to carry that out to the street."

"I know," I said. "I'm going to take it out from now on."

"Because it's full," he said. "And I haven't got the strength to drag it."

"I'll take it out this week."

"Very well," he said, as if he was giving me something. I finished my coffee and excused myself to leave.

"Would it help you if I cooked you a meal, say, once or twice a week?" I asked.

"I can't cook myself anymore. I'm very weak and I have no desire to eat."

I took that as a yes and started planning my menu.

The day after the art opening, I sent Jim an email.

> Dear Jim,
>
> *Why do some people not click? You are certainly good-looking and you have a great commitment to helping others and doing the right thing, but we have very different styles of communication and I don't feel a lot of chemistry. I have no*

doubt that you will be snatched up by the right person, quickly. I wish you luck in your future dating.

Quinn

And that was that. Whew. It was a relief, really, to end the fourth Internet dating episode. He sent me back a sweet letter, saying that he understood and he would still fix the fan belt on my car. I'd learned my lesson with men, however: they listen to actions, not words. So I never responded, and that was the last I heard of him.

Chapter 16
Westward Ho! Moving Beyond the Borders in Internet Dating

I was branching out, past Nebraska. Now, Reader, you might say, "Ah, yes. Quinn doesn't fit into Nebraska, but I could see her hitting it off with a man from New York, or Colorado. Or even California." Exactly right, my friend. But when I went through my inbox, through my "Geographically Wrong" subfolder, the only locations were Chile, Germany, Iowa, Arkansas, Texas, and Oklahoma. And most of them were creepy. Oklahoma was the only guy with a sense of humor. He was also the only liberal. Here's what he had written, about 6 weeks earlier:

> When I read your profile, I felt like I'd known you for years. You are great at conveying who you are and you make me want to learn more about you. Also, I love New Mexico, especially Taos.
>
> I am a computer programmer, but I swear, I'm not a nerd. What's a typical day for me? I usually roll into work by 9, even though the four people I manage are due in at 8. Once in a while, I pop in early to see if they all really come at 8 (as opposed to 8:56, or something). They do. Today I ate lunch with my friend Hamid, at this tiny little dive called "The Alamo." Remarkably good Tex Mex. After work, I take a run with the dog, Bonzo. About 3 miles is all that he (or I) can manage. Tonight, I'm going to a friend's house to help him paint. I should mention that I live in Oklahoma. But

wait! Don't delete me yet! I'm not tied down to this place.
I've lived here my whole life and I'm ready for a change.
Eric

The subject line was "If we only had a wheelbarrow, that would be something."

Dear Eric,

Thanks for your email. Sorry I took so long to respond. I'm not sure about the distance, but, then, I wasn't sure about Match either, and here I am so, what the hey, right? What kind of dog is Bonzo? What does that mean, about the wheelbarrow? Quinn

Quinn

Are you kidding? If I only had a wheelbarrow?!?! It's from the Princess Bride! Have you never seen that movie? Inconceivable!! Schnikes, I just reread your profile. You had a show of your paintings! A, "Take THAT creative geniuses out there," honest-to-goodness, art show?

Congratulations. Me, um, I wrote a Haiku once. ;-) Bonzo is a mutt. But a lovable one. Take care and have a beauty of an evening. Eric

This time his subject line said, "Boring conversation anyway." But I got smart. I went online, to imdb.com (Internet Movie Database, Earth's Biggest Movie Database) and used their Quotes Search to find the line. It was from Star Wars IV. When I wrote him back, I put the name of the movie in the subject line.

Eric,

Have you heard of the Honking Haiku? It's a guy in Brooklyn who started posting Haiku's on telephone posts. He lived in Cobble Hill, or some other nice neighborhood of brownstones, and commuters would sit in traffic on his residential street and honk at each other. It bothered him, so he started writing Honking Haiku poetry and taping it to light posts. He was fined for posting unauthorized signs on city property! The Man will get you every time.

I used to live in a neighborhood in Brooklyn like that, and the honking was really rude.

Quinn

Now, for those readers who are unfamiliar with Haiku, it's a form of poetry that is five syllables in the first line, seven in the second, and five again in the third. Eric's next email came quickly:

Dear Quinn,

Dog Haiku:

Mailman, go away
Bark, bark, bark, bark, bark, bark, bark!
Now I need to sleep

Eric

(His subject line said, "Everything was fine until that no-talent ass clown started winning Grammies.")

I sent him a Match haiku reply (subject line: Office Space):

Onscreen reading makes
My eyes water. Oh my burn
ing eyes. Out, spot! Out!

I'm not very good at haiku.

Eric always sent a movie quote in the subject line. I always put the title of the movie in the subject line of my reply. He never commented on this, just sent another quote in the next letter.

In between patients one day, about a week into my acquaintance with Eric, I opened my Inbox and saw an email from Mobile38568.

Spam, I assumed, but opened it anyway. (Don't worry–I wasn't going to click on any links!)

> *Hi Quinn. I'm driving to OK City. Wantde to sent you a text msg sorry for typos I cant drive and type because I'm mobilexic. Eric.*

I wrote back:

> *Hurtling through space*
> *My hands leave the wheel to type*
> *A note to my SPLAT!*

He sent back a one-liner:

> *:)*

The next day, I sent him this:

> *Dear Eric,*
>
> *I have to say, that, in spite of your dangerous texting habits, I'm rather smitten with you.*

He wrote back an email with no mention of what I'd said.

"What's he doing?" I asked Izzy. "You don't just ignore someone saying she is smitten with you!"

"He's shy or not ready to move forward that fast," she said.

I nodded. Sure. "It just seems rude. I'm out on a limb, waiting for a response and he's ignoring me."

"Just keep emailing him, like normal," Izzy suggested.

So I did. Five days later, he wrote again. The subject line was "Woman...wo-o-o-man."

Say, did you know that your profile is multi-layered? I was just back on it, checking you out (LOVE your picture, by the way) and I realized (or remembered) that you have lived in Spain. Did I mention before that I'd really like to talk to you? Not just to hear how you communicate in real time, etc, but because I'm dying to hear how a New York-Spain-New Mexico-Minnesota-Nebraskan accent sounds. So??? Can we talk? Sometime soon? Can I add that I'm smitten with you, as well? Let's face it, you're irresistible!

I wrote back:

Eric,

I would love to demonstrate my NY-Spain-NM-MN-NE accent to you. It's quite spectacular (I'm told). And I'd like to talk. Tell me a good time for you, and your number, and I'll give you a ring.

Quinn

P.S. Actually, I'm over the whole "smitten" thing.

Eric got my sense of humor. We talked that same night. Now, I'm not going to say it was easy, Reader. I was nervous. But I was also excited to talk to him. I wanted to hear what his voice sounded like, and hear how he handled himself in quasi-person.

When I said, "Hi, Eric?" He said, "Is this Omaha?" He had a deep voice. Not crazy deep, just a nice, male resonance. We ended up chatting for almost two hours. He was easy to talk to, every bit as funny as his emails, and a real conversationalist. Conversation is a lost art, my friends. Most people talk non-stop about themselves. Eric asked questions. And he didn't interrupt. He could tell when I was setting up a story, and he let me do it. At the end of our conversation, he asked if he could come for a visit.

"I have some friends in Kansas that I haven't seen in ages. I could stop by there and head on to Omaha, if that doesn't seem too fast."

"Why waste time?" I asked. "You might as well meet me. But I should warn you that I've gained about 75 lbs since that picture was taken, and my hair has gone gray."

He was silent, but I could hear laughter behind it. He said, "I should tell you that I'm calling you from my car, and I'm going about 95 miles down I-35 with my lights off. And my eyes are closed."

I laughed.

"I stole that line, sort of," he said. "From Letterman. I heard him call into some show, Larry King or something, a long, long time ago, and he said something like that. It cracked me up."

"It's cracking me up," I said.

"So how about this weekend?" he asked.

"You're on!"

Hanging up the phone
Terror hits me in the gut
What was I thinking?

But I prepared a weekend. He was arriving on Saturday. I was meeting him at a hotel on the outskirts of town. (He'd found the hotel all on his own.) His expected arrival time was 10 a.m. So, I thought we'd start with an architectural tour of the Old Market. Then lunch. Then we could go on a nature walk, or whatever he wanted. There was a poetry slam that night at the Omaha Healing Arts Center. On Sunday, I thought we could see a movie and go to a museum.

I was fine until Saturday morning, at about 9:52. I was driving to the hotel, which I'd just spotted from the interstate, when the fear struck my insides like a sledgehammer. Holy crap! What was I doing? All I could think was, "Don't break out into a sweat and trigger underarm body odor." So I started deep breathing to trick my body into thinking that I was calm and collected. As I neared the parking lot, I faced the truth. I did not want to be here. I didn't want to be anywhere near potential love matches. I was scared to death and I wanted to go back to my happy, lonely little life that revolved around stupid television, painting, crafts projects, and silent rooms.

But I pulled into the parking lot because a guy who had driven from Oklahoma was there, waiting for me to show him around Omaha.

It was a sunny, somewhat windy, warm spring day. The kind of day that triggers seasonal allergies for me. I had taken my allergy medicine before I left the house, but I was regretting that I hadn't picked up any Afrin. Eric was standing in the parking lot, next to a green car with Oklahoma plates. He looked like his picture, but much cuter. He was tall, with short, dark hair. He had a nice lean build.

"Greetings," he called as I got out of my car. "Is that a Mitsubishi?"

"Yes," I said.

He opened his arms and gave me a friendly hug. "Good to see you. I have to admit that I'm a little nervous," he said as he let go.

"How odd," I said. When I'm nervous I tend to hide it with deadpan sarcasm. Luckily, he got me. He gave a whooping laugh, and said, "So back to your car. How do you like it?"

"It's fine, I guess."

"I used to have an Eclipse, but then my neighbor, well, he has these trees on his property. Gorgeous shade trees. I used them all summer long when I gardened. But last year he decided to cut them down. I tried to talk him out of it, but he wouldn't budge. So the trees came down and one of them landed on my Eclipse. My parents were just about to trade in this Celica for something fancier, so they gave it to me and I kept the insurance money. Spent it on a scuba diving trip to Mexico."

And in an instant, I felt fine around him. What is it about some people? Their presence just puts you at ease. That's how I felt with him, like I could be myself and I'd be fine. "Say, do you mind if we stop at a drug store, on the way?" I asked. "I have to pick up some Afrin."

"Is that what you use? I find that Flonase with Claritin is really effective."

"I have a strict regimen of Astelin twice a day, plus 120 mg of Allegra, but it's been an especially bad week and since we're going to be outside, I think I need Afrin, too."

"Now, you can't use that very often, can you?"

"No. It's the addictive one. Just once every 24 hours."

"Just one squirt?"

"Yes, in each nostril. I get two squirts of Astelin in each nostril, twice a day. Plus one shot of Afrin. I try to take it in the morning."

"Have you ever tried Flonase?"

"Flonase doesn't work for me. Neither does Claritin."

"Are you mold?"

"Dust mites, but I'm also trees."

We were in my car, at this point, driving.

"Do you realize," Eric said, "that we've been talking about our nasal sprays for ten minutes?"

"We're pathetic." I pulled into a local drugstore. "Do you need anything?"

"Can you grab some Kleenex?"

"Absolutely. I'll be right back." I brought back the tissues with aloe lotion.

Eric and I ended up having dinner with Izzy and Ann. He wanted to meet my friends, and to be honest, I needed a break. It wasn't anything negative about Eric, it was just that spending a long period of time with someone you don't know requires you to talk a great deal, because you are trying to create a portrait of yourself and I was pooped. Our conversations ran like this:

"I love to cook," Eric said. "I especially like to have elaborate dinner parties."

"Me, too. In fact, I was standing in line, about to buy a KitchenAid mixer…"

"Hold that thought. I need to interrupt to tell you that my grandmother, who owns a KitchenAid mixer, stopped by the other day and left me a pound, hear that? A pound of chocolate chip cookies! She is the kindest lady, and she's been having a hard time lately, because her best friend has cancer. She's just a rock, though.'

"She sounds great."

"She is. And she's had the same mixer for decades. It's white."

"So is mine. I bought it refurbished."

"My last laptop was refurbished. I bought it 18-months ago, and it is so much better than a regular computer. Now I go to cafes with it, and look ultra cool while I drink my coffee. Of course, I also need a phone with the internet, as if one thing isn't enough."

"Well, laptops are heavy."

"Indeed. I walked home from a café recently. It's just about a mile from my house. I'd gone with friends who'd picked me up, and when they left I decided to hang out and work on my laptop. Well, that was all fine but on the walk home, I'll tell you what. My shoulder was killing me! I had it in an old knapsack."

"Yeah. But back to the KitchenAid mixer. The first thing I made, as soon as I got it, was a pound of cookie dough. I wanted to make pizza, but it felt like, for the first time, it had to be a cake or cookies. Something sweet."

"So you're a sweet tooth?"

"Not really. I'm pretty healthy. My vice is probably fatty stuff, like bacon. And cream."

"I can't eat dairy anymore."

"What? Why?"

"Allergies. It's fine, though. I was never a big dairy eater anyway."

Suffice to say that talking like that non-stop for two solid days can wear you down a little. I have friends who would become invigorated by that kind of interaction. But I'm an introvert, and it just sucked me dry. So when Eric said he wanted to meet my friends, I was relieved. Eric was not just an extrovert. He was a super-extrovert. He was thriving on our communication, and he wanted to add even more to the pot by going out with Izzy and Ann and anyone else I could bring along.

We ate at a brewery in the Old Market. He charmed them with talk like this: "So, Ann, you are originally from Portland? Do you know a little café there called the Red Onion? They've got the best French Onion soup I've ever tasted."

"I know the place well," she said. "In fact, I practically lived on that French Onion soup from the ages of 23 to 25. I have that recipe, by the way, and I'd be glad to pass it on to Quinn to send to you."

"No way! Oh, this trip just gets better and better!" Then he'd turn to Izzy and say, "I'm sensing you aren't an onion fan. What gives?"

"How'd you guess that?" she asked.

"You had a slight grimace on your face when I mentioned the soup. And anything besides a smile would have given you away. People who eat French Onion soup love it so much that they can't talk about it without looking happy."

"A real cure for the blues," Ann added.

"He's amazing!" they both said, simultaneously, when Eric had left for the bathroom.

"Have you kissed yet?" Izzy asked.

"No." I paused. "He's nice, but he's wearing me out. He's really talkative and outgoing and I'm feeling really exhausted, trying to keep up."

"Well then shut him up by kissing him," Ann said.

"I'm just not sure," I said. "I'm too tired to judge whether or not I'm attracted to him in that way."

"Please. He's gorgeous," Izzy said. "Stop thinking and act."

As we got ready to leave the restaurant, I peeked at my watch. It was 10:15. Thank God. I couldn't wait to drop Eric off and get home.

Eric looked at his watch. "Whoa, it's early. Who's up for dancing? Or what else is there to do in this town?"

"I could dance," Izzy said.

So we danced until 1 a.m. By the time I dropped him off at his hotel, I had no desire to kiss him. I just wanted to be alone. I felt like a thin rug that had been walked on for fifty years. He didn't try to kiss me, which could have meant many things. "So what time should I pick you up for breakfast?" I asked.

"Uh, how about 6:30?"

"It's 1 a.m.!" I exclaimed. That's in five hours!"

"Okay, no problem. How about 7?"

I felt bad for him. Trapped in an ugly hotel room. But I was so tired of interaction. I needed a small break. "Can we do 7:30? Or 8?"

"Absolutely," Eric said. "I'll see you at 8."

We saw a movie the next day. But instead of the art museum, Eric wanted to drive to the Husker stadium in Lincoln, Nebraska. When the Huskers play in Lincoln, the stadium becomes the third largest city in Nebraska. Not a football fan, I'd never been to the stadium.

When we got there, it was all locked up. We walked around the perimeter, peering inside, until we saw a person leaving through a locked door, and managed to slip inside before the door had shut. Ten feet in, a security guard was sitting on a stool. "The stadium is closed," he told us.

"No problem," Eric said. "We can leave. See, I dragged my friend Quinn here, because I wanted to see the stadium. It's legendary, after all." He leaned in confidentially. "She's never even been to a game, and she lives in Omaha. I drove here from Oklahoma, and dragged her down here to show her how amazing it is."

"Have you seen the Heisman trophy winners?" he asked, and before I knew it, he was up and shuffling down the hall, getting out his keys. We admired the winners display. "I can show you the field," he said, "but you can't walk on it."

"I just want a picture of me standing in front of it," Eric assured him, as they walked down the hall with me trailing behind.

We ate at a local brewery so that I could introduce him to a vanilla porter beer that I especially liked. He bought two six packs of the porter. "Have you ever had Deschutes beer, from Oregon?" he asked. "It's the best."

"It sounds familiar. Maybe when I was in Jackson Hole?"

"Probably. I think there's a good brewery there."

"So," I said. "You're leaving at the crack of dawn tomorrow."

"I am, indeed."

"So. How do you think this is going?" I asked.

"Well, I've had a great time. It's been as fun, hanging out with you, as I thought it would be. Omaha is a terrific town. Your friends are great. Gosh, I feel like I'm having an exit interview."

I laughed and said, "Sorry." But he was, really.

"Would I like to date you, if you lived nearby?" he continued. "Absolutely. Do I feel, from the 24 hours or so that we've spent together, that I would relocate to Omaha to start a relationship? Not really. I think you've gotten an idea of what I'm like. I've been myself, this weekend. I assume that you have, too. And, as a friend, I think you're great. But I'm not really feeling a big spark."

"I agree," I said. "I wish you did live closer, so we could, at the very least, hang out."

And so it is. And so it goes. We spent the evening at my apartment. I made dinner while Eric tried to get my printer to work. I drove him back to his hotel at 10 p.m., and he drove home the next day. I'd finally met an interesting and nice man on Match. So now I knew it could happen. That was something, right there.

Chapter 17
Buying a House is like Dating a Man

If Mohammed won't come to the mountain, the mountain will come to Mohammed. In spite of the 73 unanswered emails in my inbox, I started doing my own match searches. At first, my list of requirements was:

Athletic or slender
34-42 years old
5'8-6'2
Liberal or very liberal
Undergrad, or advanced degree
Within 60 miles of Omaha

That gave me two guys. One had a mullet and a wife-beater tank top. The other had grey hair and wrote, "I'm actually not 36 years old. I'm 48 but everyone says I look much younger. I changed my age on my profile because I wasn't getting any hits. I'm not attracted to women my age, probably because I look so young."

I broadened my age range to 27-47 years. That gave me three pages of matches. On page two, four profiles down, I found this one:

> *I'm a quiet, capable man. I'm about halfway through my graduate studies in biology. This works well with my interest in environmental issues and my summer job as a forest ranger. I'm also a musician. I play several instruments. I am*

originally from Maine, am tolerating Nebraska, and would like to wind up in Colorado, New Mexico, or perhaps Montana or Wyoming, if I could be guaranteed a like-minded community of liberals to hang out with. I'm active, physically. As a PhD student, I don't have a lot of money to throw around. But I'm committed to supporting organic farmers.

You are, well, I don't know what. You have a healthy lifestyle and a warm smile. You make sacrifices for worthy causes.

There was no picture. He lived in Lincoln, about a 50-minute drive south. He listed his age as 27. Cripes. That was young. Still. He was neat. I wrote him:

Wow, you're neat. ~~I've always wanted to marry~~ A forest ranger! I admire your support of organic farmers. I lived in New Mexico for five years. I'm in Nebraska for a job that I like, but I see myself ~~raising kids and~~ growing old in the mountains. Maine, eh? I'm from NY. I guess Nebraskans would see us as two peas in an east coast pod, but you and I know we are from different worlds. Even so, I'd love to hear about Maine. I have a romantic notion about the isolation, austere beauty of the land, and reticence of the people.

Take care, Quinn

He wrote back the very next day.

Quinn,

What a nice surprise, to open my email this morning and find your note. I'm an early riser, so I was up at five to grade papers. I, too, would enjoy meeting and talking about our respective states.

Caleb

Another match correspondence began. He was a little stilted, but nice. I found I was kind of just going through the motions. I had developed a spiel that I was regurgitating for every Match guy. It would be fair to say that I was getting a little burned out.

Quinn,

I'll be in Omaha, next Saturday, to drop a friend off at the airport. Would you be interested in a meeting?

Caleb

Caleb, Yes, let's meet! How about La Buvette, in the Old Market?

La Buvette was a café, based on the European model. Bottles of wine lined the walls. People smoked excessively until the restaurant smoking ban. Food was simple and good. You could sit for hours, arguing politics, and no one cared. I was nervous walking in. I timed myself to arrive at 2 p.m. on the dot. I didn't want to have to wait for him, but he wasn't there when I arrived. Of course, not knowing what he looked like, I could only tell he wasn't there because there was no man standing around at the entrance, and no man sitting alone at a table. I hate being the first to arrive for a date. It feels so inelegant. I chose a small table, by the window, and sat.

He appeared less than a minute after I'd sat down. Almost like he'd been waiting across the street for me to arrive and choose a table. He was about my height or slightly shorter, with thinning hair. He was a little stout with a weightlifting body type.

"Quinn?" He asked.

"Hi. Did you have any trouble finding the place?"

"None."

We sat. "And you got your friend dropped off at the airport okay?"

"I did."

I couldn't have pictured a man less like my ideal. If I'd seen him in a bar and someone had wanted to introduce us, I would have refused. I would have taken one look at him and said, "Nope. He's not my type." But the thing was, since we'd been emailing, I knew that he was my type, in spite of the muscles.

The conversation got off to a slow start, because he was not forthcoming in asking me questions. He seemed very nervous so I punctuated my sentences with warm smiles.

"Tell me about being a forest ranger," I asked. "What exactly do you do?"

"I used to fight fires, in the forest. In fact, I fought fires for a whole summer in New Mexico, a few years back. That was a hot place." New Mexico has had a rough time lately, with drought and forest fires.

"Was that work dangerous?"

He nodded. "Especially during the day. I was on the night shift for a lot of it. The fires drop down at night. The sun makes them stronger."

"How interesting," I said. He puffed up slightly, and eased up.

"It's incredible. As soon as the sun sets, the fires drop."

I smiled again. I was so proud of myself. I was putting him at ease, the way Izzy might have done.

We talked all afternoon. Caleb was intense, but I won several laughs from him and when he smiled, his eyes looked very blue. As the sun started to drop in the sky, the café grew dim and our waitress paused to put a lit votive candle on our table.

"I really like this place," Caleb said, looking around. "I didn't know it even existed."

"Are there places like this in Lincoln?"

"No, but there are other neat spots. Maybe some time you could come down and I could show you around my city?"

"I'd like that."

"Oh, my God!" I told Izzy, directly after the date had ended, when I called her from my car. "He was amazing! And to think I'd have never even talked to him if it hadn't been for Match!"

"He's shorter than you, you say?"

"I'm not completely sure," I said. "I had a slight heel on my shoes."

"So he's your height or shorter." Her voice was flat.

"Who cares about that?"

"It's just that Eric was way taller than you."

"He's also in Oklahoma."

"Did you get the sense that he was lying about being a fire fighter?" Ann asked.

"Not at all! Why would he lie?"

"Why not? Maybe he was just trying to impress you."

"How can you be so cynical?"

"I learned it the hard way. I just don't want to see you hurt."

"Why aren't you excited, like I am?"

"I just liked Eric."

So bringing dates home to meet the friends was backfiring.

My home inspector called me.

"Sorry about the delay," he said. "I'll do the house tomorrow at three. If you meet me there at five, I should be finished by then."

My book had suggested I follow the inspector through the whole process. "Can I come at three and watch?"

"You can. But when I'm finished, I'm going to walk you through every room and tell you what I've found. I'll go a lot faster if you wait till five."

"Okay. I'm a little concerned about the fireplace," I told him. "It doesn't look like it's been used, and I want to make sure it's working." I'd heard that fixing fireplaces could be expensive.

"You might need a fireplace inspector to come out for that," he said. "But I can take a look and give you a general idea of what to expect."

"Life is going great!" I told Izzy. "I'm about to buy a home! I feel so adult. And it's such a beautiful home. It's perfect in so many ways."

"Except the neighborhood."

"Well, sure. But still. I can't afford a house that nice in a good neighborhood. And besides, it doesn't come close to neighborhoods I lived in in Brooklyn. And now, Caleb." I let out a deep, contented sigh. "Finally, my life is turning around."

Izzy nodded, but her face was holding something back. "What's wrong," I asked her.

"Nothing."

"Come on, spill it."

She shook her head. "It's Sal. We were at his parents last night, and they were joking about us having children, and he told them he didn't want kids."

"Was he just yanking their chain?"

"No. We talked about it later. I thought maybe he meant that he didn't want kids now. He's great with kids. You should see him with his sisters' children. They all adore him."

"So you think he'll come around?"

"I don't know. He's not ready for a commitment."

"So you think, but do you really know that?"

"He said, 'I'm years away from considering marriage.'"

"Oh."

"Yeah."

"So, what are you going to do?"

"I don't know. I appreciate his honesty. But I don't have time to wait around for him. I've got to start a family."

Izzy is four years younger than me. She is always telling me I have plenty of time to start a family. I filed away the fact that she didn't actually believe this and said, "He might change his mind."

"No," Izzy said. "I don't think so."

The home inspector was in the kitchen when I arrived, typing on a laptop. A small printer was plugged in next to him. He was a tall man, with a boy next-door look about him. "The house took a little longer than I expected," he said, after shaking my hand. "Give me just a few more minutes to finish up the report."

I used the time to go back through the house, which I'd only seen that one time. It was as good as I remembered. The sunroom was larger than I recalled. I inspected the fireplace again. There was some trace of soot, which I held as a good sign.

I wandered back into the kitchen. The countertops were an uglier green color than I remembered. But there was a space where a dishwasher would fit, and I was dreaming of the day that I stopped washing all my dishes by hand. I sat down. The inspector's computer keys clicked away in the silence. I couldn't stand the suspense.

"Would you say," I began, "overall good or overall bad?"

"Overall bad," he said, without pausing in his typing.

I nodded. Hmmm. He continued to type. I looked around at the walls, the door to the rental unit. Hmmm. I nodded to myself, then looked down at my lap and realized I was wringing my hands. Suddenly, I felt afraid. Could I lose this house? I went back to the living room and looked at the stained glass windows. I heard the printer in the kitchen start to churn out paper. The inspector appeared a few minutes later holding his report.

"Is it the fireplace?" I asked. I was deeply disappointed. I had imagined sitting in front of a roaring fire, maybe playing Scrabble with Caleb.

"The fireplace is the only good news I've got," he said. "It's practically the only part of the house that passes inspection."

I heard him, but I couldn't really believe him. The house was so well kept compared to the other places I'd seen.

"Let's start in the basement, shall we?" he asked, handing me his report.

"Look at this wall," he said, motioning to the white washed cement. "It's been scraped."

"Scraped?"

"Yes, and repainted. They were probably trying to hide the presence of mold from moisture.

"Really," I said, looking at the wall.

"And then look at this floor." I followed him to a dark corner. He shone his flashlight on the ground.

"See the broom marks here?"

"Yeah." Someone had swept up the basement.

"That's silt, probably from flooding. They got most of it up, but they missed this area. And then we have the electrical system," he continued, and focused the flashlight across the room at the fuse box.

"I already know that it's fuses, instead of circuit breakers," I told him to ward off more criticism of the house.

"See this box?" He was pointing at a metal box next to the fuse box. He opened it to reveal more fuses inside. "And this one? And this one? All in all, you've got seven additional fuse boxes piggybacked onto the main one." I don't know how I'd missed that before. "As the electrical needs of the owners increased, say for central air and the like, instead of updating the electricity, they just added more fuses. "Did you ever see Chevy's Chase's movie, Christmas Vacation?" I hadn't. "He covers his house in thousands of lights, and plugs them into extensions that all end up going into a single outlet." He nodded at the fuse boxes. "That's exactly what you're looking at right here." He chuckled, then frowned. "There's no way this will pass any FHA inspection. It's hazardous. Now, about this furnace."

The furnace was the size of my apartment bathroom. "This old bear is about 75 years old," he told me. "It's working, but barely. It will certainly be dead in a month. It's possible that FHA will let it slide, but only if it hasn't died by the time they get here. Oh, and the house has virtually no water pressure."

We moved upstairs. The ground floor was fine except for a few stuck windows, ungrounded outlets, and a light switch that didn't work. The third floor, my rental unit, had a broken toilet. The sink didn't drain. "But the real issue is this paint job," he told me, standing where the sloping ceiling met the wall. "Feel this surface," he said. I put my hand up against the ceiling. "Do you notice the give?"

"It's rippled, instead of smooth."

"Exactly. They painted this place," he gestured around him, "to hide water spots in the ceiling, from a leaking roof."

"How do you know they painted it?" I was thinking he might have it wrong.

"They removed the outlet covers to paint, but never bothered to put them back."

I looked around the room. He was right. How did I miss all of this?

"But to be sure, I climbed up onto the roof. You're going to need a new roof before spring, or you'll be living in a lake. The garage roof is shot, too. Now, let me show you the front porch."

I followed him outside. There was a metal awning bolted into the front of the house. Metal railings came down and formed a front porch. Rusty chairs were scattered around. "Now, me, I wouldn't have destroyed the lines of a Tudor by putting up this kind of monstrosity," he began. "But the real problem with this porch is the wiring." He gestured to the lamp that was mounted over the front door. "Whoever put this up used indoor wiring. The insulation around the wire has since worn away." I looked up at what he was pointing to. Exposed copper wire was wrapped around the front porch. "Conceivably, you could electrocute yourself by touching the metal part of the porch," he said. I took my hand off the railing.

"How much do you think it would cost to fix all of this?"

"I'm not a contractor, but let's see. I'd estimate, oh, and the roof is made of asbestos tiles. So you'll have to hire a special team to remove that and dispose of it. But I'd say, six to ten thousand for the roof, depending on what they find when they rip up the tiles. Four thousand for the electrical. Two thousand for the plumbing. I don't know how much it would cost to rip this porch off. You could just take down the lamp. The ground slopes toward the house, which may be why the basement is wet. You could pay a landscaper to fill in the slope, that would probably be a couple of thousand dollars."

"About 18 thousand?"

"At least. You never know what else you'll uncover, as you go along."

I wrote him a check for $305. I felt like I'd been ravaged. "Thank you," I said.

"You're welcome."

"You'll find another house." I heard this line from everyone, my friends, my family, my co-workers, my landlady, and my realtor.

"Now we know why it's been on the market for a year," Flora added.

"Well, since it has, maybe we can negotiate," I said. "I'd like to revise my offer. Either lower price or have them repair everything."

"FHA won't approve it, no matter how low they go."

"Then let's put the repairs I want into the offer."

"Okay," she said, but I could tell by her face that she had no hope it would work.

"They might be tired of paying taxes on an empty house."

"Quite so," she said.

I met Caleb in Lincoln, for our second date. I had my cell phone, and a promise to call Izzy by 9 p.m. He was nervous all over again, but he took less time to warm up.

"Tell me about your graduate studies. Do you teach?"

"Yes. I enjoy teaching immensely. I have mostly undergrads."

"Are you a hard teacher?"

He shrugged. "I can be," he said. I'd noticed that he tended to be very stiff, both in what he said and how he held himself. His back was ramrod straight, and he barely turned his head when he talked. "My classes are filled with pre-med students, and one of my jobs is to weed out the weak ones."

"What about biology majors? Do you have many of them?"

"Some," he said.

"When I started my coursework in audiology, I was terrified about the science part. I had to take a graduate level class called Hearing Sciences that was all sound waves, action potentials, and the like. If

I'd taken some undergraduate version of it, I'd have done better, but my school didn't offer that, and the only science class I'd taken in art school was called Revolutionary Concepts in Modern Science. More of a weed-in class than a weed-outer."

He shrugged. "Ears aren't my specialty. Say, did you ever camp up by Jemez, when you lived in New Mexico?"

Our talk veered from camping to favorite novels to dream vacations. "I'd probably bike across the country," Caleb said.

"I'd go white water rafting in the Grand Canyon," I said.

I called Izzy from the bathroom at 8:45. "We're going to walk around the University," I told her. "I'll call you at 11." It was a beautiful night. We wandered around, talking. When it was time to go, he left me a few blocks from my car and headed home. I got in my car, locked the doors, and called Izzy. "Oh my God!" I told her.

"Good?"

"Great! He was great. We had such a good time. We talked and talked."

"Did you kiss?"

"No. That's the only negative. He's really shy. I tried to look welcoming, but, well, he just shook my hand and that was the end."

"Do you think he's not interested?"

"I don't know," I said. "It does kind of suck that I've got an hour's drive ahead of me, in the dark, I won't get home till midnight, and I didn't even get a kiss."

"He's shy. Next time, you'll have to jump him."

The sellers rejected my offer. "What?" I said. I was shocked. I'd really believed they'd come around. "Who's going to buy that house for $85,000?"

"Someone who doesn't get a home inspection," my realtor said.

When I hung up with her, I cried. See, I'd already begun to mentally pack up my apartment and unpack in my new home. I had guest lists and menus for dinner parties. I was renting the upstairs to an ER resident or a grad student who had finished his coursework and was writing his dissertation. I had adopted a dog from the Humane Society. "Damn," I said. "Stupid, dumb house, sucking me in and then breaking my heart."

Every single homeowner I knew said, "The same thing happened to us. We found a house we wanted, and lost it. But in the end, we found a better house, and so will you." But I didn't think that their first lost house had matching stained glass windows, French doors, a rental unit with built-ins, and an attached garage.

"You shouldn't have started the mental move-in," Ann said.

"I couldn't help myself," I cried.

"That house would have bankrupted you."

"Not if they had gone down on the price. If only I hadn't had to go through FHA. I could have offered them $65,000 and made the repairs myself."

"How's things with Caleb?" she asked, clearly trying to distract me.

"Fine," I said. "Actually, good. I'm going to his house on Friday, for dinner."

"He's making you dinner?"

"Yes."

"Is that safe?"

"I think so. I'm going to call Izzy when I leave."

"But he could murder you as soon as you arrive, and then no one would know for hours."

This was true. I didn't really think Caleb was out to kill me, but it always pays to be safe. "I could have Izzy call me, fifteen minutes after I arrive. Then I could tell her, 'I'll call you when I leave,' to let him know that my friends are watching me."

"Good," Ann said. "I could call you, too. Just let me know."

"I'm looking forward to this dinner," I said. "I need something happy right now. I'm so bummed about the house."

"What's he cooking?"

"I don't know. I'm bringing wine."

"Red or white?"

"I left it up to him and he chose red."

"Good man," she said.

Chapter 18
The Significance of the Third Date

Why is date number three so significant? It's when you decide, "Okay, we like each other. Let's make it official." Certainly, if you haven't kissed yet, you will on your third date, won't you?

I was so nervous the night of my dinner date that I decided to implement some strategies to keep me calm. I left work early and had a massage. I wore my best color, black. But even though I played Enya all the way down in the car, I had a stress stomach ache by the time I got to his house. I parked a block away and called Izzy.

"I'm really, really nervous."

"Can you just tell him that?" she suggested. "Maybe, when he opens the door, hand him the wine and say, 'Can we open this now? Because I am really nervous.'"

I liked her idea, but when he answered his door he didn't even smile. He said, "I've got something on the stove," and disappeared back into the building. He lived in one of those old mansions that have been split into several apartments. I followed him into the kitchen. He was back at the stove. I stood, with my coat on, holding my bottle of wine, while he ignored me and stirred a pot. Of course, he was as nervous as I was, more, perhaps. Still…he could have taken my feelings into account. I took off my coat and hung it on the chair back.

"Shall I open the wine?" I asked.

"I'm fine for now," he said, and took a sip from a mug with a tea bag hanging out. I waited for him to offer me tea. He continued to cook.

"Smells good," I said.

"Thanks."

"If you tell me where your corkscrew is, I'll just open this wine."

He finally noticed that a woman was sitting in his kitchen. "Sorry. Would you rather have tea? A good friend who's living in the Xinjiang region of China sent this to me."

"Thanks, but I think I'll stick to the wine. I'm kind of nervous." He didn't respond. I also looked great, but he didn't think to tell me so. "Smells good," I said. "What are you making?"

"Rice pilaf, lentils with bacon, and then the main course is an omelet with red peppers. You aren't a vegetarian, are you?"

"No."

He left the room and came back with a jazz cd, which he put in a cd player on the table.

"Can I help you with something?" I asked.

"Nope. It's all under control."

I sat and drank my wine. When dinner was ready, Caleb sat down, but continued to look walled up. Like a fortress. I guessed it was from nerves. "This looks delicious," I said. I had the first bite of omelet in my mouth when my phone rang. "Sorry," I said. "I don't usually leave my phone on, but my friend was worried about, well, you know, tonight." I dug the phone out of my jacket pocket. "Hello?"

"Hi. I didn't think you'd pick up." It was Ann.

"Hi. I'm at Caleb's house and we just sat down to a delicious dinner."

"Okay, well call me when you leave, okay? Or tomorrow morning first thing."

"Okay, Ann. I'll call you when I leave." I hung up. "I'm really sorry about that but I promised my friends I would leave on my phone."

"I understand," he said, but his face was stormy.

"It's nothing against you," I began. "But in this day and age, unfortunately, to stay safe, we have to be cautious of everyone."

"Sure," he said. "I completely understand. Women are at risk every day to have violence done to them." He could have been talking at a senate hearing, for all the formality he used. "And people always assume that muscular men like me are a greater risk…"

"What? No. That's not it at all. My friends don't even know what you look like. You could have been a tiny little broomstick of a guy and they would have called."

"I work out. That's true. But that doesn't mean I'm not gentle."

"You couldn't be more wrong," I said. My phone started to ring again. "Hang on. Hello?" This time it was Izzy.

"How's it going?"

"Fine. We're in the middle of dinner."

"Oops, sorry."

"It's okay. I'll call you when I leave." I started to turn my phone off, but, on second thought, left it on. "Your body type has nothing to do with it. Men are stronger than women no matter what body type they have."

"I certainly understand the need for safety." His face didn't agree with his words.

"I can see I've offended you, and I'm sorry for that. But I've met you twice and now I'm at your house, in another city. Can you honestly imagine that I wouldn't have some precautions in place? It has absolutely nothing to do with you. If I thought, even for a moment, that you were going to do me violence, I wouldn't have come."

"Fine," he said. "Let's just enjoy the dinner."

We ate. The tension started to break as we talked about writers we liked. He was surprisingly well versed in female writers. "Have you read Barbara Kingsolver's Prodigal Summer?" I asked. "The heroine is a forest ranger."

He gestured to the bookcase in the living room. "It's in my house, and on my list of books, but I won't get to it for another couple of weeks. I'm re-reading Zora Neale Hurston's works, right now."

He had two flavors of ice cream for dessert, strawberry and butter pecan. We retired to the living room. There was a large sofa. I sat down. He sat across the room, on the floor. Caleb and I shared so many interests we could have talked all night. "You listen to Jane Arden?" I asked. I was amazed. "Don't you love that album, Living Under June?"

"It reminds me of an old photo album I found in an antique store. Every time I listen, I feel as though I'm looking at intimate portraits of strangers."

He got up and put another cd on. As the first strands began, I said, "Leonard Cohen?"

He nodded. "What are your favorite songs by him?"

"'Famous Blue Raincoat' and 'Suzanne.' Although I prefer the 'Suzanne' version that's sung by Peter Gabriel. His voice is so sexy." Speaking of which, I wondered at what point Caleb was going to kiss me? I'd been putting off leaving, in the hopes he would. Now it was 2 a.m. and he was still sitting as far away from me as possible without going through the wall. There was a period of silence, but he didn't seem uncomfortable. He was listening to the music.

"I should get going," I said.

"You are welcome to stay the night."

"Thanks, but I think I'll just head out."

He nodded. "Well, the offer stands, if you want."

"Oh, okay." I paused. "And so, by staying the night…do you mean have sex?" My voice squeaked on the last word.

"Yes. If you'd like." He was sitting across the room with the same stony, bordering on haughty, expression he'd worn all night.

I almost laughed. "I'm not going to have sex with you," I began. Then I tried to soften my tone. "I'm flattered. But you have never even kissed me."

"I'm not very good at making moves on women."

We stared at each other.

I shrugged. "Make a move," I said.

He paused a moment, and then stood up and walked over to the sofa. He sat down next to me. He face was rigid. He leaned in and kissed me. Okay, so he was a little stiff, but at least he was finally kissing me. We kissed for about ten seconds, and then his hand went up my shirt and under my bra. While I was recovering from the shock, he planted his other hand on my crotch.

"Hold on, cowboy," I said, removing both hands. "You're moving awfully fast for someone who doesn't know how to make moves on women."

"Sorry." He knelt in front of me, on the floor, and started to kiss me again. I heard him knock over the water glass I'd left on the floor. We kissed for about a minute, and all of a sudden, he started pulling my shirt up over my head.

"What the hell?" I stood. "What's the matter with you? I already told you I wasn't having sex."

He sat back on the ground. His knee was wet where he'd knelt in the water. "I sensed something."

"I don't know what. I'm not going from a first kiss with you to sex."

"I've spent a lot of years in the role of confidant, for women," he said. "I'm not going to be your best friend."

"I'm not asking you to!" I stood. Here I'd thought Caleb was shy, but maybe he was just an asshole. *It's not going to work out with Caleb*, I thought. God was I disappointed. *Okay, just get out of here and you can deal with all of that later.*

"Of course, you know I'd never force you," he said. He had that wounded look he'd worn when my friends called earlier.

I shook my head at him, incredulous. *I'd like to see you try, buddy.* I finally admitted to myself that he was self-centered. That we only talked about topics that interested him. I heard all about his biology program, I knew the classes he was taking and teaching, and he knew absolutely nothing about my job or audiology. I picked up my purse. "Good bye, Caleb," I said, and walked out the door.

On the way home, it started to rain. There was construction on I-80, so I didn't get home for nearly 90 minutes. Was I so desperate for a date that I ignored gigantic character flaws in men? I had called Izzy as soon as I was off Caleb's street. She kept cutting out, though, and anyway, I needed to focus on my driving, so I told her I'd talk to her in the morning. Plus, she needed to get back to bed. It was 2:30 a.m., after all.

The next morning Caleb sent me an email.

> *Quinn,*
>
> *I enjoyed talking with you over dinner. You and I are both very busy people. I don't think either of us has time to commit to a serious relationship, but if you would like something casual I think we could arrange weekly meetings. As I said earlier, I am no longer interested in having a friendship with a woman where I'm just the ear for her relationship problems.*
>
> *Caleb*

> *Dear Caleb,*
>
> *I don't recall ever discussing any relationships with your ear. My understanding was that WE were in a relationship. I*

didn't view you as my confidant, I saw you as a man. You are too busy for something committed, but you could make time when sex is on the table? I want a man who can handle both; I'm not interested in you just for sex's sake. You, on the other hand, don't seem to hold me in the same light.

Quinn

I went back online and took my profile down. This is where dating a man is like buying a house. My house and Caleb. They both seemed fantastic. Like everything I'd ever wanted. In retrospect, I see where I made my mistake. I started to dream about them. I mentally moved in, and mentally moved Caleb in too. I had this perfect life, the built-ins, the literary conversations at dinner, the rental income, and the things I would learn about camping from a forest ranger. My kids were going to be great in science and art, because they'd have both our genes. When they were older, we'd kick out the renter and give them their own rooms. However, and I can't stress this enough, Reader, don't dream until you've had a home inspection. Infatuation is a reaction to the surface. But, as my father kept saying, "When you pull off that roof, you have no idea what you're going to find. All the beams might be rotting underneath."

Chapter 19
Burning Out on Match

"I'm sick of this stinking crap!" I told Izzy. "No more internet dating!"

"Fall seven times, stand up eight," she said. When I looked at her with incredulity, she added, "It's a Japanese proverb."

"My love affair with Match is over."

"Can you find a site for artists? Or audiologists?"

"I tried a few others, but they have almost no one from Omaha on them. There are sites for tall people and one for Ivy League graduates."

"How snooty," Izzy said. "The Ivy League one, I mean."

"Yeah. And there's nothing for me. I took my profile down."

"You've met six guys," Izzy said. "That's nothing. Everyone says you have to meet 12 before you find the one online. You're giving up too fast."

"No, I gave up just in time. Everyone else let the system break them, and now they've settled for less. Me, I'm doing great. What with the house hunting, my art, my knitting, and watching the first five seasons of Buffy on DVD, I don't have time for a man."

She said, "Last night, Sal and I broke up."

We were outside, cutting through Memorial Park on our way to our favorite coffee house. I stopped. "What?"

"He's not ready for marriage. He may never be ready for marriage. We had a good talk about it. He was honest. He says he's at least five years away, but he doesn't even know if he'll ever be ready for more."

"But he might change his mind. Maybe he just needs to figure out what he's going to do with his life. Once he's settled with that, he may feel differently about marriage."

Izzy started walking. The wind lifted her hair. With her confident, long-legged gait, she looked like a Greek goddess. "When? We've been together four years and he hasn't done a thing to figure out his life. I don't have time to wait."

"You are so courageous," I said.

She laughed. "Hardly. I'm just afraid to grow old alone."

"Number one," I said, "I wouldn't be able to dump him. I'd keep holding out, hoping he'd change. Number two, if I dumped him, it'd be a ruse, just to make him realize how much he loves me and to bring him back."

"He won't come back," she said. "He'll miss me, a lot. But he's not going to change his mind."

"Number three, I'd be bawling my eyes out."

"I've cried enough tears in my life," she said. I knew she was thinking of her divorce. "Now I'm a realist."

Chapter 20
Dating Men with Children

Like Izzy, I licked my wounds and moved on. I put my profile up again. I signed up for another internet dating site, eHarmony.com. They make you fill out a personality profile. Then, instead of browsing their site for men, eHarmony sends you the men who are your best match, based on your respective profiles. I spent two solid hours filling out that profile. The site gave me back two Nebraskan men. One was four hours away, in Kearney. The other was a member of the NRA and weighed 300 lbs.

I tried another site, GreatBoyfriends.com, "where every single man comes with a woman's stamp of approval." Two sisters, E. Jean Carroll and Cande Carroll, run it. They send you supportive emails telling you how brilliant you are. I liked the personality of this site more than the others, but I didn't have an ex-boyfriend to submit. I signed up anyway, but, as it turned out, there were no Nebraskan men currently in their file.

I had a two-year-old who needed a hearing test. Marlena. The appointment had just been made that morning, so I didn't have her chart. They came fifteen minutes late, which meant I was going to be late for my next appointment, unless this two-year-old was miraculously easy to test and had normal hearing. "Do you have any concerns for hearing?" I asked her mom.

"Nope. She hears fine."

"Is she talking much?" It's hard to rate a two-year-old's speech. The range of normal is broad.

"Just not around strangers," her mom said. "She talks all the time at home."

With Lona helping, Marlena caught on fast at putting the peg in the board when she heard the beep. If a kid is active, you might go for just a low pitch and a high pitch, to get a ballpark picture of a child's hearing. With Marlena, we got six frequencies, from 250 to 8000 Hz. And she had a hearing loss in both ears. I went into the booth and took off the headphones.

"Is she doing okay?" her mother asked.

"She's a real pro." I took another type of headphone off the wall.

"What's that?" her mother asked.

"This is a bone oscillator. It sits on her skull, behind the ear. When I play beeps with this headphone, I test the inner ear directly."

"How can she hear beeps if you don't put it in her ear?"

"Sound is a vibration, usually of air molecules. This kind of test is called bone conduction, because sound is conducted through the bone. The sound vibrates the skull. By vibrating the skull, we bypass the middle ear, where people get ear infections, and just test the inner ear, where the hair cells are."

If you have a conductive hearing loss, the nerve is working and the middle ear is blocking sound from getting to it. Sometimes a conductive loss can be treated medically and fixed. If you have a sensorineural hearing loss, it originates in the inner ear or higher (the nerve, which travels up to the brainstem). Usually, a sensorineural hearing loss is untreatable, except with hearing aids or a cochlear implant. Marlena had a moderate, flat sensorineural loss.

Lona brought them out of the booth and I sat down to talk to the mom. I started my typical explanation of what a moderate hearing loss meant, and how talking at a normal voice for Marlena will sound more like a whisper. The mom listened to my entire explanation and then said, "Well, I was told she might have a conductive loss, because she has middle ear fluid."

"So, she's had her hearing tested before?" I asked. I was surprised she knew the word "conductive." Most parents forget it five seconds after you say it.

"Yes. Here, and at her pediatricians."

For a minute, I fretted that I'd missed a conductive loss. But no, Marlena had been very reliable with her bone conduction responses. I did tympanograms on her, just to recheck my results.

Tympanograms are a quick test of how well the eardrums are

moving. If they don't move, there might be fluid. Marlena's eardrums moved fine. I explained why I thought her hearing loss was not conductive. She stopped talking and stared past me, at the wall.

"Has anyone ever mentioned hearing aids to you before?" I asked. She shook her head.

So, I talked about how hearing aids work and why Marlena would need them. I explained the next steps, taking ear impressions for ear molds, seeing an ear doctor, fitting a loaner hearing aid. "Do you have any questions about any of this?" I asked.

"Is there a bathroom around here?"

While they were in the bathroom, I tracked down Marlena's chart. Inside, there was a hearing test from a year ago, when Marlena was one. The loss was exactly like the one I had found today. Hearing aids had been recommended. When they returned, I showed Marlena's mother the test.

"That's right. They wanted to give her hearing aids. But our pediatrician said she had a conductive loss."

"Did he do a hearing test?"

"He looked in her ear and saw fluid."

I excused myself and went to find the audiologist who'd done the last hearing test. Jamie Robbins was at her desk. She had worked here about ten years. She was in her late thirties. Married. I said, "Do you remember a patient named Marlena Hanson?"

She opened her top desk drawer and pulled out a set of tiny ear molds. Purple. "I called. I wrote letters. They dropped off the face of the earth."

"Well, they're back," I told her. "Mom says the pediatrician said she had a conductive loss from fluid."

"No, the pediatrician is Dr. Mueller. I spoke to his office several times about trying to get them to come back here for the loaner aid. They were behind us, but they couldn't get mom to come in."

"So she's lying. She lied to me about hearing concerns, too. She had no hearing concerns. Then, after the test, she said Marlena had a conductive loss."

Jamie shrugged.

"Now that kid has gone an entire year without amplification," I fumed.

"A whole year of language learning, down the drain," Jamie agreed. "So much for early intervention."

"Back to the fire," I told her, picking the ear molds up as I left.

"These are the old ear molds, but they are too small now," I said as I walked into the booth. "I'm going to fit Marlena with a temporary ear mold so that she can go home with a loaner hearing aid today." I thought if I could get a hearing aid on Marlena, her mom would start to notice a difference in Marlena's response to sounds. It goes without saying that I was going to be very, very late for my other patients. Our administrative assistant was looking for another audiologist to jump in and help out.

Marlena tolerated the hearing aid well. When I put it in her ear, she didn't even seem to register it, much less pull it out. But when her mother said, "Marlena, can you hear me?" she spun around and looked at her mother with surprise.

"I don't want people to stare at her."

"Look how her hair covers the aids," I said. It really did, too. Purple ear molds would draw attention, however, so I made a note to order the molds in flesh color.

Later that day, Jamie popped her head in. "How'd it go?"

"A minor breakthrough," I said. "She cried and admitted to being in denial."

"Humph." Jamie said. I shared her cynicism. This mother had ignored letters, phone calls, and appeals from her pediatrician and us. She had finally returned, it was true, but she'd lied throughout the appointment. A few tears at the end weren't enough to convince me. But who knew? Maybe she'd surprise me.

My phone rang. It was Izzy. "You've got a new email. He sounds great. He's an artist. You should email him."

"Busy, today?" I asked. Izzy still had my email password, and she'd periodically check up on my emails, even though I was relying on her feedback less and less, now that I'd gotten the hang of interacting with Match men.

"Swamped. But, hey, guess what I'm doing tonight! You'll be so proud of me."

"Signing up for Match?"

"I'm going to a Bar Mitzvah!"

"With whom?"

"Someone from work. I can't decide what to wear. I have this great little black dress, with a low back, but I'm not sure it's appropriate.

It's sexy. The invitation said 'Black Tie Optional.'"

"Since when do you do 'sexy' at a Bar Mitzvah?"

"Since I got single. I want to meet someone!"

"You will be the nightmare of every Jewish mother in the room."

"Mothers love me, Quinn."

"You're right. Have a great time."

I checked my account to see what this guy Izzy had called about was like.

> *USERNAME: ArtForArtsSake*
>
> *TAGELINE: "Be fearless in your work and your life."*
>
> *Dear Quinn Painter,*
>
> *If you write this well, I can't wait to see your art. Do you show alot, in the Omaha area? I am a sculptor. I got my degree at the Kansas City Art Institute. Over the past few years, I've made alot of important changes in my life, including sacraficing some material comforts in order to follow my dreams.*
>
> *It's working, too! Hear I am opening my own gallery, soon, in midtown. I own a loft in the old market area, which I bought shortly after my divorce. Yes, I'm divorced, and I have a four-year-old child from that relationship. He is the best part of my life. I'm the happiest I've ever been, and I feel ready to move forward in my romantic life, as I have in my professional life. I'd love to meet with you some time, for coffee, and talk about art. I don't have a photograph posted, but I can always send you one, if you want to see that before we meet.*
>
> *Art.*

"I have some concerns about Art," I told Izzy. The Bar Mitzvah had been a bust, but she'd been a popular dance partner for a lot of adolescent boys.

"Okay, let's hear them."

"First, he's got a kid."

"Okay. Is that so bad? Instant family."

"But, they spend the weekend with their kids instead of you. And if you get serious, you inherit step-kids who hear comments like, "So daddy's little tramp thinks she can pull off a mini-skirt at her age?"

"Until you win the ex over with your non-threatening personality."

"Well, that's debatable. But there's more. He set me up with the offer of a photograph so that if I ask for it, I look superficial. I don't like men who don't post their pictures online."

"Maybe he doesn't have a digital camera."

"Everyone with a phone has a digital camera. Besides, you can send Match your picture by mail, and they'll scan and post it for you. Plus," I added, remembering, "he has a picture, he can send it to me. He just won't post it!"

"Well, I don't think you can hold that against him. Just meet him and see.

Dear Art,

Thanks for your email. Why don't we meet? Are you free this weekend? There's a nice bakery in Old Market, Delicce. I assume you know it?

Quinn,

Actually, it's spelled Delice, and I would love to go there. How does 4pm work for you, on Saturday?

Art,

~~Yes, the double c in my email was a typo, not a misspell, but thanks for pointing it out. By the way, you've had several misspells in your emails to me. "A lot" is two words, sacrifice only has one "a" and "Hear" should be "here," in your context.~~ Four o'clock sounds fine. I'll see you then.

Quinn

The corrections were all mine. I was getting the hang of this.

When I walked into Delice, there was a nice-looking man at a table with the local freebie spread out in front of him. He was in his thirties, with a shaved head, beard, and intense eyes. He was wearing jeans, a grey cotton sweater, and clogs, even though it was snowing outside. I was waiting in line to order when I saw him look up and register me. And look back down to his paper. Not Art. Too bad! By the time I'd been served my chocolate croissant, three men had walked in, none of them looking like they were meeting someone. I took a seat. It was now 4:15. I picked up one of the freebie papers and started eating my croissant. I kept shooting glances at the shaved head. I couldn't believe that he wasn't Art. At 4:25, the real Art showed up. He wore a long raincoat. His hair was thinning and spiky.

"Quinn? Right? I'm so sorry I'm late. I was meeting with contractors at my gallery. I thought I could meet them at 3:30 and still get here in time, but I couldn't." *Poor time manager*, my brain ticked. "I'm so, very, sorry. Really."

"It's fine," I said. I mean, really, what else could I say? *Get away from my table you scum sucker! A curse on your family for the next 1000 years! No one keeps Quinn Painter waiting!*

He went to get coffee. I wondered if Shaved Head was listening. Maybe he'd guess that Art and I had met on the Internet. Maybe he'd go online tonight and check me out. And then he might email me and say:

> *Hey, didn't I see you at Delice yesterday? That guy was a loser. Why don't you try me? I have my bachelors in Marine Biology and I specialized in environmental law at Harvard Law. I took three years off between degrees to work for Ameri-corps, in New Mexico, and my goal is to return there to live within the next ten years. But there's a lot of beauty in Nebraska's landscape too, and I would love the chance to show you that. I see you're a painter. My mom is a painter. She shows in New York and Paris. My father is a college professor. They live in Upstate NY, which is where I grew up, just like you. I don't smoke, I do yoga daily and have my black belt in karate. I speak French. I can't wait to have children, and I'd seriously consider going halftime at work so that I could share equally in raising the kids. By the way, you are stunningly beautiful and your picture here doesn't do justice to what you look like in person. Hope to hear from you soon, Benjamin.*"

Art returned with coffee and a plate of cookies. He pushed the plate to the center. "Please, have some."

I reached out and took one.

"I'm trying to find a way to make up for my lateness," he said.

"Don't worry," I repeated. "Tell me about your gallery. What kind of art will you show there?"

"Sculpture, mostly. And some abstract paintings. What kind of art do you make?"

"Oil paintings. Lately, portraits."

"Cool." Silence. I could picture him in his own gallery, with nothing to say to the artists that came in.

"So tell me about your child?"

"Well, he's just the greatest. He lives with his mom, but I see him all the time. He stays over at least two nights a week."

"Do you have a good relationship with his mother?"

"Let's just say that my ex is a very bitter woman," he said.

"You know, my parents are divorced. I think it's important to get along with your child's parent, even if it's just for the child that you do it."

"I'd like to, but she is so angry and hostile that it's really impossible. She basically is the reason we separated at all, and she doesn't listen to reason."

I must be honest. I'd written him off when he showed up late. Well, not completely. If he had been funny and considerate, then I would have given him a couple more chances to be on time before writing him off. But he was awkward and he had to compete with the fantasy guy I'd created while waiting for him. When he said nasty things about his ex and put all the blame for their bad relationship on her, he was history. But I stayed and chatted for another fifteen minutes. I guess it's hard for me to walk away from things. And I'm glad I did, because I learned something important from him that has stopped me from ever considering men with children again.

"So you've done a lot of traveling," Art said as he blew on his coffee.

"Yes. I've traveled quite a bit in this country, and spent a lot of time in Europe, but I've never been to any other continent."

"I'd love to go to Bolivia and Hawaii. Or even New York or San Francisco."

"I've never been to San Francisco. It sounds like a neat city."

"Yes, it does. It's got a good art scene. I'd love to live there." He sounded wistful.

"But then you'd have to leave your son."

"That's right. So I'm pretty much locked into Omaha."

And that's when it hit me. Any man with children will be locked into Omaha. Or he'll be the kind of man that would move away and leave his kids. I can't imagine not living in the same state as my children and I don't think I could allow some man who'd done that to be the father of my children. And this was the moment I'd been waiting for. The mutual realization that we weren't a match. "I don't plan on spending more than a few more years in Omaha," I said. We looked at each other with a reciprocated understanding, I thought.

When we left the café, he was parked just outside. "Let me give you a ride to your car," he said.

"I'm fine," I told him. "It's just around the corner."

"It's freezing outside. I'll drive you."

"No, it's fine. I want to walk."

"This is ridiculous. Let me drive you."

I turned to face him and said, "I want to walk. Okay? It's two blocks. I'm not an invalid."

"Can I see you again?" he asked.

"I'm not sure that's a good idea. You are tied to Omaha and I am planning on leaving."

"Will you be at that art opening on Saturday night?"

"Probably, but…"

"Okay, I'll see you then." And he hopped in his SUV and drove away.

Chapter 21
How I Stay Safe in Internet Dating

I assume that every single man I meet has the potential to be a psychopath. Even when they seem nice, I still implement the same precautions. If any of them had turned into long-term, then things would have changed. But in the initial meeting period, I give them nothing. Basically, I try to imagine what I would do to attack someone and then put safeguards up to stop that from happening. Here is a list of what I do to stay safe.

1. Match and other online dating services need your email address. I set up a dummy hotmail account, used just for Internet dating. I use false identifying information.
2. On my profile, I list my zip code incorrectly, in a neighboring town, instead of my own city, so that if someone started looking for me, they'd start in that town. I also give a fake birth date, with the right year. Viewers don't get to see the birth date, but just in case there was a good hacker among them, I want to throw him off. I use the right year because that's how your age is determined.
3. I never give my last name, even if asked outright.
4. I reveal my profession in the broadest term, "healthcare."
5. I meet in public place (no hikes or bike rides in secluded areas).
6. I park several blocks away so that dates cannot see my license plate number.
7. I do not allow the person to escort me back to car.

8. I bring my cell phone but keep it hidden on my person, not in purse. This is so that, if he were to grab my purse as we were walking away from each other, I've still got help.

9. If I leave the table for any reason, I don't drink my beverage when I return. That date-rape drug may be more prevalent than you think, so I never leave my drink unattended. Or if I do, I don't drink from it again.

10. I have a friend standing-by who expects a check-in call at a designated time.

11. I always call the friend as soon as the date is over, while walking back to my car. I don't hang up until I'm safely inside the car with the doors locked.

12. When I call a Match Man, I use a cell phone (can't trace my address as easily) or block my phone number (*82).

13. If I get their phone number, I do a reverse look-up on the Internet to verify that they are who they say they are. (Google "reverse lookup" if you want to find this.)

14. My own phone number is unlisted and blocked.

15. I periodically do Internet searches on my phone number, my name, and "Quinn Painter" to make sure they don't give anyone clues about my existence.

Chapter 22
Case Study: How to Ditch a Man

"He'll be at the art opening," I told my painting class. "So you can check him out. But we aren't going to date." They couldn't wait to meet him. It would be the first live one, after hearing so many stories.

"Poor guy's probably desperate," said my painting teacher, Jack. "Who knows what kind of women he's been meeting."

"Yeah, maybe you're right," I said, thinking of Lance's stories.

On Saturday, I dressed up for the show. Not because of Art, but in case there were any cute guys that I *did* want to meet. The show was in the Old Market area, in a used bookstore in a beautiful old pre-WWII building. Art was the first person I saw when I arrived. He was kind of tall so his head bobbed above everyone else in the crowd. He looked right at me, the moment I walked in the door, and then he looked away. Trying to be cool. I set off to find my friends. They were all in the back, drinking. Both Jack and Eli had come with their wives. Kate's husband was home with the kids. "Is he here?" They wanted to know. I pointed out Art's bobbing head, which was now moving our way. He stood about five feet from me, without approaching. I tried to look around at the paintings on the walls, but the crowd was too dense to see anything.

Finally, my art class and I went over to Art to say hi. He was next to a woman, but I couldn't tell if he was with her.

"Hi, Art. Do you want to meet my friends?" I introduced everyone. He said hello to them, but didn't introduce the woman.

We made the dumb small talk that strangers make: the turnout, the show, the weather, and the news. We were discussing some news story when the woman standing next to Art corrected us on our misuse of a political term. "Actually," she said, "that term wasn't even used until the 1940s and the meaning only applies to government."

We all stared at her. I thought, *Who the hell is this woman?* I said, "Hi. I'm Quinn."

"Hi. I'm Agatha. I am always complaining to Art about how people massacre the English language."

So they *were* together. And Art hadn't even introduce her! We eventually made our escape from them and reconvened in a corner.

"I don't like him," Eli said.

"Huge black mark for not introducing his friend," Kate said.

"And for having such a boring friend," Jack said. "It was like watching PBS. What was she talking about?"

"His hair!" Eli continued. He hadn't even heard the others' comments. "Those spikes are from high school."

"He's hiding a bald spot," I said.

"But the worst part was that he didn't make eye contact with me. He just stared at you, even when I was talking to him!" Eli shook his head and took a swig of his beer.

We continued to hang out in the back. Art stayed about five feet away, shooting looks at us, or me, which we all ignored. Everyone was drinking and getting drunk because the only food was baby carrots, broccoli spears, and Brie cheese with no crackers. By 10:30 the crowd had thinned but Art remained, shooting me looks. "What is his problem?" Eli asked. He'd taken a real dislike to Art, because of the lack of eye contact.

We were finally able to look at the work, so we started around the room. Art began to follow us, keeping about two paintings behind. Jack's wife leaned in and said, "What do you think he's trying to do?"

"I don't know. Maybe wait till I leave and try to walk with me?"

"We'll walk out with you," Jack said.

"I wouldn't put it past him to try something," Eli told me

We paused in front of a ceramic sculpture, done by an artist that you might call a Nazi-Fem. She was in her late fifties and seemed to think that all men were evil until proven innocent. I'd only interacted with her once or twice. She was a bully. We were standing around the piece, pettily trading insults about it, when Art joined us.

"Hey, Quinn. You're still here?" He asked as he stepped in between the piece and me. "How do you like the show?"

"It's good," I said.

"It reminds me of my own work. I was thinking that I never got to tell you about my own art, when we talked before. I'm doing a series on garbage. I want to show the world the magnitude of our waste problem." I nodded. Eli and Jack were on my right. Kate and Jack's wife were on my left. Eli's wife had just stepped away to chat with someone from her high school. I knew she was going to be sorry to miss meeting Art, since Eli had been grousing about him all evening. Art, meanwhile, had inserted himself in the middle of all my friends and started talking to me as if they were pieces of art. "When you look in major museums and galleries, you see a lot of stuff, but you never see garbage, do you?"

I didn't see Eli move, I just saw a blur to my right and Art was bumped against the pedestal that held the ceramic sculpture. The piece, which was a large, womblike vessel, crashed to the ground and crumbled into dust. Every person in the gallery stopped talking and looked at Art. Literally, every person was staring at him. I found out later, the Nazi-Fem was in the bathroom. He was still holding his plastic wine glass out, as if he were about to take a sip. It seemed like minutes, but probably only three seconds passed while I watched Art's face change from confusion to shock to terror. He turned, as if to look for someone of authority in the room. The crowd separated as he stepped toward the back of the gallery. Then he turned on his heel, threw his wine into the air, and tore out of the gallery so fast that I barely saw him go. The gallery remained still and silent. I felt a wave of hysteria coming at me and knew that in a few seconds I'd be laughing completely out of control. I grabbed my right hand with my left and pinched it hard to try to offset the fit. At that moment, my teacher nodded to me and said, "I've always said she's no craftsman. Look at this crap. One little poke and her work collapses into dust."

Chapter 23
Match.com:
Home of Hunchbacks, Racists, and Ageists

I called Izzy for a Match pep talk. "What are you up to?" I asked.

"I'm making a collage of women I admire. I'm going to hang it on my refrigerator. What are you doing?"

"Contemplating sterilization to stop the ticking of my biological clock."

"Suck it up. Seriously. Deal."

I called Ann for a second opinion. She said, "I'd quit it right now. The whole thing is causing you stress and, let's face it, you haven't exactly met any stellar men."

"Well, not yet."

"Not ever, I'd guess."

"Well, I'm not giving up yet," I told her. "I've only met seven men. You have to meet at least 12 before you get a good one. Everyone agrees."

Sheesh! Talk about friends not helping you when you need them.

Dear Quinn,

Hi, my name is Horace. I think you and I have a lot in common. I, too, have traveled extensively. I lived in France for ten years and have been back in the states for about five.

Horace,

Thanks for email. I notice that you are 44, but your dating range is 18-42. Do you have something against women your own age, or older?

Quinn,

I have dated many women older than me. Some were great, some were not. I have no problem with age—in my case, I'm told I look much, much younger than 44.

"I don't understand, if he has no problem dating older women, why is his dating-range so low?"

"Who cares? Just meet him and see what he's like," Izzy said.

"But why would you have such a low range? He didn't even address that in his response."

"Don't email back and ask him. Just meet him and see what he's like. He's the first local liberal you've found! He lived in France. He speaks French, for goodness sakes!"

"How are things going in your neck of the dating woods?" I asked.

"I'm going to a party tonight. Kaye from work is having a get together. She said there would be single men."

"Good."

"Yeah. Actually, I need your help role-playing something," Izzy said.

"What is it?"

"Pretend you're a guy. I'm going to walk up to you at this party." She stood and positioned me against the wall and handed me a pen. "Just put the pen in your pocket and stand like you're talking to someone." I did this and after a second, Izzy pulled up next to me and said, "Hi. Do you have a pen?"

"Sure," I said, handing her my pen. Izzy took the pen with her right hand, and holding my hand with her left, she feigned writing on my palm. "I'm Isabel. And this is my number." She let my hand drop down, still holding onto my fingers. "Call me." Then she let go, pivoted, and walked away.

"Holy shit." I told her. "You would never have the guts!"

"I think I might," she said. "I just need to work out the mechanics of it."

Hey Quinn,

You have the best profile I've seen. Can I get your friend to write mine, as well? I'm back in Omaha after living for five years in DC. I love the southwest! I try to go there on vacation as often as possible. Take a look at my profile and see if you think we are a match. I would love to hear from you.

Davey.

Dear Davey,

Thanks for your email. You seem nice but I see you list your political views as very conservative, and I'm not sure that makes us a match, as I am extremely liberal. Thanks for your email, though. Quinn

Quinn,

I don't know why I put conservative. I'm really not. In fact, I am pro-choice. I probably wrote that because it's what my parents are and without thinking I just use that term for myself. If you have any other questions about my politics (or anything else), please ask. Davey.

Now that I was back in the Match.com saddle, keeping up with the Internet dating wasn't easy. I was juggling five people:

1. Horace, the ageist.
2. Davey, the conservative.
3. Ryan, an architect who loved NY and the southwest.
4. Flash456, an entrepreneur from CA.
5. JustANiceGuy72 who loved desert camping.

I was still house hunting, too. Every house in my price range was a dump. I had learned a lot from my home inspection, and I wasn't going to be taken again. I arrived to each house with a checklist and a flashlight. While Flora clucked her tongue, I climbed into crawl spaces, felt down ceilings and walls, and examined dark basement corners. But for all my effort in uncovering hidden flaws, I was missing the forest for the trees. In the latest, a 1918 Arts and Crafts style home with bright red carpeting, silver wall paint, and gold doorknobs, I said, "The electricity is a circuit box, there's no silt on the basement floor. The built-ins are pretty." *Although not as pretty as the house I lost.*

"It's as if they tried to make this house as ugly as possible," Flora said.

"If I painted the walls…"

"Metallic paint on built-ins. Do you have any idea how hard that would be to remove? Look at the kitchen cabinets. They're plywood. And they're crooked, like someone half-cocked hung them. Did you see the neighbor's yard? There's an abandoned car in the back."

"Is that really such a big deal?" I asked.

"Yes." And that was that, as far as Flora was concerned. She put her card on the kitchen counter and headed for the front door.

I called Lonesh's mother to hear how he was doing. "He's doing just great," she said. "He wears the hearing aids all day at school."

"Great. How often does he wear them at home?"

Pause. "Does he need them at home?"

"Yes. It's just like glasses. He should wear them all the time. School is important, but he also needs to hear his family talking."

"Believe me, he hears us."

"Yes, with the way his loss is, I'm sure he does. But he probably doesn't overhear you talking…" I racked my brain to come up with an example that would show the mom some benefit from wearing the aids at home. "Or maybe the television is louder."

"The TV was softer when he wore them," she said. "And he could hear the oven timer go off."

I breathed an internal sigh of relief. Mom's agenda wasn't to prove to me that he didn't need the aids. "It's hard to remember to wear them," I said, "because he will hear some of what you say without them. Maybe you could implement a reward schedule, say, if he wears them every day for a week, he gets something very small."

"Or we could start a diary, where we record everything he can hear."

"That's a great idea," I said.

"Okay, let me work on this and I'll get back to you."

I searched around in my files until I found a child-friendly hearing aid rating system. It was designed for parents to measure the benefits of hearing aids, but was simple enough that Lonesh could participate in it, too. I made copies and sent them to his mom.

I called Izzy. "How's it going?"

"Good. I'm driving between schools."

"I just had a brainstorm. Why not try Match?"

"Nope, not ready for that."

"Okay." Pause. "Because, remember how I didn't want to do it either? And when we did it together it turned out to be so fun?"

"Not ready for Match."

"Okay. Just thought I'd ask." Sheesh!

I had to talk to a family whose one month old had just been identified with a profound hearing loss in both ears. Obviously, children that young can't raise their hand, or even turn their heads when they hear a beep. This child had just had an Auditory Brainstem Response test, or ABR. To perform an ABR, electrodes are stuck behind the ear or in the ear, and on their forehead. The electrodes pick up electrical brain activity. A sound is played in the child's ear, and when the electrical response is averaged, random responses are tossed and the activity that is timed to the sound reveals a pattern. This pattern, or response, comes from the brainstem. A normal pattern for a soft sound suggests normal hearing.

For this infant, Maddie, sound had to be 90 dB HL before we could measure a pattern. That's about as loud as a chainsaw. Her diagnosis was profound hearing loss. This was tricky, because her parents had no hearing concerns. They said she was responsive to sounds.

"Well," I said, turning to face them. "This test played different sounds in Maddie's ears, and measured the response her ear made to them. And the softest sounds her ear responded to were very loud. It suggests that sounds would have to be very loud before she would hear them." Parent report is important. You can't rely just on your objective test measures. "Will you describe how Maddie responds to sounds?"

"When we talk to her, she focuses her eyes on us," the father said. "She looks at us when we talk."

I nodded. "And when there are loud sounds? Does she startle? Does she wake from a sleep when the phone rings?"

"She hears us!" the dad said. "She looks at us when we talk!" The mom started to cry. I handed her a box of tissues.

"She doesn't wake to any sounds," the mother said. "But she seems like she hears us, when we talk to her."

"Babies are very visual. They focus on their parents' faces when they talk. Not all communication is hearing. Have you ever visited a foreign country and tried to get directions from someone who didn't speak English?" I got a slight nod from the father. "Isn't it amazing, the things you can communicate with someone you can't even understand? Maddie is communicating with you, by watching your face change and your mouth move."

"Do you think she is lip reading?" the father asked.

"No, because you can't lip read unless you understand a language, English, in this case. And Maddie is too little to understand English. But we want her to learn English, or some language. And the first step is to try to make sounds louder for her, so that she can hear them."

"Hearing aids?" The mom asked.

"Yes. We can take ear impression and order ear molds. Then we can fit Maddie with a loaner hearing aid and see how she does."

"What about a cochlear implant?" the mom asked.

"She's a candidate for that," I said. "We'd still start with hearing aids, but she could easily end up with an implant. Do you know much about them?"

The mom nodded. "Yeah, they are like, bionic ears."

"Well, kind of. Like hearing aids, they don't restore normal hearing. Cochlear implants aren't a magic cure for hearing loss, but with profound hearing losses, they usually do a better job than hearing aids would." I gave them a packet of information on implants. "There are a lot of communication options," I began. "I don't want to overwhelm you with too much information today."

"What other options?"

"Well, our goal is to teach Maddie language. That's why we care so much about her hearing, because it's hard to learn a language when you can't hear it. Do you know anyone who uses sign language to speak?"

"I have an aunt who signs," said the mom.

"Has she had hearing loss since childhood?"

"Yes."

"So you already know that sign language is one way of teaching a child a language, without them needing to hear. Do you know any sign language?"

She shook her head.

"You might want to talk to her about sign language; using a family member to help you guys communicate. Sign language would be a way to start communicating with Maddie right now."

"So, what? We learn to sign? How long will that take?" the dad asked.

"Well, in the beginning you would learn easy stuff. Like, "juice" and "diaper." The kind of things you say to a baby."

"We're not going to learn sign language," the dad said. "Realistically, how will she talk to other people? Kate can't even talk to her aunt."

I nodded. Not all kids can rely on just oral speech. Many need sign to help them out, but there was no point in getting into this with parents of a one month old. The family would have plenty of time to come to that realization, if necessary.

I had emails in my box from all five of my current matchers, plus four new people. I was spending hours online, dealing with the Match stuff. Also, my computer was old and frequently froze and had to be restarted.

Horace wanted to meet. He suggested a meeting for the next night, at the café in Barnes and Noble. From his phrasing, I got the impression he met all his Match women at this site. I suggested the same place I'd gone with Caleb. I wasn't going to let Caleb ruin a nice spot. The other Match men were still in the getting to know you stage–a back and forth of short, witty emails, designed to intrigue and impress.

My neighbor was coughing next door. I'd started to listen for him, nightly, because I'd begun to worry that he might die without anyone noticing. I'd made him another batch of food over the weekend. He'd taken it without a thank you, and returned all my Tupperware a few days later. They were so clean they looked brand new.

I knew I was pushing the envelope, but I'd scheduled a house viewing just before my meeting with Horace. Flora picked me up at work and we drove together to the home I'd found on the Internet.

The neighborhood was a little bit bad. The house was on a block where jobless men stand outside all day and talk into parked cars filled with more idle men. As I started to undo my seatbelt, my realtor hit the power locks and locked me in. I looked over at her. When we had first met, she had said, "There are two things we must have clear. First, you will not work with another agent while you are working with me. And second, if I make an appointment to see a house with you, you must go inside. I don't care if we spend three seconds in the house, I have to leave my card." Her requests seemed reasonable and I'd agreed.

Now we sat, locked in her car, and she said, "Quinn, I cannot in good conscience show you this house. You'd be liable to try to buy it and I simply could not sleep at night, knowing that you were living in this neighborhood."

I looked around. There was garbage on the street. The house itself had a sink in the yard and a broken window with a piece of cloth stuffed the hole. Sheets hung where curtains would normally be. The other houses had junk in their yards. Two of the cars parked on the street had flat tires and violation stickers on the windows. I could see her point. "But what about your rule?" I asked.

She whipped out her cell phone. "I'm calling the realtor," she said. "Hi, Martin, this is Flora. Yes, I am sitting in my car right now, outside your property on 24th Street. My client is a sweet young woman who is looking for her first house. This property just isn't a match for her. She is all alone and she's got no family in town." Flora listened to Martin and rolled her eyes at me. "No, she's allergic to dogs. And what dog will protect her on the walk from her car to her front door?" She paused. "Yes, I'll have her take a look at that property. She can decide if it's a better match." Flora snapped her phone shut.

"What property?" I asked.

"Nothing you'd be interested in," she said as she started up the engine.

So I made it to the café with about twenty minutes to spare. I did some window-shopping and finally arrived at our agreed upon time, six o'clock on the dot. Horace was not inside. About 30 seconds after I had taken a table, he appeared. Were these men hiding somewhere across the street, and waiting till they saw me before they came inside? Was that shyness? Or were they planning on bolting if they didn't like what they saw? My profile picture showed me dressed up, it's true, but it was a pretty realistic idea of what I look like.

Horace's picture had shown a man with blond hair, green eyes, and a warm, friendly smile. In real life, he had the hair and eye color, and also, a hunchback. I stood to shake his hand. He didn't look younger than 44. In fact, I would have guessed his age to be about 48. He was noticeably shorter than me. I was certain that wasn't on his profile. "Hi Quinn, it's nice to meet you." He spoke with a lisp.

As I sat back down, I wrestled with my vanity and my sense of right. *Get to know him first. You liked his personality.* "So, tell me about France."

"It was the best." He started coughing. He had a hacking, croupy cough. The waitress came to take our order. "Do you want something to eat?" he asked as I ordered a red wine.

"No, thanks."

"I'll order food."

I didn't want to be committed to dinner with this guy. "I don't want any food."

"I insist. I'll order food."

"I won't eat it."

He ordered a whiskey and left it at that. "I just got back from Australia. That country is beautiful."

"I'll bet. You know, I saw a really neat film from Australia not too long ago. 'Rabbit Proof Fence.' Did you see that? It's a true story about the government's policy to take children of mixed race and raise them in camps to be culturally white. It's about three little girls who escape the camp and travel thousands of miles by foot to get home to their aboriginal mother."

"I know all about that policy and the fence. Australians are racists."

"Well, the policy is no longer in effect. I don't think you can call an entire group of people racist."

"Even they say they are racist. It's in their museum."

"Their policies were racist. But I don't believe every person in that country is racist."

"Well, sure, the Aborigines aren't racist."

I took a sip of my wine. "If you are going to make a blanket statement like that about a country, then you might as well make it about ours. We have racial problems. Is every white American racist?"

Horace looked taken aback. "No, of course not!"

"Well then, how can you say it about the Australians?"

He spoke slowly and clearly. "Their own museum says that about them."

A little Izzy in an angel suit appeared on my right shoulder and said, *Don't fight with him. Let it go.* I took a deep breath and I let this go.

"Tell me about France."

"Well, it's a lovely place. I spent a lot of time in the south." He drew a map of France on a napkin and gave me a geography lecture.

"Did you spend much time in Paris?"

He coughed again. "Of course. I lived in Paris for several years."

"What did you think of the Centre Pompidou?"

"I saw many things there and I loved them all."

"But did you like the Pompidou?"

"I'm sure I did. I can't remember everything I did."

I thought, *If you don't know what it is, why don't you just ask me? You "taught" me about French geography for ten minutes and now you can't ask me what the Centre Pompidou is*? I was getting the feeling that he had to be the parental figure. Maybe that's why his dating range was so low. "The Centre Pompidou is the museum of modern art. It has all the brightly colored tubes coming out of it."

"So what do you do?" he asked.

"I'm an audiologist."

"Huh?" He laughed at his joke. "Actually, I saw an audiologist not too long ago. I have an inner ear problem."

"Do you?"

He had another coughing attack. He took a sip of water and continued. "Yes, I had fluid in the inner ear. I couldn't hear anything. The ear doctor had to puncture the drum to drain the fluid."

"That sounds like your middle ear," I said.

"Actually, it was the inner ear."

I thought, *Actually, your inner ear is imbedded in your temporal bone and it's supposed to have fluid and if you wanted to puncture it, you'd have to take something like an ice pick and drive it into your skull.* And then, I suddenly had an epiphany: I was not having fun Internet dating. I didn't like meeting strangers and pretending to be more outgoing than I really was. I didn't like making banal conversation with men who were probably not listening to a word I said and were just judging me based on my looks.

"So, you haven't mentioned age tonight," Horace said, unmindful of my inner thoughts.

"Should I?" I asked. I really just wanted to leave.

Horace smiled. "It's just that I expected you to comment on how young I look. Everyone is always shocked when they learn my true age."

"I know your true age."

"But if you didn't, how old would you guess I was?"

I wrestled with truth/meanness and lies/kindness.

"Come on. What would you say?" said the short, lisping hunchback in front of me. If he thought he looked young, who was I to burst his bubble?

"Thirty-eight?"

"Thirty-five is what everyone says," he told me.

"Ahh."

Horace started coughing again. This time he ended by hacking something up and spitting it into a napkin. "So, Quinn, why don't you tell me about your travels?" he asked.

I took another sip of my wine and congratulated myself for ordering no food. The wine was half gone. I would be out of here in less than fifteen minutes. "I've lived in Venice and Barcelona. And I traveled to Czechoslovakia…"

"It's the Czech Republic, actually."

"Actually, in 1992 it was still called Czechoslovakia, but they voted to split on my last day there."

"Have you ever been to Israel?"

"No, but I'd like to."

"It's incredible. If the Palestinians would just leave, it would be perfect."

"Well, it's their home, too."

He shook his head. "Actually, it belongs to the Jews. They have lived there for thousands of years."

"They weren't the only people to live there, for thousands of years, and they weren't the first either."

"Yes they were."

"There's evidence of prehistoric man there. And as far back as we have names for groups, there were many different tribes living there, including the Jebusites, Midianites, and Canaanites." Do I normally know stuff like this, Reader? No! But I had literally, the day before, started reading a tourism book about Israel. It was like…I was *fated* to contradict him!

His face faltered. "Well, they've been there longer than the Palestinians."

I peeked at my watch. I had ten minutes before I was due to call Ann, tonight's contact person. It would take that long to end this conversation and make my excuses. I swallowed the rest of my wine. "Do you think that we should give this country back to the Native Americans?"

"What? No, of course not!"

So, I'd hit a nerve. Interesting. "Because you're saying that about Israel. That the Jews were there first, as were the Native Americans."

"It's completely different. Judaism is a religion. It's sacred. God chose them to live there."

"I'll bet the Native Americans would say God chose them to live here."

He shook his head. "You're wrong."

I shrugged.

He smiled and extended his hand across the table. "Let's shake on agreeing to disagree," he said.

"I can't shake your hand," I said.

"Why not?"

"Because, you're sick. You've been coughing on your hand all night."

"Are you seriously not going to shake my hand?"

"I don't want to get sick."

"This is ridiculous." He held his hand out. "Shake my hand."

"Not unless you wash it."

"You are seriously not going to shake my hand?"

"So, tell me about your job."

"I can't believe this. You won't shake my hand?"

I shook my head.

"What if I dunk my hand in my whiskey?" he shouted. "Then will you shake my hand?"

Adjacent tables were looking at us. "Get over it," I said, quietly. "We're past that now and talking about your job."

"I'm not done with the hand conversation. God, you're so American."

"You're American too."

"I'm going to go wash my hands."

"Let's just shake hands mentally."

"No, I'm going to wash my hands." He left for the bathroom. I wondered if he was really going to wash his hands or not. When he came back, he held out his hands. "Washed."

I leaned my nose in to smell them. There was that cheap, public bathroom soap smell on them. I put my hand out. He pulled his away.

"I've changed my mind," he said. "I don't want to shake hands."

I looked at my watch and said, "Well, I should really be going."

"Wait. Let me get you another wine."

"No thanks."

He turned and called our waitress. "I'm going to order some food. And I'll have another whiskey and she'll have another wine."

"I don't want any wine."

"She'll have another wine."

I looked at the waitress and said, "No, I won't."

"I insist you have some food."

"As I've said, no."

He had a desperate look in his eye. Maybe he thought that force-feeding me food and alcohol would make the date go better. "I'm going to have another whiskey," he announced. "Please, let me get you a glass of wine."

I stood up. "It's been a pleasure, but I really must go."

"I'll walk you to your car," he said, standing and pulling out his wallet.

"Nope. I've got it from here." I put money on the table to cover my drink.

"I insist."

"I'm really fine."

"I'm walking you to your car," Horace said.

It was getting kind of funny, to see him try to take over and fail. "You aren't," I said in a friendly tone. "Good-bye."

"Wait," he said. He had followed me onto the sidewalk. "When will we see each other again?" He looked angry. He was like a spoiled child, expecting to get his way.

"I don't think we're very compatible, do you?"

"Yes, I think we are."

I was floored. "Well," I finally said, "I don't. So, good luck with your life. I'm sure you'll meet someone who's a better match for you." I turned to leave. I walked about half a block and paused at a window display to discreetly look behind me. He was walking away, in the opposite direction. He was such a freak, though, that I wouldn't be surprised if he tried to double back. I took out my cell phone and called Ann.

"It's me. He was a weirdo and angry that I don't want to see him again. I'm talking to you as I walk to my car. If it sounds like I've been tackled from behind, it's probably him. Horace."

"What happened?"

"He didn't understand basic infection control. He didn't listen to anything I said. He's racist. He is several inches shorter than me, he only dates younger women but looks four years older than his age, and he is hunchbacked and speaks with a lisp."

"Maybe you should try to date women," Ann said.

"I'd almost consider it," I said, finally reaching my car and locking myself inside. I sighed. "The first liberal I've met in Omaha. Practically the only liberal on Match." I checked my watch. "God, he went on and on. I had one glass of wine. I need to wait fifteen more minutes to make it an hour before I can drive. I don't want to walk around the market in case he's stalking me."

"Fifteen minutes seems like adequate time to tell me every detail of tonight's date. Oh, and the house? How did that go?"

"They were both a bust. Poorly maintained, bad location, and, I'm no engineer, but I think that, over time, major structural damage would have been revealed in both."

"Why don't you just get a dog?"

"I know the right man is out there," I said.

"Just probably not in Nebraska," Ann said.

The next day, Horace sent me an email:

> *Hi, Quinn. Say, I never did learn your last name. Will you pass it along? Also, I'm attaching an article on Palestine that is completely unbiased because it's written by a South American. I think you'll find it very interesting.*

I didn't respond. The next day, he sent me another email. My anti-virus software quarantined this one. After that, I blocked his address through Hotmail.

So, Horace was off the list and Dave was next on my dating queue. We were meeting at the zoo. I already had a bad feeling about Dave. Mainly because the day before, he sent me this email:

> *Did you see the news today? Apparently a teacher has been arrested for possession of a compass, protractor, and straight edge. It is claimed he is a member of the Al Gebra movement bearing weapons of math instruction.*
>
> *I'm looking forward to meeting tomorrow. Remember, if you wear your smile, we're bound to have fun.*

I arrived at the zoo right on time. Well, I waited in my car until I was one minute late, because for once, I wanted the guy to be waiting for me. Dave was later, though, I realized, as I arrived at the entrance. I wasn't wearing my smile at the ten-minute mark. It was freezing outside. Families kept arriving and staring at me. They probably thought I was a child molester, hanging out alone at the zoo like that. The more I stood, the angrier I became. I planned a couple of zinging lines for when he arrived, like "Actually, I'll be leaving now."

I felt obligated to wait for 20 minutes. One of those things you learn in college. If the teacher is more than 20 minutes late, you can leave. As I watched happy families arrive, I thought, "What am I doing here?" I could feel my allergies kicking in. I didn't want to meet Dave. I just wanted to go home. I left at the 18 minute mark. As I was driving away, I saw a young man walking alone to the front of the zoo. It was probably Dave, but I didn't bother to stop. According to the clock in my car, he was 20 minutes late A weight lifted from my shoulders. My Saturday was mine again. I wouldn't be spending it making inane conversation with a stranger in a zoo. I was free.

As a reward for being stood up, I went to Target and bought myself some house slippers and chocolate. Then I went home and spent the rest of the day eating the chocolate, while reading a novel, in my slippers. Ahhh. It was the best stand-up of my life.

Footnote to Chapter 23:

Dave emailed me four days later:

Hey, did we mix up our times? I went to the zoo, but you weren't there. I was a bit late, and I saw a cute girl walking away, with long, black hair. Could that have been you? Should we try again?

I wrote back:

You were 20 minutes late. And you didn't bother to email about it for four days? In my book, that's just plain rude. I'll pass on trying a second time.

Dave:

Wow. You're awfully quick to judge. Can't you please give me a second chance?

Me:

Sorry, but no. One time of standing outside for 20 minutes, feeling like an idiot was enough. Plus, if you were late the first time you met me, I doubt you'll improve much. You never even apologized!

Dave:

Listen, I really am sorry. I feel like we have a connection and I'd really like another chance. I'm very, very sorry. Won't you please give me another chance? I've enjoyed our emails and I'd like to make it up to you. Please? Will you?

Dave's last response is important, because it touches on something I'll discuss in more detail in Chapter 56, The Games We Play. We only want what we can't have. He was inconsiderate and not even apologetic until I rejected him. Then suddenly, he was desperate to meet me.

Chapter 24
Just Because I'm Single,
Doesn't Mean I'm A Lesbian

In your late thirties, most friends your own age will be married. This is true of the majority of my college friends and everyone from high school. I've lived in five different cities in the past fifteen years, so I make new friends as I go. These friends are also usually married, which can make me something of an oddity.

I know people wonder about my sexual orientation. It's a common enough question. "Why's she single?" But what's also commonplace is a tendency of my girlfriends to imply to their husbands, family, or co-workers that, not only am I a lesbian, but they might be experimenting in this area too, with me.

Izzy did it the other day. She had to go to an office party and at that particular moment in time, every other person she worked with was dating, engaged, or married. She wanted me to come along with her.

"Uh, no."

"Why not? It'll be fun."

"How long have you known me? I hate things like that. Besides, it's weird to take a girlfriend to something like that."

"I think it would be cool. And they can just think you're my lover."

"Izzy, just because I'm single doesn't mean I'm a lesbian!"

So, not only do we single women not get sex, not get dates, and not get a fair membership rate at the Omaha zoo (which only offers a "family" rate), but now we are the pawns of dissatisfied married women and bored, freshly single best friends. Single women out there, how much burden do they expect us to carry on our backs?

I had an audiology conference in DC. I was giving a lecture on fitting hearing aids on infants. My hotel in Chinatown had seen better days. The convention center was a ten-minute walk, or one Metro stop away. On the first morning, I walked. I'll never forget it. I was crossing a street, when, on the right side, I passed a building with these lowercase letters on the outside: npr. *Holy Cow*, I thought. National Public Radio. My Mecca. My homeland. I almost tripped. Instead of going toward the convention center, I turned right and marched straight into NPR's lobby. Pictures of NPR announcers covered the wall. I approached the security guard, a friendly-looking man. "Hi, do you give tours?"

He nodded. "Eleven o'clock. Get here about ten to."

I went back to the convention center to check in, and then I high-tailed it back to NPR for my tour. There was a large crowd in the lobby already when a young woman came downstairs and said, "Hi. I'm your tour guide. We have an especially large group today, so we're going to split into two." She gestured to a man in his early 30s. "This is Dan. He's going to take the half on this side of the room."

Dan started us at the top of the building. "If anyone has any questions, just shout them out. I love questions."

A young boy, about ten years old, raised his hand. "What kind of noise cancellation system do your engineers use to reduce background noise from satellite phones?"

"I, uh, have no Godly idea," Dan said. "You know what? I'll try to flag down an engineer and ask. But, in the meantime," he cracked his neck, "Let me show you this room." We were led into a room with waves and ridges in the concrete walls. "This is studio 4B. It has won awards for its acoustics. We built it in, uh, uh." He shook his head. "Listen. I haven't given this tour in six years, so I can't remember any of the numbers. But let me tell you a funny story about what happened in this studio on election night."

As I listened to the story, I wondered what it would be like to live in a big city again. Dan was cute and funny. And his job! How fun would it be to hear him talk about his work? Would I have better luck meeting men in a big city? Probably not. My single friends in NYC had every bit as much difficulty meeting men as I did. And when I lived there, for seven years, from ages 18-25, with my breasts the perkiest they'd ever be, I almost didn't date a soul.

"Did you ever wonder why, on a trip, you can scroll through the radio dial and always know you're listening to NPR the moment you hear it?" Dan gestured to the microphones in the studio. "That's thanks to these microphones. They're $6000 each. NPR has used them since day one and the sound engineers here think they are the best." The ten-year-old boy was standing next to one of the mics. Dan eyed him. "Don't touch that," he deadpanned. I started to laugh. He looked over at me and smiled.

One flight down, I asked a question. "How much of Morning Edition is pre-recorded and how much is live?" I'd always wondered that.

"Normally, 80% of Morning Edition is recorded, but on a day like today it's live."

We, the tour group, looked at him blankly. "Maybe you guys haven't heard, since you're traveling. Jack James died this morning." There was a murmur in the crowd. You may remember the story of the Pastor who was on a hunger strike because gay marriage had been made legal in his state? Now, I'd followed the story. I'd seen him on television. But I'm not good with names. I thought that one of the NPR newscasters had died. I let out a giant gasp.

Dan eyed me again. A couple of nanoseconds later, I realized who James was. Great, I thought. Now he probably thinks I'm a right-winger. So much for looking appealing to the liberal NPR employee.

The tour culminated in watching Steve Inskeep give the last five minutes of the news. A cheer erupted from the office when the newscast ended. "That means they feel the live broadcast went well," Dan told us.

Downstairs in the lobby, people started to disperse. "So, uh, thanks again for coming, Everyone. And, uh..." Dan pointed his finger at the boy. "Hey. Stay in school."

That night, I went to a bookstore in Dupont Circle. There was a lively café in the back. It was fun to go to a bookstore that wasn't a big chain. I felt like I was back in New York City again, where independent bookstores abound. Actually, I was missing NYC a lot on this trip. Just walking down the busy streets, riding the Metro, and looking at all the different people made me so homesick that I almost wanted to cry.

What if that guy from NPR came in here tonight? I wondered, as I pulled books off the shelves and people bumped past me. What if he said, "Hey, you're the girl from the tour."

I could say, "Great tour."

And then I had nothing. Even in my fantasy, I couldn't come up with a damn thing to say. I'll tell you what Izzy would have done. She would have reached up and touched his lips. Then she would have said, "You had some fuzz, there." Then she would have said nothing, just stared at him without looking tense. Probably she would have brought him back to her hotel room.

Or maybe, that was my fantasy, after all. I couldn't see myself doing that, but if I could dream it, couldn't I do it?

Probably not.

Chapter 25
Persuasion - How to Drag Your Friends Online with You

1. ~~Horace, the ageist.~~
2. ~~Davey, the conservative.~~
3. Ryan, an architect who loved NY and the southwest.
4. Flash456, an entrepreneur from CA.
5. JustANiceGuy72 who loved desert camping.

Just three guys left. "Match sucks!" I told Izzy.

"You have to persevere," she said. She was at my desk. It was after five and my office was empty. We were going out to dinner. "Here," she said, reaching for a Post-it. "I'll write it down." She picked up a Sharpie, wrote, "PERSIST" and stuck it to my computer screen. "Now, tell me about the three you've got left."

"Well, Ryan's picture is really cute. He has longish hair and dark eyes. He seems quiet, but his emails are witty. He's another conservative, though."

"We're in Nebraska. It carried a larger percentage of the vote for Bush than Texas. You've got to expect to get people who don't share your political views. Does it really matter?"

"Yes. Would you want to date a conservative?"

"As I've told you before, I've dated many," Izzy said.

"I just can't imagine marrying someone whose beliefs are so different from mine."

Izzy shrugged. "I don't think politics should be the deciding factor, before you've even met them. Who are the others?"

"Flash is from California. I'm not sure about him. His real name is

Derek. He says he flies all over for work and could fly here. But he lives near Oakland and I'd hate to move there. Plus, he had a hard time uploading his picture. He kept whining about it, and calling tech support. He does do yoga, though. Now, Just A Nice Guy seems like my best bet. He desert camps."

"What kind of job does he have?"

"I don't remember," I said.

"How tall is he?"

"I forget."

"How much money does he make?"

"Jeez, Izzy. I don't know. Okay? I have no idea."

"But you know he's a liberal."

"Actually, he said 'middle of the road,' but I decided to give him a try anyway."

"Is that the only thing you notice?"

"I look at their picture."

We ended up getting take-out and eating it back at my place. I heard Walter's radio as we came up the stairs. I listened with one ear for the sound of him moving around inside the apartment and eventually heard him flush a toilet.

"How goes the dating front?" I asked.

"My goal," Izzy said, as she opened her pasta, "is to be in a serious relationship, on the verge of marriage, within a year."

"Okay. And who are your prospects?"

"There's a cute guy at the 7-eleven near me."

I said nothing. We could hear my neighbor's radio program. His cough.

"I just don't feel up to dealing with a profile," Izzy said.

I jumped up to get my computer. "I'll write the whole thing! You can edit. Just sit back and drink some wine."

Of course, once I got going, Izzy got involved. "You are ready for a committed relationship, if the right woman comes along. You don't do drugs. You ..."

"Here," she said, pushing me aside, "let me finish that. You're making me sound too harsh."

"You'll be sorry," I said as I backed off to let her in front of the computer. "It's better to be clear at the start about what you're looking for."

"I'm not jaded like you. Yet." I sat in an easy chair and sipped my wine.

"Let's go get dressed up tomorrow and take pictures for our profiles," Izzy said.

"Great idea!"

She sat back and said, "Well, what do you think?"

Username: HighAndMighty
Tagline: Laugh till it hurts!
I'm happiest when I'm surrounded by people who make me think, make me laugh. I'm more optimistic than pessimistic, more introverted than extroverted, more curious than ambitious. Favorite things include running by lakes, NPR in the morning (especially the puzzle master on Sundays!), down comforters, movie matinees, card games, and laughing to tears with good friends. I'm an avid reader and they see a lot of me at the public library. I read more fiction than non-fiction, but I am always open to suggestions. A quick perusal of my bookshelves will reveal a dictionary of slang, English novels, mystery series, and a biography of Humphrey Bogart. I am a vegetarian and have been for many years- don't be frightened, I won't force-feed you tofu. It just means I tend to prefer ethnic restaurants and love trying new foods.

I love men who think of fun and unusual things to do on dates. Can you soften a situation with humor? Do you enjoy cooking (or at least trying to)? Do you ever laugh until your stomach hurts? Can you play games with good sportsmanship? Do you love language and word play? Do conversations with you range from bee keeping to the best Internet provider? Do you ever spend all afternoon reading? Do you take care of your body and live a healthy lifestyle? Complete bonus points if you a) know, and b) enjoy old movies with Cary Grant and Jimmy Stewart. I guess it goes without saying that you are single, and sane!

Izzy hit the *Make my profile visible* button. "Let the games begin," she said.

We got some great pictures the next day. With our hair done and makeup on, we tramped around in front of the Durham Western

Heritage Museum, which is an old, restored train station. We also got some good shots near the river, and in Bemis Park, where the trees look like crotchety old men. I had an especially good one of me, where Izzy lay under me and snapped my face against the stark, tangled branches as they twisted into the sky. We uploaded the pictures to our respective profiles. We'd have to wait 48-72 hours before they would appear. Meanwhile, when I checked my mail, I had another email from Flash456, from California. He wanted to call me, or have me call him.

I think I have a phone phobia. I don't even like calling married girlfriends, in case their husbands pick up and I have to make three minutes of small talk. At work, I put off phone calls till the last minute. So I didn't want to call Derek.

"Come on, call him right now," Izzy said.

"It's too late," I said.

"It's 8 p.m. in California," she said. "If you put it off, you'll just get increasingly stressed about calling."

"Fine," I said, and without another thought, I picked up the phone and dialed. After three rings, he picked up.

"Hello?"

"Hi, uh, this is Quinn, from Match.com."

"Yes?" Unfriendly tone.

"I was just calling to say hi. Is this a bad time?"

"I'm on my way out the door. What do you want?"

I was indignant. How dare he? Do you ever feel pleasure in knowing that you are 100% justified in getting angry with someone? Like, the driver in front of you who tries to make an illegal left turn? I love honking at those cars. I was going to love getting angry with Derek. And then I was going to hang up and wash my hands of him.

I took on a slight Beavis and Butthead tone and said, "Well, uh, I was calling because you *asked* me to."

"I did?"

"Uh, yeah?"

"Oh, shit!" he said. "SHIT! You're Quinn! The painter! Shit. Hmmm. What an icebreaker! Hey, well, how the hell are you? Gosh, I'm sorry. When you said Match.com, I thought you were a telemarketer." He was so funny about it, and so instantly comfortable with me, that I had to start laughing over the whole thing.

"So, are you rude to telemarketers?" I asked.

"Always!" he said. "You sound exactly like I thought you would. Kind of sweet, hippie. Like you don't wear make-up."

"All that from my voice?" I asked.

"Yeah. You have makeup on in your picture, don't you? So maybe I'm way off base."

"No, you're not. That picture is from a wedding. It was the only one I already had on my computer. But generally, I look pretty granola-y."

We had a nice talk. While Izzy watched television, we covered politics, yoga, our favorite flavor of ice cream (him: butter pecan, me: chocolate.) He called again the following day, and we had another good talk in which we covered retirement funds, financial philosophies, and our favorite brand of ice cream (him: Ben and Jerry's, me: Häagen-Dazs). At the end of the second talk, Derek said, "I have about a million frequent flyer miles. I'd really like to meet you, to see if this will go anywhere. Can I come to Omaha?"

"Sure," I said.

"How about this weekend?" It was Thursday.

"I, ah, well," I panicked. My apartment was a mess. And I needed time to prepare mentally. "I have some commitments already this weekend," I said. Knitting, the Cake Boss marathon on TLC, and my library book was due back on Saturday.

"What about the following week?"

"Sure," I said. "That would work."

"Can you hold on a second? My other line is ringing." I busied myself in my kitchen sink, doing dishes while I waited. He came back on. "Sorry about that. It was a work call."

"At this hour?"

"India is waking up."

"Oh."

"Where were we? Oh yeah, can you give me some hotel recommendations?"

"There's a Super 8 right by the airport."

Silence for a moment, then, "I don't stay at Super 8s. What about a Hilton?"

"Sure. There's one in the Old Market."

"Is that a convenient location for you? Hold on, my other line again."

He was gone two minutes, by my microwave clock. When he came back this time, I said, "Is now a bad time? Perhaps we should talk another time when you aren't so busy."

"I'm always busy. Now is as good a time as any. But, if that hotel is convenient, I'll make my reservations now."

"Super."

"Can you hold again for a minute?"

"Actually, I think I'll just hang up," I told him. "We're finished, aren't we?"

"Sure. Okay. Goodbye, then."

"I felt really comfortable talking to him," I told Ann. "But I don't want to get my hopes up. If things don't work out, at least I'll be able to say he's a hotel snob."

Ann shook her head. "Protective mechanisms can end up sabotaging you. Just keep that in the back of your mind. How hard would it be to act without a safety net?"

We were at our café. The owner had just made Ann's coffee drink himself and personally delivered it to her. "I used a new vanilla flavor," he said. "You'll have to tell me how it tastes."

"I will," Ann said. From her face, I could see that she wasn't registering his infatuation. I wanted to say something to her about it, but I was afraid she'd freak out and reject the guy. He was working to win her over. I wondered if she would ever let go of her own safety net, but I kept my mouth shut.

When I'd left my apartment that morning to meet Ann for coffee before work, Walter's laundry was hanging in the basement. Like always, he'd done the laundry at 5 a.m.

When I got home from work that evening, the laundry was still hanging. I'd never seen that before. His car was in his garage. He wasn't inside. I walked upstairs and listened at his door. No radio. I knocked. "Walter?" I called. I knocked again. Well. Here it was. The moment I'd been waiting for. Either he was asleep, severely incapacitated, or dead, and I was going to have to do something. I just didn't know what. I would have called my landlady, but she was on vacation. I went downstairs and knocked on Buzz's door. I told him what was going on.

"And I'm not sure what to do," I finished.

"I'll tell you what we'll do," he said. "We'll call 911." He was propping himself up on his cane with one hand while he dialed his cordless phone with the other. He told them our neighbor was ill and possibly dying. When he hung up, he asked, "Is the door unlocked?" I hadn't tried the door.

He propelled himself toward the door. "Well, let's go check."

"What if he's in the bathroom, or asleep? I don't want to upset him by walking in."

"I could care less if we upset him," he said, pushing past me. "He's upset me!" For the little that they interacted, Buzz really cared about Walter's welfare. I followed him upstairs, but the door was locked. He pounded on the door and shouted, but Walter didn't answer.

The cops took 40 minutes to arrive. "He could be dying in there!" Buzz shouted at them as they appeared in our lobby. A man and a woman in uniform. "Where's the ambulance? Is it just the two of you? What took you so long?"

It turned out that these two didn't have the authority to kick down Walter's door. After getting the story from us, they called in for another person, who took fifteen minutes to arrive. When there were three police officers present, they sent Buzz and me downstairs. I guess they were trying to protect Walter's privacy. We sat in Buzz's living room, an exact replica of mine except for décor and listened to them kick down Walter's door. The deadbolt must not have been thrown, because they did it in two kicks.

Buzz called up to them, but they wouldn't answer our questions. After a while, a hearse pulled into our driveway. "What's this?" Buzz asked. "Oh. I guess we have our answers. But this is a hard way to tell us." He shook his head. Then he went to his front door and repeated those last two sentences, shouted them, upstairs to the police. A few minutes later, the male police officer came down and knocked on Buzz's door, which was open so that we could watch the hallway.

"Your neighbor was dead," he said. "Is the owner of this building in town?"

"She left on vacation this morning," Buzz told him. He turned to me. "She's going to feel terrible about this. I have her number but I hate to call her and ruin her trip."

"But Walter's door is open. We have to get the lock fixed," I said.

"The door can be shut," the officer said. "We didn't break the jamb."

"Oh."

"So he was dead when you found him, then?" Buzz asked.

"He'd been dead several hours. How did you know?"

"He hadn't taken his laundry up," I said. "He was sick, with cancer. I was listening for him." A stretcher with a gray, zipped body bag passed by Buzz's door. I couldn't believe that was Walter inside. "He had a niece, in Milwaukee."

"We know," said the policeman. "He left very detailed instructions."

"Yes," I said. "In his envelope."

I emailed the desert camper.

> *Dear JustANiceGuy,*
> *I've really enjoyed our emails back and forth. Do you want to meet some time, and talk in person?*

> *Dear Quinn,*
> *Sure, we can do that. But I should warn you, I'm in school right now and so I don't own a car. If you have a problem with that, I'd just as soon you say so, up front, instead of later.*

> *JustANiceGuy,*
> *I don't have a problem with that. I remember how grad school was. What are you studying?*

> *Quinn,*
> *I'm studying to be a nurse practitioner. And also, you should know that I live with my folks. So, just say now if that's a problem.*

> *Dear JustANiceGuy,*
> *Again, no problems here.*

Quinn,
I could meet you two weeks from Saturday, between 2 and 5.
But you should know that I don't have a lot of money to
spend on things.

Dear JustANiceGuy,
Sounds good. Say, are you sure you have your heart in this
dating thing?

He never responded. So we never met.

My neighbor's funeral happened at 10 a.m., on a Tuesday. I took off two hours from work to attend. The service was performed in a church not far from my apartment. I sat down next to Buzz and my landlady. An elderly couple sat in front of us. There was a middle-aged woman in a black suit by herself in the front row. There were six of us in the church.

When the service was over, Buzz, Agnes, and I drove separately to the cemetery. It was one of those indecisive days, when the weather shifts between overcast and sunny. Only four of us had continued on to the burial. The wind picked up and whipped our hair around our heads a little.

"I feel just sick that I was out of town when Walter passed," Agnes whispered to us. "Of all the times to take a vacation."

"You couldn't have known," I said.

She clucked her tongue. "Do you know that I never raised his rent? You'll just die when you hear this, but he was paying me $200 a month for that place."

"That was good of you," I said.

"Well, I felt I had to. He came with the building, you know." She pulled her coat around her tighter. The wind looked like it might blow her away. "I bought that building more than 30 years ago. He had already been there for ten, when I got it. He wouldn't let me do any changes. Those lime green walls are the same color they were when I bought the place."

"He didn't like any changes," Buzz said. "He did everything like clockwork. Grocery shopping every Wednesday morning at 7 a.m.

Left for church on Sundays at 8 a.m." He nodded at the casket they were bringing to the open grave. "You could set your clock to him."

"Will you get a new renter right away?" I asked.

"I'll need at least two months to redo the place. I have painters coming next week. The floors need to be refinished, the windows cleaned. His oven is forty years old. He wouldn't let me replace it. He did get a new refrigerator, about fifteen years ago, but it's not a self-defroster."

"It's going to be beautiful, when it's finished."

Agnes nodded.

"So, Walter never married?" I asked.

"Oh, no. A confirmed bachelor." The priest began to talk again. Then they lowered the coffin into the grave and we all went back to our lives.

"I was looking at my future," I told Izzy. "That's what my own funeral will be. A lonely, sad little crowd."

"God, such a drama queen. You know that you've got a million friends, plus your family. Now tell me who you've got onboard on Match."

"I'm meeting another one, Ryan the Architect, for a drink after work."

"What's he like?"

"I don't really know. He seems nice by email, but they *all* seem nice by email."

Ryan the Architect was waiting for me when I arrived at the martini bar. *Finally*, I thought, *a man who arrives first*. He was good-looking, in an artsy way. He had longish brown hair that that fell a couple of inches below his ears. His glasses were funky black frames. He was wearing khakis, a long-sleeved, navy blue, cotton shirt that that showed off his biceps, and flip-flops.

"Quinn?" He asked, as he stood with his hand outstretched. We shook.

"Hi. Have you been waiting long?"

"I just got here," he said.

We sat. He ordered a chocolate martini. I ordered a vodka martini straight-up.

"My ex always made fun of me for drinking flowery martinis," he apologized.

"Chocolate is never something to apologize for!" I said. "So, how long have you been an architect for?"

"About ten years."

"Do you like your job?"

"I love it. So tell me, Quinn Painter," he leaned back in his chair, "What do you do for fun?"

"Well, I read a lot. I like movies."

"I love movies. What's your favorite?"

I shrugged, but smiled. Finally, a guy who could converse instead of monologue me to death. This date was perking up. "I just rented Super-Size Me and High Fidelity."

"Have you read the book, High Fidelity?"

"Yeah," I said. "I did. In fact, I own it. Have you read it?"

"No. But my ex-girlfriend really loved it, too."

"Oh."

"So what else do you do in your free time?" he asked.

"I've been house-hunting, lately."

"For what kind of house?"

"Something old. I don't know what. It's hard to find one in my price range."

"I'm saving for a house," he said.

"Are you? I like living in an apartment," I told him. "But I think it's time to buy."

"Yeah. I used to live in an apartment."

"You don't anymore?"

"Nah. I live with my parents."

"Oh."

We sipped our martinis.

"I moved in with them when my ex and I broke up. She got the apartment, and I planned to live with them temporarily, until I found a new place."

"But?"

"But, hey," he gave me a bashful smile, "my mom is a great cook. She does my laundry. Plus, I'm saving so much money."

"They don't make you pay rent?"

"Are you kidding? They love having me there. They don't want me to leave." He laughed. "But I know what you're thinking. I'm 34 years old. I have to move out. I know. I do. It's just that I was pretty broken up after my ex and I broke up, and it was so nice to move back into that safe little world."

"How long ago did you guys break up?" I asked.

"It's been two years."

Check please. "I couldn't even imagine living with my parents," I said. "I haven't lived with them since college. Since sophomore year, actually, because I went to Europe in my junior summer."

"Where did you go in Europe?"

"Italy. I took classes in Venice."

"Really? My ex lived in Venice for a while."

"Gee, Ryan. Your ex-girlfriend sounds swell. I bet we'd make great friends. Maybe you should give me her number and I'll give her a call."

He missed my sarcasm. "You guys are kind of similar," he said, sizing me up. "You kind of look like her, actually." He laughed. "But if you're that much like my ex, you'd probably dump me."

I didn't know how to even respond.

"You're a lot nicer than she was," he said.

"I'm probably not."

He smiled at me. "I'll bet you are." He finished off his martini in a swig. "Where do you want to go next?"

I looked at my watch. "Do you mind if I'm blunt? You're cute and you seem nice. But stop talking about your ex. And don't compare a woman you are on a date with to your ex. Not in any way. At least, not out loud." I reached into my purse and pulled out a ten-dollar bill. I put it on the table. "And for goodness sakes. You're a grown man with a good job. Move out of your parents' house! Get a roommate, if you don't want to be alone. And learn to do your own laundry." I stood. "Now, I'm going to leave. I wish you the best of luck in your future dates."

Chapter 26
Valentine's Day

"I had a meltdown on my date last night." I told Izzy.

"Meltdown or breakthrough?" she asked. "You're just getting more efficient."

Maybe she was right. Ryan didn't look particularly distressed when I left. In fact, he'd nodded and said, "Good points." And he shook my hand before I left.

"I'm loving Match!" Izzy told me. "I've been out on three dates this week. I can't believe how good it feels. This was just what the doctor ordered. I bought a six-month subscription."

"You paid for six-months? You've had three dates in one week?" I asked.

"Yes. And even just the goodnight kisses have raised my self-confidence through the roof. I feel unstoppable. Match is the best thing I've done in years."

"You've kissed people? How many?"

"All three."

"You kissed all three men you met on Match?"

"Yes."

"And they were kissable? You wanted to kiss them?"

"They were all babes. The first guy, Joe, had a kind of country boy charm to him. He was sweet. He paid for dinner."

"You let a guy pay for dinner?"

"Why not? And as we were leaving, I figured, I'm going to kiss him. So I leaned in and gave him a small kiss on the lips. He was taken completely by surprise. It was fun."

"___"

"The second guy was a banker and he was a little straight-laced. But I think I'm just what he needs to loosen up a little. And he's a little short."

"How short?"

"It's not too bad. But he's just a couple of inches taller than me. It bothers me more than I'd like it to."

"Height? Who cares? Remember Max?" I asked.

Izzy rolled her eyes. "The name rings a bell."

Max was my...how do I say this without being trite? It's not possible. He was my first love. We dated ten months before breaking up. Even though I'm the one who did the breaking up, I took the three-year plan to get over him. Izzy surely reached a point where she was so sick of Max's name that she wanted to scream. But I almost never bring him up anymore. I probably haven't mentioned him more than five times a year for the past 3-4 years.

"When I first met him," I began, "I didn't think he was good-looking at all." Izzy had never met Max. I wasn't living in Omaha back then. "I fell for him because he was so funny and because he had so much integrity."

Izzy nodded. "I still don't understand why you two broke up."

"We were moving down different paths. We had completely different life goals. He wanted a wife. I wanted a partnership. But toward the end of our dating life, I remember sitting with him at El Patio. Remember that restaurant?"

"In the student ghetto?" Izzy had visited me enough times in Albuquerque to know my haunts.

"Yeah. And I suppose I knew that we weren't going to make it. And I remember thinking that if I could just keep looking at him forever, I would." I grimaced. "We broke up that same night. About some stupid fight. I can't even remember now."

"So, by the end, you thought he was handsome."

"No. Even then, while I was staring at him, I remember thinking 'All this pain he's causing and he's not even good-looking.' I loved his looks anyway."

"He sounds like he had a lot of charisma."

"He did. Charisma is deadly," I warned. I did a little internal survey. It was still painful to talk about Max. I moved on. "But some guys just make you click, you know? And no one has it all. So if it happens with the banker, if you fall for him, you won't care about his height anyway."

Izzy nodded. "And he's a great kisser. And, we're going out on Valentine's Day!"

"Valentine's Day? When is that?"

"Saturday."

"How do you manage all this? I haven't had a single kissable guy since I started Match. Except for Caleb, who just wanted sex."

"What about the guy from California?"

"Derek. He flies in next Saturday."

"You should kiss him."

"I don't know if he's kissable."

"He's cute. He's flying across the country to see you."

"I'll try. Okay. That will be my weekend goal. To kiss him."

"You won't regret it," Izzy said.

On Valentine's Day, I had Moo Shu Pork take out and listened to the Cowboy Junkies' Trinity Session cd until I felt completely desolate. Izzy called. "How are you doing?"

"Aren't you on your date?"

"Uh-oh. You don't sound good. Do I hear the Cowboy Junkies?"

I felt my eyes tear up. "I don't know why I do this to myself," I said. "It's just a stupid greeting card holiday."

"Yesterday, everyone at work was saying 'Happy Valentine's Day.' I told everyone, 'Happy Friday the 13th!'"

That made me smile, a little bit. "What about your date?"

"I'm dressing for it right now. So tell me, what are you going to do to make yourself feel better?"

"Eat a pint of Häagen-Dazs?"

"No. First, turn off the Cowboy Junkies. Second, watch a movie. Go rent something you haven't seen before but always wanted to."

"I'm kind of settled at home," I said. "I thought I'd stay in for the night."

"It's 6:30!" she snapped.

"I don't know how safe the roads are, what with all those happy couples driving around on dates."

"Listen to me," Izzy said. "You have a guy flying in from California next week, to see you! Now march yourself outside right now and rent something funny that will get you out of this state you've gotten yourself into."

"Okay."

"Promise?"

"Yes."

I rented Buffy the Vampire Slayer, the movie. It wasn't as good as the television series. Izzy was right, though. It did make me feel better.

The following Saturday, Derek was flying in to see me. I wanted to be calm and centered when I met him at the airport at noon. I went to yoga at 6 a.m. Upon my return, I made a nice strong cup of coffee and painted while listening to NPR. By ten I was feeling terrific. I had two hours to clean my kitchen and sweep. I wasn't sure if Derek would get to see my place, but I wanted to make a good impression if he did. At 10:05 my phone rang.

"Hello?"

"Hi, it's Derek."

"Hi Derek. Where are you?"

"I'm in Omaha. I took an earlier flight."

"You did?"

"Yes. I was at the airport, and they had a plane leaving for Omaha. I asked if they had room, they did, so I jumped on it."

"Okay. Great. Well, then let me come get you." There are a lot of people online who claim to want spontaneous women. No matter how cute they are, I always click right past.

Derek was a giant. Tall, with a gut. The added weight made him seem middle-aged, instead of his actual 38 years. He was cute, though. And nice. He hugged me when he spotted me. His sternum crushed my nose.

"Hi. How was your flight?" I asked.

"Great." He looked Greek, with a long nose and a darkish coloring around his eyes. His hair was a medium brown. He was nice-looking, but he didn't make my stomach flip. There are some men who make my insides flip-flop the moment I see them. What does it mean? True love? A message from my genetic coding that this is the ultimate father of my children? Random, meaningless attraction? I tend to think that I recognize them from a former life. Not that I necessarily believe in reincarnation, but, if I was going to pick my favorite afterlife option, that would be it.

"Do you have bag?" I had a crick in my neck just from making eye contact.

"Nope, I just did carry-on."

"Terrific."

After he had checked in to his hotel, I suggested we take a walk. There was a walking path through the city. Nothing special, but it was a nice day out. "Yeah, that'd be great," he said.

We drove to the path. I got mixed up on which road to take and asked him to pull my laminated Omaha map out of my glove box. He opened the glove box, which was filled to the brink with maps. "Am I going to get bit?" he asked, hand poised over the glove box. Then he straightened up the box for me.

On the path, we had different walking speeds. I'm a racer. He was a meanderer. "Look at this," he'd say. I'd backtrack and he'd be pointing to a flower, a waterhole, or a pile of stones.

"Tell me about your job." I said. "What does your company do?"

"We are hired by drug companies. Mostly herbal or homeopathic businesses. Once in a while, a pharmaceuticals company calls us. When the FCC tries to fine someone or close them down for making false claims, we find the research out there to support those claims."

"Hmmm," I said. I had Izzy on one shoulder, telling me to shut up and smile and kiss him. I had me on the other shoulder. Me won. "That's interesting," I began. "But it sounds a little unethical. Usually, in medicine, if you tell a patient that a drug works, you can back it up. For example, I can give you research to support my assertion that most people do better with two hearing aids than one. If I made that up to sell more hearing aids, and then searched for research to support my claim, that would be misleading the public. I would be lying to raise my profit margin, instead of helping people to hear better."

"Yeah," he said, and he had the decency to look ashamed. "That is probably the best way to do things. But this is working for me right now. I'm not saying I want to necessarily do it long term. Right now my goal is solvency."

We went to the Old Market for lunch. While we ate, I thought about what he'd said. I kept my voice and facial expression friendly when I asked him, "So why the rush for solvency? Are you in debt?"

"Not at all. But I've found that it is a lot easier to be a good person, and to treat people kindly, when you are rich. I want to help others."

"Except the others who buy herbal remedies."

He gave me smooth smile. "I want to live a good life, and the more money I have, the more people I'll help."

I considered going into the bathroom to phone Izzy, but just then the check appeared. We argued over who should pay.

"I insist," I said. "You FLEW here. You're paying for your hotel (I wasn't even going to offer to split the cost of the Hilton with him.) I think I can treat you to lunch."

"Dinner. Okay? You can treat me to dinner. I'm picking up lunch." He handed the waiter his credit card and shooed him away. Too late, I remembered to be gracious and thanked him.

As we left the restaurant, I began listing activities to fill the afternoon. He wanted to see Warren Buffett's house. Warren Buffett lived nearby, actually. In a nice but regular looking house. We sat outside, in the car. I wondered if security cameras were filming us. "Wow," Derek said. "The Oracle of Omaha." He shook his head in amazement.

"He's just a guy who got rich," I said. "It's not like he's changed the world in any meaningful way."

"He's a genius."

At making money. I couldn't see the draw. "Well?" I asked. "What's next on the agenda?"

"Actually, if you don't mind, I'd like to just go back to my hotel room. I'm a little tired and I'd like to rest."

I felt a little hurt, but who knew what time he'd gotten up to catch his flight? As we reached the front of the hotel, he turned and said, "I still want to have dinner with you."

"Of course," I told him, confused. "Where do you want to go for dinner?"

"What are my choices?"

"Italian, Indian, Persian, French…"

"French."

"Okay." The French restaurant was the most expensive place in Omaha. It had a three or four star rating. Oh well. I could handle it. "I'll pick you up at seven."

"Sounds great," he said.

I spent the afternoon re-reading The Beekeeper's Apprentice, by Laurie King, to remind myself that love doesn't always come in the package you're looking for.

Derek ordered a $60 bottle of wine. I had a sick feeling in my stomach about how much the bill was going to be. His entrée was $46. I went into damage control and ordered the cheapest entrée, which was still $24. "Yum, pasta," I said, to cover my stinginess. "My favorite."

He was fun to chat with, at least. We were talking about an article we'd both read in the New Yorker, a long time ago, about a woman who sold pianos. "It made me want to learn to play," he said. "So that I could someday hear those subtle differences between the various pianos."

"It made me want to quit my job and write," I said. "Imagine that journalist? A piano player himself, and he gets to have a series of interviews with this woman. And write it up. And someone actually buys it. And it's something he was already interested in, anyway."

"Whom would you interview, if you could?" he asked.

"Hmm. I always want to interview my favorite singers. Like, Tori Amos, and ask her things like, 'So, in this song, when you talk about Neil, is that your dog?'" I laughed. "I'd probably suck at interviews. Like that guy on Saturday Night Live, who would do interviews and say things like, 'You know that movie you did? That was so cool.'"

"Chris Farley. He was funny as hell."

I smiled. Derek had some wealth issues, but we did have conversational topics in common. "I remember that you do yoga. Maybe tomorrow we could go to my yoga class," I suggested.

"I'd love to," he said. "But I won't be able to, because I've moved my flight up and I'm flying out at 8:10 tomorrow morning."

"You are?" My first reaction: relief. A second later: hurt. Massive hurt. Crashing self-worth.

"Listen," he leaned forward and looked me in the eye. "This has nothing to do with you. I have really enjoyed meeting you. You are really wonderful and I am looking forward to many more phone conversations with you and the chance for you to come visit me in California. I'm just exhausted and I need to get home and get some rest. But I don't want you to think I'm leaving early for anything more than that."

"Okay," I said. I didn't believe him for a second.

So, this is over, I thought, watching him across the table. We were still eating and drinking together, but it wouldn't go past this evening. Or at least past 8 a.m. tomorrow. What a waste, to spend this much money on a dinner with someone I would never see again. It was funny how important it was for him to maintain the façade that we would continue to correspond. He told me about his family, about his friends and his hope that his future spouse (maybe me) would enjoy living in California with him. He had a really nice house, built in the 1960s. Well, the house wasn't anything special but the yard was big. He was waiting to decorate it. Waiting for The One, so that they could choose the color scheme together.

The waitress offered us dessert. The bill was already so high. What could two more ten-dollar desserts matter? I ordered the crème Brulee.

"What I want isn't on your menu," Derek began. "But I think you can make it for me anyway. I want a dish of vanilla ice cream, with chocolate sauce on top. I don't want any nuts. I don't want any whipped cream. I don't want a cherry. I just want a dish of plain vanilla ice cream, with chocolate sauce on top. Understand?"

I watched the waitress' face. She smiled and told him, "I'm sure we can give you that." A few minutes after she left, another waitress passed us with a tray of cherries jubilee.

"Oh my God. Our waitress didn't tell us they had cherries jubilee."

I confirmed that she had.

"Well I missed it. And that is my all-time favorite dessert."

Another waitress was walking by, laden with two trays of entrees. "Excuse me, miss, but you must find our waitress immediately!" The waitress turned, with her trays of hot food, and headed back into the kitchen. A minute later, our waitress appeared. "I'm sorry but I need to cancel my dessert order," Derek said. "I must have the cherries jubilee."

"The dish of ice cream is already made," she told him. That was my first inkling that she had disliked his behavior from before. And maybe all through dinner. He could be domineering, I'd noticed. Derek looked at me. "I'll have to pay for dinner," he said. "Because I am going to order two desserts."

As she left, I said, "You can tip, if you want. But dinner is on me."

He shrugged.

But when the check came, Derek pulled out his credit card and tried to pay for it all. I opened my purse. "Take mine," I told the waitress. "Dinner was supposed to be on me." She took his.

"This is crazy," I said, even though the crazy part was that I was even arguing with him about it. I should have just let him pay.

"This is my insurance policy," he told me. "This insures that you will come and visit me. You'll incur expenses when you come. But I do want you to come. So let me pay for this, knowing that you will pay for things when you're in California."

He was really going all the way with the charade. "Okay," I told him. Who was I to burst our pretend bubble?

The waitress returned, with the manager. "I'm sorry, Sir," she said, and she really did look upset. "But your card has been rejected."

"It was never activated," the manager explained to me. I guess she thought she was saving him some embarrassment. All I could think was, "So I have to pay?" I went for my purse, but Derek had already pulled out another card.

"Not a problem," he said, but his cool was obviously feigned. So maybe he was some kind of con-artist. He was definitely a fraud in the herbal medicine department.

Even though the Omaha airport doesn't require check-in more than an hour in advance, he insisted on arriving two hours early. At 6:10 a.m., I pulled up to passenger drop-off and popped the trunk. "Thanks for coming," I said.

He pulled his bag out of the trunk. "I had a wonderful time. I'll see you soon, in California." He gave me one last nose-crunching hug. "I'll call you," he said.

When has that line ever been true? No, Reader, he never did call. And no, I wasn't sorry.

Chapter 27
Buying a House
Will Get You a Marriage Proposal

Several married women I know firmly believe that buying a house gets you a marriage proposal. WARNING: This only works if you're *already dating someone*. I wasn't dating anyone when I finally bought my home, thus, no proposal.

A week before my 39th birthday, I went solo, without Flora, to some open houses. I had a list of four homes, ordered by preference. Flora's coaching was paying off. Even I could see that the first two were dumps. The third was on a major thoroughfare, with no place to park. I swung a right, behind the house, to see if there was an alley for parking, and that's when I realized the backyard of the house looked out over the interstate. A semi shook my window as it sped past. I was crisscrossing through the neighborhood, trying to get on a major street, when I came upon another house for sale. It turned out to be the last house on my list. There was a giant dumpster in the driveway. They'd obviously been doing some work inside. It was an Arts and Crafts style home, a simple four-corner design. The outside was freshly painted. Inside, the place was empty except for the realtor, but all I noticed was the turning oak staircase with the built-in bench at the bottom. "That's called a 'Deacon's seat,'" the realtor said as she followed my eyes.

"Is it?" I asked. "It's charming." I wandered through the downstairs. The realtor was good; she left me to explore the house alone. The layout was typical of old-style homes: the front door

opened to an entry hall, beyond which was the kitchen. To the right
was the living room, which opened up into the dining room. There
was a built-in pantry at the back, which connected the dining room to
the kitchen with swinging doors. Upstairs there were three bedrooms
and a bath. The basement was dry as a bone and it had been raining
almost non-stop for three days. The electricity was a circuit box.
Central air had just been installed in the past month. The furnace was
brand new. The roof was new. The water heater was five years old.

"The previous owner left at the age of 95," the realtor told me.
"She's in assisted-living. She was only the second owner. She lived
here 60 years." I nodded. "They've redone the kitchen and the
bathroom wiring," she added. The house was $12,500 below my
price limit. Back outside, I looked at the other houses on the block.
There was a giant mansion a couple of doors down on a huge plot of
land. The other houses were like mine or smaller. The neighborhood
wasn't too great, but also, not too bad.

I called my realtor. "I found a house. I want to make an offer." She
wasn't thrilled about the neighborhood. "It's fine," I told her.
"People have flower pots on their porches."

"You should go door to door and talk to the neighbors." So I did.
After work, I talked to three people, who all said it was a nice place
to live. I also called the police station, but they wouldn't give me
crime statistics for a particular neighborhood. I called the
neighborhood association and spoke to the president, who led me to
believe that my street was like a country club, compared to the rest
of the area the association covered.

"How much are you going to offer?" Lucy asked.

"I thought I'd offer them asking price, but ask them to pay half my
closing costs."

"Asking price? Why don't you go lower?"

"Well, I have this theory," I said. "I think it insults people when
you ask for lower. And besides, the house is very fairly priced. But,
if they pay half my closing costs, I'd have enough money to finish
the wood floors before I moved in."

They accepted my offer. Flora wanted me to use her home
inspector. "He could do the inspection tomorrow," she said.

"I'm going with the guy I used before. He's the only one I trust."

She shook her head. I wouldn't budge.

And I stayed guarded this time. I wasn't going to be disappointed
again. But I was smarter now, and I thought this house would pass

inspection.

I hadn't been able to get Marlena back for follow-up. She was the two-year-old whose mother had let the hearing loss go for a year before coming back. "I think I've just lost one of our loaner hearing aids," I told Lucy. "I fit that little two-year-old with it because I wanted her mother to see the difference. But their phone is disconnected and they haven't responded to my letters.

Lucy shrugged. "What can you do? Not fit someone because they look unreliable?"

"I just hate to lose a loaner." Our loaner program is mostly funded by donations.

A package arrived in the mail from my mother. One of the workers at Walter's apartment handed it to me when I came home. His apartment was looking fantastic. The floors were stunning. The walls were freshly painted. Forty years of Walter was gone in a week's time. He wouldn't recognize the place if he walked inside, I thought. In my own apartment, I opened a beer and sat down with my package. My 39th birthday was coming up. My mom always gives the greatest birthday gifts. This looked simple. It was a padded manila envelope. It felt like a book. It was a book. It was a book called *How To Find A Husband After 35*. I put the book down. I drank my beer. I stood. I called Izzy.

"Throw it away," she said.

"I should."

"I mean it. Just toss it without opening it."

"I can't believe she sent this, right before my 39th birthday."

"Speaking of which, how do you want to celebrate?"

"Sushi and martinis?"

"The woman's got a plan."

"Okay," I said, tucking the book under the sofa cushion. "Let me hear about you. Where are you at with the men?"

"Well, the banker, Josh, is kind of blowing the rest out of the water."

"Is he? Why?"

"He's just so cute and sweet in such a geeky way. He's teaching me chess. And this weekend, he's competing in a chess tournament. I'm going to go to cheer him on."

"Oh my God! I want to meet this guy."

"I want you to. I want your opinion on him. He just seems so amazing and calming. He's passionate about the most original things, like clock repair. And gardens. His garden is gorgeous. It could be in magazines."

"And the banking?"

"Banking sounds boring," she said, "but it's really quite fascinating."

"Are you falling for this guy?" I was incredulous.

"Maybe," she said.

"Izzy, he is your second Internet date."

"I know. I'm going to keep looking. But it's hard to find the time. We saw each other three times this week and we talk every day. And he's so sweet. He's already asked me how many kids I want and whether I think I'll be a stay-at-home mom."

"You paid for six months online. Can you just keep up email conversations with two other men? You don't have to date them, just email them."

"Why?"

I didn't want to tell her what I was thinking. That she needed a couple of other men in the reserves for when she and Josh crashed and burned. I didn't know if I was being cynical or if I was jealous of her for finding someone right away when I'd been on Match for so long. When I looked into my heart, I just felt afraid for her. She'd been terribly hurt by her ex-husband and now she was falling hard for a guy she barely knew.

"Now, a house like this is ideal," the home inspector told me, "because you've got the same person living in it for sixty years. With no children. Plus, she had a family that took care of her." I nodded. He hadn't remembered me, when I arrived for this second inspection.

"Remember? The house was a very flawed Tudor? The metal front porch could have electrocuted someone?"

"I see so many flawed homes, every day. I honestly can't keep them straight."

I couldn't believe it.

"Now this plumbing," he said, gesturing to the exposed basement ceilings, "was updated four years ago. The circuit box was put in two years ago." We walked upstairs. "About ten years ago, they punched holes in the walls and pumped insulation inside. The roof is spotless, except for a couple of dents that must have been made by ladders when they painted the outside of the house." We went into the bathroom. "Let me show you something." He turned on the shower and the sink faucets, and flushed the toilet. "Do you see how the water stream is continuous in the shower? You're not going to get reduced water pressure if someone else in the house runs water while you're in the shower." He shook his head. "Do you know how rare that is?"

"I got the house," I told Ann.

"Cheers," she said, holding up her mug of coffee, specially prepared by the owner.

"I might get a dog."

"Is the yard fenced in?"

"Not yet. But that will force me to take walks. And don't you think a dog is a good conversation starter?"

"How's the dating scene?"

"Dire. Ugly." I took a sip of coffee. "Very, very bad. But on the bright side, I'm about to turn 39!"

Ann laughed. She held up her mug. "To homeownership!"

"Here, here!"

Chapter 28
Thirty Days on the Mountain

I decided to go thirty days without complaining about being single. If I was sick of me whining, then others must be, too. So, absolutely no complaining, no jokes, no comments about eggs dive-bombing out of my body every month. If I met my goal, I was going to reward myself with one of the following:

1. A robotic vacuum cleaner
2. A watch from the J.Jill catalog
3. Composting worms to eat my kitchen scraps

Breaking the habit was harder than I thought. When people said, "How's it going?" I wanted to reply, "Fine, except that I'm pretty sure I'm going to end up an old maid, because I never meet any men." Instead, I'd just say, "Really well," and wonder why I wore my self-pity about singledom around like it was a trophy.

"Hi, Quinn? It's Debbie. Listen, uh, I'm going to have to cancel my appointment for this afternoon." My toothless, eyeless patient.

"Okay. Thanks for calling to let me know. Do you want to reschedule it?"

"Uh, yeah, but I'm not sure when. See, the thing is, I'm in jail right now and I don't know when I'll get out. My mom can't post the bail."

"You're in jail?"

"Yeah, and I'm supposed to go in front of the judge today, but I don't know if he'll let me out."

"What happened?"

"Well, I went after JJ again with a hammer, and knocked out some of his teeth. And I did a lot of damage to his car. I don't know what it is, Quinn. Sometimes I just lose it. He kept calling me a cow, and most days I don't even hear him, but that day it struck me hard. I don't know, Quinn, I just wanted to kill him."

I didn't know what to say. I hoped the jail didn't record their phone calls.

"So I thought I'd better call you and let you know I won't be there. I didn't really have the gas to get there, anyway, if it wasn't for this jail thing, I mean."

How many people would go through the hassle of canceling their hearing aid appointment from jail? She was 37-years-old. I couldn't believe how hard her life was, and how much longer she had of this crappy life to live.

Chapter 29
Men Who Don't Read Your Profile

I was starting to realize that many of the men who emailed me on Match.com were not reading my profile. I first discovered what men were doing when I decided not to consider conservatives anymore, no matter how funny they were. The easy way to do this would be to search for men by their politics. When I first started on Match, you could search by eye color, hair color, body type, salary, turn-ons and turn-offs (tattoos, dancing, public displays of affection, etc.), but you could not search by politics.

So every search I made required a painstaking process of looking up each person's political stance individually. I'd written that I wanted liberal in my profile, so I thought it would be faster to just go through the men I had (89 in my inbox), instead of seeking out new ones. It took me four days to do it, but after going through every emailer's profile, I had 7 that marked themselves as liberal. Four of those were from different states. The other three were over my age limit by seven to fifteen years.

Instead, I emailed men who called their politics "Middle of the Road." One negative of Match is that they give you pre-written categories that imply personality you may not have. For instance, on the question of smoking, you can't say "no." The only negative option is "No way!" For politics, when I first began, you could choose Ultra-conservative, Conservative, Middle of the Road, Liberal, Anarchist." To me, Middle of the Road means, "I don't care," or "I don't keep up with political events." But I didn't know what it meant to anyone else. I had 53 Middle-of-the-Roaders. I emailed five, and asked them their thoughts on gay marriage. All five were either opposed to gays getting married or refused to answer my question.

So I decided to rewrite my profile. Izzy had written the last line of my profile. It said, "If you're not any of this but you think I should still know you, write me anyway." I liked the idea that I might not even know what I was looking for and that I'd miss the right guy if I were too restrictive. But I didn't want to waste my time going through so many emails to find a liberal. So my new profile ended like this:

"If you're not any of this but you think I should still know you, write me anyway. FOOTNOTE: If you are conservative, please do not email me. We won't get along."

I waited a week, but that footnote seemed to have no impact on the number of conservatives who emailed me. A couple of peopled did write to tell me I was close-minded, but everyone else acted like they hadn't even read it.

And politics weren't the only thing that was clogging my inbox. Men with inappropriate age ranges wasted my time, too. So one night, I rewrote my footnote.

FOOTNOTES: 1. Please don't email me if you are conservative. 2. If you are in my age range and willing to date an 18-year-old girl, OR if you are seeking women 10 years younger than you but not any older, or only a couple of years older, don't email me—you won't be able to hold up your end of a conversation with me.

My new, rude footnote had absolutely no impact on the politics or age ranges of the men who continued to email me. Nine out of ten were still conservative. I got one liberal about every forty emails. And the liberals, well, they were not a stellar bunch.

Emails from Nebraskan liberals:

> *USERNAME: HOTBOD*
> *TAGLINE: Hurry, I'm not getting any younger!*
>
> *Your gorgeous, marry me, just joking. im 35 no kids/3 cats. email me soon.*

USERNAME: LOOKING653
TAGLINE: Let's see if I can rope the moon for you.

Hi Quinn: First I must compliment you on the best personal I have ever read. Your words speak such import that I had forgotten I searched for them. If you would, indulge me for yet a few more moments as I want to pose a question: Does your painting ever speak of a reflection of life deliberately, or is it just a picture that sometimes reveals something beyond the surface of your conceptual self?

USERNAME: XMANRULES
TAGLINE: Love all things and God is at the top of the list.

Quinn, I could also love you.

USERNAME: GreatGuy201
TAGLINE: Everyone says I'm a great guy.

You have very beautiful eyes. And two other things, I don't have a mustache anymore and I need to update my photo since I lost 55 pounds in the last 4 months.

USERNAME: TryMe696
TAGLINE: My friends made me do this!

Hi, your smile simply leaped off the screen to me…Oh my! So, was Santa good to you…No fruitcake I hope. Why don't you give me a try?

"That must be why women put pictures of themselves with their kids in their profiles," I told Izzy one day. We were hanging out at my place, doing a marathon of Kirsten Dunst movies. *Crazy/Beautiful* was on. "Because they know that no one reads the profiles and they only want men who can deal with kids."

"Probably," Izzy said. "So? Any good prospects lately?"

I wanted to say, *There's no one out there for me!* But that would have been complaining about being single and I was 14 days from getting that robotic vacuum cleaner.

"There are too many emails to sort through."

"Let's go through them right now," Izzy said. "We'll clear them out tonight." Her optimism just made me feel even more depressed. But then I realized I was letting something like an internet dating site make me feel hopeless.

"You know what?" I said, sitting up from the sofa. "I'm going to rewrite my profile. I'm going to find a way, in the first line, the one you can see in your search results, to stop those photo-cruisers from contacting me."

I fired-up my laptop. We tried to keep watching Crazy/Beautiful, but we couldn't pay attention, so Izzy ended up turning it off.

I wrote, "If you are not liberal, don't email me."

"Say 'please don't email me,'" Izzy suggested.

"I want to be forceful," I told her.

"You can be forceful but still nice."

"If you are not liberal, please don't email me. If your dating range is two years older than you and fifteen years younger…don't email me." Izzy opened her mouth and I said, "I am not being polite to the men who only date younger women."

Izzy shrugged and sat back in her chair. "Do what you have to do." She is so supportive!

The re-write took a lot less time than writing the original profile. When I finished, I felt immense satisfaction. It was direct, but also funny. "It's time to clear away all the noise," I said to Izzy.

USERNAME: QuinnPainter
TAGLINE: My Therapist Says I'm A Real Catch.
"Don't worship me until I've earned it"–Shirley Mcclaine, Terms of Endearment. You know, I used to laugh at all the bitter profiles I read on this site. Now, I completely understand where they're coming from. I'll save you some time and be blunt, okay? There is no point in your reading on unless you are 1. liberal (And I mean it–not "I'm an open-minded conservative, blah, blah, blah." If the word conservative is any part of your self-description, please, don't try to convince me otherwise, just click on to the next profile) 2. I'm 39. If you want to date me, you can't also be willing to date 18-year-olds. Really. We'll have nothing to talk about. I want a man who can meet me at my intellectual level and I can't do that with a man who could

also accompany his girlfriend to see the Jonas Brothers in concert.
3. If you only date women your age or younger, move on. Ok, now
that the undesirables aren't reading any more, I've got 900 words to
show you that I'm actually temperate, kind, and compassionate. If
you're new to this, you may think my comments are extreme. But, if
you're a seasoned veteran like I am, you know that you must be
explicit or you'll wind up sorting through 75 emails a week from
people you would never, ever be able bring to your ex-hippie
parents. I'm an artist, from NY, with a deep love of the desert and
mountains. I also have a Masters in an unrelated field that supports
my painting habit. I am an introvert but I can fake extroversion when
I need to. I care about living a healthy lifestyle. I like being around
people but I need time to myself. I read a lot. I watch a lot of PBS
and I'm addicted to teenage drama series. If I won the lottery, I'd
quit my job and go camping for a year.

I love men who are compassionate, funny, healthy, sane, well-read,
happy, active, dog-lovers, environmentalists. Are you ready for a
committed relationship if you meet the right person? Are you part of
a strong circle of friends who think you're awesome? Can you go off
on your own, or out with your friends, without me having to always
come along and are you unthreatened by my strong ties to friends
and my need for having time to myself? Are you a good
conversationalist? Do you like to camp? Hike? Travel? Read away
your entire Saturday? Do you like good food? Are you smart about
money but understand that money doesn't make you happy? If you
think we might be a match, write me an email with essays on your
opinions re: 1. stem cell research, 2. gay marriage, 3. drilling in the
artic wildlife refuge, (1500 words or more), and I'll get back to you.
(Just joking. We can wait till we meet in person to discuss those
issues. Again, joking.)

The essay component was Izzy's idea. I loved it. I reset my hit
counter, so I could monitor how many people opened my profile.
With my new profile awaiting approval, I was ready to turn my
attention to Izzy's personal life. "So, how go the men?"
   "The banker is fabulous. I think he's the one."
   "Slow down, Nellie. You've known him three weeks."
   "I know, but he's already told me he loves me."
   "What!" I sat forward. "Are you serious? Oh, no." I slumped back

in my seat. "Too bad."

"Why is it too bad?" she asked.

"Because it's too soon to be…" I eyed her glow. "Have you slept with him?

"No, not yet. But it's been hard not to."

"He's moving so fast."

"Is that bad?" Izzy asked.

"It makes him seem kind of desperate."

She shrugged and nodded, as if to say, *I hear you, but I'm not sure I agree*. "I think that, at a certain age, you just know."

I agreed with her about that.

"And he had already been in a six month relationship with another Match woman, who I gather was a little crazy."

"When did they break-up?" I asked.

"A month ago."

"A week before he meets you and he's already told you he loves you!"

"I know it seems fast, but when you know, you know."

"Izzy, I have serious concerns about this guy. I want to meet him and I want you to continue to correspond with other men."

"I definitely want you to meet him."

"Izzy, I'm worried."

She clucked me on the chin. "Your concern is really cute. Why can't you convey THAT in your profile instead of sounding like such a witch?"

Chapter 30
Common Lines in Male Profiles

One of the good guys.

I'm new to this.

I don't like the bar scene.

I'm generous to a fault.

I am very loyal and honest.

I just got out of a long-term relationship.

I know about new beginnings.

I'm your Prince Charming.

I have a large heart and a lot to offer someone.

I work hard and I play hard.

I know how to treat a lady.

I love holding hands and moonlit walks.

I love to spoil women.

You must be trustworthy.

You should enjoy dressing up for a night on the town but feel equally comfortable in old jeans and a t-shirt.

I love cuddling at home with a movie and a bottle of wine.

You should be good-looking and fit.

I don't have an "ideal" woman in mind, but you should be honest and good-looking.

Man seeks lying slut.

I'm joking on the last one, of course.

Chapter 31
Men Who Say They Want Honesty but Are
Actually Frightened of the Truth

Day 1 of new profile. 203 hits. Two emails. That was fine. It meant that, of 203 people who read me, 201 decided we weren't a match, hopefully because of my explicit comments. I clicked open the first email. It was a 41-year-old man who lived in the Dominican Republic. I was invited to travel there, as his guest. I opened his profile to read his stats. His age range was 18-35. While I was looking at his profile, I got an instant messaging thing from Match saying that he was online right now and wanted to chat with me. I declined, deleted, and opened the second email.

> *Username: Ready_To_Try*
> *Tagline: Single Again and It's Rather Daunting.*

His email subject line said, "Just ask MY therapist."

> *"Well, I'm back in the dating scene, after 11 years. I'm ready to jump in, but I'm kind of new at this. Your profile intrigues me. You have a thorny attractiveness that piques my interest. Your comments about the desert remind me of a writer I know. In the secret desire that you'll actually know of whom I speak, I'll only drop the title of one of his books...Desert Solitaire."*

I didn't appreciate his little "test" of my literacy. Why not just say Edward Abbey? I had read *Desert Solitaire* and it didn't blow me away. And "thorny attractiveness?" Was that supposed to be a compliment?

Day two—407 hits. Four emails.

> *Did you say* blunt*? Man, do NOT mess with Edgy QuinnPainter. (33, Middle of the Road. Dating range: 18-34 year-olds)*

> *I just broke off my gay relationship with an 18-year-old. We were picketing an oil field up in the Arctic Circle. And now I'm nuts about you!!! (30. Conservative. Dating range 18-30)*

> *I live in California, but I grew up in Omaha, and had to check the match scene back in the heartland. You make me want to come home. I really, really like your profile and truly find you interesting and sexy. (38. Liberal. Dating range: 28-42)*

> *Somebody has been getting lots of responses from knuckle draggers. Sheesh! Well, I must say, I was intrigued by your profile. You say what you mean—I like that! (35. Liberal. Dating range 25-40)*

Day three—513 hits. Two emails

> *It's a shame you're looking for a liberal person because you and I would get along great if you weren't so closed-minded. Remember this: smile and the world smiles with you… frown and you'll frown alone!" (28. Conservative. Dating range: 18-38)*

Hi. Well you have a lot of requirements, and I don't even know if you are bothering to read this, but I'll try to respond:

1. I don't know much about stems cells but I am opposed to cloning so I am probably not a supporter of stem cells if that is what they are about.

2. I have a lot of friends who are gay. (No, I'm not gay myself). I don't know if you are even reading this, but I hope you are because I am putting a lot of work into it. I am not a bigot. I support equal rights for gays. Just not the word "marriage." That word is a sacred bond between a man and a woman. They can use whatever "bond" they want for themselves, but they can't have ours. My gay friend agrees. ARE YOU EVEN READING THIS???

3. About the artic wildlife refuge. How can you be so stupid as to think that some animals in Alaska are more important than our freedom from Middle Eastern oil???? Have you forgotten about 9-11???Why won't you date a conservative??? (Not that I am one. I'm kind of in the middle.) Do you just want someone who only agrees with you?

I've edited that letter down a lot. It ran about two pages. His age range was 18-34. He was 34. I wrote him back:

I did read all of your email and I disagree with all of your opinions. Good luck in your future ventures.

His reply:

A bit cold, but blunt. So you just want someone who parrots you... I've seen you on Match.com for a long time. Do you know why? (rhetorical question–no need to answer back)

"Why do you write these people back?" Izzy asked at breakfast on Day 4 of my new, smarmy profile. I'd filled her in on the emails from the provoked men.

"Because I must," I said.

"Well at least you get mail," she said. "I only get winks, and it appears to be because they are too cheap to join and so they cannot email me. They include little riddles like 'All of America can see me online at the same username,' or 'on the mail that is hot.' I mean, please. Cough up a few bucks."

I was careful not to react to the fact that she was back on Match. "I never even look at winks," I told her.

"All my winks are from 40-year-old men in Ohio." She took a sip of coffee. "One guy has a picture of his penis up."

"What! That's impossible. They screen the photos."

"It was murky, but that's what I think it was." She shook her head.

"I'm sorry I got you into this," I told her. "It really sucks."

"Are you nuts?" she asked. "It's fun because, unlike you, I'm open to dating anyone as long as he's taller than 5' 10", makes more than $28,000, and is under the age of 48. See, for gals like us, the sky's the limit. We aren't obsessed with dating range and politics. So tell me about the two guys who liked your profile."

"I emailed them both back, and neither one has responded. Yet."

"Right. It's only been a day or two."

"Exactly," I said. "Some people don't check their email every day, like we do."

"The selfish bastards," Izzy said.

Chapter 32
You've Got (angry) Mail

My new profile was starting to gather more responses.

QuinnPainter,

What do you mean about stem cell research? Are you referring to abortion?

QP,

Is "conservative" code for some kind of religious thing? Do you have something against Christianity? You radicals are trying to single-handedly break the back of this great country. If you had your way, we'd open the borders and give our country away to the terrorist. Why don't you just leave, if you hate it so much here?

QuinnP,

So I guess you'd rather see our troops die in the Middle East than drill? People like you are stupid. We'll be overrun by terrorist, but the wakihaki butterfly will be alive. I hope you and the butterfly will be happy. And I guess you'd never deem me worthy to date. Which is too bad because I would probably make you really happy. But you'll never know, because you're an idiot.

Quinn,

It's true that I only date younger women. But I have a good reason why. Women who are my age want to fast forward into marriage. I want to take my time in a relationship, and get to know someone before I start a family. I can't do that with someone who's 36.

Quinn,

Gee, I own a home in Santa Fe, in the mountains. I think you'd like to come see it, some day, but I only date younger women. Are you still so sure you want to exclude me from your list of potential dates? I only date younger women because I look very young myself. Also, I have nothing in common with women my age. So that's why. I'd still like to take you out sometime, and show you a fun night. You obviously need it.

Chapter 33
What You Can't Get From Emails - Chemistry

I took a page from Izzy's book and tried another search without marking "liberal." But I got over 200 matches–too many to sort through. I went back to liberal and I had three. Two were men I'd already corresponded with. I emailed the third, who was in the technical/engineering field, earned $60,000/year, and was six foot one. I was getting so inured to interaction with strange men that, instead of regurgitating my normal spiel, I whipped off a new email and sent it off without a second thought:

> *Hi. You sound neat. I'm not an engineer, but I do appreciate bridges and other engineering feats. I enjoyed reading your profile. You're a good writer. You seem thoughtful, intelligent, and genuine. Also, you're really good-looking! My challenge to you is to read my profile. It's got a "thorny attractiveness," I'm told. I've gotten so tired of meeting people I'm not a match for that I've now included an essay component. I dare you!!!*

Jonathan and his mom returned for a follow-up. I'd fit him with hearing aids about two weeks earlier. His mom had cried again, but only for a minute.

"How are things going?" I asked.

"Great," his mom said.

"Are you wearing your hearing aids?" I asked him, turning my head for a better look at his ears. His mom opened her purse.

"I don't make him wear them in the car," she said as she pulled his aids out. I examined the aids before putting them in Jonathan's ear. The molds were pristine. Not a speck of earwax on them.

"About how many hours a day are you wearing these?" I asked him. I had a friendly smile on my face. "I weigh tem moey all tay," he said. His mom nodded a confirmation.

"What?" I asked.

"He wears them mostly all day," his mom said.

"Is that, what, three to four hours a day?" I asked, still smiling and nodding.

He shrugged. Kids his age have no real sense of time. His mom said, "About that. Maybe a little less."

My heart was breaking for this little boy and his mom. His speech was unclear and delayed. He needed hearing aids to help him with his speech. But his mom didn't see the relationship between the two things. By the time she did, the window to language learning could be mostly closed. "Could he start wearing them at dinnertime and story time?" I asked.

"There's not time at dinner," she said. "Our lives are too hectic. And by the end of the night, I'm just too tired to fuss with them for story time." At least she was honest.

I spent a few minutes talking about the benefits of hearing aids, especially in terms of learning language. She nodded, and then said, "He hears us, when we talk."

"He hears parts of what you say. But you can tell by his speech that he's not hearing everything." Jonathan had what you might call "mushy" speech. He left out a lot of consonants, because he couldn't hear them. He was intelligible if I knew the context, but when he said things out of the blue, I couldn't understand him.

"I understand everything he says," his mom said.

"How about strangers?" I asked.

"Yep. Everyone understands him."

I didn't know how to turn this mom around. Something about my approach wasn't getting through to her. So I was failing them both. You could blame the mom, but I felt that the real fault rested with me. A different kind of approach might have made her understand. My way was definitely not working.

There's something that's often in the room with you, when you are fitting children. No one talks about it. It's a big, invisible monster called Denial. Kind of like Big Bird's Snuffleupagus. Parents can't see the monster. It's as if it's chained to their ankle but they don't even know they are dragging it around. They do their best. I do my best. Sometimes, the kids do okay anyway. I hoped Jonathan was one of those kids.

"You did your best," my supervisor, Marta, said when I told her the story.

"Then why wouldn't she listen to me?" I asked.

"Someday, when you have kids of your own, you might have a different perspective," she said.

So now my childless state was impacting my job. "Great," I said. "And I'm getting older by the minute, with no men in sight." Duf! And there went my robotic vacuum cleaner. I'd been just five days shy of it, too.

The engineer wrote me back:
> *Damn! How did I miss you? I LOVE your profile. That's right, just tell it like it is. I'm hooked. When can we meet?*

We set up a time to meet. I was moving that week, so we scheduled it for the next week, on a Wednesday. Maybe things were going my way. I'd taken a risk with my profile and I'd been rewarded. I was getting less mail, I was meeting men who knew what I was like and were still interested. I was moving to a house. My house!

I met Izzy's boyfriend, if you could call a guy who'd just broken up with someone else and told a new woman he loved her two weeks after meeting her, a boyfriend. Izzy brought Josh to my "moving party." I have that in quotes, because you can hardly call asking people to come to your house to help you move a party. I did have beer and planned to order pizza. But still.

I'd spent four days packing everything up. My apartment was a city of cardboard boxes. I'd also bought a used washer, dryer, and refrigerator, all of which had to be loaded.

Helping me were Izzy, Lucy and her husband, Ernie, Ann, and Ann's brother, Alfred. No, Ann's brother is not an option. He had a girlfriend; a soldier stationed in Afghanistan. How's that for role reversal? And Izzy's boyfriend, Josh, made six. Josh had good people skills, I had to give him credit for that. He immediately bonded with the men, although, that's not a big challenge. Men make it easy to bond, because they require only an initial handshake and then a simple grunt pattern for the rest of the evening. Now, women want to know how often you do your highlights, where you bought your shoes, an itemization of ex-loves, and what workouts you like at the gym. Very tricky stuff.

I kept my eye on Josh. He didn't shrink from the work, which I liked. He had some good ideas about taking off my back door to get the washer down to the basement. He'd even planned ahead by bringing his tool case in his trunk.

"Well?" Izzy asked, when we found ourselves momentarily alone in the back of the truck.

"He's hard working and nice. I like him. He looks at you with real affection, too," I told her. She walked away with a big, smug grin on her face. And no, Reader, the sight of him nuzzling her didn't make me sick with envy.

Besides, I was living something of my own kind of high life. I owned a home! I sat in the living room on Saturday and just watched the sun creep across my pine floors. Everything was stunningly quiet. True, I was surrounded by boxes, but who cared about that? And I had a date with an engineer. Owning a home gives you a whole new kind of confidence in dating. Now, when I walked into the martini bar in mid-town to meet the engineer, I wasn't just Quinn, accomplished painter with good job. I was Quinn the homeowner. Quinn of the good-credit score. Quinn the independent women who takes care of her own future.

Dan the engineer of unknown real estate holdings was tall and blond, with friendly eyes and a strong handshake. I liked him immediately.

"Your voice is much softer than I expected," he said.

"You were expecting a yeller, after my profile?"

"Well, sort of." He smiled. "I guess I was expecting a New York accent. Kind of grating. But you were so cute in your picture that I thought I'd be able to get past it."

I felt my cheeks turn red.

"And here you are in person. Just as cute, but with a sweet, melodious voice."

"You're laying it on kind of thick," I finally said, with a smile. "I liked you the moment you walked in the door, so you can relax a little."

"Ah, there's the blunt edge I've been waiting for," he said. But he was smiling.

Reader? I was feeling very pleased about this guy, Dan. And I was starting to realize something. It wasn't what he said that made me like him. It was something else. Something you can't judge online or by email. It was his aura. Or it was chemistry. Or I recognized him from a previous life. Whatever it was, if I replayed our conversation, you would think, "So what's special about him?" Because you weren't there to feel the chemistry. We had a drink and it was time to go. He squeezed my hand as we parted on the sidewalk outside. "I'm glad you emailed me, Quinn Painter."

I smiled. "Me, too." We had plans to go out again that Friday night.

At work, my jailbird patient, Debbie was back. Her left hearing aid was completely crushed. It looked like she'd driven a car over it.

"What happened?" I asked.

"It fell out of my ear."

"And?"

"I don't know."

Properly inserted hearing aids don't just fall out of someone's ear. You could safely turn cartwheels with a hearing aid on. But I wasn't going to have that conversation. "You're still within the warranty," I said. "The company will replace it, but just this one time."

"Good, because I just can't hear without them."

This was true. I put the crushed aid into a box and filled out a loss/damage claim form for the hearing aid manufacturer.

On Friday, I got a phone message from Dan the Engineer. "Hey, Quinn. It's Dan. I'm sorry for the short notice, but I have to cancel tonight. Something has come up. A family matter. I'll be in touch."

I sent him a note, telling him that I hope all was well and that I was keeping him and his family in my thoughts.

On Saturday, I got an email.

Dear Quinn,

I don't really know how to begin, except to say that I really enjoyed the time we spent together, last week. I didn't mention before, that I'd been engaged, a while back, and broken off the engagement after a lot of soul searching. Anyway, on Thursday I ran into my ex-fiancé. Actually, Friday was our original wedding date before we called it off. (I said "I" before but the decision was mutual.) In any case, we got to talking and both realized that there are still deep feelings there. After an intense night, we have decided to try again. I feel bad telling you this by email. I would have liked to have told you in person but I thought that I could explain myself better this way. I really think that you are truly a very special person and I wish you all the luck in the world in finding someone you can honestly and truly love, like I have.
Dan

I wrote back: "I'm happy for you, Dan. Good luck." And I moved forward. As Izzy says, fall seven times, stand up eight. There was already another email in my inbox.

WildNKrazy

Hey, Quinn. I'm a long-time fan. Meaning that I've seen your profile for at least six months. Then, last night, I logged on and look! A new, gnarly profile! Fantastic! Boy, I've bet you've got some stories. Where was your picture taken? Is that water in the background? Greece?

I should have started with this line: I'm liberal. My parents are also hippies.

Oliver

His picture was cute. He had blond hair that was long and in dread locks. Did you see A Knights Tale? The first few scenes, when Heath Ledger still has long hair? That's what he looked like. And a beard. His eyes looked kind. The only problem was that he lived in Colorado. Ouray. But I still wrote him back.

Oliver,

*Thanks for the email. That water shot is the good ol'
Missouri River, as it passes through Omaha. What's it like to
live in Ouray? I've been there, and it's gorgeous. But I'd
think that the smallness of the town could be hard to take
year-round. Are you from there? What do you do?*

Quinn

Quinn,

*Great to hear from you! I love Ouray, but I'm originally
from Denver. I wanted to see how I liked rural life, so I
bought an old building just off the main strip, and I'm slowly
restoring it. I work as a photographer, so the first thing I did
was set up a darkroom and post a sign out front. This is an
incredible place for an artist to live. Yes, the town is small,
especially when you contrast it with the vastness of the
surrounding country. I'm not sure I completely like it. But
it's a great experiment.*

Oliver

He'd attached a photograph. A shot of the town of Ouray, the main
strip, at dawn, with a light frost over everything. Streams of sunlight
were traveling, almost horizontally, across the picture, lighting up
the ridges of a frost that covered everything. It was a meditative,
calming picture. I remembered the time I'd been to Ouray. It was
with Max, that ex of mine, many years before. We'd been camping
high in the mountains and we'd driven into town to get more coffee.
I studied the photograph. Ouray looked exactly the same, except it
was white.

"So tell me more about this new guy," Lucy said.
"His name is Oliver." I tried to suppress my grin. "He sends me his
photographs." I showed her the latest, of a dirty little boy and a dirty
dog, sitting together on a curbside, near an old Ford truck. "He's so
cute, in an earthy, alluring way." I pulled up his profile on Match.

"He looks unclean," Lucy said.

"That's not dirty, it's hippie."

"Yuck. Would you really want to touch his hair?"

"I love his hair!" I said. "It's sexy. It says so much about his personality."

Lucy spun back around in her chair. "Each to his own, I guess."

I looked at Oliver's picture. He had one of those smiles that just looks genuine. He was wearing a green linen shirt with his sleeves rolled up. The picture was taken in the woods and the sun was behind him, lighting up the outside of his head like a gold halo. "He's beautiful," I said.

"Just remember," Lucy said, "you're choosing the father of your children."

"His name is Oliver," I told Ann. "He sends me pictures of old women knitting."

Ann nodded encouragingly.

"I can't seem to stop smiling."

Ann laughed.

"The only real negative is that he lives in Colorado."

"Hmmm. Not the worst thing in the world."

"That's what I think. I would love to live in Colorado."

"Except that the house you just bought is in Nebraska."

"Yeah. I'm not too worried about that. If it came to moving for love, who cares about losing some money on a house? Maybe I could even rent it out."

"So you're moving for love now?"

"No! See? Don't let me do that!"

"Do what?"

"Jump ahead like that with plans. Every guy looks good on email. It's only after I meet them that their flaws come out." I shook my head. "Or ex-fiancés reappear."

"Okay, I won't let you make mental plans for your future with Oliver."

"I just love that name, Oliver. It's so sweet, but virile."

Ann turned to the counter. "Jackson? Can you get another coffee for my smitten friend here? But better make it decaf."

When Jackson arrived with my coffee, he said, "So, you've been bit by the smit bug, eh?"

"Apparently so," I said.

"Look at her glow," Ann told him.

"What about you guys?" I asked. "Have you never been bit?"

Jackson blushed. Ann blew her nose, loudly, before saying, "Nope. I think I'm immune. Five percent of the population is immune to every other disease."

"So, love is a disease?" I asked her.

"No, but infatuation is a sickness," she said.

I looked up at Jackson. I almost didn't, but in the end I couldn't stop myself. "What about you, Jackson? Smitten lately?"

He smiled at me. His blush was gone. "Nope. I'm in complete agreement with Ann. Who has time for that kind of business?"

Ann smiled at him. "See, Quinn? It's a rare finding, but today you are outnumbered by rational people."

"I guess I am," I said, eyeing Jackson.

Chapter 34
Mothers Are Always Right

"I like Josh," I told Izzy. "But can't you slow things down a little?" We were at my house.

"Why?"

"I'm afraid he's saying he loves you because he's got some other agenda. You are awesome. You are amazing. Who wouldn't fall in love with you, once he got to know you? But, he doesn't know you!" My home was a mad maze of half unpacked boxes, so we were drinking beer on my new front porch.

"He's so much fun, though. We took a class on clock repair. I like how he introduces me to new things. Doesn't that count for a lot?"

"It does."

"We run every morning. Then we eat a healthy breakfast. He has improved my quality of life," she paused. "How do you know when someone is the right one for you?" Izzy asked.

"Don't you just know?" I asked.

"What if I just know, now?"

I shook my head. "It doesn't feel right."

She laughed. "Why not?"

I stood. "Because he only knows your good points, right now. And you his." I paused and looked through my living room window. My bookcase was half loaded. "Hold on."

I returned with a book and more beer. "Let's find out what a Harvard Business School graduate says."

Izzy looked at the book I was holding. "I thought you threw that thing out!"

"I can't throw away a book," I said, and I sat down and opened

Find A Husband After 35, by Rachel Greenwald, M.B.A. This author, whom you may have seen on Oprah, was using her Harvard degree to sell her 18-month plan to finding a husband. On the inside cover, my mother had written, "Sweetheart, We love you single, but you also seem like you would like to meet someone. I've read most of this book and I think she has some good ideas. Love, Mom."

I found the Table of Contents. Step 15 looked promising. "Ah-ha!" I said. "Phase One, Keep Your Options Open." I looked up. "Have you had sex yet?"

"Not yet, but it's getting hard to say no."

"She says," I was skimming the pages, "You must have two dates a week for at least two months before having sex."

"Let's see," Izzy said, adding up in the air. "We are just at that point. We've been dating almost two months and we're seeing each other twice a week and talking daily."

Basically, Rachel Greenwald recommended making a list of the two or three things most important in a man. "She says to wait till you're in this stage to make the list, because a list you might have made a year ago could be completely different from the list you'll make when you've met a man you're serious about."

"That's a good insight," Izzy commented. "I guess my list would be, good with children, good with money, comfortable with public displays of affection."

"Okay. Does Josh win?"

"I haven't seen him with kids. He talks about his nephews a lot, though. He is good with money. And he's comfortable with public displays of affection."

"That's all good."

"What does she say next?"

"To put him in situations that will test him. Like, have him baby-sit with you. Or ask him for a loan."

"Hmmm." Izzy was thinking. I kept reading.

"Phase Three is called 'Don't Throw Good Money After Bad.' She says, 'Smart daters have the discipline to end the relationship and move on…you have to do it quickly and emphatically. It's an amputation, not a taffy pull…you don't give it one more try. You don't suggest therapy. You don't answer his calls.' Hmmm," I said. "Rachel Greenwald makes a solid point."

Izzy laughed. "You know, your mom may have had a good idea

after all."

"She really might."

One of the things I dislike about my job is the paperwork. It probably takes me as long to write most of my reports as it does to actually see the patient. It's not the body of the report that takes so much time. It's hunting down the addresses of the doctors, schools, and state organizations that the reports go to. It's filling out the billing sheet that itemizes all the testing I've done, and doing the paperwork to bill Medicaid for hearing aids. In the middle of one of these tedious tasks, I got an email from Oliver.

> *Hey! I was just sitting around re-reading your profile, and I see that you've traveled quite a bit in Europe. I've never been there, but I did live in Alaska for a summer. I lived with an Inuit family and they accepted me as one of their own.*
>
> *Say, do you think I could call you sometime, so we could talk? Or, if you'd rather, you can call me. I'll put my number below. I'm imagining your voice as soft and kind of feminine, but with a steely will just below the surface. I'd like to find out how close I am to the truth. Call anytime.*

I called Oliver that night, when I got home from work. He picked up on the second ring.

"Heeeellloooo? Is this Quinn calling?"

"Hi, Oliver. Yes, it's Quinn."

"Quinn! Nice to hear your voice. How are you, out there in Omaha?"

It felt awkward for a while. He sounded nervous. His voice cracked a few times. But he was warm and friendly. I started to loosen up after the first ten minutes or so. We ended up chatting for an hour.

"How does it feel to have a dream job?" I asked.

"Dream job? Is that because I work in the arts?"

"Yeah."

"Well, to be honest, it has pros and cons. Since my art pays my bills, I don't always show the integrity that I thought I'd have, when I was an 18-year-old student in art school."

"I took some photography, in school," I said.

"I took some painting. In fact, I paint on the side, just for fun. I'm told that my pieces are pretty good. I'll email you some."

"Okay, I'll email you some of my paintings, too." I said.

"Great. Now, let's talk about your day job. Are you passionate about it?"

Am I? I wondered. "I'm passionate about hearing loss. I didn't realize till I got into the field how hard life is when you can't hear. But interacting all day with patients can be stressful and heartbreaking, at times. I don't know if I have it in me to make this my lifelong career."

"I've always thought how terrible it would be to not be able to hear music," he said. "But if I had to choose, I'd rather be deaf than blind."

"I don't know if I would."

"Come on! You're a painter!"

"Being deaf is a lot worse than just not hearing music," I said. "If you are born with enough hearing loss, it can make learning a language very hard. Even as an adult, hearing loss prevents you from easily communicating with people around you."

"Yeah, but there's sign language," he said.

"Yes, but the reality is that most families don't learn it. Or they learn to speak at a very low level. You want a child to experience the richness of language, but most families who go with sign probably know less than 1000 words. A normal hearing high school senior knows about 60,000 words. Of course, the exception is deaf parents of deaf children. Many of them are native signers, so they sign fluently and teach their children the same."

"But then, when the kid goes to McDonalds, how does he order a hamburger?"

"It's restrictive," I agreed. "But a very beautiful, poetic language."

"Do you sign?" he asked.

"No. I've taken classes in it, but like any language, you need a lot more than two courses to be able to have a conversation that goes beyond 'Hello, my name is Quinn.'" I paused. "Do you speak any languages?"

"Just Japanese."

"*Just* Japanese? How did you learn that?"

"I lived in Japan for two years, in high school."

"Really? How come?"

"Er, my parents were…missionaries."

Ding, ding, ding! Fire on the deck! "Oh?"

"Pentacostalists."

I REPEAT, FIRE ON THE DECK. FIRE ON THE DECK!! ABANDON SHIP! ABANDON SHIP! "Didn't you list yourself as spiritual but not religious on Match?"

"Yes. I've been opposed to their belief system since I was about eight years old. By the time I was in high school, I was an out and out rebel. For example, I stole short-sleeved shirts from the Gap and wore them when I was at school."

I laughed.

"Yeah, I was pretty wild. They basically moved to Japan because they thought American culture was bad for me."

"Are you an only child?"

"I have a sister who's just like them. She's in South America right now, trading food for people's acceptance of Jesus in their lives."

"How did you like Japan?"

"I loved it. There's a lot of subversion in that country, if you scratch below the surface. I have a lot of good friends from there, still. Although my Japanese is rusty, people tell me that I have almost no accent. A limited vocabulary," he chuckled, "maybe 1000 words, I don't know. But no accent. How about with sign? I guess you can't really have an accent in sign?"

"You can have what's called lazy sign, where your hand movements aren't crisp. And there's something called a "wooden face." Sign language relies heavily on facial expressions to convey meaning. A lot of hearing people talk with a 'wooden face' because English doesn't require as much facial expression." I paused. "So, are you in touch with your parents?"

"We have a kind of truce. It's hard, because they honestly fear for my soul. I cause them a lot of grief."

"That would be difficult."

"It might be, except that it's been that way for so long. For almost as long as I can remember, I've disapproved of them, so I hardly know what it's like to have any other relationship."

"That's tough."

"Nah. I have so many other friends who fill in the gaps. I've really got a full happy life."

Chapter 35
Getting a Dog Will
Stop Your Biological Clock

Problem: Single girl is afraid to sleep alone in her new house. Solution: Get a dog. Problem: Single girl spends many evenings home alone, feeling lonely. Solution: Get a dog. Problem: Shy, single girl needs conversation starter with men. Solution: Get a dog.

Reader, I got a dog! And now I'm seriously questioning my ability to be a good mother, which could mean that there's no point in even bothering with men. I used to toy with the idea of having kids on my own. Now I see that not only could I not do it alone, I'm not sure I could do it with a husband.

After nearly a month, my house was only halfway unpacked. It was exhausting work to decide where everything should go. Also, I was sleeping downstairs, under the window with the broken latch. I wasn't comfortable alone in the house. Actually, I was downright scared. In my second floor apartment, someone would have to bust down the front door to come inside. In my house, there were eight ground-level windows and three doors. The house was full of unfamiliar noises and I woke to all of them.

That doesn't mean I didn't love my house. I marveled at the woodwork, the turn of the staircase, the history of the place. I relished the silence. There was no coughing or television noise unless I was coughing or watching TV. After work, I sometimes came home and just sat in the living room, reveling in the space. I wandered through all the rooms, amazed that the entire house was mine!

But I was tired all the time. I interacted with patients forty hours a week and then came home to boxes and lifting and decision-making about where things should go. I couldn't help but think that, if I were married, I'd have someone to help me. And to protect me. Or at least, make me feel safe. My painting class thought that getting a dog would make me feel safe. I tried to imagine how it would feel to share this house with another living creature; to come home to a wagging tail at the door. To sweep up dog hair and clean up poop. Also, could I swing it financially?

I'd been toying with the idea of getting a dog for months. I always expected to have a dog. My family has dogs. My friends have dogs. Absolutely everyone who had a dog advised me to do it.

So I went to the Nebraska Humane Society. About 15 million dogs a year are put to death. I saved one. In the room with the kennels, there were thirty dogs and the attendant told me there were more in back, waiting for openings in the front kennels. Ann came along to help me decide. They had every breed imaginable. There were eight-year-old dogs and puppies. I wouldn't even let myself look at the puppies. I was getting an adult dog and I didn't want to be swayed by cute little puppy dogs.

"Well?" Ann asked. "Who do you like?"

"I want a three-year-old," I said. I didn't want to have to deal with chewing and rowdy behavior or toilet training. "And my first choice is a Dalmatian." I'd grown up with a Beagle, but that was too small. In college, my parents got a Yellow Labrador, but I wanted to strike out on my own.

"Dalmatians have a lot of energy," Ann said. "They require a ton of exercise."

"Is that right?"

There was only one Dalmatian up for adoption. He had a big spot right between his eyes that made him look angry. We watched him for a few minutes. Like the other dogs, he was stressed and jumpy. Every time someone opened the door to the viewing room, the Dalmatian and all the dogs went nuts, barking and howling.

"Well? What do you think?" Ann asked.

"Uh, I don't know if I'm up for a dog who needs a lot of exercise." In the cage next to the Dalmatian was a white dog. The sign said he was a 2 ½ year-old Shepherd mix.

"That's a Shepherd?" I asked.

"Looks like a Yellow Lab to me," Ann said. His name was Onyx. The door to the viewing room opened again. In the din of a room of barking dogs, the Shepherd never took his eyes off us. He didn't bark. He just wagged his tail, calm and friendly.

"He's the one," I told Ann.

Before I could take my dog home, I had to meet with him and a facilitator. Onyx was friendly, considering the circumstances. I answered the facilitator's questions, like whether my yard was fenced (no) and would I be willing and able to walk the dog every day (yes).

"Have you thought about an older dog?" the facilitator asked. "We have a wonderful, seven-year-old lab that is well trained. His owner died and his family couldn't take him."

So I can get him, fall in love with him, and watch him die on me? No thanks. "I'm really looking for a younger dog," I said.

She didn't look convinced.

"Is this dog really a Shepherd?" I asked her. "He looks like a Yellow Lab."

"He's a White German Shepherd," she said.

"I didn't know such a breed existed," I said.

"This dog was surrendered to us without any information. We fixed him."

"And he's a White German Shepherd? Even though his hair is short, like a Labrador's?"

"Yes," she said. "The Nazis tried to eradicate them from the population because they thought they were an impure part of the Shepherd breed."

"Really?" I asked.

"To this day, the American Kennel Club doesn't acknowledge them as a legitimate breed."

I went home with the White German Shepherd. Screw you, Nazis. And AKC.

He cost me $112. I guess I had thought a dog from the pound would be free. Maybe the cost prevented frivolous adoptions. He was 78 lbs. In the parking lot, Ann and I tried to get him to look when we said "Onyx." He didn't acknowledge us.

"He hasn't been here that long," Ann said. "I'll bet he never even noticed that they'd renamed him."

"I wonder what his old name was," I said. I tried to go through the

alphabet, but he didn't perk up to any particular sound. Ann had
driven in a separate car. "Goodbye, for now," she told him. He
wagged his tail. I put him in the backseat, opened the window two
inches, and started home. I thought about names for him. It was hard
to come up with a name.

"Well, Dog. You don't know where we're going yet, but I'm going
to show you your new home." He looked at me in the rear view
mirror like he was trying to decipher my language. Halfway home,
he tried to climb into the front seat. I blocked him with my forearm.
A mile later, he tried again, this time much faster, with virtually no
warning movements. One minute, he was sitting in the backseat, the
next he was halfway into the front. "No!" I told him. "NO!" I
couldn't push him back. He was locked in like he'd grown out of the
front seat. I pulled into the parking lot of an attorney's office. There
was one car in front of the small, free-standing building. *The lawyer,
working late*, I thought.

I tried to push the dog into the backseat, but he was un-moveable. I
got out of the car and dragged him out with me. I opened the
backdoor of the car and tried to force him into the back seat. He
fought me, digging his nails into the asphalt, so I had to practically
lift him up and push him into place. He immediately jumped into the
front seat. I could imagine the attorney, working late, watching me
out the window of his office.

"No means no!" I yelled at the dog. It wouldn't be the last time I
said that to him. I grabbed him by the $10 collar I'd just bought from
the Society's gift shop and dragged him back outside. We did it three
times before he stayed in the backseat.

A mile from home, he was back in the front seat again. I pulled
over again and dragged him out the driver's side door and into the
back seat. This time, we only did it once, and he stayed in the
backseat until I pulled into my driveway. "Well, this is your
homecoming," I told him. "Which you've kind of ruined by making
me mad at you." I took a deep breath. "Okay. Welcome home."

I walked him around my yard and up and down my street, but he
didn't seem to have to go. I brought him up onto the front porch.

"Would you like to see your new home?" I asked him. I opened the
front door and let him loose. He ran through the house, sniffing and
getting his bearings. Then he crouched and peed on my living room
floor. His bladder was horse-sized. I couldn't believe how much
came out. "No! No! Bad dog!" I tried to drag him outside, but he

couldn't stop urinating and it seemed easier to let him go in one place. "Bad dog!" I said, as he peed. When he was done, I left him to get paper towels and soap. I came back to find a neat pile of poop in the middle of my $300 living room rug. He'd done a number one and a number two in the first five minutes of being in his new house.

Sunlight was streaming through the west-facing windows at the front of the house, but Dog didn't seem to notice. While I cleaned up the rug and floor, he went tearing around, sniffing and trying to put everything in his mouth.

We went on another walk, and I fed him (bag of dog food $22). Then, I followed him around, taking things out of his mouth. He couldn't settle down, so finally I locked us in the bedroom to keep him contained. This would be my first night sleeping in my bed, since I'd moved. I laid a blanket on the ground for him and climbed into my bed with a book. He wasn't interested in the Kong toy I'd bought, for $12. He wanted to pick up socks, shoes, and books. He circled the room like a wolf, whining the whole time. "Try to relax," I told him. "Go to sleep."

I got about four hours of sleep. In the morning, after a bathroom walk and food, I dog proofed my bathroom, by removing absolutely everything and looping the shower curtain around the rod and out of reach. I opened the window halfway. Enough for air, but not enough for him to squeeze through if he got it in his head to jump.

Reader, was I glad to go to work! It was a relief to get away from him. But at my desk, I found that I couldn't stop worrying about him. Was he lonely? Had he destroyed the bathroom? Ripped the toilet out of the floor? Had he managed to jump out the window anyway? Was he barking non-stop? I went home at lunch. The house was silent. Was he dead? Had he managed to somehow electrocute himself? I opened the bathroom door. Dog was sitting, watching me. The picture of self-control. He *had* scratched a hole in the screen, so my fears weren't completely unfounded. The toilet plunger was chewed to bits. The Kong toy was exactly where I'd left it.

I took him outside on a leash and he immediately peed, buckets. "Good boy," I praised. "Good, good boy!" He seemed fine until I tried to put him back in the bathroom. He didn't want to go back inside. He shrieked like I was murdering him. I'd never heard a dog make a sound like that. I forced him in and left. I could hear him howling from outside as I fumbled with my keys to open my car.

"So, how's your dog?" Lucy asked.
"He's active," I said.
"Will they give you your money back if you return him?"
I looked at my computer screen. "I don't know."

When I came home after work, I could hear him from the driveway, howling and whining. Had he cried all afternoon? It was hard to say. In an attempt to wear him out, we went on an hour-long walk. Dog was terrible on the leash. He made a game of cutting in front of me as I walked, like he was intentionally trying to trip me.

After our walk, we drove to a pet store to purchase a dog run for the backyard. Izzy came over to meet Dog and help me string the run from my back porch to a telephone pole at the end of my property. We put Dog back in the bathroom while we hung the run.

"What are you going to name him?"
"Pacey, I think."
"Why's he howling?"
I rubbed my eyes. "He doesn't like being locked in the bathroom. But I can't let him out unsupervised. He eats everything. And he peed and pooped again in the house." I paused. "After I walked him for fifteen minutes. He pooped on the white carpet in my bedroom."

Izzy shook her head.

"First, he peed, again, on my living room carpet. And then he snuck off to poop." I tried to take the high-pitched squeal out of my voice. "He was sitting, watching me clean up his urine. When he went upstairs, I was right behind him, but he pooped it all out in seconds. I couldn't stop him."

"You wouldn't have that problem with cats," Izzy said.

Starting that night, I began removing every object he picked up, and replacing it with his Kong toy. We were in No-Chew Boot Camp. By 10 p.m. I was so tired my eyes hurt, so we went to bed. But at 2 a.m., Pacey was at my bed, tail thumping against my nightstand. I opened my eyes and he had my iron in his mouth! I could only imagine the damage a dropped iron would do to my hard wood floors. I removed the iron and stuck his Kong toy in his mouth. I heard it bounce to the ground as I put the iron on a shelf in my closet. "Go to sleep!" I said, patting the blanket. Pacey stood next to the bedroom door and fired three sharp barks at me. Did he have to go to the bathroom? I got my shoes on, and took him downstairs.

Outside, he did nothing but sniff. Then he sat down next to me and barked three more times. We went back upstairs. I locked us in the bedroom and climbed into bed.

Pacey sat by the door and whined under his breath. "Shut up!" I yelled, but he apparently didn't understand English.

In the morning, I called my mom. "How are you, Honey?"

"Good," I told her. "In fact, I have some great news." Then I started sobbing. "I got a dog," I sputtered out in gasps. I tried to take some deep breaths. "Sorry, I'm just sleep-deprived." I breathed again, then started bawling so hard that snot came out of my nose. "He's awful. He won't let me sleep and he runs around here like a maniac."

I think the last time I cried like this to her was when I was 19. I had a waitressing job in Brooklyn. The owner and chef, an Italian guy, screamed at the waitresses all night. When I'd started crying that time, my mom had said, "Honey, why don't you quit?"

"I'm not going to quit!" I'd said. "I'm not a quitter."

And my mom had said, "Sometimes it takes more courage to quit something than to stay with it." So this time, I was expecting her to say, "Honey, it's okay for you to return that dog to the Humane Society." But instead, she said, "Listen, you are upset right now, but give yourself a week and you are going to love this dog. What's his name?"

"Pacey," I sobbed.

"You...saved...Pacey's...life!" she said. "And he is going to love you so much. And you are going to love him so much."

"I don't even like him!"

"Write down all the feelings you're having about him right now," she said. "I promise you that in the next week, you will read what you wrote and you won't feel it anymore. Hold on." I could hear her shouting to my stepfather. "Quinn got a dog. He's a maniac." They had a private, muffled conversation that I couldn't hear.

My stepfather got on the phone. "Quinn, do you have a cage for him?"

"No. I've been locking him in the bathroom."

"We're sending you a check. I'll put it in the mail today. Go out and buy a cage. Put the dog in the cage at night so that you can get some sleep. Once you do that, you'll be fine." A few hours later, my sister called and gave me a pep talk, too. Then my brother. Mi familia. They are dog people.

On the morning of our first visit to the veterinarian, Pacey and I had probably gotten four hours of sleep. The vet waiting room was very small. Next to me sat a woman with a cat in a cat carrier. I was worried that Pacey would make a sudden break and attack, but he just sat with his ears cocked and studied the cat, as if he'd never seen anything like it in his life.

The vets in the area don't charge for the first office visit when you adopt a dog from the pound. I would only have to pay for his shots. When the vet came in, she said, "Hi, I'm Dr. Jones. Who have we got here?" She was a middle-aged woman with sandy hair. There were pictures of Labradors in frames on the wall.

"This is Pacey."

She got down on the ground to pet him and he rolled over. "He likes his belly scratched. Good boy." She turned to me. "How are things going?"

Again, I burst into tears. I couldn't believe it. How embarrassing. "He's just a little wilder than I thought he'd be," I said as I tried to get a grip. I could guess what she was thinking. *Wimp.* "I'm just kind of sleep-deprived. He kept me up all night."

She nodded. "You need to get yourself into an obedience class, pronto. Now, tell him to sit."

I made my voice firm. "Pacey, sit."

"Sharper and deeper," the vet said, "like this. SIT!" She sounded so scary that I jumped backward and Pacey sat.

"Just be firm with him," she said. "And get yourself into a class. If you don't, you won't be able to keep him and he'll wind up right back in the Humane Society."

The vet technician appeared, with instruments for a shot. The doctor took the needle and filled it, while the tech held Pacey down.

"Aren't you going to muzzle him?" I asked. "I don't know him well enough to judge what he'll do."

The tech shook her head.

The vet said, "You just know, with some dogs."

They gave Pacey a shot. He didn't even yelp. His ears went back as the shot went in. That was the only way you'd guess it hurt.

I paid at the front desk while Pacey pulled at his leash.

"Sixty-nine dollars," the front desk person said.

"Sixty-nine? I thought you waived the office visit."

"We did. That was for the shots and the heartworm."

On the way home from the vet, I stopped at a pet store and bought a cage. $120.00. That afternoon, I signed up for a training class at the community college. $80.00. The first class didn't begin for three weeks. It was six weeks long. Two hours a week. Two hours of my Saturday gone to obedience training. It seemed unfair. I couldn't help but think that if I had a husband we could alternate. Are you sick of me whining about not having a husband with whom to share life's duties? I'm sick of me too.

"I used to have a White German Shepherd when I was a kid," Oliver from Colorado said, on our next phone call. I'd had Pacey for a week now. He was leaps and bounds better than the first night, but still a trial.

"I'd never even heard of that breed before," I told him. He knew about the Nazi thing.

"And it goes on today," he said. "The German Kennel Club refuses to recognize them as a competitive breed. And the American Kennel Club has followed suit."

"I heard that."

"Yeah. You and Pacey would be barred from competing."

I looked down at Pacey, who was sitting a few feet away, watching me. When he saw me look, he stood up and barked at me. I turned my back to him and he rammed me with his head.

"He'd be barred anyway," I said. "He's nuts. He's just standing here, barking at me."

"Does he have to go out?"

"He just came in," I said. But I stood up and took Pacey to the back door and hooked him to the dog run. He stood on the back porch and continued to bark. Who knew why? "He's really active," I told Oliver. "I walk him every day, for thirty minutes to an hour, and he still runs all over the house and scratches my hardwood floors with his nails."

"He sounds like a puppy still."

"He's supposed to be 2 ½."

"Hmmm."

"I specifically got an older dog so I didn't have to work so hard."

"When I was a kid, I trained my dog to walk with me, off-leash. I'm really good around animals. They listen to me," Oliver said.

"Can I hold the phone up and have you talk to Pacey?" I joked. I paused. "Say, did you get the paintings I emailed you?" I'd sent him pictures of two of my latest works. Whenever he sent me his photos, I always sent him a note back immediately, talking about the piece and praising him. I'd sent him my two paintings five days ago and he still hadn't even acknowledged them.

"Yes. They were great. Thanks for mailing them."

"You're welcome…"

"You know, you are always welcome to call me."

"Okay, thanks."

"I mean, you know, you can call me anytime. You don't have to set it up in advance, like you've been doing."

"Okay. I just do that so I don't interrupt you, or wake you."

"Quinn, you are welcome to wake me. And you won't interrupt me from anything that I'd rather be doing than talking to you. What I'm trying to say is, some woman won't answer my phone if you call unexpectedly."

"Oh. Okay." After hanging up, I wondered what he'd meant by that comment. Was he saying he wouldn't date other people while we worked out our relationship? Or was he just talking nonsense?

My father was coming for a visit. We'd been planning it since I bought the house. He was going to do work on the house. I'd made a list of things I needed done, like change ceiling lights, add ceiling fan, fix doorbell.

By the time he arrived, I'd had Pacey for two weeks. We were sleeping through the night, thanks to the cage. Did it matter that I was wracked with guilt over confining him to a cage all night and then most of the day?

"Dogs love their cages," my dad said. "Your sister's dog still sleeps in his cage, even though he doesn't have to anymore. The cages remind them of caves."

I was using hotdogs to lure Pacey in before work. Initially, I'd put his water in the cage and left the door open. As thirsty as he may be, Pacey would not enter his cage for water if I were in the room with him. Even with hotdogs, Pacey would refuse to go into the cage if I was there, so I'd leave the room, stomp loudly to the bathroom, then creep back down the hall on tip-toes. Pacey would spend some time debating the value of freedom over a piece of processed meat. Then he'd tried to reach the hotdog with just his head. Eventually, he'd have to put his two front paws into the cage. As he reached his goal, I'd jump out from behind the door and push his butt into the cage. He'd howl the rest of the time I was in the house, so I always tried to leave immediately after Operation Cage. I mean, Operation Cave.

I was looking forward to having my father around, in part because then Pacey could be loose in the house for most of the day. Thanks to my constant removal of household items from his mouth, coupled with the insertion of a toy, he'd almost completely stopped picking up my things. What he was still doing, however, was mouthing. He didn't bite, he just tried to take your hand or wrist in his teeth.

"We had that same problem with our German Shepherd when I was a kid," Lucy said. "Shepherds are big mouthers."

"They are?" I asked. I felt happy to think that it wasn't just Pacey, being bad.

"My mother took a spray bottle of water and lemon juice and sprayed his mouth every time he did it."

"That worked?"

"You betcha."

I bought a lemon ball and a little spray bottle on my way home from work. The next time Pacey mouthed me, which was seconds after mixing lemon juice into water, I forced his mouth open and sprayed him. He blinked in surprise. A few minutes later, he mouthed again. I sprayed. He blinked. I breathed a sigh of relief. It looked like this was going to work.

"That sounds kind of extreme," Oliver said. "Why don't you just tell him no?"

"He doesn't understand 'no.'"

"Hmmm."

"It's working," I said.

"It's just so mean."

I felt a pang. "It's not that mean," I said. "He makes the choice, mouth me and get zapped. Don't mouth me, don't get zapped."

The truth was that Pacey had already become immune to the spray bottle. He didn't mind the water and lemon juice mixture anymore. I'd switched to water and vinegar, but this only worked for a couple of days. Since then, I'd been spraying the lemon ball directly into his mouth. Now, this was effective. In fact, it was so effective that, if Pacey saw the lemon ball, he no longer mouthed me.

I'd bought four lemon balls and stashed them around the house so that one was always within easy reach. Also, I frequently walked around with one hidden in the waistband of my jeans, near the small of my back. I'd say, "Hi, Pacey," and wave my hands around so that he could see I wasn't holding the lemon ball. He'd mouth me and zing! I'd whip the lemon ball out from the back of my jeans and nail him. "The lemon ball always knows," I told Pacey.

But I didn't tell Oliver any of this. "If I don't teach him not to mouth," I said, "then I'm an irresponsible dog owner. Mouthing seems harmless, but he's a big dog, with big teeth. He needs to learn that he can't chew on people's hands."

"I just think there are other ways to accomplish that goal. When does your obedience class begin?"

"Not soon enough."

My dad arrived. I'd taken four days off from work and we settled right away into a routine. First on the agenda was a tour of the house. "This is a good, solid house," he told me, pointing to the stone walls in the basement. "My aunt had a house like this. Almost the exact same layout, except she had a door on the side of the house for the milkman to slip jugs into." By the end of the walk-through, he had added about ten other repairs to my list.

That night, I heard him on the phone to my stepmother. "She's got a beautiful, dry basement," he was saying. I felt a stab of pride. I'd done a good job of choosing a house.

My dad was a workhorse. We'd spent the rest of the first day at the home store, and by the end of the second day, we had ripped up the porch stairs, cut wood for new stairs, installed a programmable thermostat, replaced the doorbell, and installed motion-detector light switches in my front and upstairs hallways. I'd learned how to replace ceiling lights and light switches.

I walked Pacey in the mornings and evenings. My father preferred to work through the walks. "I have to walk him," I explained, "or he'll drive us nuts. He's very hyper."

My father looked at me. He'd been outside, cutting down tree branches. He had on gloves, goggles, and a yellow hard hat with a piece of cloth hanging from behind to shield his neck from the sun. "He seems fine," he said.

"He's a lunatic."

At night, we relaxed by sitting in the living room, doing crossword puzzles. We both liked Will Shortz's puzzles, from the New York Times. "What's an 'MS follower?' Three letters," I asked. "Someone who reads Ms. Magazine?"

"D-O-S?" He suggested.

"Huh? Ohhh. Thanks." I continued to do the puzzle. "What's a melon from Turkey? Six letters."

"Casaba."

"I'm sitting here with a crossword puzzle dictionary, a regular dictionary, and a thesaurus. You have nothing over there and yet you know all the answers."

He shook his head. "I don't know them all. But I've been doing crossword puzzles since I was 12 or 13. So, for over 50 years."

"But 'casaba'?"

"It's always the answer for melon. It has a lot of As."

Pacey got up from his bed and did a big stretch in the middle of the rug. He let out a long, loud yawn.

"He sounds like a dolphin," my dad said.

When Pacey was done stretching, he came over to my seat, to say hello. I patted him on the head and tweaked his ear. Then he trotted over to my father, on the sofa, and sat down. "Hi there, fellow" my dad said, peering at Pacey over his bifocals.

I got lost in my puzzle again. My father was petting Pacey and chatting with him, then I heard him say, "Oh, I don't think you should do that. Quinn's not going to like that."

I looked up. Pacey had his two front paws on the sofa. I went straight for the lemon ball and zapped him while his paws were still on the sofa. "Bad dog!" I said, as I zapped. Then, "Good dog!" when he dropped all four paws to the floor.

"Training dogs is a mind-game," I told my dad. "It seems messed up, to praise right after yelling, but every book I've read says to do it that way."

"He knew he wasn't supposed to be up here," my dad said. "He looked over at you first, and when he saw that you weren't looking, he put his paws up."

"You should zap him with the lemon ball," I said. I'd given my dad a lemon ball when he first arrived, but he was being very bad about using it.

"You're too hard on him," my dad said. "He's a good dog."

"He just tried to climb onto the sofa! That's a bad dog."

"He's just a dog," my dad said, stroking Pacey's ears. Pacey leaned into him and made the dolphin sound again.

I looked at Pacey. He barked at me, as if to say, "What are you looking at?"

My stepmother came for the last half of the visit. "She feeds table scraps to dogs," my father warned me.

"This dog isn't allowed any human food," I told her, the moment she walked in the door. She looked appalled that I'd even suggest such a thing. But she'd brought almost a suitcase full of dog toys and treats. She took out a disposable camera and took a picture of Pacey with one of his new toys, a doll that squeaked each time he chewed it. He couldn't make the connection between the squeak and his chew. Every time it squeaked, he dropped the toy to look around.

"I've wanted a dog since we got married," she told me. "Your father promised me a dog."

Pacey was seated at my dad's feet, getting a neck massage. "If we could get a dog just like Pacey," my father said, "I'd say yes."

On the last day of their visit, my father and I had coffee at the dining room table while my step-mom slept in. I'd enjoyed having people in the house with me, to drink coffee with in the morning and talk to in the evenings. I was going to miss them when they left. My stepmother was scheduled for knee surgery later that week. Walking was painful and stairs were nearly impossible. She'd been coming down my staircase on her butt and going up the same way. This didn't stop her from taking a dustpan and sweeping up Pacey's dog hair as she inched her way up and down the stairs.

As she came down on the last morning with the dustpan, I whispered to my father, "I just swept those stairs last night." He laughed.

My stepmother paused at the landing to lay down the dustpan and snap a picture of my father and me. Then she handed over the dustpan to me. "Even with dog hair," she said, "I want a dog."

A week after they left, a pack of photos arrived in the mail from my stepmother. Of the two rolls of film, four pictures had shots of me and my dad. Every other shot was of Pacey.

Three weeks after knee surgery, my stepmom and my dad adopted a White German Shepherd from their local Humane Society. They named her Selby. So, in a way, you could say that Pacey saved the life of another dog.

"I'm thinking, I haven't had a road trip in a while," Oliver said. My parents had left a few days earlier. "What would you say if I came to Omaha?"

"I'd love it," I said.

"What weekend would work best for you?"

"Anytime," I said.

"Let's see what I've got going. What about the weekend of the 15th?"

"Sure," I said.

"And a hotel. Can you recommend a good one? And by good I mean, do you have Super 8 or Motel 6 in your area?"

I smiled. "We do. We certainly do."

"Josh and I have started house hunting," Izzy said.

"Huh?"

"Yes. We went out house hunting on Saturday. We both want the same type of house. A modest bungalow. Two bedrooms. Small yard."

"Wow. So, can I take it from this comment that you've slept with him?"

"Yes. It was great. He's good in bed."

"Wow." I couldn't seem to stop saying that. "Great. What order did all this, uh, happen in?"

Izzy laughed. "He suggested we go to a couple of open houses. So we did. And we were so in sync. He's planning for our future and I find that incredibly sexy."

I nodded. "Well, I'm glad. Good for you!"

"How are things with Oliver?"

"Oh, hey, he's coming to town next weekend!"

Izzy let out a whoop. "Fantastic. I want to meet him, of course."

"Oh, you're going to meet him. Can I tell you he is just so...neat! So sexy, so smart. So interesting. I feel giddy, thinking about him."

Izzy smiled. "Good for you."

"He also basically told me that he's not dating anyone. Doesn't that mean he's serious about a committed relationship?"

"It sounds like it."

"I'm trying to think of fun things to do. I was planning on the zoo and maybe a movie at the Dundee Theater."

"Take my advice," Izzy said. "Have sex with him. He's such a babe."

Chapter 36
You Want Milk with That Cow? Men Who Talk Commitment to Get Sex

"So, have you ever been engaged or married?" Oliver was asking. We were talking on the phone again. We'd been talking at least once every two days and he was due to come out in a week.

"Uh, no. Have you?"

"I guess I'm old-fashioned, but I believe in committed relationships. I'm looking forward to making a home with the right woman someday. You know, get married, have a bunch of kids. Mow the lawn on the weekends. Fix the toilet. That sort of thing."

"Is that a line you use to get women into bed?" I joked.

"Not at all!" He sounded wounded. "Unlike many men, I'm not afraid of commitment. I've been in two relationships that were headed for the altar, but in the end they failed. I guess I should tell you right now that both times the women told me that my biggest flaws were that I am superior and critical."

"Oh." I didn't really know what to say to that.

"You know, I think I can be that way because before we moved to Japan I went to a very exclusive, private high school. Eight-five percent of its graduates go to Ivy League schools. I was there on full scholarship. But the thing was, even though I got good grades, actually, excellent grades, I didn't need to work for them."

"Really? That's great, huh?"

"I guess. I mean, I just read comics in school. That's how I kept myself occupied. And that's why college was so good for me. I had to work, there."

"What year did you graduate?"

"I didn't actually graduate. I realized by my sophomore year that I knew enough to get me what I needed, so I left. I'm lucky, too. My friends who stayed to graduate got all commercial and designy."

I yawned. "I should probably get to bed," I said. "I have to get up early for yoga."

"Do you? I've tried yoga before, but I've found it doesn't work for me, because I already know how to stretch and I know my body better than any teacher in a class could. So I just maintain my flexibility on my own."

"I go to yoga in a hot room. It helps increase my flexibility."

"Some people need that," he said. "But hey, I forgot to tell you, I got a cat."

"You did?"

"A kitten, actually. I named her Pumpkin. She's trying to climb up on my phone cord right now. She's jealous of you, I think."

"How cute! Did you get her from the Humane Society?"

"Uh, no. I bought her. My neighbor breeds cats. She gave me a deal, though."

"Oh. So, listen, I really need to get some shut eye."

"Oh, absolutely. Sweet dreams!"

"To you, too. And give Pumpkin a little kiss for me."

Dog walks had become a staple of my daily life. Pacey was beginning to sleep through the night. He'd still tear around the house every evening, but I'd realized that if I sat on the sofa and ignored him, he would stop after ten or twenty minutes and fall asleep. Our walks helped to tire him out. I was just getting ready to go on my favorite walk when Izzy called.

"Can we talk?"

"Sure. I was about to leave with Pacey on a walk. Do you want to come along?"

"Yes! Pick me up on your way. I'll be waiting out front."

We went to a big, usually deserted lake, on the north side of town. Today, the sky was steel gray, nearly the same color as the water. Izzy looked great, as usual. Her skin was clear and had a lot of color. She seemed more tranquil than normal. We were walking at a fast pace to get everyone's heart rate up.

"So," I said. "How's Josh?"

"We're having a little bit of a problem," Izzy said. "We were out on a jog the other morning, and we passed, get this, his mother and father."

"Really?"

"Yeah. They were at a garage sale in his neighborhood. They were so cute. They look like a pair of old academics. The mom had long grey hair; the dad had these wire-rimmed glasses. They had planned to stop by Josh's house after making their purchases. She was buying an old, wooden loom, with a rug already started halfway. He had a brass spigot."

"I like them!" I said. "Great in-laws."

"Yes! But then Josh didn't introduce us."

"What?"

"We were both standing there, sweating. Clearly on a run together. They kept looking from him to me, but he never introduced us!"

"Sometimes people forget to introduce. I wouldn't read too much into it."

"I don't know. So finally, I said 'Hi, I'm Isabel.'"

"Good."

"And he said, 'Yes, this is my running partner, Isabel."

"Uh-oh."

"Later, I asked him why he didn't introduce me as his girlfriend, and he told me I was rushing things."

"*You're* rushing things? Who is house hunting? Who said 'I love you' after two weeks?"

"I mentioned that. And he said 'I think we have different ideas about what "I love you" means.'"

"Different ideas of what that phrase means! What is he, nuts? What else does 'I love you' mean?"

"Suddenly, I'm starting to wonder if he is actually as ready for commitment as I thought. I'm going to give him a little more time, but then I'm going to go back online."

"I think that's a good idea."

"I'm not ready to totally give up on him," she warned. "He is so much fun to hang out with. But now he's backing out of house hunting, too. He thinks we need to slow things down."

"Doesn't it seem like he started slowing everything down after you guys had sex?"

"It kind of does," she said.

"It's like he used the commitment talk to get you into bed and once he got sex, he dropped it."

"I don't think he was doing that intentionally," Izzy said.

"Maybe there's a reason why everyone always says don't put out until you get a ring."

"Those prudes were wiser than we thought."

"He's not going to buy the cow if he gets the milk for free," I said, in an old lady voice.

"Stop!" Izzy said, laughing. "I don't believe Josh is that conniving. He's just freaking out a little about how serious we are. But he wants to be serious. I know he does. He's just starting to panic. I'm going to help him get through this."

"You should also get back on Match."

"I just might," she said.

I started to sing. "*She said nohuggynokissy, till I get a wedding ring.*"

Izzy laughed. "I love the Georgia Satellites. Maybe I need to buy him that album."

That night, I was reading in bed when I heard a crashing sound. I leaned over to look at Pacey, who was asleep in his kennel. He was sound asleep on his side, but all four feet were running, banging against the side of the cage.

Chapter 37
Getting What You Wished For

I smiled at my computer. Oliver. He'd sent me a picture of Pumpkin. She was sitting inside a cookie jar, gazing out at the camera with big, almond-shaped eyes. Oliver had written:

> *Hey, Yoga-Queen! How are you today? At one with the universe? Sending out good karma to all around you? It's only 10 AM and already Pumpkin and I are facing off from different corners. She kept me up all night by playfully clawing my face as I slept. Oh, the joy of pet ownership. Pacey is, what, 75 lbs? When I first got Pumpkin, I thought, "Hmmm. How would she do in a room alone with Pacey? Would she be safe?" I didn't think so. But now, I'm reconsidering. Seriously, we have to get them together. We have to put our animals in a room and see them brawl. I honestly don't know if Pacey would come out on top. You are looking at that picture of Pumpkin in the cookie jar, right? And you're thinking, "What a cutie!" But she's tough. Rough and tough and full of spit and vinegar. Pet ownership is harder than I realized. I have new admiration for you and your 75 lb white German Shepherd.*
>
> *Take care,*
>
> *Oliver.*

I was staring at the screen with a goofy grin when a new message

popped up. From PetersonM. My heart stopped. M. Peterson was
Max. My ex-boyfriend from nine years ago.

"Holy shit," I said.

"What?" Lucy asked. She was getting ready to take a patient.

"Nothing, it's probably just spam." I couldn't open the email. I
stood and left the office. In the outer area, I didn't know where to go.
I checked my mailbox, which was stuffed to overflow. I sat down
next to the recycle bin and began to sort through the envelopes. My
heart was beating so fast that I could barely breathe. What could he
be writing for? I could guess:

> *Hey. How've you been? Sorry I haven't written before. I do
> want to stay in touch. Where are you now? Still in Iowa? I'm
> doing really well here. I'm the happiest I've ever been, I just
> got married about six months ago to a wonderful girl named
> June. You'd really like her. What is happening in your
> world?*
>
> *I'm going on some field trips, so I won't be able to respond
> for a month or so.*
>
> *Peace,*
>
> *Max*

My mail pile was gone. I drummed my fingers on the table. I'd
have to read the email eventually. I returned to my desk. When I
opened my inbox, his letter actually ran like this:

> *Dear Quinn,*
>
> *Are you the Quinn I knew in New Mexico? She exuded an
> intoxicating mixture of intelligence and sexiness. I was a
> complete ass to her because she utterly terrified me. Now
> I'm realizing that there are no other women like her in the
> world. I don't deserve her, but I'm hoping she's still single
> and possibly maimed so that she might just be willing to
> settle for a man who was young and foolish and is now full
> of regret.*
>
> *Quinn, when I think back on our time together, I think of it
> as the most fulfilling, fun, and challenging period of my life.
> My current life is good, except that I miss your energy, your*

*honesty, and your sweetness. I'm job-hunting, looking for
faculty positions around the country. The Department of
Biology at UNO is looking for an ecologist. They've offered
me an interview. I won't come if you don't want me to. But
before you say no, could you let me fly out and see you?*

*And if you're not that Quinn, well, thanks for listening, and
wish me luck!*

Yours,

Max

My ears were ringing. Did I start hyperventilating? I don't know. I
broke out in a sweat and saw spots in front of my eyes. I closed the
email and tried to slow down my heart rate with controlled, deep
breathing. My head was spinning. I felt like it was going to break off
and fly out of my office. I went into the bathroom and sat in one of
the two stalls. Okay. Now I could think. And my thought was, "Why
did he wait until now, when I was actually excited about meeting
Oliver?" It was like he had some kind of radar. Or was this the
Universe intervening for me?

Back at my desk, I called Izzy. "You're not going to believe this," I
told her. "I just got an email from M." Suddenly, I couldn't even say
his name, just his first initial.

"Who? Uh-oh," Izzy caught on fast. "Have you guys been
corresponding?"

"No. He must have Googled me."

"What did he want?"

In a whisper, I read Izzy the email.

"Damn." She was silent for a moment. "That's good writing. He's
dead on right about you. You're unforgettable."

"Izzy, I'm on the nerve of a vergous breakdown." I shook my head.
My tongue was tied. "On the verge of a nervous breakdown."

"Why? This is great news! It's Max! Remember him? Ding, ding,
ding, ding, ding! The love of your life? Your soul mate? Remember
how you used to burst into tears when people mentioned his name?
He wants you back! He's willing to move to Omaha to get you back.
Omaha."

I took a deep breath. "But what about Oliver?"

"Still check out Oliver. See who you like best."

"God, you've got nerves of steel," I told her. "I don't think I can pull this off."

"Of course you can."

I was going to wait a day to respond, but in the end, I couldn't feign that kind of nonchalance.

> *Max,*
>
> *I'm mostly speechless. I don't know what I'm feeling, and I'm dating other people, but so far, there is nothing serious. So of course I want you to come. I have a guest room here, and you're welcome to it, if you like.*
>
> *Quinn*

I'd put my home phone number at the bottom of the letter. Now I was going to panic every time the phone rang.

Pacey hated his kennel. The hotdogs had stopped working. Now, every morning, Pacey would look at the meat, turn to me, and begin a stream of angry barking. Translation: I see what you are trying to do and I resent you for using something I love to force me into a cage. Then, without breaking eye contact, he would lay down, as if to say: "You in a rush to get to work? Oh well..."

"He'll learn to love the cage," is what everyone kept telling me. "Dogs love small spaces. They sleep for 20 hours a day."

So far, Pacey wasn't like most dogs. Maybe he did sleep all day in his cage. But I didn't think so, because he barely slept when I was home on the weekend. Frankly, I didn't think he slept at all. He spent half the night turning in his cage, whining.

Parents have told me that the sound of their crying infant is heart piercing. Pacey's whining was that kind of disturbing. I couldn't bear to hear him cry, maybe in part because I didn't know what he wanted. Well, I guess I did. He wanted to run around the house, poop, pee, and eat my possessions.

"You got a dog?" Max asked when he called.

"Yes, a White German Shepherd."

"I can totally see you with a dog. Good for you."

"Thanks." I had missed him. It was good to hear his deep, mellow voice. When I first heard him on the other end of the phone, I felt like I'd fallen back into my old, comfortable life in Albuquerque. I'd missed his green eyes and his soft smile. I'd missed his humor and the fun things we used to do, like camping and hiking. I'd missed his muscular body and the way his skin darkened in the summer. I'd missed kissing him. I'd missed making love.

Pacey had started barking the moment I got on the phone. I put him outside on his chain.

"What was he barking at?"

"Me. He likes my undivided attention, so when I'm on the phone he sits in front of me and barks like he's actually saying something."

"He sounds like he has a great personality."

"That's one way to put it. So, how are you?"

"I'm good. I'm excited to come to Omaha."

"I don't even know where you're living right now."

"I'm in Seattle."

"Seattle?"

"Yeah. I've been working for an engineering firm. I love Seattle. But I really want to teach." I just sat back and enjoyed the sound of his voice. It was a relief to hear from him and know that he was doing well. I'd forgotten that a few years after we broke up I was seized by a fear that he would die and no one would remember to tell me. *If it never goes beyond this call*, I thought, *I'm glad I got to hear from him. I'm glad to know that he's okay.*

"Anyway, without boring you, suffice to say that I wound up with a chunk of savings and a lot of money in my IRA. And my life feels empty."

"I can relate," I said.

"Can you?" He sounded excited.

"Well, except for the savings and the fat IRA. But I wonder what I'm doing with my life."

"Are you still painting?"

"Yes. In fact, the painting I'm working on now is of my 6-year-old self glaring at the current me. She's wondering what in the heck I've done to wreck her dreams of being a ballerina."

Max laughed. "That's fantastic. I'd love to see it when I visit. I miss seeing your paintings and hearing about what they mean. I really miss you."

I wanted to say that I missed him, too. But for some reason I couldn't. My throat got a frog stuck in it, I guess. There was an awkward pause, and then Max continued. "The way I came to this decision was that I had a lot of vacation saved, so I took off four weeks and went camping in the Boundary Waters. I was thinking about what I would do if I could do things differently. And two things kept coming up. Teaching and you."

I didn't respond. That frog was just getting bigger. I could feel tears prickling at my eyes.

"So," he cleared his throat, "I have my interview set up for next Friday. I'm flying in on Thursday night. The department chair wants to pick me up at the airport, but I think I'll just spend a few hours with them. I could get to your house by 8 or 9. I interview all day Friday. Then I thought I'd stay on a few more days to spend with you."

The same weekend that Oliver was coming. Gulp. "Perfect. Just great. It'll be so good to see you."

I checked on Pacey after we'd hung up. My neighbor was tying up a rose bush in her yard. Pacey was as close to her as his chain would allow, his tail thumping the ground. He saw me out of the corner of his eye, turned to me, and barked, I guess to say, "What are you looking at? Leave us alone!"

I went back inside. I wanted to sit and relish my conversation with Max, but I had to call Oliver. He answered on the fourth ring. "Hey, it's Quinn. There's a problem with this weekend." My face felt flush. Adrenaline was running through me from my conversation with Max. I tried to calm down my voice.

"What's wrong? You sound tense."

"Sorry. I just got a phone call from a friend I haven't seen in nine years, who's coming into Omaha this weekend to interview for a teaching job. I feel like if you come this weekend I'm going to have to split my time up and I wanted to give you all my attention. Do you think we could change to the following weekend?"

"Sure. I completely understand. You didn't really have any control about when your friend was coming."

"None at all. And it's not like the interview can be changed."

"You'll enjoy your visit with her though."

"I will. Nine years is a long time." I paused. "Thanks for being so understanding," I said.

"Not a problem. It just means I take off next Friday instead of this Friday. So just stop worrying. I can still hear the tension in your voice."

"Well, I just feel bad about this short notice. It's crazy, the timing."

"It's fine. I'll see you next weekend."

I hung up the phone. Max was coming.

Pacey and I had had our first obedience class. My instructor, Myna, was an ancient woman who owned three terrier show dogs. The class was a mix of large and small dogs. A cursory glance confirmed: no single men in my age range. Honestly, Reader. It's like I can't turn it off. I've got two men in the wings, and yet I'm still checking out my options.

We met in a school gym. Metal folding chairs lined the walls. Myna lectured for the first hour. Pacey was shockingly well behaved at first. He sat when other people approached him. I rubbed his stomach with my foot as Myna talked. After about forty minutes of sitting still and resisting the nearby dogs, Pacey stood up and started to whine softly, under his breath. When I did nothing, his whining accelerated to a yelping, which quickly moved on to a howl. He actually sat next to me, in class, and began to howl like a coyote. The class thought he was a riot.

The teacher said, "My goodness, are we keeping you from something, Dear? Have you got someplace you need to be?"

Frankly, I thought Pacey was speaking for all of us. We were tired of trying to control our dogs while we listened to her talk.

"Let's have a ten minute bathroom break and we'll learn to sit when we come back."

Pacey already knew sit. He picked up "stay" immediately. I had to show him about ten times and then he nailed it. Maybe there was hope for him, after all.

As we broke up to leave, Myna announced, "Next week, we'll learn "down" and "heel." Love-of-my-life coming into town or not, I wasn't going to miss that class.

The night before Max arrived I had a dream about him. He was unrecognizable. There was absolutely nothing in him that I knew, including his eyes, voice, personality, smile, or body. Yet, I believed this was Max. I don't remember what our conversation was about. But while we talked, I made mental notes on his physical flaws (skinny legs, baggy eyes, pot belly) to arm myself for the regret I'd feel when he was gone. He was visiting on some work related thing, I guess. Because another person was with us the whole time.

The next day, the real Max appeared at my door at 9 p.m. A pair of car lights flashed through my front window. A car was backing out of my driveway as I opened the door. And there was Max, standing on my front porch. Max. Tall, dirty blond, green-eyed Max. He had a warm, sweet face and the kind of smile that just lifted you off your feet. He looked great. He was definitely older. He had thin lines around his mouth, but they just made him look like he'd spent a lifetime smiling at people. He dropped his bags and swept me up into his arms. He was so tall that my feet lifted off the floor. I just inhaled him. He smelled the same as always. I felt like I was back in New Mexico. I felt like I was home.

Pacey was racing around us, whining and wondering why he wasn't part of the group hug. Max put me down and dropped to one knee to offer an upturned hand to Pacey. Pacey was thrilled to have a second person in his house. Especially someone who got down to his level. He sniffed the hand and immediately rolled onto his back, offering up his belly for scratching. Max obliged.

"He's a love," he said.

"Sometimes."

He stood up from Pacey and gave me another long, tight hug. Then he pushed me away from him and eyeballed me. "You haven't changed a bit," he said. "So this is your house?"

"Yes," I said. "I'm only the third owner, ever, and it's 93 years old." He wandered past me into the kitchen, which led to the built in pantry. I wanted him to love the house. "It was built in 1912," I said. "A tornado came down this street a year later, on Easter Sunday. It took out a house across the street, but left this house and the two on either side."

He came back grinning. "I love it. And it looks like it's in great condition, too." He gestured to the stairwell. "My grandmother's house had this exact same seat in the staircase. She had a stained glass window right there. Quinn, I can totally picture you here, when you're old like my grandma, telling your grandchildren about the tornado of 1913."

As usual, Max reeked with charisma. I felt giddy just being around him.

We settled down in the living room with beers. "How was your interview?" I asked.

"Tiring, but good. Everyone here is really nice. I just…"

"What?"

"Quinn, Omaha? Of all the places I thought I'd find you, Omaha was not one of them."

"Max, you've never been to Omaha. How do you know what it's like?"

He nodded his head in agreement. But after a minute he said, "I just pictured you near mountains, or in a giant city, or around the ocean."

"I wouldn't want to live near the ocean," I said. "Too expensive."

"But what about Boulder, or Berkeley? Or Seattle?"

"What about them?"

"Could you see yourself there, Quinn?"

I narrowed my eyes. "Maybe," I said.

"Because I have interviews there, too. And I think you'd love any of those cities."

"I can't have my job anywhere in the country but here. There's no other center in the country that does as much with pediatric audiology."

"Okay. Well, I was just checking. Just, you know, exploring all options." He reached over and picked up a strand of my hair. My heart started beating in my ears. "I've missed you so much. I've wondered so many times what you were up to, how you were. And here I am, sitting right across from you, in your home, which you bought, and you're an audiologist. I feel like I'm in an alternate universe. Audiology. Jeez. I would never have pegged you for that career. I thought you'd be a fine artist, or a coffee house owner, or running a shelter for some group in need. But I don't even know what an audiologist does. You're going to have to catch me up, here. Tell me about an average day in the life of Quinn Malone, Audiologist and Omahan."

We talked for hours with Pacey curled up at our feet. About halfway through he reached out and took hold of my hand. I realized, talking to him, that in the back of my mind when I bought this house I had imagined the possibility of this moment. This moment of Max, with me and Pacey, in this house. I was picturing my dream of someday having a family in this house.

It was after midnight when Max finally said he needed to take a shower and go to bed. He had a full day of interviews tomorrow. I took Pacey outside to pee. It was good to be in the cool darkness after the intensity of the past several hours. Pacey was so excited about Max's presence that he didn't want to pee. Eventually, we came inside and went upstairs. Max was dressed in cotton pajama bottoms and a blue t-shirt that made his green eyes vivid. "Do you need anything?" I asked. He was standing in the guest room, which I'd made up earlier in the day. "I'm set. Will you wake me at seven?"

"Sure." I wanted to give him a hug goodnight, but I felt timid. As I turned to leave, he touched my shoulder.

"Quinn." When I turned around he gave a big bear hug.

"It's good to see you," I said into his shoulder.

"You too," he said. I closed his door behind me as I left. Pacey lay down in the hallway outside Max's room.

I brushed my teeth and climbed into bed. My mind was whirling. I thought I'd never fall asleep. But by the time I had read three pages of my novel my eyelids were drooping. I turned off my light and went to bed.

"Quinn? Hi, this is Lonesh's mom. Listen, I had to call and tell you. Lonesh had a spelling test on Monday."

"Did he?"

"Yes. He always does poorly on them. As much as we practice, he never does better than a C." She paused. "This week, he got a B+."

"Really?"

"Yes. It's those hearing aids. He hears so many new sounds. S and F and TH. It's been so wonderful to watch him grow. He seems to pick up new things every week."

"I'm happy," I said. "Thank you for calling and telling me." As I hung up, I was grinning ear to ear. I couldn't wait to tell Max. I guess that's what companionship is all about. I wanted to share all my happy moments with him. *I just hope he gets the job*, I thought.

Max didn't get home till nine o'clock again. "Beer?" I asked.
He shook his head. "Do you have any herbal tea?"
I put the kettle on the stove. I was already in my sleeping clothes, a

grey, v-necked t-shirt, and light blue, cotton bottoms with a blue silk ribbon sewn around the bottom of each leg. I was aiming for casual sexy. Picture a JCrew catalog. "How did it go?" I asked.

"Fine. They'll let me know next week."

"Do they have other candidates?"

"Sure."

"How did the interviews go? What was your day like?"

He told me about his day. Then I told him about mine. When our tea was empty and Pacey was asleep at my feet, Max yawned and cracked his neck.

"Does Pacey need to go out?"

"He will, one more time tonight."

"I could use some exercise. Let's take him out on a nice, long walk."

Normally, I wouldn't have felt safe, walking around the neighborhood that late at night. But with a man and a dog…I shrugged. "Okay." I left to change out of my PJs.

Pacey was thrilled, of course. He was going to enjoy Max living here, too. *IF that's how this plays out*, I reminded myself. Pacey pranced out ahead of us on the sidewalk, his tail wagging. "The faculty says you live in a bad area," he said.

I shrugged. "I wouldn't call it bad. A little north of me, it's scarier. This area is kind of like the border."

"The only reason anyone gave for it being a bad neighborhood today was that the place is 'mixed.'"

I nodded. "Yeah, this city is still pretty segregated. The western part of the city is like a giant suburb for white flight. But my block has about an even split between black, white, and Latino people."

"What are your neighbors like?"

"Some are good, some don't mow their lawns or shovel their snow. It's not a racial thing." I paused. The lights were off in most of the houses. "When I moved in, the only neighbors who came over to introduce themselves and welcome me to the neighborhood were my black neighbors. Even though I'm white, not a single white neighbor came by to say hello."

We walked in silence for a while. Max said, "Talking to you is like the same as always, except that it's different, too. You're the same, but then you're not. You're…"

"Older."

Max laughed. "You're more complex. Less naïve."

I didn't answer him. I didn't think he was right. I was about the same as before. I was naïve when I left my suburbs at eighteen to live in Brooklyn, but I hadn't met Max till several years later, in New Mexico.

At bedtime, Max yawned and kissed me on the top of my head. "I'll see you in the morning," he said, and went into the guest room. Pacey took his place outside Max's door.

I read for an hour in bed, then went downstairs. Pacey waited till he knew I wasn't coming back up, and then followed me. I dialed Izzy.

"Hello?"

"Hi, it's Quinn. Did I wake you?"

"No, what are you doing up so late?"

"I was waiting for Max to fall asleep." I paused. "I don't know how things are going. We haven't kissed or anything."

"What? Why not?"

"Well, I guess I thought he would kiss me. Plus, he's not just interviewing here. He sort of tried to convince me that I should move to somewhere with him, like Berkeley."

"Well, why not? Berkeley is great."

"Because I have a great job here. And a house. And I've put so much work into my garden that I want to see how it comes out. I'll be able to harvest raspberries from my bush next year."

"Quinn, this is Max, we're talking about. Remember? Three years ago, you wouldn't have hesitated to move anywhere with him."

I thought about that. "But we haven't seen each other in nine years."

"What are you doing with him tomorrow?"

"I don't know. I want to show him how nice Omaha can be," I paused. "How do I do that?"

"Well, what were you going to do with Oliver?"

"Oh, no. Oliver things won't impress Max. Max's a snob. He won't want to go to the zoo. Maybe good food. I wish we could drive to the Black Hills, to camp, but that's too far away."

"Quinn, he's here to see you. You could sit in your living room and talk all day, and he would be happy."

I nodded, tapping my finger on the phone as Pacey lay across the room and closed his eyes. "Yeah. Okay."

"Remember Groundhog Day, the movie? If you could do anything you wanted and no one would remember it the next day, some people would rob a bank or tell off their boss. Remember our conversations about what we would do, if we were trapped in that movie? What have you always said you would do?"

"Track down Max and tell him I want a second chance to make our relationship work," I whispered.

"Get some sleep. Enjoy tomorrow. It's a dream come true."

Chapter 38
How Would I Act If I Had No Fear?

Reader, I was terrified. I was scared of losing Max, I was scared of having him. I was pretending that Oliver was in the mix, but he wasn't. This was all about Max and me. Max was who I wanted. So why was I so scared?

Going back in time to see how things could turn out different is a common theme in movies and television. The movie Groundhog Day is the popular example, but there are others:

1. The WB's season finale of Felicity. Felicity, torn for five seasons between two men, ends the series with her first love, but then gets to go back in time and chooses differently. (In the end, it turns out that she was right the first time.)

2. Me Myself I. Rachel Griffiths, unhappy single woman, gets to move into an alternate universe, where she's married with kids. (Singledom totally won out, by the way. This movie was clearly made by a responsible, single woman filmmaker).

3. Drew Barrymore. 50 First Dates.

4. It's A Wonderful Life–what would the world be like if Jimmy Stewart had never been born?

Unfortunately, I wasn't in a movie, and I couldn't go back in time or redo things later. I just got to go forward. Suddenly I remembered my class in petitioning the Universe, and one phrase popped into my head. *How would I act if I had no fear?*

On Saturday, I woke up at six. While Max slept, I listened to *Only a Game* on NPR and made sandwiches for lunch. For breakfast, I had fresh raspberries and blueberries in yogurt and granola. Max wandered downstairs at 8. He found me outside, gardening. (I'd left a note propped up against the coffeemaker.) Pacey rose immediately to greet him, tail wagging.

"Good morning," I said. "Sleep well?"

I was on the south side of the house, digging a trench to outline a future flowerbed with stones. He was barefoot in jeans and a grey t-shirt. He had the mug I'd put out for him, presumably filled with coffee. He looked sleepy headed and handsome. I wanted to kiss him. So I stood up and kissed him. No fear. He fell right into it. I could feel his chest against mine. I could smell his detergent. It felt like our mouths were built just for each other.

"God, you're a good kisser," he said when I let go. I smiled and sat back down by my flower bed. He squatted down next to me. "I also forgot how early you rise."

"I didn't wake you, did I?"

"No. Did you do all this today?"

The trench was nearly dug. "It's only taken half an hour."

"It's the weekend, Quinn. Try to relax."

"This is how I relax. Besides, when else would I do it? I have a job."

We didn't talk much over breakfast. Max is not a morning person. "Did you see that movie, Groundhog Day?"

"Sure," he said.

"What would you do, if you could do something and no one would remember it?"

He shrugged. "Rob a bank?"

Max came with me to obedience class. Pacey mastered commands quickly, except that he had a bit of an attitude problem. I'd say, "Sit," and Pacey would glance around the room, up at the ceiling, and down at the floor. Then he'd sit.

"He does things in his own time," Max said.

"I'm beginning to see that he has a real stubborn streak," I said.

"Next up is the 'down' position," the instructor announced, from the middle of the gym. "Some of the more dominant dogs," she glanced at Pacey, "may become aggressive when you make them go into a down position."

"Pacey's not aggressive," I said as she walked over to us. "He's rambunctious, but he's never even growled at me."

The instructor raised her eyebrows at me, as if to say, "I seriously doubt that."

"It's true," I said, as if she'd spoken.

"Does he growl when you go near his food?" she asked.

"No. In fact, I can take rawhides right out of his mouth. He's not aggressive. He's just stubborn."

She didn't believe me. I could tell by her face. As she walked away, I said to Max, "Do you think he's aggressive?"

He shook his head. "Of course not. He's a sweetheart. Don't worry about her."

Within minutes, Pacey knew what "down" meant. That didn't mean he liked it. When I held a treat to the ground and said, "Pacey, down," he would watch me out of the corner of his eye as he scratched his left ear or sniffed the floor. I waited and eventually he'd let out a sigh and drop to the ground.

"Damn dog!" I whispered. "You're making me look bad!"

After class, we walked around my favorite walk in Omaha, the lake on the north side of town. Pacey was in hog heaven.

"What have you been up to?" I asked. "Since last I saw you? Have you dated anyone special?"

He shrugged. "A couple people. I dated a biologist for two years. Maria. I was in an on-and-off relationship with a secretary in the office I'm at now, in Seattle. Lisa. There've been others, but those were the two longest."

"Why didn't they work?" I asked.

"Lisa pretty much wanted to get married and start a family. I wasn't ready for that, at least, not with her. And Maria, well, our relationship was turbulent. We fought like cats and dogs. It was fun for a while, but not for a lifetime." He put his arm around my shoulder as we walked. "I guess I've been using you as my yard stick. No one quite measured up."

We were walking up an incline. I turned to look at Max. I had a big smile on my face. Because of the hill, we were eye level. Max reached his arms around my waist and gave me a long, sweet kiss. I was holding Pacey's leash. I felt the tug as he reached the end of the lead. I felt the slack as he walked back toward us and sat. Max kept one hand on the small of my back and brushed the fingers of his other hand across my throat. The longer we kissed, the more I remembered. I remembered kissing him once at the top of a summit in the Sandia Mountains. I remember kissing under shooting stars in the cold, mountainous woods of southwestern Colorado. I remembered kissing him to hide my anger and hurt feeling, to put off the end of our deteriorating relationship. All at once I felt sweet love and a terrible pain. I ended the kiss.

He held my forearms to keep me from moving away. "What's the matter?"

"I don't know. I just remembered the end of our relationship."

He slung an arm around my shoulder and squeezed me into him as we resumed walking. "That was a long time ago. We've both changed a lot. We don't have to hurt each other this time."

Izzy was right. We didn't need to go anywhere to be happy. We spent the day talking, eating, and going on walks. Like Izzy, Max liked taking walks. I showed Max my paintings. We talked about geology, ecology, and the great dust bowl, which stretched into Nebraska. Max was going to make a great teacher because he had the ability to make almost anything he talked about fascinating. We gossiped about old friends and caught up on our families. The thing about Max, probably the thing that kept me pining for him for so many years, was how much I enjoyed his personality, his intellect, and his humor. Our day was like a dream. I had to keep pinching myself to believe that Max was here, in Omaha. That he was back in my life. I was happy. But when it came time for bed, and he leaned in to kiss me, and we fell backwards on the sofa, wrapping our arms around each other as we kissed, I stopped him after a few minutes, and sat up.

"Too fast?" Max asked.

"Maybe a little bit," I said. I knew that Izzy would be ripping her hair out if she knew, but I couldn't help myself. I didn't want to completely lose myself in Max.

Max embraced me. "I want to take it slow, too," he whispered. "Let's just sleep together, like we used to when we were first dating. I miss that as much as all the rest."

"Liar," I said. He laughed. But that's what we did. We slept together, without sleeping together. I fell asleep in his arms, and woke up to hear him breathing next to me in the morning. He was sound asleep, so I crept out of bed and went outside to garden and marvel in my great fortune.

He found me in the yard about an hour later. "Good morning," he said, handing me a cup of coffee.

"Thanks." I took my gardening gloves off so I could hold the mug without spilling it. We were sitting in my flower bed, surrounded by poppies and chives. Curling my feet up under me, I turned to face him. "Every morning should be this good. Digging in soil, separating peonies, a handsome man bringing me coffee."

He sat down beside me. "Every morning could be like this," he said.

I put my coffee down. "I've missed you," I said. But then this niggling part of my brain asked if it was him I missed, or the idea of him?

"I've missed you too." He leaned over and kissed me. He tasted like toothpaste. I felt an overwhelming need for him. My need felt so vast that I didn't think that Max alone would be able to fill it. And that reminded me of how I used to feel with him. Even after sex, I felt like I hadn't gotten enough of him. Was I was expecting a man to give me fulfillment? Or was Max not giving enough of himself?

Max slid his hands up my back, under my shirt, and leaned me supine into the damp dirt. "Wait," I said, struggling to get up.

"Your neighbor can't see," he said, and he slid one hand around my front until he found my breast.

"My poppies," I said.

"I love your poppies," he murmured. "God, I love your poppies."

I pushed myself back up. "My poppy plants." I said. "I'm crushing them."

He took a deep breath. Then he pulled me onto his lap. His hands went back up my shirt, this time with both hands in front. "Quinn," he whispered.

"Let's go inside," I said.

"Come on. Be spontaneous," he said, blowing softly on my neck.

"We're not in the woods," I said. "This is a city." I grabbed his hands to pull him up as I stood. "Let's go inside."

Max stood too, and brushed the dirt off his pants. "Actually, let's wait. I wanted to go on a run this morning. And besides, I was thinking. Let's go out on a date tonight. Let's make reservations and eat at the fanciest restaurant in town. You can get dressed up, and I'll get dressed up, and we'll make a night of it."

"Okay," I said. "But I'm still game for going inside if you want to check out my poppies."

He flushed, which made me smile.

"I can't," he said. "I just remembered that I forgot to pick up condoms."

"What? You think women don't know how to buy condoms?"

He took a step toward me, a big smile on his face. "You have some?"

"No. But I might have."

His smile sank. He shook his head. "Then I guess I'll be off on my run," he said. He took off. Half a block away, I called to him.

"Wait!" He slowed to a stop and turned on his heel. He had a cocky grin on his face. "Yes?" he asked.

"Bring Pacey."

His smile fell, but he came back and leashed Pacey for the run. I watched them go down the block, with Pacey running in front of Max and nearly tripping him twice before they turned a corner.

Inside the house, I brushed dirt off my back and washed my hands. Then I phoned Oliver. "Hey, it's Quinn."

"Hey back at ya!" He sounded warm and friendly. Happy to hear from me. "How's your friend? Does she like Omaha?"

"She's a he, actually," I said. "Max."

"Oh. I thought you said it was a girl. I must have misunderstood." But I could tell by his voice that he didn't really think he had misunderstood.

"No, you made an assumption, and I didn't correct you." I sat down in my living room. "Max is an ex-boyfriend. I hadn't seen him in nine years. He's in town for an interview. I needed to see what was going to happen with him, before I started up something with you."

We sat in silence for a while. Probably it was only a few minutes, but it seemed to go on and on. I could hear kids playing outside, and dogs barking.

"How are things going?" he asked.

"The jury's still out."

More silence.

"So this was a serious relationship, nine years ago?"

"Uh, yes."

He was quiet again. What could I do, Reader? I waited.

"I can see where you're coming from," Oliver finally said. "I guess, in your shoes I probably would have done the same thing. And I appreciate the honesty."

"I understand if you don't want me to call again."

"No, you can still call. Yeah. Definitely call."

"Max? My goodness, less than a week in town and you already know the best place to eat. Have you got some kind of sixth sense?"

We were standing in the foyer of the restaurant, and a young, stunningly attractive blond woman in a red dress was greeting Max. She inserted herself in between us and gave him a pretentious kiss on each cheek. She was with an older man, probably in his late fifties.

"Shasta. Hi. This is my friend, Quinn." When he gestured to me, Shasta turned around and looked at me like I was a spot on her expensive Persian rug. She barely even acknowledged me with her eyes before turning back to Max to say, "You'll have to join us. I'm here with Pappy." Her "pappy" had wandered several feet away and was talking with the maître-d.

"Shasta," Max said to me, "is a biologist at the university."

Ahhh.

"She came here from Brown."

Ugh.

"I insist you join us," Shasta said to Max. "So we can talk more about your music. I want a copy of your cd. I mean it!"

Music? Max had played the guitar when I knew him. This was the first I'd heard of a compact disc.

"I told you I'd send you a copy."

"I want you to personally deliver it, when you come here to teach." She was just two inches from his mouth when she said that. I wanted to murder her. I'm serious. Her Pappy appeared at her elbow and we were all introduced again. Me as an afterthought.

"Max is joining us for dinner," Shasta told her father.

Max looked at me with an "Is that cool?" expression.

With just a narrowing of my eyes, I was able to convey that, no, it was not cool.

"Actually," Max said, putting his arm around my shoulder, "Quinn and I don't have much time together. I fly out tomorrow, and we wanted this time on our own. Thank you for the invitation," he said. "Another time, when I'm living here, I hope."

"Oh, I'm disappointed!" Shasta said. Max glanced back at me, but quickly saw that I wasn't going to reconsider.

"Another time," he said.

Luckily, we sat on opposite sides of the dining room, me with my back to her. I was having trouble gaining control of my jealous rage.

Max didn't look uncomfortable. He unfolded his napkin and began to study the wine list.

"What the hell is a 'pappy?'" I snapped.

Max raised his eyebrows. "That's uncalled for." He put down the wine list. "Great menu," he said. I felt like our evening was ruined. He'd already moved on to appetizers.

"Did you notice that she was totally hitting on you?"

"No she wasn't."

"Yes, she was."

"Calm down, Quinn."

I'm not normally a jealous person, but my hands were shaking. "That's who you had dinner with, on Friday?"

He looked surprised at my leap of logic, but nodded. "She's on the selection committee. It was completely above board."

"So, if you come here, instead of going to Princeton or Berkeley, what will happen? Will we start a serious relationship? Or will we take some time to get to know each other?"

"I guess we're better off taking some time to get to know each other again," he said.

"Does that mean we'll date other people?"

"No! Jeez, Quinn." He held my gaze for a minute. "I'd be moving here for one reason. You. Okay? Now, are you seriously going to let jealousy ruin this special night?"

"No," I said. "I just…she was hitting on you, very hard. You might not have seen the signals, but she sent out plenty to me, warning me that she was going to be some serious competition. I don't like being threatened."

He picked up my hand across the table. "I'm not interested in her. I'm interested in you. So let's just drop it."

I picked up the menu. I needed to drop it, but I didn't know how. I was so upset I felt nauseated. I waited till the waiter had taken our drink order, then I went to the bathroom.

From the stall, I called Izzy, who was out. I tried Ann next and breathed a sigh of relief when she answered. As quickly as possible, I outlined the situation.

"Why are you so upset?"

"If she was a dog, she would have urinated on him!"

"So what? It's you he loves, not some stranger," she paused. "It's not like you to be jealous, Quinn."

I took a deep breath. "He just seems so clueless. He seriously doesn't believe that she is hitting on him. So she would be able to gain a lot of ground before he figures things out." The toilet flushed next to me. I peered out the crack of my stall and saw a gray-haired lady walk over to the sink to wash her hands.

"What is it about her that makes her such a threat?"

"She's gorgeous, for one," I whispered. "And smart."

"I think you have to trust Max until he proves you wrong," Ann said. I couldn't believe that Ann, the biggest man-hater I knew, was backing Max up. The gray-haired lady left the bathroom.

I sat on the toilet and stared at the drain in the floor. But she was right. "Okay." I hated to hang up with Ann. "I'm overreacting and I need to calm down." I paused. "Give me a theme song," I said. "To help me stay afloat. What's a good one?"

"Uh, what about that one by Natalie Merchant, that goes "Da, da, dee da." Ann's strength is not song lyrics.

"How about the Golden Earring song?" I suggested. "It's *2 a.m. The fear is gone. I'm sitting here waiting. The gun's still warm.*"

"Yeah! That's a good one. Or what about that one about the planets?"

"Venus? She's got it?"

"Yeah." Do we know each other, or what?

"Okay. That's a good one."

"Try to have fun," Ann said.

"Okay. I will."

I hung up and exited the stall. Washed my hands and checked my lipstick. I looked at my reflection and said, "Get a grip. Jealousy is poison. Go enjoy yourself." Then I left the bathroom and began the long trek across the dining hall. *She's got it! Yeah baby, she's got it.*

He was sitting, facing me, his back to the window. I was going to be okay. I sat down across from Max and drank half my wine in one gulp. *I'm your Venus, I'm your fire at your desire.* Kiss my ass, Shasta.

Max held my hand during most of dinner, and that helped.

Later that night, we were sitting on his bed, in the guest room, kissing in the moonlight. He gathered my hair up in one hand and started to kiss the back of my neck while his other hand unzipped my dress. And just then, I remembered what we were fighting about, that night, nine years ago, at El Patio Restaurant in Albuquerque.

He was flirting with our waitress. She was younger than us, about 20. She was pretty, of course, and she stumbled through the dinner specials like it was her first day on the job. Max fixed his gaze on her and asked, "And what's your name?"

She said, "It's uh, uh. I, uh. Bonnie. I'm Bonnie." A deep blush rose up from her neckline to her cheeks.

"Thank you, Bonnie," he said, cool as a cucumber. "I'll have a Corona." He raised his eyebrows at me and I ordered a Guinness.

When she was gone, he said, "Our waitress forgot her name." He seemed pleased with himself.

"Because she's just a kid and you made her nervous by flirting with her."

"I wasn't flirting."

I remember I felt so tired that I wanted to lay my head down on the table and sleep. "Why can't you be a good man?" I asked.

"I am a good man."

"Except for your wandering eye." I should clarify, Reader, that he had never cheated on me. At least, that I knew. But he flirted, and women flung themselves at him. I also knew that he had cheated before, on two previous girlfriends.

"I haven't done anything," he said. He was angry. Maybe he had a right to be.

"Will we be having this conversation in ten years about our children's baby sitter?" I had asked.

That made him hopping mad. He took his napkin out of his lap and threw it on the table before rising out of his seat. I felt somehow triumphant. Because I had finally upset him as much as he had upset me.

When the waitress returned with our beers, I was alone at the table. I drank my beer slowly, enjoying the feel of the cold glass against my hand. Max's beer sat across from me, untouched. When I was finished, I paid our bill and left.

Up until now, when I've told the story of our demise, I've always said it was because Max wanted to move back to New York, where we were from, and I wanted to stay in New Mexico. I've always said he had a job offer. And he did. But he didn't take that job. He stayed in Albuquerque for three months after our break-up before accepting a different New York job. I've told people it was because we were going in different life directions. He wanted a job that made him rich and required him to work 70-hour work weeks. He wanted a wife who supported his career, ran his house, and raised his kids, while he earned piles of money. I've always said that I wanted my own career. I've always said we had different life goals.

Not so. The truth is, we broke up because I thought he was a philanderer. I had completely forgotten that, up till now. Isn't memory a tricky thing?

I pulled away from him and stood up, in my guest room.

"What? What's wrong?" he asked.

"What's going to happen, if you come here?" I asked. "Are we going to fight the whole time about Shasta? Or some other pretty woman who hits on you?"

"I'm not doing anything with Shasta, or anyone else!"

"And if you are so certain you want to come here, why are you applying at so many other schools?"

"Because I may not get this job."

"If you are applying to Berkeley, and Princeton, don't you think that Omaha is a shoe-in?"

He rubbed his eyes. I didn't know what I was doing. He hadn't done anything wrong. But finally the frog was leaving my throat. "Be honest. If things work out between us, and I get a job somewhere like Boulder, where would you rather live?"

"I love this house," I said.

"I'm just saying, do you really want to stay in Omaha forever? The industrial farms, as far as the eye can see. The conservatives, the football, the steak. Quinn. It's like, if you picked a state that was your polar opposite, you'd pick Nebraska."

He was right. He knew me. He really did. But I said, "There's more to Omaha than football and steak." Which is true. Then I asked, "Who have you dated since we broke up?"

"What?"

"How many girlfriends have you had?"

"I don't know! It's been ten years!"

"Who did you last date?"

"The secretary, Lisa."

"And how long ago did you break up?"

He sighed and shook his head. See, the thing about Max is, he feels compelled to be honest, even when it makes him brutal. "We stopped officially dating three months ago."

"But you still have sex."

He looked at me. "Yes."

"When did you last have sex?"

He rubbed his eyes with his thumb and index finger. "The night before I came here."

I chewed on the inside of my lip and concentrated on not letting my emotions fly across my face. *Please, God, don't let me cry.* "Remember when we broke up, in Albuquerque? You didn't leave for another three months. Did you date someone during those three months?"

"God, Quinn!"

I didn't say anything.

He shook his head. "Yeah, I dated someone."

"Who was it?"

"A waitress."

"The waitress from El Patio who forgot her name?"

He nodded.

As I was dropping through space, I suddenly found a foothold. I sounded as bad as Max, but I suddenly thought, *there's still Oliver.* And I felt better.

I zipped up the back of my dress. I went over to Max and gave him a long, hard hug. "Max," I said. "I care about you. And I'm afraid for you. You don't treat women well. And what you want, a meaningful relationship with an intelligent woman, you're never going to get, until you put women on the same plane as you."

I doubt he agreed with what I said, but he was wise enough to just let me say it. That was another thing I'd always liked about him. He understood when people needed to say things uncontested.

I drove him to the airport, the next day. I was sad, but I wasn't full of despair. That's the power of having a guy-in-waiting.

Chapter 39
Getting F***ed Over by the Universe

I called Oliver the day after Max left. I was kind of nervous. I didn't know how he was handling the Max thing. "It's Quinn," I said.

"Quinn. So? Is Max gone or are you engaged?"

"He's gone," I said.

"What went wrong?" he asked.

"Nothing, really," I said. I picked at some lint on my shirt. "Time can make it easy to idealize relationships. But usually, if two people were meant to be together, they wouldn't have broken up in the first place."

"I have to admit, I was feeling kind of jealous."

"I'm really sorry about that," I said. "I just, well, he called out of nowhere and I had to see where it led. I've always held him as an ideal," I said. "Now, I don't know why." I sounded fine. I was fine. I wasn't grieving for Max. It was like I was on some kind of high, maybe because I'd cleared away nine years of delusional longing.

"Am I still invited next week?"

"Yes, if you still want to come."

"I do. Actually, I feel kind of glad that your Max has already come and gone. Now we can get down to business without any ghosts. You know, I had an ex-girlfriend who was always comparing me to this guy she'd lived with for ten years. He was one of those alpha males who would stage little events in an effort to prove to me that he could have her back at the snap of his fingers. It drove me nuts."

"Did she ever go back to him?"

"No. In fact, I think she's married now to someone else."

"I don't usually get jealous of my boyfriends' ex-girlfriends," I said. "But I guess it depends on whether the person gives me a reason to be jealous."

"Well, I'm told I'm the jealous type. But in a way it's good, because I won't do anything to make you jealous, if we end up in a relationship. I'm really careful about that."

"How's Pumpkin?"

"She's great. She's been a real pain this weekend. I've been brewing beer and she keeps getting in the way."

"You brew your own beer?"

"I'm a newbie. A friend of mine came over to show me how a while back. He came back last night, and when I gave him a bottle of my first solo batch, he told me it took him two years to make a batch as good as mine."

"You must be a natural."

"I guess so. I'm just that way, though. I'm naturally good at almost everything."

"I've noticed." I was being kind of teasingly sarcastic, but he missed it.

"Yeah. Like oil painting. I did my first painting a couple of years ago. I was dating this girl who had painted for like, ten years. My painting blew her away. She was just, like, blown."

"Why don't you tell me about something you do that doesn't come easily?" I asked.

"Uh, I don't know. I don't like to clean. Although, I can be extremely neat, when I set my mind to it."

"Well," I said. "Maybe that can be a goal for you. When you come next week, tell me about something that was hard for you to master."

"A challenge. Okay," he said. "I'll give it some thought."

"Oliver, I'm looking forward to meeting you," I said.

"Me too, Quinn the Painter."

Marlena's mother called. I couldn't believe it when I heard her voice on the phone.

"How's Marlena doing with the loaner aid?" I asked.

"She doesn't like how big they are. Anyway, I'm just calling to ask you to send me a copy of her hearing test."

"Okay. Do you need it for a pre-school program?"

"No, I found a hearing aid guy in town who can fit those little hearing aids on her."

"Little?"

"Yeah. The ones that go all the way into the ears."

I couldn't believe my ears. "CICs? Completely-in-the-canals?"

"Yes, CICs."

"She is too young to have them," I began. "She'll be grown out of them within a year, at the most. Then you'll have to pay to have them recased." My boss walked by and signaled me that our staff meeting was starting. "And she won't be able to use an FM system with them, when she starts school. Who's fitting her?" I asked.

"The place on 108th Street."

I didn't know it. I paused to rally my thoughts. "Marlena's hearing test is more than six months old," I said. "They'll have to do a new test. It's against the law to fit a child with hearing aids without a new test."

"They don't test kids," she said.

And they obviously don't fit them, I thought.

"They told me to come to you for a new hearing test."

I was completely astounded. I wanted to deny her a hearing test. I wanted to call the federal government and have the hearing aid people on 108th Street arrested. I wanted to hang up, stand up from my chair, and walk out of my office forever. Ever feel that way? Instead, I took a deep breath and scheduled her to come in. Then I went to the staff meeting. I decided to make "Whatever" my mantra of the day.

"Can she even afford them?" Lucy asked. Our staff meeting was over and we were talking about Marlena's mom.

"Probably. They live in Happy Hollow." A very wealthy part of town. "The mom drives a Lexus."

"How do you know that?"

"She told me."

Lucy shook her head. "All these months, when you've talked about them, I've been picturing trailer trash. They're rich?"

"Well-to-do, at least. Or they seem so. They dress really well. The mom's hands are always manicured."

"And here I am, stereotyping trailer trash. You know, some of my most reliable parents are on Medicaid. Some of the moms I follow have four kids from three different men, and yet, I tell them to wear those hearing aids from morning till night, and, by God, they do."

She looked at me. "So why do I continue to judge people by their socio-economic level?"

I shrugged. "I do it too. I expect rich people to be able to deal better. But they rarely do. Maybe they don't worry about making the rent this month, or being deported, but they still have stressful lives. Heck, I have a stressful life. Although I don't know why."

"So what about this mom of Marlena?" she asked.

"I want to kill her," I told Lucy.

I took Pacey on a long walk that night to help relieve stress caused by idiot parents. When I got home, I was still mad. Pacey, for once, was exhausted. He flopped out on the floor in the entryway and fell asleep.

I looked around my house. It was still clean and orderly from Max's visit. Assuming all was a go, and Oliver wasn't a freak, I was going to invite him to my house on Saturday night, for a fancy dinner. Upstairs, I had seven more boxes to unpack, but the place was starting to look like a home. For just a minute, I let myself imagine kissing Oliver. Wrapping his long hair in my fingers.

I sat down. I looked at my watch. Only 8 p.m. in Colorado. I picked up the phone. Oliver had said to call anytime.

"Hello?" A woman.

I thought I had the wrong number, but I asked anyway. "Hi, could I speak with Oliver?"

"Who's calling, please?" Her voice was challenging.

What the hell is this? I thought. "It's Quinn," I said, trying to sound as friendly as possible.

"Hi, Quinn. This is Marsha."

"Hi, Marsha."

"Oliver is in the shower."

I didn't know what to say. What was he doing in the shower when a hostile woman was in the house?

"Is there something *I* can help you with?"

"I really don't know how," I said, "since I was calling for Oliver."

"He'll have to call you back. Does he have your number?"

"He does, Marsha. Thank you. Goodbye."

My heart was thumping when I hung up. The house suddenly felt dead quiet. Pacey was on his side. His four legs were moving in his sleep. His nose was twitching and while I watched, he started growling in his sleep. I thought, *If he calls back within the next ten minutes, it was a misunderstanding. She was a neighbor or friend.* I kept my mind blank, to avoid jumping to conclusions. When fifteen minutes had passed, I thought, "Damn."

"That was no girlfriend," Jack said.

"It was a wife," Kate said.

Eli nodded.

"No way," I told them, putting my paintbrush down. "He wouldn't have done that."

"Has he called yet?" Kate asked.

I shook my head. It had been 24-hours. He was due to arrive in two days.

"He is married," she said.

I shook my fist at the ceiling. "Damn you, Internet dating!" I shouted.

"It's not like you guys were being exclusive," Izzy suggested. "Maybe she didn't even tell him you called."

"If that's the case, then why hasn't he called? He's coming tomorrow," I said. "To visit me."

"Are you going to call him?"

I shook my head. "No way."

Pacey, at least, was benefiting from my stress. We went on another two-hour hike around the lake. I could tell he was tired on the walk back to the car, because he kept bumping into me. The walks were a good way to tire him out, but the lake was 30 minutes away, so they took up most of my evening.

When we got home, I went upstairs to bed. My bed is like my office. I have papers and books, crossword puzzles, my laptop, and a phone on one side, my pillows and comforter on the other. I kept Pacey locked in with me, because he hadn't yet proven that he wouldn't use my house as his bathroom. In spite of his exhaustion, Pacey was pacing the room, whining. He sat down and watched me, quietly whimpering under his breath. He didn't like being trapped in my bedroom. His eyelids were drooping as he whined. I pretended to ignore him by turning my face away. With a disgruntled bark, he lay down and watched me. Every few minutes, I peered at him out of the corner of my eye. He had to shake his head once in a while, to stop sleep from overpowering him. Then, I heard a thump. Pacey's head had hit the ground. And it hadn't even woken him up.

I logged onto Match to see if I had any mail. None. I checked out Oliver's profile. He hadn't logged on in more than a week. I did a couple of searches for new matches, but my heart wasn't in it. I needed to find other ways of meeting men.

I closed my laptop and started to jot down brainstorming ideas on the backside of an envelope.

1. classes: whiskey tasting, woodworking, history
2. lectures at the university: science, art
3. Planetarium lectures
4. join a gym
5. salsa classes
6. walk Pacey in the park? Enroll him in agility classes?

Couldn't I do one of these a week? I thought the gym was my best option, in terms of meeting a steady stream of men, but I didn't really want to spend the time, or money, on a gym.

Oliver's arrival day came and went. He didn't. At least my house was clean.

Chapter 40
Why Men with Long Hair
Can't Give Women Multiple Orgasms

There's no chapter here, Readers. I just wanted to see that sentence in print.

Chapter 41
Revenge

At obedience class, we learned how to stop dogs from jumping (turn your back to them) and how to roll over. Pacey was really getting the hang of learning tricks. If I showed him something five times, he had it. The problem was, he still didn't like obeying me. He knew what I wanted him to do; he just didn't like to be commanded.

Izzy was having man problems. She and Josh had agreed to slow down their relationship.

"And that includes dating other people," she said. "It's like your book says, don't be idle. Date others while you figure someone out."

"Actually, the *Find A Husband* book says to cut your losses and move on. I think she says something like, 'Don't call, don't write, don't do couple's therapy.'"

"I can't be that drastic," Izzy said. "I really care about Josh."

"But you're dating again, online?"

"I have three guys going. I'm meeting one of them tonight, and one tomorrow after work. Then Josh and I are having dinner."

"My, you are spreading yourself thin!"

"Yes, well. I am. But I feel so under the gun. I don't have a lot of time."

"Do you remember how opposed you used to be to marriage? Remember how you would act at other people's weddings, getting drunk and telling the guests at your table that the couple was doomed? We could hardly keep you quiet during the service. Do you remember what you always wanted to shout?"

"Good fucking luck," Izzy said. She smiled. "It was the hurt talking. I distrusted the institution because it had failed me. Now, I'm ready to embrace it again. I miss married life."

"Do you think I'm ever going to meet anyone?" I asked. "I feel like I've been dating forever, yet I haven't made it to a single fourth date. I'm starting to lose hope."

"You'll meet someone. You just aren't going to settle for a slouch."

Oliver called four days after he was due to arrive. "Hey, what's up?"

"Not much," I said. "What's up with you?" Was he going to act like nothing had happened?

"Nothing really. How are you doing?"

"Well, in terms of you, not well. You were coming here and you didn't even call to cancel! And who is Marsha and why is she acting like she's your exclusive girlfriend?"

"Oh. Marsha. Yeah, I wondered if that was what upset you. She told me you called and when I didn't hear from you, I figured the trip was off. But Marsha and I are no longer together. I had been dating her very causally. Honestly, I barely know her. I don't know where she got off, answering my phone."

"So why didn't you call me back?"

"I was waiting to hear from you. I wasn't sure if you still wanted me to come for a visit. Anyway, I've had a really rough week. I've been working on a bunch of projects, and three of them failed completely. I was actually pretty depressed about it. I mean, I'd put almost sixty work hours into each one."

He went on like that, for 14 minutes straight. I timed him while I unloaded my dishwasher and cleaned my stovetop.

"So, what have you been up to?" he finally asked.

"Not much," I told him. "I've been…"

"You know, I was really surprised when you never called. I could have used a friendly voice this week."

"Sorry," I told him. My kitchen was clean, so the phone call hadn't been a complete waste. "Here, maybe I can cheer you up with a haiku."

"I'd like that," he said.

"Okay," I said. I came up with it off the top of my head. I had to count on my fingers, as I spoke, to make sure I got the number of syllables right.

The brilliant college
Drop-out lives a pointless life
but doesn't notice.

He didn't say anything.

I said, "It's called, "Why Men with Long Hair Are Selfish Assholes."

Long silence. Then he said, "That was very bitter. I don't think I want to know you after all, Quinn. I'm going to hang-up now."

"Goodbye," I said. And then he hung up.

Sometimes it feels good to just be petty and small, Reader. It really does.

Chapter 42
Destructive Lists

Here are some lists that women make in idle moments. They begin about the age of 8 and continue on indefinitely. We girls should be listing the world's most needed inventions, or best cities. Best careers. Best ice cream flavors. Instead, we make lists like this:

Best Baby Names

Girls
1. Sahra (means "awakening")
2. Clara
3. Faith
4. Mercedes (nickname: Mercy)
5. Ivy
6. Hazel
7. Madison
8. Ruby Rose
9. Lotus

Boys
1. Benjamin
2. Moses
3. Johnson
4. Nicolas
5. Joseph
6. Alexander
7. Austin

8. Seth
9. Zane

Best Wedding Locations
1. Under ponderosa pines in Colorado or New Mexican mountains
2. Sedona, AZ, outside at sunset
3. A meadow with wild flowers
4. Cherry Esplanade in the Brooklyn Botanical Gardens
5. Jamaica
6. Hawaii

Best songs to play at my wedding
1. Crush (Dave Matthews Band)
2. Let My Love Open the Door (Pearl Jam)
3. Two Step (Dave Matthews Band)
4. You Are My Kind (Seal)
5. When I'm 64 (Beatles)
6. In Your Eyes (Peter Gabriel)
7. Radar Love (Golden Earring)
8. Play Me (Neil Diamond)
9. At Last (Joan Osbourne)

After each break-up, I remember my destructive little lists and grieve for my girlhood dreams and what could have been.

How many people have private lists like mine? I know there are "What to pack lists" and "Things to do lists" in most people's history. But are there "Cities I want to live in" lists and "How will I spend my money when I become rich" lists in the pockets of people we work with or stand next to in church? What about "Ways I will be good," and "How I will be happy" lists?

Chapter 43
Listening to My Mother

But whatever. I moved on. I didn't take my profile down, this time. I even read my Match emails. Everyone seemed so drab and boring, next to Oliver, but maybe that's because his megalomania created its own light. One Friday night, after Pacey had been walked and I was settling in for the night, my phone rang. It was Lucy.

"Hey, Lucy, what's up?"

"I'm out at a bar," she shouted. I could hear a lot of noise behind her. "We're watching the game. My husband's college roommate is out with us. He works for the Huskers. He's in their PR department. He's single and all of a sudden, I thought of you."

"Oh, thank you," I said.

"He's a catch because he gets great seats to all the games. It's just that tonight he is staying in Omaha, so he's watching the game at the bar. Why don't you meet us?"

"I don't know," I said. "You know how I hate football."

"Not with his seats," she said. "You'd be right in the middle of the action. Hell, I wish I could date him!"

"He deserves a woman who would appreciate that part of him. I would never want to go to the games."

"Are you sure?"

"Thanks for thinking of me, though. I really appreciate it."

I hung up with Lucy, opened a beer, and settled into my sofa to watch the television shows I'd taped for the week. The Office, a PBS special on Alzheimer's disease, America's Test Kitchen, and Ask This Old House. Pacey was asleep on the other side of the room.

Suddenly I realized that I'd turned down a chance to meet a guy so that I could stay home with my dog and watch television. Taped television.

Desperate times call for desperate measures. I turned off the TV and got my mother's book, *Find a Husband After 35 (Using What I Learned At Harvard Business School)*. The author, Rachel Greenwald, had gotten her M.B.A at Harvard. What a gimmick! I began with the table of contents, which was actually a little more interesting than I thought it would be. There were chapters like, "Market Expansion: Cast a Wider Net" and "Branding: Identify What Makes You Different." Opening the book up to chapter 14, I read this line. "If you have a dog, ask yourself whether you use him as a tool to meet men, or an excuse to stay home on Friday nights?" I shut the book and put it back on the shelf. Who needed truth-telling on a Friday night, when I had 3 ½ hours of television to fill my head?

But the next day I read *Find A Husband After 35* cover to cover. There were things in there that I would never do. But she had a lot of good ideas. One was to alert everyone in your life, and everyone you come into contact with, to your interest in meeting a man. I wasn't going to be as direct as Rachel Greenwald recommended, but I did like the idea. She also suggested creating your own slogan. I could use my Match tagline, "Funny, but introverted artist." Her idea was to tell people your slogan so that, when they are talking you up to potential dates, they know how to describe you.

She had some good ideas for how to dress, too. For example, in spite of how great you feel in it, don't wear a power suit on a date. I don't own a power suit, but I saw her point. What makes me feel good might not make me look feminine. For instance, my best colors are black and brown. My new idea was to wear more pink. Also, she said not to dress too sexy or men won't view you as a possible future wife. She also suggested getting your hair professionally blown dry before each first date.

This author guaranteed that you would get married within 18-months if you followed her plan. I couldn't do everything she said, though. There were too many things that were just impossible for me to do. Like, call up everyone I know, including hairdressers and neighbors from childhood and tell them that this was the year I'd decided I wanted to find someone special and that I'd like their help. Impossible for me. And I don't think I was alone, because after some of her toughest steps, Rachel Greenwald said something like, "Now, you may be thinking that you could never do that. But I ask you to go back to the beginning of this book, when I had you answer a series of questions to help determine whether this book was for you. I asked if you were willing to do *whatever it takes* to find a husband, as long as it wasn't immoral or illegal." Turns out I wasn't, so I guess I didn't want a husband as much as I thought I did. Good to know.

I went out shopping for pink clothes. I've despised pink since I stopped having single digit ages. But things were going to change. I got two pink shirts and two pink skirts. The sales lady, a woman in her mid-twenties, told me, "Nice choices! You like pink, I see."

"I don't really like it that much," I said. "But I'm trying to meet men, and I thought that looking more feminine would make it easier."

"Hmmm, what kind of guy are you looking for?"

"I don't know. Someone nice and healthy."

"Do you mind bald?"

"No, not at all."

"I have a bald friend who's a lawyer. He's really nice, but he's kind of fat."

"The only thing is the weight," I said. "I like to do a lot of outdoors things. I've always envisioned a man that could backpack into the wilderness with me for two months."

She nodded. "I completely understand. I wish I knew someone else." She gave me my receipt and credit card.

"Thanks for trying," I said, taking my bags. I felt giddy on my way to the car. I was *doing* the book. It was in my own way, but still, I was alerting even strangers to the fact that I wanted to meet someone.

Chapter 44
A Kinder, Gentler Me

"I was online, the other day," Jack said. "So I looked up your profile on Match."

"Really? What'd you think?" I asked. I stopped painting to hear what he had to say. I was pretty proud of my profile.

"It's a little bitter," he said.

I feel like I've spent half my life working to avoid being called bitter, angry, or desperate. If a man thinks you are any of those things, forget about it.

"In what way?" I asked.

"You comment about not dating men who only date younger than themselves."

"What's wrong with that?"

He shrugged. "You put asterisks around it. It was the first thing my eye went to."

"I don't want those men to email me."

"So tell them, when they email."

I pondered this. "I want to set a public example," I said. "It's my protest corner."

But I guess I'm starting to mature, Reader. Because when I got home from class, I went into my profile and removed that line. I figured, why be so strident? Once that line was gone, I took out a few more, and before I knew it, I had a kinder, gentler profile. The new me. Basically, the same profile, without all the zip.

"I like it," Ann said. I had printed out a copy and taken it to our morning coffee. "But I've liked all of your profiles so far."

"Thanks," I said, looking around. We were meeting at a new coffee house, downtown. "This place," I began, "is very cavernous. I'm not sure I like it here."

Ann shrugged. "It's nice to try new places."

I narrowed my eyes. "You've never gone anywhere but Jackson's place," I said. "What gives?"

She picked at the table, then put her hands in her lap and looked at me. "I can't go back to that place anymore." She shook her head. "He turns out to have some kind of crush on me. He got me alone the other day, and told me all this stuff about his feelings for me."

"Jackson is great," I said. "Why not see where it takes you?"

She shook her head. "I don't date."

"But, why not?"

"I don't like men. Haven't I made that clear before?"

"You like men!"

"Not for dating."

"Yes, but you liked Jackson just fine, until he told you he had romantic feelings for you."

"I don't think he's any good now—he seems damaged. He must be, if he likes me."

I didn't know what to say. I looked at Ann. "You're brilliant and gorgeous. You're a total catch. Any guy would be lucky to have you."

"Men just screw you over," she said.

"But Jackson wouldn't do that. He's nice. You know that. You know him."

"Nice men don't like me. I'm desperate, needy, obnoxiously opinionated, quick to anger, resentful, insecure, and difficult."

I couldn't speak for a minute. Then I said, "Why, we're *all* those things! So what?"

She shook her head. "I'm just not going to waste my time on a guy. I've had enough of that for a lifetime. I'm happier alone than I'd ever be with someone else."

"I don't understand."

"Everyone acts like your life isn't complete without marriage. I'm not buying into that myth."

I gripped her wrists and said, in a wide-eyed, urgent way, "It's not a myth." Then I laughed, but she didn't.

"Why do you want to get married?" she asked.

I shrugged. "To have kids."

"What if you didn't want kids? Would you still want to get married?"

"Sure. Because being married means that there's someone else out there for whom you always come first."

"Why do you need that? You seem to be doing fine on your own. You own a home, you travel, you take care of yourself."

"True. But if I was married, then I'd have…"

"Someone to share it with?" she sniped.

I took a sip of coffee and thought about it. "If I was married," I said, "I'd have someone to deflect the stress from social outings. I'd have someone to drink coffee with in the morning. I'd have someone to kiss and touch and have sex with. I could split my heating bill in half. I'd be able to buy the 60 lbs bags of dog food without breaking my back to carry it into the house. I'd only cook dinner half as often. I'd have someone around me who cared about me more than anyone else in the world. When my parents die, I'll have no one around me who will always put me first."

"And," Ann said, "you'd have the television playing when you're not watching it. You'd have a mother-in-law who probably thinks you aren't good enough for her son. You'd have to listen to someone else's chewing during every meal. And you wouldn't be able to go on vacation wherever you wanted, or spend every Christmas with your family, or buy your next house without compromising on the style or size or location."

"All good points," I conceded. "I know I won't be any happier married, than I am now. But I think you gain something from traveling through life with a permanent companion. A comrade. I think that sacrifice and compromise are good for your character, and if you're single, you don't have to do it too often."

Ann shrugged. "I don't think you need a mate to learn that stuff. A man is not the end all. I like my life."

Chapter 45
Leaving the Matrix:
Searching for Men Outside of Match

"I'm so sorry," Izzy was saying. She'd forgotten our plans to meet for pizza, and I'd sat in the bar for 35 minutes before heading home. She'd come by my house an hour later, with pizza. "I'm just so frazzled lately. I can't seem to stay on top of anything."

"Maybe you're pregnant," I said, mostly just to be mean.

"Don't even say it," she said. "It's just that life is hectic. Josh is coming back around to getting serious. He wants to start house hunting again. On Friday, he introduced me to his sister."

"What about the other people you'd been emailing?" I asked.

"No time. Plus, my sister's due next week and I'm driving to Denver as soon as she goes into labor."

"What happened to the musician you went out with last week? He sounded cool."

She shook her head. "Too mercurial. Artists don't make for reliable husbands. This time around, I'm going to be smart."

This reminded me of how I decided to get my master's in audiology. My undergrad was in art and I'd decided that, if I were going to go back to school, it would be for a more marketable degree. Money magazine rated audiology as the tenth best job in the country the year I was looking. As I recall, they based their assessment on things like years of schooling (just a master's at the time), demand (there'll be a deficit as the baby boomers hit old age), salary (upper average), and flexibility (you could live virtually anywhere in the country and probably find a job). My art degree was a great growing experience, I learned a lot, and I had absolutely no regrets. But I also worked as a secretary to pay my rent. My second degree would be for the job, not the personal growth. That's what Izzy was doing with her men. She was being pragmatic. I decided to keep my mouth shut. "That makes sense," I said.

"I'm thinking, what's a reasonable amount of time to date before getting married?"

"A year?" I asked.

"Yeah. I was thinking that, too. Or, definitely six months."

"Six months?"

"Yeah. And Josh and I have already been dating for four."

"Are you nuts? You barely know him!"

"I know enough. I'll learn the rest as I go."

"Jeez, Izzy. You were supposed to play the field for a while."

"I did. I'm done with that. I want to get married."

"But…"

"I'm ready." She gripped my hand with hers. "I'm ready."

My kinder, gentler profile was up, and my emails dropped from four a day to one a week. The Liberals still weren't emailing and the Indignant Conservatives didn't care anymore.

In my next attempt to meet men, I took Pacey to a dog fair that was supposed to have agility and fly ball demonstrations. The fair was set up in a city park. I wore a pink shirt. Pacey turned in circles, he was so happy to see so many people and dogs. After a lot of practice, he was getting much better at walking. He rarely cut in front of me anymore.

"That's a White German Shepherd if I ever saw one," said a man who was passing out maps. He had a teenage son. "Look at that Shepherd," he said to his son. "He'd love to play with our dogs, wouldn't he?"

"Do you have White Shepherds?" I asked.

He nodded. "Got three of 'em. We always have White Shepherds."

"Three?" I looked down at Pacey, who was sitting next to the man, tall and straight while being petted. "How old would you say my dog is?" I asked.

The man backed up and sized Pacey up and down. "Not a day over one year old," he said. Ah-hah! That explained why he was such a maniac! The Humane Society was wrong! He wasn't three, he was one, and still a puppy.

After watching agility demonstrations, we headed over to the nail clipping line. Pacey waited patiently, watching the other people and dogs with a dignity I wouldn't have thought possible, till that moment.

A middle-aged woman behind me was on her cell phone. "Hi. I'm here, at the dog fair, where you guys were supposed to meet me. I don't know where you are. I'm holding a spot in line, but I feel pretty silly without a dog, so when you get this, hurry up and get here." She hung up. "What kind of dog is that?" she asked me.

"White German Shepherd."

"I'm supposed to have a chow. My kids are late," she said. "My husband's probably lost."

I smiled sympathetically and was about to turn away when she said, "Where'd you get him?"

"From the Humane Society," I said.

"Mine, too," she said. "And we just love our dog." She kept up a steady chatter that only required me to nod occasionally. After about ten minutes, her kids arrived with their dog, a puppy named Ruby.

"Where's your father?"

"He's parking the car," said the oldest child, a teenage girl. Ruby wanted to play with Pacey, but Pacey turned his head away and sniffed the air, as if he was above a dog so young.

"Are you from here?" the mom asked.

"No," I told her. "I'm from NY."

She smiled. "What do you think of our city?" she asked.

"It's very nice," I said. Then I remembered my goal, to alert people to the fact that I was actively searching for a man. "But it's hard to meet people."

"Really?" she seemed surprised. "Are you single?"

I nodded.

"Looking?"

"Sure."

"Hmmm." She scrunched her eyebrows together while she thought.

"Mom?" the daughter asked. When she didn't get an answer, she said, "MOM!"

Her mom looked up. "What? Why are you yelling?"

"Because you weren't listening. What about David?"

"Who?"

"David. What about him. He'd like to meet someone."

Go, little girl! I thought.

"Oh, David. Well he would be good, except that he's got a lot of baggage," she said. To me she said, "Three kids. Who live with him."

I nodded and tried to look appealing.

"What about Greg?" the mom asked her daughter.

"Ew! Gross!" the daughter said.

The mom looked at me. "How old are you?"

"Thirty-nine."

"Oh, he's too young. Twenty-two, fresh out of college, but still a kid. You know, do you have an email address?" she asked. "I can't think of anyone else, but if someone comes to mind, I could contact you."

"Sure," I said, digging through my purse for a piece of paper.

She took my email and tucked it into her purse. "Do you have strong feelings about religion?"

I shook my head.

"Okay. Let me think about it."

I was noticing that Pacey didn't seem to know basic dog things. He didn't bark at the mailman. In fact, he didn't even notice the mailman, even when he was chained up in the front yard. Usually, he looked the other way as the mailman made his way up the lawn to our porch. If Pacey did acknowledge him, it was with a tail-wag. Pacey didn't seem to hear the doorbell, either. He cocked his head to honking horns, oven timers, and dogs on TV, but he never registered the doorbell, and always seemed surprised when I opened the door to reveal someone standing on the other side. He loved greeting visitors. He'd watch someone approach through the window and thump his tail on the floor when they hit the porch.

By the sixth month of our time together, however, things had started to change. One day, I had three visitors in a row. The first time the doorbell rang, Pacey opened his eyes from a nap, but didn't get up until I stood to answer the door. When he saw Ann behind the door, he twirled around, wagging his tail and trying to nudge past me. She came into the living room, and he sat next to her. Ten minutes later, when the doorbell rang again, he looked at me as if to say, "Something exciting is going to happen, but I don't know what!" He stayed by Ann in the living room until he saw me go to the door. It was the mailman, who had a package. Pacey wagged his tail as I opened to door to take the padded envelope.

"Look," I told Ann. "The entire first season of Veronica Mars on DVD."

"Get a life," she said.

The third time the doorbell rang, Pacey went straight for the door. He'd finally made the connection. It was a tall man, in his fifties. He looked at me strangely. "Do I have the wrong address?"

"I don't know," I said.

"I'm looking for Penny," he said. Penny was my neighbor. She was black, I was white.

"Next door," I told him, pointing north and pulling a tail-wagging Pacey away to shut the door.

"Not much of a guard dog, is he?" Ann asked.

"He doesn't even bark at the mailman," I said.

"Give him time," Ann said. "He'll come around."

Ann was correct. A few weeks after he learned about the doorbell, Pacey decided that strangers were not allowed on our lawn. The first time I noticed his new behavior was when a telephone repairman pulled up in front of our house. I was outside gardening again, and Pacey was in his usual spot, on the front porch. He watched with interest as the repairman parallel parked and got out of his vehicle. He even wagged his tail. But when the man put his first foot on our walkway, Pacey lunged to the end of his chain, teeth bared, growling and barking. The man jumped backward and put the truck between himself and my dog. "He's on a leash," I said as I hurried to stand between the man and a snarling Pacey. I had to repeat myself several times before the telephone man registered my words. Pacey continued to growl while I showed the man to the side of the house, where the phone box was mounted.

Overnight, Pacey started to go ballistic when the mailman came. If he was inside, he threw himself against the door, scratching and growling. I was scared he was going to break the glass. On the other hand, I liked the protection. When strangers came to the door, Pacey lunged and barked the entire time I talked to them. People were afraid of Pacey, and seeing him in defense-action, I didn't blame them. He was as tall as me when he stood on his hind legs.

"He's like a completely different dog," Izzy said, the first time he growled and barked at her as she approached the house. "Doesn't he recognize me?"

"I don't know. It's like he suddenly realized, 'This is my home,' and so now he defends it. As soon as I let her inside, Pacey stopped growling and sat down next to Izzy, tail thumping.

"I'm kind of scared to touch him," Izzy said. She stroked his head. He leaned into her and licked her hand.

Chapter 46
Using Hypnosis to Smile at Men

So I've been watching old episodes of *Sex and the City*. You know what I've noticed? Sarah Jessica Parker's face when she interacts with strange men. She kind of smiles, in sort of an oddball way. She rolls her eyes up in a self-deprecating style, she crunches her face around in a curious, interested, friendly manner. I don't think I do any of that. I look interested in an intense, serious way. But, I don't convey lightheartedness in the first ten minutes of a meeting. Partly, this is just my personality. But also, I'm usually too nervous around men to smile. I should clarify. I smile, but it's a hard smile, not my normal grin, which can be very warm, if I know you well.

When I was four years old, or so, my favorite song was on my Sesame Street album; it was an Oscar the Grouch's song: Just Let A Frown Be Your Umbrella. I think I took the lyrics to heart, because now, I would venture to say that the number one reason why I can't get a man is because of my frown. I used to think that this was no big deal because the right man, that self-assured extrovert, would see through my crusty exterior. Then, a while back, Izzy said, "Men won't approach you if they think you aren't going to go out with them." A revelation. And as I looked back on the past fifteen years, I realized that she was right.

So I set about rectifying more than a decade of scowls, but it was harder than I'd anticipated. On day one, I resolved to smile at every man I saw. And every woman, too, so it wouldn't seem like I was some kind of flirt. In the park, a man pushing a stroller walked by. I flashed him a warm smile, and threw in another for the baby. He smiled back. Perfect. Then two women. Neither smiled back at me.

Okay, okay. Whatever, ladies. Another woman came by. I couldn't smile at her after the last rejection, though. I took a moment for myself. Then a 40-ish chubby man came by with a dog. I gave him a smile. He didn't smile back. I was done for the day.

But on my way back to the car, an attractive jogger appeared on the horizon. "One last smile," I told myself, and geared up as he came down the hill. But before I could smile, he smiled at me. And Reader, do you know what I did? I sent him a killer scowl. Then, I actually thought, *What do you think this is? A meat market, buddy? Get back to your jog and stop trying to hit on women who are just out getting some air.*

A week later, I decided to try again, but I didn't even get out of my car before changing my mind and thinking, "I'm too exhausted to smile at men today." So, I gave myself a week off, which turned into three. When I finally got back to smiling at men, I realized that I could only smile at men I wasn't attracted to. Every time a cute guy came by, my knee jerk reaction was to scowl. And Readers? I'm like Medusa when I scowl. My scowl is so powerful that it scares people. Hell, even my neutral look makes strangers to say, "What's the matter? Smile!" (Which is a sure-fire way to trigger a mega-scowl.) Even my friends have told me to smile more. So that gives you an idea about my face—intensely expressive. Maybe a little too much so.

Could I get control of my smile? The prosperity teacher told us, "choose love or fear." *Choose love or fear.* Could I do it? I've done other things that were hard. I didn't drop Public Speaking in high school, even when all my friends dropped after the first day. I traveled alone through Europe at the age of 20. I spent an entire day interviewing at the Mayo Clinic, in 3-inch heels. I sent Max, love of my life, packing because hoping someone is the right man for you doesn't make it true.

For me, the first ten seconds of an interaction with a cute guy are the hardest. I want to choose love over fear, but there's no time to make that choice. When the moment arrives, the room disappears and I'm rooted to the ground, in Mordor, wind whistling through my hair, Orcs charging me, while I wish with every ounce of my soul that the earth would open up and swallow me whole. I actually want the Earth to open and swallow me. It's uncontrollable, and it's terrifying. Thus, I fail at the smile.

One of my patients was hypnotized for smoking and it worked. Her office paid everyone half the cost of whatever smoking cessation method they wanted to take, and if they stayed cigarette-free for six months, they got the second half paid for, too. Twelve people in her office were hypnotized for smoking. Of the twelve, only four had to go back for a recharge. The recharges were free if you called within seven days of smoking. As far as she knew, all twelve had gone for a year without smoking.

I couldn't stop thinking about her story, and wondering if I could get hypnotized to not be so nervous around attractive men. I had the hypnotist's card. His name was Barry Harker. I called him.

"What hypnotism could do," he began, "is stop the fear, before it causes the physical reaction in you that makes you seem unfriendly."

There was no research to back this guy up. He didn't follow-up or document his success rate. Still, why not give it a shot? So I made an appointment. He worked out of an office in a strip mall, but so does everyone in middle America. His receptionist was his wife. Barry was tall and skinny, with a handlebar mustache. We went into his office, and he sat me down in a big, fake leather recliner.

He explained the process, which was counting backwards as I went into a highly suggestive state. I had given him a list of things I wanted to change:

1. Smile at strangers, including attractive men
2. Feel calm around men I'm attracted to
3. Stop grinding my teeth at night

He dimmed the lights and asked me to close my eyes. Then he started the "You are getting very sleepy" thing, just like you see in the movies. "You are walking down a staircase. There are twelve steps. With each step you will feel more relaxed and calmer. On the last step you will be completely calm and peaceful. Ten…you are calming down. Nine…you feel your muscles loosen…"

The whole way down, all I could think was, "It's not working! I'm not getting hypnotized!" But I didn't know whether telling him this would interrupt the hypnosis or not. When we got to the last step, I felt no different from when I walked into the office.

"You feel friendly toward men. They are no barrier to your inner peace and tranquility. You smile at them and it makes you happy. It's easy to smile at them. They are no threat to you…"

I tried to stay open to what he was saying, but my mind kept wandering to the hypnotist who visited our school when I was in 10th grade. He performed in the auditorium in front of all four grades. Danny Horowicz volunteered to get onstage, and the hypnotist told him to quack like a duck every time he heard the word "banana." It worked, too. Danny put his heart and soul into that quacking. Even when he'd been taken out of hypnosis, every time someone said "banana," he started to quack. So, twenty years later, all I wanted to do, in this recliner in this strip mall, was burst out laughing.

When I'd gone back up the "steps" and he had turned up the lights, I said, "I'm not sure this worked. I don't think I went into a trance."

"It's not a trance," he said. "It's simply a highly suggestive state. I'd told you you'd be completely conscious the whole time." He stood up. His next patient was waiting. I went into the lobby and paid his wife $95.00. I really didn't see how that could make someone quack when they heard the word banana.

Leaving the office, I fingered my keys as I walked to my car. I was going to have a positive attitude about this. He'd made people stop smoking. I was going to believe he would help me with men, and my molars. As I unlocked my door, a red pick-up truck pulled up next to me. A young man, about 28, climbed out. He wore Levi jeans, work boots, and a black sweatshirt. As he hopped to the ground, he gave me a big grin. "Mornin'" he said. I froze him with a cold glare. He shrugged and walked away. *Damn. Wait. You just scared me because you were so cute.* I climbed in my car and looked at myself in the rearview mirror. "Ninety-five dollars to learn that hypnosis doesn't work? Priceless." My jaw squeezed my molars together as I turned my key in the ignition.

Izzy and Josh had found a home. And now she was canceling her road trip to Denver.

"You've been planning this trip for months!" I said.

"Josh just didn't want me to go," she said. "He's worried about me driving alone for 8 hours. He thinks I should fly." She gave a self-satisfied little sigh. "I have to say, it's nice to have someone show concern."

"Concern or control?" I asked.

Izzy laughed. "I appreciated it."

"And that, my friend, is why I'm still single and you're not."

Chapter 47
Falling for a Match Man

I'd moved outside of Match, but I was reading my emails.

Dear Quinn Painter,

Okay, I can see I'm going to have to impress you fast, because you've got the best profile on Match, so you must be besieged by mail. But, before you pass me by, let me say a couple of things: I worked for the ACLU in NY, I spent one summer camping near the Alaskan Wildlife Refuge, and I currently restore old homes in Omaha. I share a lot of your interests, including reading and gardening. Actually, I own a home in a very old part of Omaha, and there was this ancient garden there that I had to leave alone for a year, so that I could watch the full cycle of all the plants before I started pulling. I like to cook time-consuming, elaborate meals, but not very often. I'm a big dog fan, but I haven't taken the plunge of ownership, yet.

Oh, and I'm from your neck of the woods—Massachusetts. I have a very heavy Boston accent, so you'll feel right at home, with your New York accent (if we can understand each other).

Zach

I responded right away.

Zach,

Normally I'd put some real effort into a witty, but guarded response, but since you're from the East Coast, I can just be my normal, blunt self. You sound neat. What did you do for the ACLU, and how did you get interested in restoring...actually, do you just want to meet, sometime, for a drink or coffee, instead of doing this back and forth with the email?

Quinn

Quinn, You name the time and place, and I'll be there.

Zach

Reader, I'm such a wimp. I read his email and freaked out. So I called Izzy. She wasn't home.

"Izzy, where are you? I tried to flirt online, and now I'm in way over my head, and I need your help! I have to send an email back to a really neat guy on Match and I don't know what to say. Call me!"

Pacey was sleeping across the room. As I paced, he woke up, left, and returned with one of his toys in his mouth. It was a green plastic toy, shaped like a small dumbbell. One of the balls was in his mouth, the other popping out at a crooked angle. He looked so pleased with himself. He came over to me to get pet, then he crossed the room and sat down to chew. Every few minutes, his tail thumped the floor. He was just such a happy dog.

My phone rang. "Hello?"

"This is Dating Central. How may we help you?"

Izzy. "Thank goodness you're back!" I outlined my daring response to Zach's email.

"You are totally ready for this guy. Keep your eye on the goal. Just email him back and say, "The French Café, bar. Seven p.m. Tonight."

"Tonight?"

"Okay. Tomorrow. In case he doesn't check his email again."

"Wait. So soon? And the bar at the French Café?"

"Yes. Why wait? You are showing him that you're romantic and sophisticated. It's sexy. Now go do it."

I could feel my anxiety puffing up like a hairball. But I asked myself, "Love or fear?" Then I made a decision. I pushed my worry away and acted like a normal person. I emailed him back and he replied with one line. "I'll be there."

He was a babe. He had that look that I love, lean and kind. A swimmer's physique. Sandy brown hair that was cut kind of longish. A warm, friendly smile. About my age or a couple of years older. I walked into the bar, and he stood immediately and said, "Quinn!" and shook my hand. He had a firm, but not crushing grip. He looked me right in the eye and said, "It's good to meet you." Then he smiled and said, "Great location."

I could only say, "You don't have a Boston accent."

"You don't have a New York accent."

I smiled. "I didn't say I did."

He bowed. "That is true. You didn't. Actually, mine pops out now and then. Usually when I'm upset."

We sat down at the bar. I could feel a sarcastic comment rising out of me. I tend to have a barbed sense of humor when I'm nervous because it gives my fear an outlet. I tried to coach myself out of it: *Don't fuck this up. Don't fuck this up*. Then I made the best choice I'd made in a while: *Say nothing*. I gave him a warm smile.

"God, you're beautiful," Zach said.

I was mortified. Who talks like that? How could I talk to someone like this? He was too cute, too intense. I was scared-to-freaking-death.

But I came through with my usual biting alacrity. I suppressed my blush, looked right into his eyes and said, in a very intense way, "And you are obviously smart. Our children will be stunning." He was totally taken aback. It took a lot of control to keep my face straight, but I did. After about 5 seconds, he burst out laughing, and then I laughed too.

He shook his head, like I'd impressed him. I don't know what men expect us to do when they tell us we're beautiful in the first five minutes of meeting us. On the one hand, it's very flattering. But it's also embarrassing. And there is *so much more* to me than my looks. And some day I was going to be wrinkled and grey.

We ordered drinks. He had a beer. I had a vodka martini, straight up. I mean, I was at the French Café!

"So what did you do at the ACLU?"

"I was a lawyer, so I did lawyerly things."

"How long did you work there?"

"Four years. I lived on the lower East side."

We chatted about NYC for a while. "What exactly is your job now?" I asked. "Do you do the actual construction on old homes?"

"Yeah. I wasn't really happy as a lawyer. So I got a job as an apprentice to a Master Carpenter. I have always loved old homes. I specialize in restoration."

"Okay. So there you were, in a very old city, with lots of money for restoration. What brought you to Omaha, where such a tiny portion of the city is old?"

He shrugged. "I met a contractor from Nebraska. He offered me three long-term jobs in Dundee. I spent two years here, working on those projects, and by then I'd found this decrepit but amazing old home to buy. It cost me $40,000. I couldn't find something like that in New York for less than two million."

Billie Holiday was singing in the background. Zach's aura was gentle and sexy at once. I felt like I was falling into him. "So you were suckered in by the ol' good cost of living," I said.

He took a swig of his beer. "I could be house poor and live in New York, or live in a beautiful home, with a good disposable income, and be in Omaha." He looked around at the space we were in. The room was an old Art Nouveax design. There was a beautiful stained glass window on one wall, and another stained glass window encasing the entryway to the bar. "And Omaha has some real gems."

He was right about that. Omaha had wonderful restaurants, beautiful old buildings, and a good cost of living.

"What brought you here?" he asked. I told him about audiology. He listened intently while I talked, without interrupting. "So, what do you think about digital hearing aids?" he asked. "Are they really so great? My neighbor has one, and he spent, like, $5,000. And I don't think he hears me very well at all."

We parted with a handshake and an exchange of phone numbers. He called the next day. "I was going to play hard to get," he began. "But then I just wanted to talk to you." He didn't even introduce himself, but I recognized his deep voice immediately.

"Why, *I* was going to play hard to get!" I said.

"I've already got our second date planned," he said, "so don't play too hard."

"What have you got in mind?" I asked.

"All I can say is, wear a calve-length dress or skirt, and comfortable but stylish shoes."

"What if I don't own stylish shoes?" I asked.

"Sneakers, then. Do you own sneakers?" I could hear laughter in his voice.

I was silent as I tried to think of what he was planning for this, our second date. "Why calve-length?" I finally asked.

"You'll find out. I'll see you at 7." And he hung up.

As I dressed, Pacey sat in the bedroom, watching me. He had to come over and smell every skirt I tried on.

"We're going dancing?"

Zach had picked me up at seven, dressed in a snazzy suit. I'd come outside, as soon as he pulled up, to avoid a big barking scene with Pacey. I was in a dress that was fitted on top and flared out to just below my knees. I had on a pair of black heels. Unfortunately, I my face had broken out and I had an ugly red zit on my chin.

Zach had been mum about our destination, and even when we pulled up in front of the old ballroom in midtown, I hadn't been sure what he was up to. But now we were standing in a room with chairs around the perimeter and a boom box was playing big band music. There were other couples milling around, and a fair number of single men on the make. "You took us dancing?" I asked, my voice rising with panic.

"Yes," Zach said, proudly. He completely missed my tone.

We were going dancing. I had to admit it was pretty romantic, even though I couldn't dance.

Zach was saying hi to several people. I guess he was a regular here. "Are you a regular here?"

"I come pretty often," he said. He steered me over to a refreshment area and got me a glass of punch. "I really like to dance. My mom is a dance instructor."

"Oh really?" We sat down at a table.

"Yeah. She's amazing." He looked down at his punch, then back up at me. "She's blind, actually. My mom is. And she can still teach

dance. It's pretty phenomenal. Sometimes I think she has an extra
sense. Even as a kid, you could think you weren't making a sound,
and yet, she always seemed to know exactly what you were doing."
 "Wow."
 "With dancing, she can tell by the sound of your feet, whether or
not you're in step."
 "So, she taught you to dance?"
 "Yup. I've been dancing since I was six, I think."

When we got up to dance to the first song, I smiled and said, "Be
gentle with me, this is my first time." He wrapped his right hand
around my waist, and took my right hand in his left and we started to
move. I was awful. I stepped forward instead of backward. I
stumbled. I lost my shoe more than once. I know many women love
the idea of dancing. Here's what I was thinking: *Could we just put
these stupid mating rituals aside and have sex?*
 "You're doing a great job," Zach said. "You've got real grace."
 "You're a terrible liar," I said.
 "What?" He looked sincerely surprised. "You've got a nice
rhythm."
 How accurate are our self-views? Was I a bad dancer, or was Zach
blind to my lack of grace? I'm going with the latter.
 Once, at a party in college, some friends pointed out a guy who
supposedly had a huge crush on me. Over the course of the evening,
we ignored each other, as I was too shy to approach him, and he was
apparently too shy to approach me. The party was in a brownstone,
and almost everyone was in the backyard, enjoying the warm, spring
night. When I left, I had to walk back through the house to leave. As
I entered the long dining room/living room, I saw the guy sitting at
the far end of the room, on a sofa by the front door. There was
almost no one else in the room.
 Back then, at age 19, I was particularly nervous about people
watching me when I walked. So you can imagine my dread when I
realized I had to cross the length of the floor while this guy stared at
me. Halfway across the room I slipped in a puddle of beer and fell
flat on my back. In a white mini-skirt. After I'd re-righted myself, I
straightened my wet skirt and waved a quick goodbye to him as I
hurried out the door, completely mortified.
 Months later, that guy worked up the nerve to talk to me. And

here's what he said. He said, "That night at the party, when I was sitting alone in the front room, you appeared across the way, and you looked like an angel."

"I slipped in beer," I said, still humiliated by the memory.

"You were so graceful," he said. "It was like little bubbles of air lifted you back up onto your feet."

Men see what they want to see. Which brings me back to present day, and my dance with Zach. Here we were, nose to nose, and me with a zit on my chin. Plus, my underarms were sweating and I worried that Zach would be able to smell body odor when he held my arms up. Zits, B.O. But he thought I was graceful.

When we left, he took my hand and swung it as we crossed the parking lot. He drove an old Honda Civic hatchback. His car made me like him even more. I love those old hatchbacks. They give storage *and* good gas mileage.

He walked me to my front door. "I had fun tonight," he said, taking hold of my hand again. With my other hand, I pulled my keys out of my purse. The idea that he might kiss me made me unreasonably nervous. *Get a grip*, I told myself. *You're 39 years old, for God's sake!*

"I did, too," I said. "Thanks for showing me how to dance."

"You're a natural," he said, still holding my hand and wrapping his other hand around my waist. He started humming, *The Way You Look Tonight*, and moved us to the tune. Then he kissed me. There was no warning, really. No staring into my eyes, or awkward pauses. Just humming, swaying, and then kissing. He was a good, clean kisser. After the kiss, he pulled me into him and kissed the top of my head. Then he whispered in my ear. "I know you hated all of that," he said. "You're a real trooper."

"You could tell?" I asked. I was astounded.

"Your face is like a pane of glass." He leaned in and kissed me again. "You're horrible at hiding your emotions," he said, rubbing my chin with his thumb. I thought, *Great, make the zit worse*. Then he kissed my nose and took my keys from my fist. He took his time finding the right key and unlocked my door.

"I'll call you tomorrow," he said. He waited until I was inside, then ambled back to his car. All I could think was, "Wow."

My world was suddenly flowering outward. The year before, my life had revolved around work, a few outings with friends, and a lot of television. Now I had a house, a dog, and a boyfriend added into the mix. Jonathan and his mother came in for a hearing aid repair and I didn't even bother to ask her how often he was wearing the aids. Suddenly, I was less emotionally tied to my job.

"No rant about Jonathan?" Lucy asked when I returned to my desk.

"People do what they do," I said. "I can't change them, why make myself sick about it?"

Izzy and Josh got engaged. "We've set the date for two months from Saturday. It's going to be really simple. Nothing too stressful. Just a nice, relaxing, special time with friends and family."

I swallowed my worries and gave her a hug. "I'm happy for you," I said.

Zach and I went out again.

"How was your week?" I asked.

"Typical," he said. He started playing with my fingers across the table. We were at a small wine bar. The same place I'd been to with Caleb. I felt like I'd come full circle. Here I was again, but this time I was with a guy who really liked me. A guy who was funny and sexy and smart.

"Do you work long hours?" I asked. He looked tired.

He nodded. "I don't mean to," he said. "I haven't always been a work-a-holic. It's just that I haven't had much else better to do with my time."

I nodded. "What would you do if you could do anything in the world?" I asked. "What kind of schedule would you keep?"

He leaned back and considered my question. That was something else I liked about him. He didn't just answer. He really thought about what I was asking.

"Well, I love my job. I wouldn't mind going back to school someday, though, and getting a degree in landscape architecture. I'd really like to design gardens. And maybe I could become some kind of a consultant, because I do miss some aspects of law. Actually, I think I'd like to teach. Have a couple of kids to mentor. I could donate some time to a legal aid organization."

I sat back and watched his face light up as he talked. Reader, did you ever see those movies in Science class about erosion? Where giant slabs of rock and earth slide down into the ocean? That's what my insides were doing. They were caving in while I listened to him, and I wondered if this was what love felt like.

Even though Izzy wasn't married yet, she was having in-law problems. Josh had bought the house they'd found, and the two of them had moved in together. We were hanging out in her new home and I felt like my head was spinning from how quickly everything had shifted. Josh had paid for movers, so one day she was in her apartment, the next day she was in her home, and I never even helped her through the transition.

"His parents invited us over for dinner. I brought them a pie," Izzy was saying, "and Margaret, the mom, thanked me and took it, but never set it out on the table for dessert."

"Maybe they had too much dessert already?" I asked.

"So what?" she snapped. "So damn what?"

At this moment, I got the unbidden vision of Zach, laughing in sunlight. He doesn't really look attractive when he laughs. The center of his face almost falls in on itself. He looks like a cartoon character, of, say, a banana, laughing. Are there any Smug Marrieds still reading? If so, this is where you might be thinking, "Oh, falling in love. I wish I could do that, again." Falling in love must be like childbirth, where your mind erases the pain of labor so that you're willing to have more kids. I was not enjoying the sensation of falling for Zach. I felt psychotically happy. I was unable to focus on one thing for more than 30 seconds, my stomach had an almost permanent knot, I'd had diarrhea for the past seven days, and I was biting my nails. It was like eating chocolate, vodka, and bacon, all at once.

So here I was, trying to listen to Izzy, with all this uncomfortable crap getting in my way. Meanwhile, Izzy had a real crisis on her hands. Her future in-laws were openly snubbing her.

"Maybe they were allergic to the fruit?"

"They weren't! I checked with Josh before I made it!"

"What did Josh say about it?"

"He didn't know, but he was sure they didn't mean any offense."

"Well," I said, weakly, "there you go."

"They don't think I'm good enough for their son!"

"You're jumping to conclusions. They probably just need time to get to know you."

"I'm trying to do that. I brought them a pie! Do you know how hard it is to make a pie?"

I did, because I'd taught Izzy how to make pies, and they did not come easily to her, yet. "Listen," I said, rallying my forces. "You are going to have to deal." I can't say I didn't get a little pleasure from my next remark. "You're engaged to someone you've only known for three months. On your wedding day, you'll have known him for less than six months. Everyone who loves you is scared you jumped in too fast. You have to accept that and be glad people love you enough to worry. If his parents feel the same way, then they are just showing how much they care about him. Give them time."

"But I wanted them to see how nice I am."

"They will, but they need time."

"But I made them a pie!"

"My mother would say, 'Offer it up to God.'"

"But I don't believe in God."

"Then I would say, 'Suck it up.'"

I was seeing Zach at least once every three days. Pacey growled and snarled at him every time he walked up to the house. He'd really evolved into a ferocious guard dog, but as soon as Zach stepped inside, Pacey followed him around like he was the one with the crush.

We played Scrabble. We painted my living room. We listened to Fresh Air on NPR. We gardened in his yard and mine.

One Saturday, I helped him rewire the outlets in his living room. Afterward, we made love in his bedroom. He had kissed me downstairs, pressing his body into mine until we were up against the wall. The feel of him against me made me lose my breath. His hands ran down my back, then under my shirt. As we kissed, I ran my hands up his back. "Quinn," Zach murmured. "I can't stop touching you."

"Don't stop," I whispered. In that moment, he lifted me off the ground. We kept kissing as he carried me upstairs. In his bed we pulled off each other's clothes. Zach had a beautiful body. His skin was golden and he was lean and muscular all over. The feel of his skin against mine sent me reeling. I couldn't stop running my hands over him. He brushed his lips against my nipples and I let out a quiet moan. This time, I had condoms in my purse, but Zach was prepared, too. He stood to get a condom from his dresser drawer. Standing above me, naked and aroused, he looked like a Greek god.

"Zach," I said.

He climbed back into bed and started kissing my belly. He ran his lips down to my inner thighs. I closed my eyes and let my head explode. After a bit, I sat up and pushed him backward. I climbed on top of him as his mouth found my breasts. I reached for him. He was as hard as a rock and as smooth as silk. I put his condom on and guided him into me. There was a moment, as soon as he got inside, where it seemed like we connected in more than a physical way. I felt like a piece of Zach had appeared inside of my head. Then we started moving and all thought left my mind. Panting, watching Zach's face contort in ecstasy, my mind started popping, like mini explosions of red as I came. Zach started moaning. His fingers dug into my back. I felt his entire body freeze. His eyes were closed. Then everything ended and he fell backwards down into the pillows. He was still holding me tightly, his eyes were still closed, but he had started breathing again.

After a few minutes, he slid out of me and opened his eyes. He gave me a crinkled smiled and reached up to touch my cheek. "Quinn," he said. Then he closed his eyes and snuggled into me. I was still panting a little. I felt fantastic. On his bedroom wall, he had a poster of Degas dancers. As Zach dozed, I looked at the Degas, relishing the feel of Zach's arms, still wrapped around me.

"I'm getting a piano," Zach said. "One of my clients is giving it to me. I just have to pay to move it."

"Can you play?"

He shrugged. We were sitting on my front porch, where we'd just installed a porch swing. I'd made homemade lemonade. It was late Sunday morning, and we were watching the people come and go at the church across the street. "I studied it as a kid. I wasn't very good, but I've wanted to pick it up again."

"Will you take lessons?"

"Probably."

"Will you teach me how to play?"

His eyes lit up. "Yes. That'd be great. Then we can play Heart and Soul together."

I smiled. "You're the best boyfriend…"

He smiled. "Say, my parents are coming into town tomorrow."

"They are?"

"Yeah. From Boston. I thought maybe you could meet them."

"I'd love to!"

"Great. Are you free on Tuesday night? I took the day off, and I thought I'd make a big meal and we could all hang out.

"Okay."

"His parents are coming!" I told Izzy. "I'm already stressing."

"Are you insane?" Izzy asked. We were at her house. Josh was at work. I wondered how it would be to have him around while I was visiting Izzy. I guess it would put a damper on some of our talks. "Parents love you," Izzy continued. "My parents still send you a Christmas present every year. Whenever I get on the phone with them they say, 'How's Quinn?' Last time I talked to them, my mother said, 'I hope you're not spending so much time with Josh that you aren't seeing enough of Quinn. Remember that boyfriends come and go, but good friends last a lifetime.'"

I laughed.

"It's ridiculous how much they like you," Izzy said. "I told my mother, 'Josh isn't just a boyfriend. We're getting married,' and she said, 'Honey, I hope that Quinn isn't feeling excluded. Does she like Josh?'"

"Heh, heh, heh. Well, yes, now that you mention it, you're right. Parents do love me. I still get birthday cards from my college roommate's mom."

"So relax. Just glide in and be your sweet self, and everything will be fine."

On the big night, I dressed in a sundress and headed over to Zach's. I'd made a salad and brought a bottle of wine. Zach answered the door in an apron. "Quinn," he gave me a warm hug, and then pulled me into the living room. "Mom and Dad, this is Quinn. Quinn, these are my parents, Margot and Mike."

Both parents stood up and came over to shake my hand. They were in their sixties and grey haired. Both were trim and clearly physically active. The dad wore jeans and an oxford shirt. The mom had on a simple, flowered dress. I could see the dancer in her, by her muscle tone and something about how she carried herself. I don't think I would have realized she was blind if Zach hadn't told me. She walked right up to me, looked me in the eye, and shook my hand.

"It's really nice to meet you both," I said.

"You, too," she said. "Please, come sit down and visit with us while Zach finishes dinner."

"Do you need any help?" I asked him.

He shook his head. "No. Sit down and relax. Who needs a refill? Mom?"

"I'm fine, son. Mike?"

"I'll take some more wine," his dad said.

Zach went into the kitchen and we settled ourselves in the living room.

"So, what do you do?" his mother asked.

Now that we were seated, she wasn't as good at making eye contact with me. That probably would have been my first inkling that something was up. "I'm an audiologist," I said.

"What?" Mike asked. Then he laughed. I smiled. "But really, what exactly does that mean?" he asked.

"Hearing testing, hearing aids, and balance testing. I work at a hospital that specializes in pediatrics, but I see about equal amounts of adults and children."

"Interesting. So you like children?" Margot asked.

"Yes."

"And are your parents together?"

"They are divorced."

"And how old were you when they divorced?"

"Uh, middle school."

Zach appeared with wine for his dad. He also gave me a glass. "Mom, don't give Quinn the third degree."

"I'm just trying to get to know her."

"It's okay," I said. "I don't mind. Both my parents are happily remarried," I added.

She nodded. When Zach left she said, "And Zach says you own your own home?"

"Yes. It's a foursquare, from 1912. And I hear that you're a dance instructor. Did Zach tell you he took me dancing on our second date?"

"No, he didn't. How wonderful. I always wonder whether he keeps up with his dancing."

"Everyone at the dance place knew him," I said. "He told me he comes there when he gets homesick, because it reminds him of you." She was touched. I could see it in her face.

"And do you dance?" she asked.

"That was my first time," I said.

"Did you enjoy yourself?"

"Well, I'm pretty awkward and clumsy, but Zach made it easy. He's very graceful and he's a good teacher."

"Yes he is," she said.

"Zach tells us you paint," his father said.

"Yes."

"We'd love to see your work," he said.

"Sure. Anytime."

"Maybe after dinner?" Margot said.

"Sure." I was wondering what Margot would get from my paintings.

Dinner was simple, but delicious. Zach grilled steaks and roasted vegetables. "These veggies are great," I said.

"Is that garlic I taste?" his mom asked.

Zach smiled. He seemed to derive great pleasure from cooking for his parents.

During dinner, Zach's father grilled him on his latest jobs. "Be careful when you take that roof off," he cautioned. "You have no idea what you're going to find. That estimate you gave the owners could go much higher if the beams are rotted."

Zach nodded politely. "Thanks, Dad. I will."

I helped Zach clean up in the kitchen, while his parents drank coffee on the front porch.

"You're so respectful," I whispered. "And your parents are really cool." Zach took his sudsy hands out of the sink, gripped my shoulders, and gave me a kiss.

We spent the rest of the evening on Zach's front porch. At one point, I went upstairs to the bathroom. As I came back down, I heard Zach's father talking. "She's a sweet girl, Zach. Make sure you don't hurt her."

"I won't," Zach said.

"I'm just saying that she's kind and sweet. Be careful with her."

"I know, Dad. Okay? I know."

"What was that business about you not hurting me about?" I asked later, when the evening was over and he had walked me to my car. His parents had gone back inside.

"I don't know." He smiled, but he looked annoyed. "They really liked you a lot."

"I'm glad," I said. "I liked them too."

"Thanks for coming," he said. "It's been fun to have you here tonight."

I don't know why, but I had a funny feeling as I pulled away. It was almost like my success with his parents had backfired.

Zach's parents were in town for a few more days, but he didn't invite me over again, and they never came by to see my paintings. He stopped by my house the night that they left. "Did you get your parents off okay?"

"Yeah," he handed me the salad bowl I'd brought over, cleaned. When I put it down, he gave me a big hug. "It's hard to go so long without seeing you."

"You could have invited me back," I said. "I enjoyed your parents."

He dropped his head. "Sorry. I just...they were getting too intense about you. I want our relationship to develop naturally. I don't want to be propelled forward by them."

I nodded. "Totally," I said.

"Honey, I am so sick of people telling me that I'm not listening because I don't want to." My first patient of the morning, Carmel, was an 88-year-old woman with auburn hair. She'd driven herself to the appointment.

I nodded.

"I have a lot of friends who own hearing aids that they don't wear," she said. "But I just feel like I need to do something! So," she cocked her head and looked at me. "What have you got?"

We'd just done a hearing test. "Well, there are basically three levels of hearing aid technology," I said. "It's kind of like the difference behind driving a Honda Civic and a Lexus. Both have good track records for dependability. Both get you where you want to go, but one gets you there in more style. Now, if we start at the entry-level technology..."

Carmel held up her hand to interrupt. "I drive a Mercedes-Benz," she said. "Just show me the best."

I was in love with Zach. I first realized it one afternoon, when I was sitting home alone and registered that The Partridge Family song lyric "I Think I Love You" was going through my head. Then I realized that the day before, Sarah McLaughlin's "I Love You," had been stuck in my head. Then I remembered that earlier in the week, a line from a Melissa Etheridge song, "Come To My Window," had made me burst into tears. I'd been driving and I'd chalked it up to PMS. But it wasn't. It was love. I hadn't fallen in love with anyone since Max. Back in my early twenties, before my heart had ever been broken, falling in love with Max was thrilling and easy. Now, in my late thirties, it was both thrilling and terrifying.

Ann and I went to see Bright Eyes, a local Omaha band. There was chair seating, but we had paid extra to be in the pit. We were surrounded by girls with pants hung so low we could see their butt cracks. "I can't believe how young everyone is," Ann marveled.

We'd come early, and even though we were close to the front, girls and boys kept shoving past us to squeeze their bodies in between us and the stage. About half of them had lit cigarettes, which made us wary of burn holes in our clothes, or worse. By the time the opening act came on, we'd been pushed far away from the stage.

"Why are teeny-boppers so short?" I asked.

"They don't eat well. And they smoke." Ann sighed. "Are we too old to be here?"

"No way!" I said. "They are lucky to have women in their late thirties in the audience. We add a touch of class."

She smiled at me. "Let's just move back," she said. I sighed. She was right. We retreated to just outside the crush of bodies. Ann bumped my shoulder and motioned to a figure standing a few feet away. He was wearing a hooded jacket and jamming out to the opening act, dancing and mouthing the lyrics. It was the lead singer of Bright Eyes, Conor Oberst. He stayed for a couple of songs and left.

"Those punk teenagers stole our spots and then they missed their hero when he was right next to them," I said, triumphantly.

Ann nodded. "They don't know nothin."

The music was so loud that we didn't know it was thundering and lightning until we got back out in the parking lot. Rain was coming down in sheets. We got soaking wet running to Ann's car, then sat for thirty minutes in a traffic snarl, waiting our turn to exit the lot.

"Do you wish you were sixteen again?" I asked Ann.

"Definitely."

I laughed, then looked at her. She had the shadows of raindrops sliding down her face from the light through the windshield. "Really?"

"Sure. Those years were great. I was popular, I was a straight-A student. My mom made dinner and did my laundry. She changed my bed sheets every week. Do you remember how great it is to have freshly washed sheets on your bed every week? On weekends, my friends and I went to the movies and then McDonalds. Life was good."

"Where are your friends now?" I asked.

"I don't know. Mostly married and with families, I guess. I stopped paying attention after the fifth wedding. It gets so boring. I'm sure all they talk about are babies and toilet training."

We watched the traffic inch forward.

"Back then, my life still had so much potential," Ann continued. "I was poised for greatness. Now I work retail jobs. I rent. I don't have a boyfriend."

"You could get a boyfriend. And you could get a job in your field. In…what did you major in again?"

Ann shook her head. "No, I don't want that. I'm just saying that, at age 16, I was the envy of everyone." She fiddled with the radio but didn't turn it on. "I like my life now. It's just that, when someone asks me what I'm doing, they want to hear about the job, the husband, the house, and the kids. I don't have any of that. And it bothers me that they aren't impressed."

"It's status. I think you're courageous for going against the stream." But what I was wondering was, What *is* she doing? She went from dumb job to dumb job. And she wasn't even doing it to work on a novel, or her music, or …something. "Do you have any long-term goals for your life?" I asked.

"Well, right now, I'm just trying to focus on staying healthy. I don't want to get swept up in the mainstream culture and lose myself. If I were religious, I'd say that I was trying to commune with God." We finally got an opening in the line of cars and made it out of the parking lot. As we sped toward the interstate, she said, "I wish you could be a nun without belonging to a religion. That's what I'd be. Single, meditative, and untouched by the mighty dollar."

"I had no idea," I said. "I thought you were just in crisis."

Ann laughed. "*Just* in crisis?"

"You know. I didn't realize you were planning on being this way your whole life. What about health insurance when you're older?"

"Maybe then I'll join a church and become a nun. To get the health insurance."

I laughed.

"Maybe by then I won't care that other people don't envy me, and I won't miss age 16, when everyone wanted to be me."

My patient, Carmel, was back after three weeks with her new, top of the line hearing aids. I'd fit her with them the day before she and her granddaughter drove to California to visit her grandniece. "I have serious misgivings about giving you your first set of hearing aids just before a road trip. Lots of people complain about road noise, and I won't be around to make any adjustments."

"I'm a tough old bird," she had told me. "If you set them right, I'll wear them."

Now, 21 days later, I nervously called her in from the waiting room. "Well?" I asked.

"I thought they were squeaking on the first day, and it turned out that I was hearing the birds."

I smiled.

"I wasn't bothered by the road noise and I felt that people were much clearer than they'd been. I still didn't get everything when I was in a group, but I had a much stronger footing."

I couldn't stop smiling. "I wasn't sure how you were going to do," I said, "being a first-time user and all. "How many hours a day do you wear them?"

"From the moment I get up till I go to sleep at night, of course." She gave me a look of impatience. "Quinn, if I'm going to do something, then I do it right."

I smiled. Then I yawned. "Sorry. I was out late last night."

"A big date?" she asked, smiling.

"No. I went to see Bright Eyes." Then I added, "They're a local band."

"That Oberst fellow?" asked my 88-year-old patient. Conor Oberst was the lead singer. My jaw dropped to the ground. "I supposed they'll all end up with hearing aids, too, someday," Carmel said. "If they keep playing their loud music without ear plugs."

I was going to tell Zach how I felt. I was going to choose love over fear. I decided to make him a dinner. An amazing, unforgettable dinner. And then I was going to tell him. After scouring all my cookbooks I'd finally settled on a pasta dish. An intricate, complicated dish from Marcella Hazan's Essentials of Classic Italian Cooking. I made Pasta Wrappers Filled with Spinach Fettuccine, Porcini Mushrooms, and Ham. I made the pasta by hand. It took me three hours to assemble the pieces together. I'd also cleaned the whole house, and shaved my legs. Finally, my life was starting to look like *Sex and the City*. (Except for the cooking and cleaning.)

When Zach came over, I felt surprisingly calm. I was flying solo with my plan. I hadn't even told Izzy or Ann. I didn't think that anyone should know how I felt until Zach knew.

Zach brought a bottle of red wine. He'd been in Chicago for business the day before and had only just flown home that morning. There was a big renovation company there.

We had a nice dinner. I won't pretend that I was calm enough to enjoy it, or even to taste it. I wasn't. And I became increasingly nervous as the moment approached. I was going to tell him during dessert. I'd made homemade ice cream and homemade brownies. Why? Because Zach had told me, nine days ago, that it was his favorite dessert as a child. Now, sitting at my dining room table, he didn't seem to remember. He just said, "Yum," and started eating.

I felt like a kid again, in a bathing cap and sagging bathing suit, standing on the edge of the pool in early summer, when the water is still very cold. Okay. I was going to plug my nose, close my eyes, and jump in.

"Zach, I'm falling in love with you."

Zach had just taken a big bite of vanilla ice cream and brownie. We waited while he chewed. He chewed eight times before I saw his Adam's apple bob in a swallow.

"Quinn," he said. "I'm moving to England."

Chapter 48
Pick Your Pride Up from the Floor, Dust it Off, Put it in Your Pocket, and Keep Walking

I couldn't talk, but I think I did a pretty good job of composing my features in an interested and surprised expression. I think my countenance said, "Oh really? England? Lovely!" But on the inside, my defenses were jumping into place. Giant metal doors were slamming shut and everyone was running around, trying to help me prop myself up and get out of there with just a little bit of face.

"I had an interview with a new company, while I was in Chicago. They offered me a job, in London." He put his fork down. "They make exact replications of old light switches, lamps, vents, you name it. Plus, they go in and restore old homes for people so rich that you basically have a carte blanche. And the restorations they do are on homes that are 500 years old! Or more! And it's England!"

"Wow." I said. "Fantastic. Congratulations."

His face took on a horrible, feeling-sorry-for-me look. I stood to clear the table, even though half his dessert was still on his plate. "Here, let me help," he said.

"I've got it. You sit." I made it to the kitchen alone, where I took a deep breath, steeled myself, and re-evaluated my goals for the evening. My new goal was, *Get him out of here as quickly as possible.*

"When do you go?" I asked, coming back into the room. I had a sudden flash of how I'd kissed him when he came in. How pathetic.

"In three weeks. Not a lot of time to get everything in order. I have to get my stuff in storage. Luckily, I've only got two jobs going and I think I know someone who could take my contracts for me, if I can't get them done." He cleared his throat. "But I'm going to try to finish them before I go. So I'm going to be super busy."

Isn't it amazing, how some people just side step the big issues? We were *dating*, and all he was talking about was his stupid, stupid job.

"Well, then you won't have a lot of time," I said, brightly. "In fact, you probably want to go home and get to bed, so you can start bright and early tomorrow."

"Uh, Quinn." I was standing in the middle of the living room. He was still sitting at the table. "Quinn, would you sit down for a minute?"

"I'm fine," I said. "I want to get these dishes in the dishwasher."

"Quinn, I really like you." He stood up and took the glasses out of my hands. I watched as he laid them on the table. He took my hands in his. "You are the most amazing person I've met in a long, long, time."

For a minute, I wondered. Would I move to England? Would I leave all this behind for a man I barely knew? I thought I might. I was a big Bronte fan, and how often do you meet a guy as special as this?

"I'm sorry we didn't have a chance to see where this was going," Zach said.

I shrugged. "It's fine. No big deal." I pulled my hands free. "You really need to go," I said.

"Okay." He got his coat. He gave me a hug. "Thanks for dinner," he said. "I'll call you before I leave."

"Okay," I said. When the door shut, I started to cry. I sat down on the floor in my foyer and cried. After a few minutes, Pacey came down to see what the noise was. He climbed right into my lap, all 78 lbs of him. I wrapped my arms around him and cried into his coat, but it didn't stop the awful feeling of despair.

I was thinking, *What is wrong with me that no men fall in love with me? Why am I fated to grow old alone? Why am I so pathetic?*

Stupidly, I'd already started the mental move-in, otherwise known as Fantasyland. I'd been thinking we'd move in together. That I'd be able to snuggle up against someone at night. And I'd have someone to talk to about my day. But once again, none of that was true. Zach and I weren't in love. I'd apparently imagined the whole, damn thing.

That night, in bed, I started making a list of every crush I'd ever had, to remind myself that once I was outside the throes of the crush, I usually didn't even like the person anymore. There was the teacher in NY. I could clearly see now that he had a drinking problem. And the doctor whose good looks had made me blind to his morose nature. And the other doctor who, as smart as he was, had no personality. And the other doctor who talked like a duck. (I was seeing a pattern here–don't date doctors.) But even though each of those crushes had consumed me in that moment, time was all I'd needed to get past them.

After that list, I began to write down every guy I'd dated since I came to Omaha. I was going to pay myself a dollar, for each guy, and buy myself something good, like a massage.

1. Ted—Star Trek writer
2. Chris—drunken caller from bars
3. Bob—bad poet
4. Lance—my first conservative
5. Dick—wanted more pictures before driving to see me
6. Jacob—does he count? The doctor who blew me off by email
7. Jim—gay
8. Eric—Oklahoma
9. Caleb—repressed ex-Pentecostalist
10. Art—divorced, with child
11. Horace—racist
12. Davey—stood me up at the zoo
13. Ryan—not over his ex-girlfriend
14. Derek—California
15. Dan—got back together with ex-fiancé
16. Oliver—"This is Marsha. Can *I* help you with something?"

I couldn't believe there were only 16 men on that list. I felt like I'd dated at least fifty. I felt old and worn out. And $16 bucks wasn't going to get me a massage. I decided to pay myself $5 per man, and even that only amounted to $80! I deserved $1000 for everything I'd been through with these men. But $80 would have to do. I got on the phone and made an appointment for a Swedish massage. It wasn't sex, but it was the best I was going to get. Maybe I'd never have sex again.

In graduate school, when things got too busy, too bad, I'd think, "That's it. I quit." I'd pretend I was quitting school and my secretarial job, and getting a position as a bread maker for a neighborhood bakery. I'd fantasize about breaking the news to my professors and bosses. About how they'd all try to convince me I was throwing my life away, and how I'd listen, Zen-like, and then still quit it all. I even had a theme song for the fantasy. "Circle" by Edie Brikell and the New Bohemians. "I quit, I give up. Nothing's good enough for anybody else, it seems."

The morning after my dinner with Zach, I woke up to sun on my face, and that song was going through my head. I decided that the bottomless pit of despair was an ugly place, and I was going to do whatever it took to avoid it, from here on out. It was that simple. I wasn't 27 anymore. I was capable of better self-control. And I was also ready to leave the self-pity behind. I reminded myself that I have a better quality of life than more than half the world population. I wrote NO SP in ballpoint pen on the fold between my thumb and index finger. Then I went to work.

"How was your weekend?" Lucy asked.

"Zach's moving to England in three weeks," I said. Lucy was the first person I'd told. My voice sounded gravely and angry. Or maybe the expletive I put in front of England is what sounded angry. Tears welled in my eyes. I looked down at my hand. NO SP!

"What? Oh, rats."

Tears were falling down my cheeks. "I thought he was the one. And now I'm going to grow old alone and childless." I felt myself sinking into that sludgy black hole. "And don't let me slide into self-pity!" I snapped.

"You aren't going to grow old alone," Lucy said. When she had no idea. If I really was going to meet someone, then when? At my age, if I still hadn't met the love of my life, it probably wasn't about the men. It was me. But what was wrong with me? I had no idea, and I had no idea how to find out.

Fear. I woke up in the middle of the night. I'd been dreaming about Zach and England. I could hear traffic sounds from the street north of me. And I suddenly realized that it must be a deep-rooted fear that was sabotaging me. It wasn't my inability to smile, for God's sake. I was afraid of men. I was scared of letting myself go, of getting hurt, of being betrayed, of making compromises, of pregnancy, of childbirth, of messing up my children, of losing someone I loved. The way that I had just lost Zach. Pacey was making little noises in his sleep. His tail started wagging but his eyes stayed closed.

I finally told Izzy. Her response was immediate. "Forget about Zach. Let's move on and work on some other guy."

"But that's the thing," I said, squelching my rising anger. My throat was so tight that it hurt to talk. I took a deep breath. "There are no other men."

"So you'll meet some more. Have you heard of that dating service, JustLunch.com?"

"I'm not doing any more Internet dating," I said.

"Okay. We'll think of some other ideas. What about the Unitarian church?"

I knew she was trying to help, but I wanted to start screaming. I looked at my hand. NO SP. "Okay. I'll try."

Zach wasn't a bad guy. He called twice, trying to make arrangements to see me before he left. I hadn't returned the first call. The second time was a Friday night. I was home, of course, eating Häagen-Dazs and watching Pretty Woman on dvd. I let the machine pick up and ate ice cream while Zach invited me to dinner in a guilt-ridden voice. A few weeks later he was gone.

I was angry at the whole world and I wanted everyone to know. I thought about taking down my Match profile, but who would notice? I thought about erasing my spiel and just writing, "Screw you all!" on my profile, but that wouldn't accomplish anything either. The one person in the world who deserved my anger was now living an ocean away. And he hadn't done anything wrong, except that he hadn't fallen in love with me.

I didn't want to see Izzy. For the first time, I resented her for getting engaged to a stranger instead of sticking it out with me and dating a lot of men. So I avoided her, and she didn't even notice because she was so busy with wedding plans.

Ann said, "You deserve to be angry. Who could blame you?

You've put yourself out there, on the line, again and again, and for what? A bunch of substandard men. And when you finally meet one of quality, events take a very unlucky turn."

We were at yet another Jackson-less Café, and her words made tears well up in my eyes.

"I promised Izzy I'd go to the Unitarian church today," I said. "To get back into the dating saddle. I put a dress on, and drove there, but I couldn't get out of my car."

"Why not?"

"A family of four parked next to me."

"So what?"

"They are raising their kids in that religion. And I'm using it to meet men? It seemed hypocritical."

"I don't think the Unitarians would mind," she said.

"I mind! I'm not going to pretend to be some religion in order to meet men. It's like using them."

Ann reached across the table and squeezed my hand. "I've been meaning to tell you that I admire how much energy you've put into this," she said.

"Thanks." I sniffed. "You know, I don't think I'm ever going to find a man."

She didn't say "Yes you are." She nodded her head in understanding. See, she is the only friend I know who accepts that as a possible truth. All my other friends insist that I'll meet someone. Often, I'm relieved at their insistence. But sometimes I wonder if they are just trying to keep up appearances, or make their lives easier, by not facing the truth along with me.

"May I ask you a question?" Ann asked. When I nodded, she said, "You have one life to live. How are you going to make that life meaningful? Is finding a man the thing that will allow you to live your best possible life?"

It was a good question. Did I need a man to achieve my life goals? Married women do tell you that all the time that husbands are too much work. It's why Smug-Marrieds are so annoying. They act nostalgic for their own single days and they bash their spouses like it's going out of style. Why can't they just be happy to have a family? And if a family wasn't in my future, what could I do to still live a life with meaning?

Chapter 49
Done With Dating!

I did nothing about dating men for a month. I didn't check my Match account. I didn't ask for set-ups or complain to co-workers about my singledom. I didn't look at men in the grocery store. I didn't even register them.

I asked a co-worker, the other day, what sucked most about married life. "Men are filthy pigs," she told me.

I went back to focusing on my single life. I knitted and gardened. I did crossword puzzles, painted, walked Pacey, and signed up for a stained glass window making class. I tried to watch less television. I came home at night and appreciated the silence of my home.

At some point, I realized that I had stopped feeling despair over Zach. I kind of wondered if he would call, but I honestly didn't expect him to. His house sold quickly. No surprise there. Good neighborhood, good workmanship. I read in the realty listings that it went for $230,000. Not a bad investment.

"How many years do you have before you get taxed on capital gains?" I asked Lucy, one day. I was thinking, if it was just a year, he might come home within the year, and maybe he'd resettle here in Omaha.

"I don't think they have capital gains taxes anymore, unless you sell a house that's crazy expensive."

"Oh." I felt my face fall.

"Go to England and tell him you like him," Lucy suggested. I appreciated her romantic heart, but I knew I'd never do that. Am I wrong in suggesting that a man could do that and be perceived as romantic, but a woman would just look desperate? Which I was.

Tick, tick, tick.

My office had a going away party for a co-worker. Toward the end of the evening, a large group of us were sitting together on the patio, eating dessert and drinking, when someone suggested I consider dating a fellow employee from a different department. The man she was talking about was 54 years old and when I told her I wasn't interested, she said I was too picky.

I didn't even have the energy to get riled up about this unfair assessment. I mean, if I had a nickel for every time someone told me I was too choosy…I'd buy a husband. Before I knew it, everyone was trying to think of how I could find the right guy. No one knew anyone, but they never do. I told everyone about Rachel Greenwald, author of *Find a Husband After 35*, and how she suggested you give your friends a tagline, like an ad slogan for your friends to use when they talk about you to a potential husband.

"What is your tagline?" Marta asked. She was married about ten years.

"Funny but introverted artist," I said. All eyes were on me, so I told them about not wearing power suits on dates, and about wearing pink. I told them Rachel Greenwald's suggestion to hold a party that introduces me to the world as someone who wants to date and get married. Everyone enjoyed the stories, and they all had comments about which of her ideas would work best. All in all, it was an okay night. I got my tagline out to upwards of ten people. And my heart wasn't even in it. Wouldn't Rachel Greenwald be proud?

One day, I woke up and I was over it. I had some wounds still to nurse, but I was ready to stop crying about Zach. Thank God for growing older. For a moment, I wondered if my heart was harder. But whatever the reason, I was done.

Chapter 50
Best Songs to Get You through a Break-up

I won't put a time frame on this. The acute stage could last years, or weeks, or you could cycle in and out of it.

Acute stage
Cowboy Junkies - *Trinity Session*, the album. *DO NOT listen to this while drinking or if you are contemplating suicide*
Tori Amos
   "In Your Hand" (*Little Earthquakes*)
   "Cloud on my Tongue" (*Under the Pink*)
   "Hey Jupiter" (*Boys for Pele*)
No Doubt - "Don't Speak" (*Tragic Kingdom*)
Bright Eyes - "Haligh, Haligh, A Lie, Haligh" (*Fevers and Mirrors*)

Rallying Stage
Natalie Merchant - "Life Is Sweet" (*Ophelia*)
Hair (movie soundtrack) - "I've Got Life"
Gloria Gaynor - "I Will Survive" (*Love Tracks*)
Cowboy Junkies
   "Sun Comes Up It's Tuesday Morning" and "'Cause Cheap Is How I Feel" (*The Caution Horses*)

Chapter 51
You'll Meet a Man
as Soon as You Stop Looking

For those of you who went straight to this chapter, maybe you want a quick validation for this long held belief. Maybe you're even still standing in the bookstore or library, unsure whether or not to commit to this book. My friend, you especially need to read this book. The truth is, you never meet a man just because you've stopped looking. Do you think that plucking gray hairs makes them grow back tenfold? Or that masturbation makes you go blind? If you've read the preceding two chapters, you know that when I stopped looking, I met no one. I never believed that line anyway, but it was still nice to have evidence to support my lack of belief.

When the time came that I was ready to pick up the cross of dating again, I went online and read the Match emails I'd ignored for the past two months. There was nothing good. No surprise there. One email was kind of interesting. It was from Davey, the guy who'd stood me up at the zoo. He'd written, "Hi, remember me? I stood you up at the zoo? Don't be afraid. I was just writing because I've noticed that you are still on Match. You've been on Match for a long time, now. We are both a year older. Why not give me a try?" I deleted him.

The next thing I did was take down my Match profile. I didn't completely sign out of Match. I just made it "not visible." I can't tell you how good it felt to take myself off Match. I didn't know how I was going to meet men, but it wasn't going to be through Match.

Chapter 52
On Being a Good Little Single Girl

Around this time, Eric, from Oklahoma, started emailing me. We'd kept loosely in touch after he'd left Omaha. I wouldn't hear from him for several months, and then he'd write, we'd have a flurry of conversation, then nothing for a few more months. I hadn't heard from him in a while when he wrote:

> *Hey Quinn,*
> *I'm confused. I was in the middle of a back-and-forth with a girl on Match. Then, after several weeks, she just stopped. I waited a week or so, then asked her if she wasn't interested in emailing anymore, or if she'd just been waylaid by a bunch of damn, dirty apes. She never responded. It's been more than a month. Then, today, she winked at me. (Reader, a "wink" is sort of a "Like" on Facebook. I never responded to winks, but a lot of people use them.)*

> *So, do I swallow my pride (what there is of it, anyway) and write a "thanks for winking" note...or do I write a "what part of interested...a MONTH and a HALF ago...do you not understand" kind of thing?*

> *Dear Eric,*
> *You would never send the mean part of that note, and you know it.*

Dear Quinn,
You are right. Damn my niceness, as it were! Oh hey, how are you? Excuse my ME ME ME streak there. How are things there?

Eric,
Things here are not so hot. I was recently burned by the Match Monster. Everything was going really great with this guy and then one day he said, "Guess what, I'm moving to England!" The things some men will do to get away from me. What part of "I love you and want to bear your children" scares them off?

Now, about your question–definitely just be nice to her. Who knows what happened? Sometimes people just drop the ball. I'd give her another shot.

Quinn,
I get a very bad vibe from Mr. England. He might be the type to kick dogs. Thanks for the advice on my winker, whose name is MonaLisa7. How's this for a response? (I sent her pretty detailed notes before...)

"Here's a wink coming right back at you. I knew if I bludgeoned you with enough emails, you'd respond. ;-) Now tell me a bit about MonaLisa."

Is that still too surly?

Eric,
Yes, too surly. try again. :)

Quinn,
Another try:
"Good afternoon, Mona (or is it Lisa?). Thanks for zipping a wink my way. Hey, I'm all about having eyelashes batted before me. ;-)" (Ok Quinn, I wrote her three emails telling about myself and asking her questions...and those are

questions she still hasn't answered...there's only so much you can glean from one profile! Bah! I'll work on it.)

Eric,
Much better email this time. You don't have to write more, although one question would not be a bad idea because it gives her a reason to respond. By the way, I like the dirty apes comment. When people didn't responded to me, I sometimes sent an email that said, "Strong, silent type?" It always worked.

Quinn,
Well, I sent it out, with your suggested question. No reply yet from winker chick. I'll try your line if she doesn't respond by tomorrow. I'm starting to burn out of Match. I've met at least five women now, and none of them have worked out.

Eric,
Give her a few days, in case she doesn't check her email much.

Quinn,
A few days??? Ah yes, patience, grasshopper. But I want instant gratification!!! ;-)

Eric,
I'm told, by several different match success stories (friends of friends) that you need to date at least 12 people before you'll meet the right one. Now, you may be thinking, "But Quinn, I DROVE to other states. Doesn't that count as at least two?" I see your point, Grasshopper, but no, it's still only one. So be a good soldier and get back out there.

Chapter 53
The Weddings of Friends -
A Bittersweet Day for the Single Woman

The morning of Izzy's wedding, I was outside early, gardening. In a nod to propriety, Izzy had slept in my guest room instead of at Josh's. She was the only bride I've ever known who slept in on her wedding day. Several of my friends didn't sleep, period, but Izzy was out like a light. While I gardened, Pacey sat, tied to my porch. He liked to watch the churchgoers across the street as they got out of their cars. That church hopped every day of the week, but Sunday brought in the most people. I was digging up a prickly shrub that I was going to replace with a lilac bush. Even with gloves, I got a lot of prickers in my fingers, but by 8:30 a.m., the old shrub was gone and the new one was in place.

I moved on to my screen door, which I was taking down. I was going to put up an iron security gate. I decided that Izzy had slept long enough and used my power drill to unscrew the doorframe. That door was probably twenty years old. I got every screw out except one: the threads were gone. I ended up prying it out with a screwdriver and pliers. It took me a solid hour. Izzy was either still asleep or in the shower. With one final wrench, I wrestled the screw out. "Look!" I said to Pacey. "I got it!" He sniffed the air and decided the screw was nothing of interest. Then his ears perked up and he turned to the street. There was a guy, about my age, jogging by. I'd never seen him before. Interesting. He had dark brown hair and a swimmer's build. Pacey stood up, but didn't bark. The guy looked at me and nodded. I said, "Morning." He stopped. My heart stopped.

"What kind of dog is that?" he asked.

"A White German Shepherd," I said. I suppose, if I were Carrie from *Sex and the City*, I would have been clothed in some stylish, if ridiculous outfit. My hair would have been highlighted and blown dry. I would be wearing a $400 pair of Manolo Blahniks strappy sandals. Instead, my hair was frizzing out of its bun. My white painters paints were mud and grass stained at the knees. My nails had dirt under them and my torso was covered with twenty-year-old door dust. Plus, I was holding the doorframe. I put it down and tried to smooth my hair. But then I remembered that I was wearing protective goggles! The ugliest ones you've ever seen in your life. They were big and thick with dark grey frames. Readers, all protective goggles are ugly, but these were worse than any others. I mean, you couldn't look for a more nerdish pair of goggles on the planet. I ripped them off. My dad would say, "They look better than a missing eye." But not much.

"How old is he?" the guy asked.

"I don't know. I got him from the pound. One or two."

The front door opened and Izzy appeared, un-showered, holding a cup of coffee. In an instant, she'd assessed the situation. "Great morning for a run," she said. He nodded. "You from here?" she asked.

"God, no," he said. "I'm from NY."

"So am I!" I exclaimed. "Where in NY?"

"Schenectady."

"Troy!" I said. They were close to each other.

"What brought you here?" Izzy asked.

"A job," he said.

"Me, too," I answered. "Do you live around here?" I didn't recognize him.

"Over on Myrtle," he said. He was just a few blocks away, on another street of beautiful, old homes that had fallen into disrepair, mainly because they were rentals.

"How do you like it here?" I asked.

"Fine. I mean, Nebraskans are really friendly and all."

"That's what everyone says," I commented. "But yet, I'm still not friends with anyone who's from here. I think they are hard to get to know."

"What kind of job did you come here for?" Izzy asked, cutting off my rant. I shot her a mental thank you.

"I'm the chef at le four rouge." The place I had eaten at with Max.

"Is that a good restaurant?" Izzy asked.

"It's the only four-star restaurant in Omaha," he said.

Suddenly, I didn't care to "brag" about the really great job that brought me to Omaha. (*I'm an audiolo-zzzzzz, oops, sorry. I fell asleep trying to tell you what I do.*)

We chatted with him for about fifteen minutes. On my own, I would have started to get panicky, worried that I was keeping him from something, or talking too much. But with Izzy running the show, I didn't have to take responsibility. Plus, I trusted her. She was much better at talking to men than I was, so I followed her lead. His name was Peter. He'd lived here about the same amount of time that I had.

He re-clarified our names before he left. "You're Quinn," he said to me. "And, what's your name again?"

"Izzy." We stood on the porch and watched Peter go around the corner. As soon as he was gone, she said, "Oh, by the way, there's a really cute guy who jogs past my house every weekend. I keep meaning to tell you about him."

"I've never seen him before," I said. "And look at me." I put my goggles back on. "This is what he saw."

"You look adorable!" Izzy said. Given the choice between support and honesty, she will support me every time. She yawned into her coffee.

"His restaurant is the place I took Max to. And California guy."

"Was the food good?"

"I can't even remember. I think of that place and I feel sick to my stomach. But enough about me. Good morning, Bride-to-Be," I said, hugging her. "Did you sleep well?"

"Like a log."

"You seem calm."

"I am. Very calm. It's so nice to have a simple wedding. I figure, I'll shower by 11, then we'll head out and I'll get married."

"Who's making sure everything is running smoothly?"

"Huh?"

"I mean, who's meeting the person who rents the hall? Who's getting the doors opened and the lights turned on? Who will be there when the caterer arrives, or the band, or the cake?"

"Uh. I've got no idea." She smiled. "See, Quinn, that's the beauty of an anal retentive fiancé. He's got everything under control. He'll do it better than I could. And he wants to do it." She stretched back and yawned again. "My only job is to show up, looking beautiful."

We showed up at the hall at one. Izzy wore a long, off-white, silk dress. To Josh's dismay, she'd found it in a thrift store for $35. There had been a brown stain on the front, but the drycleaner had made it look like new. She carried a bouquet of tiny white roses and lavender. Her hair was tied up in a simple knot she'd fashioned herself in my bathroom mirror. She looked beautiful, in a natural, easy way.

As Izzy predicted, Josh had everything under control. About fifty people were at the wedding. Everyone sat at dinner tables. Izzy and Josh were going to get married in the center of the room and Izzy had made it clear that she wasn't going to walk down any type of aisle. "I just want to be there, with Josh, not be presented for everyone to stare at," she'd said. So she'd been mingling with the guests since her arrival. At 1:30, she and Josh wandered to the center of the room. When the judge appeared, the room hushed down. They were married in three minutes. The moment the judge pronounced them husband and wife, the band began to play, "We Are Family." It was touching, in a modern sort of way. The rest of the afternoon was given over to eating and socializing.

Did I feel jealous, Reader? No, I did not. I appreciated the irony that I got her to sign up for Match, practically forced her to sign up, and she had met and married someone in less than a year, while I continued to flounder. But she and I were very different beings, and I wouldn't have done it her way anyway. I wouldn't have gotten serious that quickly. Or married so soon. So comparing us was like comparing apples to oranges. You could peel them both and squeeze them into juice, but you'd get two completely different tasting drinks. Some day, when people are talking about bad writers, they'll probably mock that line above. I'm going to leave it in anyway. After all, my best friend just abandoned me in singledom. I think I'm entitled to some cheesy comments.

Chapter 54
Letting an MBA from Harvard
Market You as Single

Marta came into my office a few days after Izzy's wedding. "I thought of someone you should meet," she said. "He's my neighbor's brother. He's got a good job, he owns a home, and he seems really nice. Her kids love him."

"Great," I said. "He sounds great."

"I gave her your tagline, an "introverted, but funny artist," and she thought he'd like that. So, next time he's over, I could invite you and you guys could meet."

"Thank you!" I told her. Later that same day, another co-worker, Theresa, popped her head in and asked me, "What's your tagline again?"

I decided to tell painting class my tagline, too. When I walked in the door, Kate said, "I had a dream about you last night."

"Did you?"

"Yes. I dreamed that I stood up on a chair at a party and announced, 'This is the year that I find Quinn Malone a husband.'"

"Wow," I said. "So, uh, what are you going to do about that?"

"I decided I'd start asking friends."

She worked at the University. "Do you know any science people?" I asked. "I know it sounds nuts, after Max and all, but one of the things I liked best about him was that he was so interesting to talk to. I loved hearing about his work. I like science if I'm not studying it for an exam."

"I could see. One of my friends teaches Chemistry."

"Oh, cool. A chemist."

Dating is like dipping your big toe into black water. It may feel like a good temperature, but seriously, what do we really know about someone we've had a few dates with? It's kind of scary, when you think about it.

Theresa came through with a man first. "I want you to meet this guy from my yoga class."

"Yoga?" Already, I was excited.

"Yes. His name is David. He's a sweetheart. He's in good shape. He's a little older than you."

"How old?"

"Forty-four."

"No problem."

"I told him about you, using your tagline, and he's intrigued."

"Great."

"I'll give him your email?" she asked.

I nodded. "Thanks, Theresa."

I got an email a day later and we started up a dialog. He'd been doing Vinyasa yoga for five years, he was a tax attorney from South Dakota but had lived here 12 years.

Just talking about him at lunch got other co-workers thinking. I could imagine a scenario where everyone was competing to find me a man. In fact, I thought it would be good for morale if the administration offered a prize to the person who found me a husband.

Per Rachel Greenwald, I was carrying a book around with me, so that men could use it as a conversation starter. She advised (and I was completely behind her on this) that women not approach men first. Let them come to you. But give them a prop, like an interesting book. So I had an account of Ernest Shackleton's trip across Antarctica by sled (South: The Endurance Expedition). I thought it was a good man's subject, plus, it was a good read. I took that book everywhere, including the grocery store. In addition, I was walking Pacey at parks and I was going to join a gym.

In other words, I was being a good little single girl, just like Charlotte on *Sex and the City*. That character breaks my heart. She tries so hard, and even though she can be annoying and a little heartless, I think she is the most honest portrayal of a 30-something, single career woman on the show.

I was at Whole Foods, an organic grocery store, prop book in hand, when I saw him. Do you remember MedicalMania? Real name Jacob? He was my first email blow off? He just completely stopped writing to me, even when I sent him that crushingly sincere note? In the middle of grocery shopping, I looked up and saw him. He was standing ten feet from me in the dairy section. I froze for a moment and then decided that I was going to approach him.

I walked over to the yogurt section. He was now four feet from me. I wanted him to look over at me. When he did, I was going to look up and smile at him. Medical Mania was investigating hormone-free milk. He made a selection and was just turning my way, when a 300 lb man stepped in between us and blocked his view of me. Med Mania abruptly changed direction and started walking away from me, toward the registers.

I put down the yogurt and tried to cut off Med Mania by circling around past the olives and deli area. It seemed like every person in the store shared the same goal: blocking my path. By the time I got to the register area, he was checking out with two people already in line behind him. I dallied nearby, but he never even looked up. He left, bags in hand, without a backward glance.

I was cursing the other customers in the store when someone said, "Is that book any good?"

A sweet-faced, blond guy was looking down at me. I needed a minute to remember my prop. "Yes, it's a fascinating story," I said.

He nodded. "I've read some of the other accounts, but not that one, yet."

"Can you recommend any of the other accounts?"

"Um, one was by Caroline Alexander. The other was Alfred Lansing. "

I nodded. *The prop was working!* "I'll check them out." I remembered to smile. He smiled back at me and held out his hand. "I'm Joe," he said.

"Hi, Joe. I'm Quinn."

He nodded. "Well, Quinn, enjoy your book."

"Thanks." He walked away from me backwards, still smiling. *Ask me for my number! Ask me for a cup of coffee!* I could have done it myself, of course, instead of waiting for him. But the book said not to. Plus, well, you know me by now. Joe continued to back away, then he turned and walked away. I nodded. Take it easy, I coached myself. You don't have to jump the first guy who talks to you. The point is, you are sending a message to the Universe, and the Universe is answering.

Marta came into my office. "Well, it turns out that my neighbor's brother is actually dating someone. She thought they'd broken up, but they hadn't. So he's a no go. But she thought of another guy. This one is only 33. He has a daughter, though, who is eight and lives with him part-time."

"I don't date men with kids," I told her.

"Why not?"

"Because I want to leave Omaha one day and a guy with a child will always be tied down to where the mother is."

"Okay, but listen," Marta said, pulling a seat over to sit. "What if you meet someone with a child and then you fall in love with him? If you love him, you won't mind staying."

"Alright. Give him my number." Things were finally starting to happen for me. I had several irons in the fire. The grocery store guy, Theresa's guy, and Marta's guy. And see folks? I was looking when all these men popped up.

Theresa's guy asked me to call him. I did, with very little sweat. I was getting good at this!

"Hi, this is Quinn," I said. He'd said he'd be home between six and seven, that evening, so I called at 6:15.

"Hi there! You sound exactly like I thought you would."

"Oh?"

"Yes. Let me guess. Hippy. Long hair. Vegetarian. Am I right?"

"Well, I have long hair. But I'm not a vegetarian. I am liberal, though."

"That's okay."

"Thanks," I said, sort of sarcastically. "Are you a vegetarian?"

"No, I just love meat too much for that."

"I understand. So, what do you like to do in your free time?"

"Well, today I'm going skating with some friends. Actually, you're calling at kind of a bad time. I'm about to leave."

"Oh, okay. I'll let you go."

"I can give you five minutes," he said.

I digested this.

"Are you there? Hello?" he said.

"I'm here. I was just thinking that you told me to call between six and seven."

"Yeah, well, my plans changed."

"Well, that's understandable," I said.

"I can always call you later," he said. "Maybe tomorrow night. Is that Friday already? What do you usually do on the weekends?"

"Oh, I paint, or garden, or read."

"Do you go out?"

"Sure," I said. "Not every Friday night, but sometimes."

"You know, Quinn. I have a feeling, from talking to you, that you are looking for a serious relationship. I'm not interested in that right now, so I think it's a good idea to end things here, instead of playing a charade."

"What?"

"I'm just not the guy I think you want."

"You could tell that about me from what? This conversation?"

"Basically, yes. But hey, no hard feelings, right?"

"Right."

"Okay, Quinn. Goodbye and good luck."

Whatever. One down, two to go.

I started frequenting Whole Foods, wandering through the aisles, new book in hand (The Life of Pi), but neither Joe nor Medical Mania, ever turned up again.

Chapter 55
You Won't Meet a Man Planting Rhubarb - Revised

A few weeks after Izzy's wedding, I was outside in my garden when Peter ran by again. Now, I'd considered putting on make-up, in case he passed, but that would look stupid, wouldn't it?

He walked up onto my sidewalk to say hi. Pacey greeted him enthusiastically. For some reason, Pacey didn't object to Peter stepping on own lawn. Maybe it was the lack of a uniform. Peter petted him as he talked to me. We were talking about the homes in our neighborhood.

"That house on the corner was the childhood home of our governor," Peter said.

"Really?"

"And the woman in that white house? The one with heavy make-up who talks to herself as she walks her dog?"

"Yeah?"

"She's a he."

"Wow," I said.

I wracked my brain to think of something good to tell him. "Did you see that they just poured a foundation on that vacant lot?" I asked.

He nodded. "The people in that brown house are building a garage.

"How'd you know that?" I asked.

"I asked them."

"Jeez. I've lived here for more than a year, and you know more about my block than I do."

He shrugged. "By the time I hit this block, I'm in the cool down section of my run, so lots of times I just walk it, and talk to people as I go."

So it was nothing special then, that he was talking to me. Oh well. Then, suddenly he seemed to stiffen up, just a bit. It was like he turned awkward. He said, "Say, last week, you said…" Just as he started to talk, an ambulance went by and Pacey started howling. We sat and watched him, laughing.

"It's okay, Pacey," I said as the ambulance went away. I was wondering what Peter had been about to say. He hadn't sounded nervous but he'd looked nervous. When the siren stopped, Peter started playing around a little with Pacey, as if he wasn't going to ask whatever question he had planned. Still, there was something about him that made me think he wouldn't chicken out. That if I waited, he'd get around to asking me whatever he meant to ask. Pacey was playing with Peter, but getting a little overwrought. I wanted to hear what Peter had to say, so, I told Pacey to sit. Then I petted his ear, ready also to grab it if he got up before I said he could. He recognized this maneuver from previous experience and stayed seated.

"Last time we talked," Peter began again, "you said that Nebraskans are hard to get to know. So I thought that you could hang out with my friends, because they aren't your friends, so then you'd know even more people."

"I'd love that." I said. "Are they Nebraskans?"

"Hell no," he laughed. "I don't know any Nebraskans either."

"Well, that would be great," I told him.

"So, I could, uh, give you my number," he said. I appreciated that he wasn't going to ask for my number. That was showing a polite respect for my privacy.

"Yes. Let me get a pen and paper, to exchange numbers."

I ended up using discarded paint samples because I couldn't find any regular paper on such short notice. I debated whether to write my full name, or my first name, or my name and Pacey's. I finally went with just my first name. He had written just his first name, too.

That very same night, he called to invite me out with his friends. I was at RibFest, so I missed his call. (Have I acclimated or what?) He said, "Hey, it's Peter. The guy who runs by your house? I'm going out tonight with that group of friends I told you about. We're leaving soon, in the next thirty minutes or so. So if you get this message in time, and want to come, give me a call."

If you know me at all, by now, Reader, you know that I fretted all the next morning about having to call him back. At two in the afternoon, I sucked it up and called. I don't know why I was so nervous. Ann told me exactly what to say and I said it verbatim on his answering machine.

Hi, Peter, it's Quinn. The girl with the dog? I got your message. It sounded like fun. I'm sorry I missed it. I was at Ribfest! I'll talk to you later. Bye.

With the phone call behind me, I could relax and enjoy the fact that a neat guy had invited me out. For the first day, I was just happy. On day 2, I began to imagine dating him. Our first kiss. Tasting his newest culinary creations. Making out with him. Going on eating tours to France. Sitting in bed at night, with our reading glasses on, reading each other the funny parts of our books. He seemed like he'd be a good dad, because he was good with Pacey.

And that, my friends, is how I screw up potential relationships: My vivid imagination. My mental move-in. Unlike Izzy, I don't particularly like dating. I'm ready for a lifetime together. So I don't deal with the real person, I deal with the fantasy my mind has created.

Poor Peter. He had no idea what he was getting into.

Eric from Oklahoma had emailed me.

Hey, Quinn. Guess what! I met someone! A real sweetheart of a girl. I don't know if I told you this, but I got so fed up with Match, and the women who wouldn't email me back, that I took down my profile. Then, a couple months ago, I thought, "Oh, what the heck?" and put it back up. This really neat woman, Louise, wrote me, and I wrote her, and so on, and so on. We met, and hit it off, and now we've been dating for two months. How are things in your neck of the woods?

Dear Eric, Up yours.

He sent me back a sideways smiley face and wrote:

Don't worry. If I can meet someone, then anyone can.

(By the way, I did write him a nice note back, telling him how happy I was for him.)

Marta came by my office with a heartbroken look on her face. "I don't know how to tell you this," she began, "but that guy I mentioned turns out to be moving to Denver."

"That's okay," I said.

"I feel terrible!"

"Don't worry," I reassured her. "I've got lots of irons in the fire." Which wasn't exactly true anymore. But when she left, Lucy told me about a childhood friend of her husband's.

"I think you'd like him. He's in school right now, getting his master's in counseling."

"Let me see where things are going with the running guy."

"You should keep your options open," she said.

I knew she was right. My pager went off. "Add on from ENT clinic," I told Lucy. "I have to go." She shrugged.

I took Pacey to a park one evening, to give him more exercise. We'd been walking around our neighborhood, in the hopes of running into Peter, until I decided that enough was enough. There's a really steep hill at a park a few miles away and I ran Pacey up and down it, to tire him out. The park was almost always deserted. I had him tied to a long clothesline so he could run free but not escape. The pitch of the hill was steep, even for my very active dog, and he was panting after just a few minutes. I congratulated myself for thinking of such a quick way to tire him out. He was utterly exhausted after twenty minutes. I'd brought water along and he guzzled down a quart.

On the drive home, Pacey, who wore a dog seatbelt on in the back seat, stuck his head forward between the two front seats and vomited all over the stick shift, the seats, and me.

With windows rolled all the way down, we made it home. Pacey went to the backyard. I went upstairs to shower and change my clothes. I tried to clean up the vomit from the car, but it had gone into the cracks between the seats. I could only imagine the stench from the first hot day.

I ended up paying $75 to have the car detailed. Which got me adding up all of Pacey's other expenses. His cage, his vet bills, the kennel. The toys, the food, the leashes. I'd spent nearly $700 on him in our first year together. Plus, I was getting a fence installed.

"He's worth every cent," Jack said, at painting class. "That dog will save your life, one day. He may have already saved it."

It was true that Pacey had taken to standing up on two legs to look out my living room window when people walked by. He looked like a polar bear. And I wasn't sleeping under the downstairs window anymore. Plus, the walks were exercise for both of us. And he cracked me up. Every day he made me laugh. Every day.

Peter invited me out again, a few weeks later. "My friends are Gamers," he said. He'd gone out of his way to tell me they were married and I wondered if this was to put me at ease. Like, to let me know that they would be safe.

"Gamers?" I asked.

"Pictionary, Trivial Pursuit, that kind of thing. They are having a Trivial Pursuit party next week, if you want to come."

Do you want to compete with a group of strangers to see who is smartest? You betcha, Peter. "Sure," I said. "It sounds like fun." Great. I was totally misrepresenting myself as an extrovert to this guy.

"Okay," he said. "Here's their address. We're meeting around six."

So, not a date, I thought. "I might be a little late," I said. I couldn't get home from work, walk Pacey, eat, and mentally prepare for this in one hour.

"Sure," he said. "Just come when you can."

"So it's not a date," Lucy said. "That's okay. He barely knows you. It sounds kind of respectful to just let you come on your own."

"Right," I said. "Exactly. And it will be good to meet new people." My mantra. I said it all day long.

ItwillbegoodtomeetnewpeopleItwillbegoodtomeetnewpeople. I thought it as I walked Pacey and as I got ready to go out. I wore the most casual, sexy outfit I had. Jeans, a tight brown shirt, and a pink cotton jacket. I used minimal makeup, blush, mascara, and rubbed-off lipstick (lipstick applied and rubbed off to give my lips a tint). I didn't want anyone to think I was overdressing for Trivial Pursuit. Before going, I listened to Natalie Merchant's "Life Is Sweet." There is this one part: "I tell you, life is sweet, in spite of the misery. There's so much more. Be grateful." For me, this song is about choosing to put your fears to bed and focusing on the good things that life has to offer you. Like meeting a group of new people for an evening of games.

But I still had a sick feeling in my stomach as I pulled up to the house of Peter's friends. When I shut off the car engine, I thought, "I'm grateful for this opportunity to enrich my life." Then I put my fear to bed and got out of the car. I could see inside the house as I came up the walk. There was a group of about ten people at a table in the front window. Every single head looked up and watched me approach.

I don't normally think about my walking like I did when I was a 19-year old college student. But when people are staring at me, I feel like I have short-circuiting-robot gait. If it had been dark out, I probably would have left. But it was still light, and they could see me, so I had no choice but to keep going.

I thought Peter would come to the door, but instead a woman answered. "Hi," I said. "I'm Quinn. I'm a friend of Peter's."

"I'm Grace," she said. "It's really nice to meet you. Come on in." I'd brought a crawler of beer from a local brewery, so I handed it over. It had spilled in the car a little and I worried that she smelled beer on me and thought I'd been drinking and driving. Reader, this is my mind, on fear.

I walked into the room and Peter, who was seated at the far end of the table, made introductions. Everyone in the room was a couple, except for him and me. I was seated at the opposite side of the table from him. Grace got out glasses and passed my beer around. They had already started, but I was put on the team that was one man short.

Everyone was really nice. And I was fine, on the surface. That's the thing about me. I can be great in social situations, even though I loathe them. I faced the sea of unknown faces and said, "So, what do you all do?" I was thinking that they all worked at the restaurant, but in fact, two were musicians, one was a veterinarian, one was a stay-at-home dad. There was a record producer, a copywriter, and the co-owners of the restaurant. Of the two people who were waiters, one was also a poet and the other was also a yoga instructor.

There were several different conversations going on at the same time. Twice, people asked me, "How do you know Peter?" And both times, before I could answer, Peter broke across conversations and said, "We're neighbors."

The only time I betrayed my true state of nervousness was when someone asked, "So, what do you do?" When I opened my mouth to answer, all conversation at the table stopped and eleven heads turned to face me.

"I'm an au-au-audiologist." I couldn't believe it. I mean, I've given four-hour lectures for two hundred people. I presented at national audiology conferences in front of six hundred people, including some of the most well known people in my field, and I stutter on a three-word sentence in front of ten people?

Of course, the musicians were interested in hearing protection, so I got to talk to them for a while about that. And I had a couple of moments when I was funny enough to get a group laugh. I was too nervous to have any fun, but I thought that everyone liked me. I stayed till the game was over and then headed home. Peter didn't leave with me like I'd hoped he would. As everyone left, he stayed behind with Grace and her husband, Joe. When I got in my car, I had serious doubts that he had any feelings for me besides friendship.

But hope springs eternal. Which was why I continued to garden every weekend, in case he walked by. A week after Trivial Pursuit, Grace called.

"Hi, Quinn. This is Grace, from Trivial Pursuit night." Not, *This is Peter's friend.*

"Hi, Grace."

"Say, I was calling to see if you wanted to go to the movies with us. That new Spanish film, I've forgotten the name, just opened at the Dundee."

The Dundee was an art/foreign film theatre in Omaha. She must have gotten my phone number from Peter. "Sure," I said. But why hadn't Peter called? "Will Peter be there?" I asked.

"Uh, I think so."

Uh? What did "uh" mean? "Okay. Yeah, I'd like to see that film." The film I've never even heard of before.

"Great. We'll pick you up."

Peter wasn't in the car when Grace and her husband, Joe, came for me. They were a little older than me. I guessed in their late forties. They had that alternative, California-calm look. Like they ate healthy and meditated daily. I liked them. "No Peter?" I asked. I wanted to make it clear that I was a little interested in Peter.

"He's coming," Joe said. "He's going to meet us there."

"Was that a dog I saw in the window?" Grace asked.

"Yes. Pacey. Normally, he's kenneled when I'm gone, but last week, I started trying him out in the house alone, first for fifteen minutes, then thirty. Yesterday he went four hours without doing any damage. We'll see how he does tonight."

"Are you nervous?"

"A bit. Last night I dreamed that he ate my television." That got a laugh from Grace and Joe. I took a breath. I was doing okay.

Peter arrived during the previews. He came down the west aisle and sat next to Joe. When the movie ended and the lights came up, he looked a little surprised to see me. "Who's up for a beer?" Grace asked.

We went next door to a local joint for a beer. "So, tell us about your painting," Joe said. "Can we see your work sometime?"

I gave him my web page address.

"We're always looking for art to hang in our restaurant," Grace said.

"Look at my web page," I told them. "I'm not sure people want to see my work while they are eating."

"Do you paint in acrylics?"

"Oils."

They nodded. They seemed interested in me, which I took to be a sign that they thought Peter liked me romantically. It was sweet, the way that they were trying so hard for him.

"You should see her yard," Peter told them. "It's like a painting all on its own. She paints with flowers."

I shook my head. "I can barely stay ahead of the weeds."

"How long have you lived there?" Peter asked.

"Just this year." I turned to Grace. "So how long have you been running your restaurant?"

"It'll be fifteen years in November," Joe said.

"And four stars. That's pretty amazing."

"Well, we have Peter to thank for that," Joe said. "He gave us the last star."

"You let me do what I want in the kitchen." Peter looked at me. "That's very rare. It's why I came here."

"Is it hard to have control over your kitchen, then?"

"I guess it depends on the chefs, and the owners," Peter said. "But yes. It's like any production. The director and the producer have to find some common ground to work on."

A phone started to ring. Grace stood. "Excuse me," she said. "Duty calls." I heard her say "Hello?" as she stepped away from the table.

"The restaurant?" I asked.

Joe nodded. "There's always one crisis or another. We've worked hard to not have to be there full-time, though."

"Dual ownership in a restaurant can destroy a marriage," Peter said.

"Because you tend to start working opposite shifts to keep the restaurant afloat," Joe explained. "But Grace and I have a great general manager."

"And you?" I asked Peter. "You don't work every night?"

"I work every day," he said. "I was there this morning at 6 a.m. But on weeknights, I tend to leave by six or seven." He looked at Joe. "That's why I was late tonight. The cherries were rotten."

"That distributor is getting worse and worse."

Peter looked at me. "No cherries jubilee tonight."

I laughed. Grace sat back down. Both men turned to her to hear what the call had been about, but she put the phone away and said, "Quinn, what did you think of the film?"

At 11 p.m., I said, "I'm sorry to be a party pooper, but I really have to get home and get some sleep."

"Me, too," Peter said. I wondered if he would offer me a ride home, but he didn't. Grace and Joe dropped me off. Pacey greeted me at the door and he hadn't destroyed anything. I knelt down and gave him a hug. "Good boy!" I told him. "Good, good, good puppy dog!"

"There's something missing," Izzy said, when I described the night. "He's not giving you a dating vibe."

"Not everyone says they love you in the first two weeks of meeting you," I snapped. She was getting harder to talk to by the minute. Totally turning into a Smug-Married.

"It's clear that his friends like him a lot," I said to Painting Class. "Or they wouldn't have been so nice to me."

"There's something not right with him," Jack said.

"Is he gay?" Eli asked.

"No!" I said. "He's not gay."

"It's strange, the way he didn't offer to drive you to their house that first night," Kate said. "It's like he's going out of his way to make it not a date."

"He's not acting like a normal guy," Jack said. "Maybe he's just gotten out of relationship. Maybe he's going through a divorce."

"How have we verified that he's not gay?" Kate asked.

"He elevator-eyed me."

"He seems conflicted," Kate said

"Maybe he and his friends are swingers," Jack continued till I told him to shut up. In fact, I told everyone to shut up. Izzy, Ann, Lucy, and the rest of the lot. I was angry at my friends for giving stupid, negative reasons why he hadn't called. They were all such doom and gloomers! The truth was that he was taking his time. He didn't want to rush things, so he was slowly getting to know me. He was also very busy. (A little Internet stalking had told me that his restaurant was premiering a new menu this month.) So what was the big deal that he didn't have time to call?

"Yeah, that's true…" Izzy said, doubtfully.

"It's still strange," Jack said.

"Hmmm. Well. I guess," Ann said.

When Pacey first moved in, he'd wake me in the morning by poking my face with his nose. I took to sleeping with the lemon ball. I could come out of a deep sleep and still zap him right in the nose with the juice. Pacey had become a quick student of the lemon ball. Within a couple of nights, he was completely cured of waking me up. He was a very bright dog.

And now we had a routine. He no longer needed to be in the cage at night. He'd get up, about an hour before me, and play quietly near my bed. The moment my alarm went off, he'd come over and climb into bed with me. He'd curl his body into mine, and lay his head on my pillow. I'd hit snooze and go back to sleep, with my arm curled around Pacey.

When the alarm went off the second time, Pacey didn't budge. It's like he thought that if he ignored it, I would too. If I started to get up, he'd make a noise like, "Errrrrr." Like a dog's version of a purr. Maybe he used to live with cats.

I'd turn off the alarm and head to the bathroom. A minute later, he'd get up and follow me. While I brushed my teeth, he'd collapse on the floor, like he'd just run a marathon. "Silly dog," I'd mutter as I rinsed.

Lucy was still pushing her Psych major blind date. "He doesn't even have the gold tooth anymore," she said.

"What?"

"He had a gold tooth, for a long time. I told him, 'You are not going to get any women with that.' He pretended not to care, but I just saw him this weekend and the tooth is back to white."

"His tooth was gold?"

"He was getting a crown, and that's what happened. It was stupid, but there you have it."

Pacey had proven himself, and he was now allowed free-range of the house while I was at work. I had started taking him on 20-minute walks before work. One morning, when we got inside, Pacey went straight upstairs. I thought he went for water, but he never came down again. He heard me put my shoes on, a sound that normally sends him running to the front door. He heard me open the front door and yet I saw neither hide nor hair of him. As I pulled out of my driveway, I saw him watching me from the upstairs window, the one you can look out when you're sitting in bed. *You lazy slob*, I thought, as I drove away.

My garden was looking fantastic because I was out there every weekend, hoping Peter would pass by. "Gay men don't hang out with married straight couples," I told Pacey. "And men don't become friends with women to be friends." He barked at me. "Anyone who's seen *When Harry Met Sally* knows that," I told him. "It's basic."

Two weeks after the movies, Peter jogged by my house. "Hey," I said. He looked tired and not so attractive anymore. I think my brain was trying to take a couple of steps back.

"Hey," he said back.

"You look tired," I said. Insert foot into mouth.

He nodded. "I'm exhausted. I don't think I've slept more than four hours a night for the past two weeks. I haven't had a run in forever." He rubbed his eyes. "We're really busy at work. We're premiering a new menu on Friday night. It's pure craziness."

"It sounds like it. But good crazy."

He smiled at me. "Definitely good crazy."

"Your friends are nice," I said.

He nodded in agreement.

"How'd you meet such a diverse group?"

"I met most of them through the restaurant. Some were customers or used to work there. A few are investors. It's a nice crowd. Grace and Joe are especially wonderful. They came here from California. It's cheaper and a lot less competitive to open a restaurant like this here. The only problem is establishing a solid clientele base."

I nodded.

"But, listen, I'd better run. Busy day."

"Good luck on your menu," I said.

"You should read this book I saw on Oprah. *He's Just Not That Into You,*" Lucy said when I started giving her the blow by blow of my conversation with Peter.

"What a mean title!"

"It's the truth. You should read it so you don't waste any more time on this guy."

I didn't agree with Lucy, but there was no one left to talk to who would tell me what I wanted to hear. So, one Saturday afternoon, I found myself in the self-help section of the bookstore.

This is a sampling of the relationship books at Barnes and Noble, on a random Saturday afternoon in Omaha, Nebraska: *Men Fake Foreplay*; *How to Make Anyone Fall in Love with You*; *Men Who Hate Women And the Women Who Love Them*; *The Commitment Cure (What to do when you fall for an ambivalent man)*; *The Nice Guy's Guide to Getting Girls*; *How to Survive Dating*; *How to Get Your Lover Back*; *Men–A Users Guide*; *How to Live with An Idiot*; *The Curse of the Singles Table–A true story of 1001 nights without sex*.

One-thousand-and-one nights without sex and you get to write a book? Please, move over and let a real Old Maid step in!

I guess that people desperate for answers will believe anything. It's the backbone of most religions–providing comfort. Those books offer a couple of minutes of "Oh, that's what's going on." But they generalize too much to be effective. Despite their claims, they can't get you a man, or even answer a question like, 'Does he like me?' It's impossible to decipher what the opposite sex is thinking. You can't think, "He jogs by my house every week, so he must like me." He might. But he also might just be jogging by your house.

I found the Oprah book, *He's Just Not That Into You*. It was so thin that I stood in Barnes and Noble and read the whole thing. And if you've read the title, you've read the book. If he liked you, he'd have asked you out by now. So move on. And don't ask men out yourself because they like a challenge. Basically, the author is telling women that the only action they can take is to stop liking the guy. They can't take the initiative and ask him out, and they can't stay friends and hope the guy will fall for them.

Not every man acts the way the author and his friends acted when they were single. I've known men who had crushes on women for months and years before they asked them out. And I've known women who have asked out men and eventually married them. So, standing there in Barnes and Noble, I thought, "Don't single women have a hard enough time of it without men writing advice in mean-titled books?" Then I thought, "I'm going to prove that this book is wrong. So there, stupid book! Put THAT on Oprah!" (Not that anything is on Oprah anymore.)

The one good idea in the book is this: do not waste your time on a vision. If the guy you like acts selfish or thoughtless, he probably is. Don't ignore his actions. Forget about the man you want him to be, and look at the man he is. Then dump him.

But this is easier said than done, isn't it? I gave Peter another week, then I called and invited him out. After all, I'm not some passive little girl and I wasn't following the advice in that dumb book!

I guessed that he was off on Mondays, because the restaurant was closed. I decided to invite him to a poetry slam. I wrote out a script before I called. More like a flow chart, with several conversation options and a pep talk at the end in case he was home and turned me down. He wasn't home, so I followed my message flow chart. Then the nail biting began. I figured he'd come home late on Saturday. He'd sleep in Sunday. He'd call me back at 2-ish Sunday afternoon. But he didn't call at two. Or three, or four. By 10 p.m. Sunday, I accepted that he wasn't going to call. Maybe he was shy and preferred to call when he knew I wouldn't be home.

"Why would he do that?" Izzy asked. "He knows you're a sure thing. You've already asked him out. I'd just call him again."

"That is so not going to happen," I said. "Besides, I'm thinking he'll call today. Maybe while I'm at work."

"Maybe."

"Do you want to go to the poetry slam?" I asked.

"I would love to. But I can't. Josh's sister is coming over for dinner. I think we're really bonding. I'm hoping that when his parents see how much she likes me, they'll start to come around."

"I'm sure they will."

But who had time for Izzy's married life problems? I was a woman in unrequited love. There was no message when I got home from work. I didn't want to, but I went alone to the slam, mainly so that, if Peter called that night, he wouldn't find out that I hadn't gone. The last time I'd gone was with Bob, the four-minute dater. This time, I sat alone and tried not to look tense. The married poet wasn't there, but there were lots of other men. Eighty percent of the slammers were male. Many were very young–they looked like college students. Most all of the men performed poems about love. It was remarkable. I sat there, listening to them pour their hearts out, and I thought, "They are as tortured and conflicted about love as I am."

Sure enough, my message light was blinking when I got home. "Hey, Quinn, it's Peter. Sorry it's taken me so long to get back to you. I can't make the slam. But I guess you figured that out, already. Hope it was fun. Talk to you later."

Okay. He didn't like me. So that's a wrap, Jack. But was it? A few nights later, he left me this message: "So, I am sick of my co-workers complaining that I can't hear them. And I'm thinking that I need my hearing tested, and I'm wondering, how do I do that? And then I remember, I know an audiologist! This is Peter, by the way. And I'm wondering, how do I find out if they are right, or just a bunch of mumblers? Can you call me? Please?" He was nervous on the message. I could hear it in his voice. I played the message back to everyone who would listen. Eighty-three percent agreed that he sounded scared.

He came in for a hearing test the following week. Now it was my turn to be scared. I kept my voice level as I looked in his ears with an otoscope. Suddenly, after testing hearing for years, I realized how unimaginative and stupid our "push the button when you hear the beeps" spiel was.

Back behind the audiometer, I sniffed my underarms. So far, so good. I was dressed nicer than usual, for work. My normal look is chinos and a solid-colored cotton shirt. Hair down or in a bun. No make-up, or blush. Today I had on a pink shirt, brown tights, and a black skirt. Plus, tinted moisturizer, eyeliner, eye shadow, mascara, blush, and lipstick. Lucy said, "Wow, you should dress like that more often. Hot date tonight?"

"The chef is coming in for a hearing test," I said.

"You should really call my friend. Or let him call you. Just to keep your options open."

I nodded. "So anyway, I'm just going to act natural. Do a hearing test. No big deal."

"Absolutely," Lucy said. "But remember how hot you look."

Peter's hearing was normal. "Whew, what a relief!"

"Yeah. And now you have a good baseline for later."

"Thanks for getting me in so quickly," he said.

"No problem. How did the new menu premiere go?"

"Great. Really terrific. A few minor crisis moments, but overall great. Now I just have to think about getting back in shape again."

"You should come with me and Pacey on a long hike sometime," I said. "This weekend is supposed to be in the 60s, and I was thinking of taking Pacey on a walk around Lake Cunningham. That usually tires him out."

Peter nodded. "Maybe. I'm kind of busy this weekend. I've got to do laundry. And clean my bathroom."

"Oh?" I asked.

"I've got about two months of laundry stacked up."

"Absolutely," I said, giving him a commiserating smile. "Well, now you know your co-workers are mumblers."

Peter stood when I did and followed me into the lobby. "See you around," he said.

"Yeah. I'll see ya."

If Peter could choose laundry over me, then I needed to branch out. But I didn't want to lose my new circle of friends, so I decided two things. First, to ask Lucy to set me up with Gold Tooth. Second, to have a party. I was going to make a bunch of Indian food and rent *Monsoon Wedding*. I would invite all my friends, including Grace, Joe, and Peter. And maybe Gold Tooth, if things worked out.

I wanted to move forward, but I still sort of hoped that if Peter saw me with another man, he might realize I could be snatched up at any minute. It had happened on a *Buffy the Vampire Slayer* re-run last week. A guy asked her out, but she was too hung-up on her dead, vampire-boyfriend to say yes. Then another woman flirted with the guy. Buffy got jealous and the next time he asked her out she said yes. Yes, I know it's television. But jealousy happens.

Chapter 56
The Games We Play

So I had this blind date, in order to make Peter jealous. Was Peter playing games too? Or did he truly just want to be friends? I've already talked about how some people only work to win someone over after that person has rejected them. But, there's more. Remember a while back, when I said that some men use commitment talk to get women into the sack? Well, some women pretend to be interested in casual dating, when all they really want is a husband. Here's my party line: "I like being single. I enjoy time to myself. But I'd like to have a family someday. So if the right man comes along, I'm definitely interested in a committed relationship." Here's the truth: I don't enjoy the stress of dating so if I'm going to give up my evenings for a man, it's going to be a man I think I might marry. I'm not dating a man unless I think he has the potential to be the love of my life. Am I game playing? I don't mean to be deceptive. I just want the guy to give me a fair shake.

The blind date with Lucy's friend was the night before my Indian food dinner. I was kind of hoping that I'd fall for the blind date and stop liking Peter. But I'm not going to tell you about the blind date, just yet. I want to jump ahead to the day of the party. I was cooking for eight, and Indian food, if you've never made it, takes a lot of prep. I started at 7 a.m. and when the guests arrived at 7 p.m., I was still at the stove.

Was I nervous cooking for a four-star chef and two restaurant owners? You bet. But I figured, no one ever cooks for them, for that very reason, so this would be a treat.

I love that movie, *Monsoon Wedding*. It's really beautifully staged. The many plots are perfectly choreographed to work together to tell a tale about a wedding. I thought my two groups of friends would meet, we'd get plates of food, and sit down to watch the movie.

Lucy and her husband Ernie arrived first. She'd brought homemade naan, which is Indian bread. "This looks fantastic!" I said. "I was too scared to even try naan. Was it hard?"

"Just a little bit," she said. "How was your date with Frankie?" she asked.

"Didn't Ernie talk to him?" I said.

"No. He meant to call today, and forgot."

The doorbell rang. It was Peter, Grace, and Joe. We made introductions. They'd brought beer and a fancy bottle of red wine. "It's good with curry," Peter said.

Lucy followed me back into the kitchen. "He's cute!" She said.

"Yeah." I was tired of trying so hard and getting nowhere with men. Time and time again.

"Well? What happened with Frankie? I thought he might be here," she said.

I opened my mouth to talk, but at that moment, Peter walked into the kitchen. "Can I stir something?" he asked.

"Uh..." I didn't really want a chef to watch how I cooked.

"I don't know anything about Indian food, so you'll have to tell me exactly what to do," he said.

"Oh, it's so easy," I said, stepping away from the stove. "Can you stir this?"

"Absolutely. Everything smells terrific."

Lucy looked like she was about to make an exit, when Grace and Ernie entered the room. "Ernie tells me you had a blind date with his best friend last night?" Grace asked.

My heart sank. This was going all wrong. "Er, well, yes." Lucy's face looked as stressed as mine. Peter's back was to me.

"What do you mean, 'Er, well, yes.'?" Ernie asked. "Frankie's a great guy. I've known him since the first grade."

"Have you talked to him today?"

"No."

"Well, he might not be your best friend anymore. He's certainly not going to want to go on another blind date that you set up."

"Why not?"

"Because he absolutely hated me." In awkward situations, I think it puts everyone else at ease if I drag myself through the mud.

"Impossible," Ernie said.

"He used to have a gold tooth, but he's a nice guy," Lucy told Grace and Peter. "He's getting his master's degree in counseling."

Everyone in the room was waiting to hear about the date. "I don't want to be a snob," I began. I had already developed three goals while Lucy was giving them background: 1. Amuse, 2. Alert that I'm Single, 3. Remind Peter that a man could snatch me up at any moment. "But one of his hobbies was monster truck racing." I saw a smile curl up the corners of Peter's mouth as he stirred. "But so be it. He is a friend of Ernie and Lucy's, so I planned to apply the three-date rule, to give myself a chance to really get to know him."

At that point, Joe wandered into the kitchen. "Quinn's telling us about her blind date last night with Ernie's best friend," Grace told him. I saw Joe look at Peter, but Peter's face was neutral.

I took a sip of wine. "About halfway through dinner, I made some comment about going home for Christmas. You know, some general thing how siblings can be a pain in the neck. And he said, 'Have you always felt such animosity toward your brother and sister?'"

"Uh-oh," Grace said.

"I said, 'It's not animosity. It's just that, when I spend too much time with them, they drive me a little crazy.' And he said, 'Is it because you don't think your mother loved you as much as she loved them?'"

Ernie let out a whoop. He shook his head. "I love that guy," he said. "But this counseling thing has really gone to his head!"

"He tries to psychoanalyze everyone since he started that program," Lucy said.

I nodded. "So, I said, 'Listen, I don't really have an issue with my family, but even if I did, it's not something I would talk about to you, in this setting.' He said, 'If you continue to push your bad feelings away, you'll never be able to work through them.' At that point, I just got mad, so I said, 'I don't know what they are teaching you in your program, but a good counselor doesn't decide in advance what someone's issue is and force-feed it to them.'"

Grace and Joe nodded approvingly. Peter had turned down the heat and stopped stirring.

I took a deep breath and kept talking. "Then he said, 'You have some serious jealously toward your siblings, and you better face up to that.' So, I tossed my napkin on the table, stood up and said, 'You are going to make a lousy therapist.' And I left." Ernie started laughing.

"I love getting the last word!" Joe said.

"So do I," I told him. "But I didn't get it last night. We were eating at M's Pub, and it was dead quiet. And when I was halfway across the room, he yelled, 'You need some serious psychological help!'"

Everyone started laughing. I had accomplished my goals. Peter was laughing. He knew I was single. He knew I was dating.

The rest of the evening was basically uneventful, except that our two groups of friends bonded really well with each other. Izzy and Josh came a little late, but it turned out that Josh and Joe knew each other from a soccer league. Sitting around, watching my friends chat, I felt proud that everyone I knew was so sociable and polite. Once again, Peter and I were the only two single people at the gathering.

Because of his growling issue, Pacey waited outside until everyone was inside. Then he got the run of the place. He had the time of his life that night. During the movie, Pacey traveled from person to person, greeting them and sitting in front of them till they petted him. For people who were sitting on the floor, he climbed right onto their lap. Luckily, the room was all dog lovers.

I hadn't seen much of Josh since the wedding. Or really, at all. Of everyone there, he was the most personable. He kept the conversation rolling, and engaged the quieter people in the group. Izzy looked content and proud of him. I started to wonder if she had not been rash, after all, in marrying him so quickly.

When everyone was gone, Pacey wandered through the house while I cleaned up. He didn't seem able to believe that the house had been so full, and now it was empty. He kept sniffing the floor, running upstairs, and coming back down. The phone rang. I looked at my watch. It was 2 a.m.

"Hello?"

"It's Lucy. We're driving home. I have to say, Peter was more tuned into you than anyone else in the room. Ernie thought so, too. Peter clearly thinks well of you."

"So you think he likes me?"

"I'd say yes. But Ernie thinks he's conflicted." Ernie got on the phone.

"Hey, Quinn. Great dinner, by the way. I don't know about this guy. He seems to admire you, but he also hasn't made a move. I'd guess it's not going to happen. But I think it's more to do with him, than you."

"Yeah. I see your point." I was starting to feel bummed.

"But I could be totally wrong," Ernie added. "I married my high school sweetheart. When I stopped dating, boys were chasing the girls they liked, and girls had their friends send you notes in homeroom to tell you someone liked you."

I hung up with Ernie. Pacey was still sniffing around. I gave him a bear hug. "I have good friends," I told him.

The phone rang again, five minutes later. It was Izzy. "That was a great party."

"Does he seem like he likes me?" I asked.

"I can't tell. I mean, yes, he clearly likes you, but I didn't get any sense that he liked you romantically."

"Did Josh?" I asked.

"He didn't think so either. Although he agrees with me that Peter likes you as a friend. Are you sure he's not gay?"

"He said girls with belly rings were hot."

"Oh, yeah. Well, you've got a good friend out of it, at the least. That's not bad."

"No."

"And Pacey was a doll. So much fun."

"He is still running around the house, looking for people. He must think everyone's hiding. He'd be so much happier if I lived with ten people all the time."

"You're doing a great job with him."

"Thanks. Josh was a big hit tonight. Everyone loved him."

"Do you think?"

"Yes. I think I've been underestimating him. He's really personable and considerate."

"Thanks," Izzy said. Her voice was glowing.

The following week, I flew to Chicago for an audiology conference. Being away gave me some perspective. I agreed with my friends that Peter probably didn't like me romantically. And by not seeing him, and having no expectation or hope to see him, I was able to think about him less. Crushes are oppressive. It was good to get away from my infatuation. I came home revived. "This is the end," I told myself. "You need to start branching out and get past Peter."

I picked Pacey up at the kennel on my way home from the airport. Some dogs are traumatized by kennels. I had been worried sick about leaving Pacey for four days. When the attendant brought Pacey out, he ignored me. He stayed by the attendant, wagging his tail. Then he took off to the far side of the hallway to sniff around a little.

"Pacey!" I called. "Pacey! Come here!" No response. I had to chase him down to get his leash on. I told myself that it was a good thing to have a dog that wasn't traumatized by your absence.

On the drive home, he leaned forward from the backseat and rested his chin on my right shoulder. My face broke into a silly grin. I felt like he was saying, "Quinn, I had to play it cool in there, but I'm really glad to see you."

Instead of taking Pacey for a walk, I decided to play fetch with him in the backyard. When I first got Pacey, he couldn't catch a ball to save his soul. But he'd come a long way since then and now catch was his favorite game. He was good at it, too.

We were still in the backyard when Peter came by. "Welcome back," he said. "How was your trip?"

"Fabulous," I said. "If you love being pulled out of line to stand with your arms outstretched while security waves wands over you and everyone in line stares at you because they've got nothing better to look at."

Peter chuckled at this. Then he said, "Your friends are really nice."

"I think so," I said.

"And good gamers. They creamed everyone at Pictionary."

"At what?"

"Pictionary."

"When did you guys play Pictionary?"

"While you were away. Lucy and Ernie came by the restaurant. We got to talking and they came over on game night. They beat everyone," he said. "They've definitely got a married-couples communication thing going."

"Married couples always win at those games," I said. "It's unfair to singletons."

"Totally."

"So they went out with you guys."

"Didn't they tell you?"

"I haven't talked to them since I came back," I said. And they hadn't left a message.

As soon as Peter left, I called Lucy. "So," I said. "Anything you want to tell me?"

"We went to Peter's restaurant, and it was delicious, by the way. Then we ended up playing Pictionary at Peter's house. They were a nice group."

"You went to his house? What was it like?"

"Old, like yours. Can you hang on a second?" I heard her yell to Ernie. "Ernie, Quinn is on the phone. What did Peter say to you?"

Ernie got on the phone. "Hey, Quinn. He said, 'I don't have a girlfriend, so I'm always the odd man out at these games.'"

Lucy took the phone back. "And when he was talking to me he said, 'So, do audiologists like to dance?'"

"Really? He said that?"

"Yeah." Ernie took the phone back.

"Also, Quinn? He was so solicitous to us. He went out of his way to be interested in our lives and I felt it must have been because we are your friends."

"Did you talk about me?"

"Ummm. Let's see…no. No, I don't believe we did."

"Really? You didn't say something like, 'That Quinn is just so beautiful and funny. Who wouldn't give anything to be her husband?'"

Ernie started laughing. "Those words were on the tip of my tongue," he said. "I almost said them, and then I thought, why state the obvious?"

I laughed. I realized I liked Ernie. I guess I'd never talked to him at office parties. Lucy said something in the background.

"Oh, that's right. I did say that you have led a really interesting life and that it's probably because you never married."

Lucy took the phone back. "It was in this context. Peter said that life is harder for single people. He was talking about bearing the responsibility of shoveling all the snow and paying for the heating bill. Ernie said that you are free to live however you like when you aren't married. He used you as the example. He said "Quinn's lived abroad, she's moved all over the country. She always has an interesting story and if she had married young, like we did, maybe she would have just settled into one job and picked up a mortgage, like we did."

"What did Peter say?"

"He said, 'Quinn is something special.'"

"No," Ernie said from next to her. "He said, 'She's a remarkable girl.'"

They had a brief argument and then Lucy came back on and said, "We don't remember verbatim, but we both thought he was basking in your amazingness when he said it."

All my self-growth in Chicago flew out the window, along with my sanity. I felt a little grief to see it go. Then I shrugged and jumped back onto the stomach-churning, joy-sucking roller coaster ride that is commonly called a "crush."

"This is all very promising," I said. "But, since I saw him today, I won't see him again for two more weeks. He's got a pattern."

"Which he's about to break," Lucy said. "Because we're holding the next gamer party at our house. And it's tomorrow night."

Reader, how many times in this book have I attacked the Smug-Marrieds? I take it all back. The Smug-Marrieds came through for me. They analyzed Peter's motives, they listened to me whine and complain. They invited him out so that we could get to know each other without any pressure.

I stayed on after Lucy and Ernie's party to help them clean up.

"Why don't you just tell him you like him?" Ernie asked as he washed dishes in the sink.

"I can't do that. What if he doesn't like me? I'll be humiliated." I had a brief flash of Zach, which I pushed away. No point in thinking about him right now.

"There's nothing wrong with having feelings for someone who doesn't return them. That way, you'll just know. And then you can continue to be friends."

But I couldn't do that. I was scared to confront Peter with my feelings because, deep in my heart, I already knew what his answer would be. And if Peter didn't like me, then that meant I would have to go back out there. Go back to petitioning the Universe and soliciting my friends and co-workers for set-ups. Back to carrying around a prop, and smiling at men, and wearing pink. Go back to internet dating. And I didn't want to. I was tired, tired, tired.

Now, Reader, maybe you are thinking, "Ahh, he's just not that into you." Maybe. But I prefer to draw my conclusion from a different writer. Dave Barry. He has a column titled, "How Guys Think." (The Boston Sunday Globe, 8/20/89). Maybe you've already read it. It's passed around the Internet a lot. And basically, what he says is this: If a man you had a great time with doesn't call you back, it's probably because you were so amazing that he thinks you might be The One. And if he's not ready for marriage, he's not going to date the girl who is The One.

Now, if I'm going to believe anything, that's what I'm going to believe. That Peter thinks I'm the funniest, sexiest, smartest, most compassionate and interesting woman he's ever met. And he's thinking, "Holy shit. She's the type of woman I want to marry. And I'm not ready for that!" And that's why he hasn't asked me out.

Chapter 57
Tick, tock, TICK, TOCK!

"I'm pregnant," Izzy told me.

"You are?" I grabbed her hands. "Oh, my God! Congratulations!"

"I only just found out, so don't tell anyone."

"I won't, but I'm so happy for you!"

Izzy smiled. Her cheeks were red, which made her eyes look especially blue. "I'm happy for me, too!"

"You're already glowing."

"I feel fantastic. Like my body was meant to be pregnant."

"And Josh?"

"Is a little freaked out, but I warned him I wanted kids right away. He's coming on board. He is a little too focused on money, but that's just his nature. He needs time to adjust to things. He isn't his best when things are sprung on him."

"You seem to understand each other well."

"Yeah. I can see how he processes things, and it's different from me, but it makes us a good match. We balance each other."

Marlena was back on my schedule. The note next to her name said, "Check hearing aids." I went out to the lobby and called them. Her mom scooped up their bags and coats, and followed me into a room. "So," I said. "How's it going?"

"That other audiologist? He couldn't get the small hearing aids to work."

"Oh?"

"Yeah. They wouldn't fit in her ears. They popped out because they were too big, and they whistled all the time."

Justified!!! I thought. "Well, they're not meant for children," I said. "Even some adults don't have big enough canals to get a good fit. Do you still have our loaner?"

"Yes, it's broken." She handed it over. I took it. The battery door was broken off. "It just broke, this week. That's why we're here. Marlena won't listen to me without that hearing aid."

Because she can't hear you, I thought. "Well, maybe it's time to think about purchasing a pair of hearing aids for her."

"The smallest ones you've got," her mother said.

"Why so glum?" Lucy asked.

"Izzy's pregnant, and she's four years younger than me."

"So what? You've got plenty of time."

"That's easy for you to say," I snapped. "You're already married. You've got all the time in the world to have kids. It's different for me. My ovaries are old!"

"My ovaries are scarred," Lucy said. "From endometriosis. We've been trying to have kids since I was 25. Last year our fertility doctor told us that I have the ovaries of a fifty-year-old."

"Lucy," I said. Then I didn't know what else to say.

"I know. It's sad and crappy. But it's the cards I was dealt. Sometimes you don't get what you deserve."

"Are you going to adopt?"

"Do you know how much adoption costs?" she asked. "Ten to thirty thousand dollars, depending on the child's race, the age, the country of origin." She flicked a piece of lint off her sleeve. "Do you know how much my sister paid, to have a child? Total? Including hospitalization and prenatal visits?"

"How much?"

"Two-hundred and fifty dollars. Her insurance covered the rest. Ernie and I have already spent ten thousand dollars on in-vitro fertilization. What a waste."

"Can your parents help you out?"

"My dad is sixty-five and he's still working the land. Ernie's dad isn't any better off. He's retired, but Ernie's mom is still teaching to add to his pension."

I shook my head. What could I say? That it was unfair and our society had messed up priorities? That adoption should be free? That fertility treatments should be covered by health insurance? It was nothing she hadn't heard or thought already.

My last patient of the day was an 89-year-old woman. "I've got hearing aids," she said. "But they don't work right. Never have."
"How old are they?" I asked.
"Six months."
She'd purchased hearing aids from a hearing aid dispenser in town. I took a look at the brand, stamped on the sides of the aids. It was a national chain that we didn't work with. "I can run these, to look at how they are set, but I won't be able to make any changes."
"Well, I paid $5200 for these aids and they have never been any good."
"You should have returned them at the end of your trial period."
"I didn't want to offend anyone," she said.

I did a hearing test on her. Then I put a small microphone in her ear, with the hearing aid, and measured how the hearing aids were amplifying conversational speech.
"These aids don't look too bad," I said. "They are matching most targets. They're just a little too soft in the low frequencies, and my guess is that your dispenser turned the lows down because you thought your voice was echoing."
"I don't know what the hell he did," she snapped. "I just know that I want to bean every robin in my yard with a rock."
I raised my eyebrows.
"The noise," she clarified. "They are too loud with these things."
"Well, you might need him to make some small adjustments," I said. "Sometimes people have to go back to their audiologist or dispenser every few weeks for a couple of months until everything is just right." I gestured to the computer screen that showed the measures I'd made. "These aren't a bad fit. You just need some fine tuning."
"I'll call him," she said.
"Good. And be prepared to go back as often as it takes, until you're wearing the aids full-time."
She gripped my arm as she stood. "Don't get old," she said after she'd finally managed to stand up.
"I'll try not to," I said.
"Are you married?" she asked.
"No."

"Are you a lesbian?" When I started, she said, "Don't get all flushed on me. I'm just asking."

"No," I sighed. "I'm just having a hard time meeting the right guy."

She positioned her cane in her right hand. "Let me tell you something, uh, Quinn, is it? I was married for 55 years. There were good times and bad times in my marriage. When Walter died, I didn't know what I was going to do. But life went on. Now I'm taking a photography class and last year I entered a watercolor into a statewide exhibit and won third prize."

"That's wonderful," I said.

"You can pine away all you want for the perfect life. But no life is perfect."

Chapter 58
The Pleasures of Singledom

"I don't even own a bike!" Ann and I were at yet another coffee house.

"You could borrow from someone, couldn't you?"

"I don't like to bike."

"But this is going to be fun! And none of us are bikers, except for Joe."

I was trying to get her to sign up for BRAN (Bike Ride Across Nebraska). It's an annual biking trip. "We're going to ride together, in a group. There'll be fast people in the group and slow ones. You can choose your own speed. Plus, in the little towns where we spend the night, the residents come together and make dinner. How fun is that? They have these giant serving lines where everyone comes up and eats."

"I don't know," Ann said.

"You'll love it. And you don't come to basketball with us. So the least you can do is the biking tour."

"I don't come to basketball because you play it at 7 a.m. I don't like to start my morning by bouncing."

I could see her point.

"Your birthday is coming up," Ann said

"Yeah. The big 4-0."

"Are you happy?"

"I haven't been happy about a birthday since I turned thirty," I said. "But I don't think 40 will be that bad. And I've got a good night planned. We're going salsa dancing."

"I don't know how to salsa dance," Ann said.

"Neither do I. But I wanted to do something a little different on my 40th birthday. I wanted to do something I wouldn't normally do. And I know everyone will go along with me, because it's my birthday."

"You're right about that."

"Listen," I said. "Why don't you invite Jackson to come out with us?" Ann shook her head. I could see from her face that she was annoyed. "So, it's not going to happen for you guys?"

"Nope."

I played with my coffee mug. "I just wanted a happy ending."

"I've got a happy ending," Ann said.

I nodded. "Maybe it's about time I start to realize that. Hey, do you want to take a glass blowing class?" I asked.

Ann smiled. "Now that's more like it. None of this sports crap. Sports will destroy your knees."

"It's on Wednesday nights," I continued.

"Who's going?" she asked.

"Izzy, Ernie, me, maybe Grace."

"Those restaurant folks sure have jazzed up the quality of your life," Ann said.

"I know. Isn't it wonderful? It makes not knowing whether or not Peter likes me almost secondary."

"Almost?"

"Almost."

Chapter 59
And We Lived Happily Ever After

But he did like me, Reader. After we'd known each other for eight solid months, he asked me out on a date. He invited me to a wolf sanctuary in western Nebraska. We drove there, one Saturday when he was off from work. On the way home, we stopped in Lincoln and ate at an intimate Italian restaurant. I was a little worn out from the day, so I didn't talk much over dinner. The lights in the restaurant were dim, and our table had three votive candles that gave a peaceful, romantic feeling. I was thinking, *This would be a great place to go on a date.*

"I'm kind of nervous to tell you something," Peter began.

"What is it?" I asked.

"I have a crush on you. Not a crush. I really like you. And it's not because you donated all the money in your pockets to the wolf preserve. Or because your skin looks like carved ivory against your hair in this light. It's something I've been feeling about you for a long time. But I haven't been sure how you would react to me telling you. I totally understand if you don't have romantic feelings for me, but before you say anything, there are a few things I want to tell you."

"Okay," I said. My appetite was gone.

"I like you because you make me laugh, every time I see you. I like how naïve you can be, even though you're also a world-weary traveler. I like how much your friends love you. I like the freckle you have under your left eye, and the little hair that's growing out of the freckle on your cheek."

That hair was getting yanked as soon as I got home. Honestly

Reader, I had no idea it was there.

"I like how you make sure that everyone in a conversation gets a chance to speak, and how you put the fear of God into people when you warn them about wearing ear plugs around loud music. Mostly, though, I just like being around you, to hear your thoughts on the day's news and to watch you when you sit with your stocking feet curled up underneath you in restaurants."

I was sitting that way, right then. I didn't know how he could tell from his side of the table.

"So, why don't you just nod, or shake your head, depending on how you feel?" he continued. "And if you shake your head, it's no problem. I have a topic of conversation that will get us through the rest of evening." He smiled. "You can tell me the entire storyline of the TV show, Felicity, from Freshman year to the season finale."

In the silence after he stopped speaking, I felt like I could hear the candles burning.

"Well," I finally said. "You've put us both in an uncomfortable position. Because I've had a crush on you, nearly since I met you, but I've also always wanted to tell you the four-season plot of Felicity. So now I really don't know which way to go."

Reader, I got laid, that night. The Heavens opened, the angels sang, and I learned that multiple orgasms are real. Within six months, he had proposed. Reader, I married him! Our wedding was beautiful. It was on the beach. At sunset. And we lived happily ever after.

Well? Was that what you were expecting? Seriously? No, I didn't think so. After reading my book, you know me well enough to recognize when I tell you an untruth. What you just read is the ending that Hollywood will give my story, if they purchase the rights and make this into a movie. I think that Lauren Graham should play me.

But that is not the true ending and this book is about the truth. As I write this last chapter, I'm 40 and I'm still single. I'm not even seeing anyone. Peter is just a friend and I realize now that that's all he'll ever be. I'm back on Match.

The thing is, this is just the ending of my book, but not the ending of my life. Maybe I'll meet a guy on my book tour! Then I can write a sequel called *The Truth about Marriage: The Real Reason Smug-*

Marrieds Are Smug.

Sure, a husband might clean up the dog poop in the yard, or come dig you out of a snowdrift, but he can't protect you from pain and grief. Even with love, your life is still ultimately yours alone. If you think a spouse rescues you from the bad parts of life, you're in for rough times ahead.

What I learned from my two years of dating was to put myself on the line and take risks. Dating is hard work. Two years of serious dating changed me, for the better. And if an introvert like me can put myself out there to change my life, then you can too. You don't have to start dating. But if you live your life well, with integrity and joy. If you do what you love. If you try not to be afraid. If you step outside of what's expected of you and be true to the dreams you had when you were fourteen, or seven, or four. Or forty. Well, you still might not meet a guy, but you'll have an exciting, meaningful, unique life. That's better than no guy and no life, isn't it? And with no life, you probably won't get a guy. So, to tell you the truth about dating: there are no guarantees. The best you can do is accept that, and then set about honoring the life that was bestowed on you.

Now, if you'll excuse me, I need to run upstairs and pluck that hair from my mole.

The end

Searching For Meredith Love

Searching for
Meredith
Love

Julie Christensen

Meredith Love thought her life was just fine. Fresh out of graduate school, she had a shiny new job in the medical office where she used to be a secretary. Sure, she didn't really like all her co-workers, and yes, her bosses still asked her to drop everything to send a fax. And, okay, she had an irritatingly successful best friend who was always telling Meredith that her life sucked. But Meredith was content with her quiet life in Albuquerque, New Mexico.

Then Ben Abel, second-year medical resident, appears on the scene, and Meredith realizes how miserable she is and what happiness could be. Suddenly, her life looks as bad as her best friend always said and it's getting worse by the minute. Now Meredith is going to have to learn how to fight for the life she wants instead of the life she's got. And even if she succeeds, a secret from her past could ruin everything.

Also By Julie Christensen

Murder Beyond Words - *A Ruby Neptune Mystery*

During a heat wave in New York City, a literary agent is murdered in her Brooklyn apartment. Across the hall in 3B, aspiring writer Ruby Neptune finds herself sucked into the murder investigation of a neighbor she barely knew and didn't really like. The agent seems to have known her killer, as there was no forced entry. Ruby slowly discovers that many of her neighbor's friends had strong reasons to want her dead.

Determined to find the killer, Ruby puts her own life on hold, which upsets her closest friends, one of whom suspect that her new boyfriend is capable of the murder. As the list of suspects narrows, it hits uncomfortably close to home and Ruby finds herself lying to friends and even putting aside her writing career to solve the case. But will Ruby be able to identify the killer before she becomes the next victim?

Murder With Art - *A Ruby Neptune Mystery (Book 2)*

Still struggling with the aftermath of a murder in her apartment building, Ruby Neptune is further involved murder when a banker is murdered and her best friend becomes the prime suspect. But is someone she's trying to protect actually a killer?

About the Author

Julie Christensen is the author of four novels. A native New York, she studied painting at Pratt Institute and worked briefly in advertising on Fifth Avenue before she realized that her "creative" job was sucking the life out of her soul. Julie worked as a live-in Au Pair in Brooklyn, taught preschool, and lived in Barcelona and New Mexico before finally going back to school to get her Masters in Audiology. After graduation, Julie did her fellowship at the Mayo Clinic in Minnesota before moving to Omaha to work at a center for pediatric audiology. It was in Omaha that she discovered how hard dating is when you are an old thirty-something. She began writing about her horrible dates to amuse her single friends and make her married friends appreciate their husbands. *The Truth About Dating* is based on these experiences. Julie was introduced to her future husband by an acquaintance who, after reading a draft of *The Truth About Dating*, realized that she knew the perfect man for Julie. They now have two children, ages 2 and 3. Julie continues to paint (juliechristensen.net) and write (julielivingthedream.blogspot.com). She is currently at work the sequel to *The Truth About Dating*.

Made in the USA
Lexington, KY
14 August 2013